CRAZY FOR LOVING YOU

PIPPA GRANT

Editing by Jessica Snyder, HEA Author Services
Cover Design by Kari March

1

Daisy Carter-Kincaid, aka a (semi-self-made) billionaire who's never met a challenge she couldn't take down in a dance-off while wearing Manolos and shooting Fireball. Until very, very soon...

When I die, they might not call me the classiest lady to ever live. Or the smartest. Or even the richest.

But there's nothing like a funeral with very few tears to inspire a person to at least want to be *missed*.

"I wonder if she would've given the flowers one star for the orchids being *peach* instead of *apricot*," my mother murmurs over her mai tai.

I choke on my own Bahama mama, smuggled into the funeral in black metal water bottles to make them look somber. "*Mom.*"

"What? I wouldn't speak ill of the dead if the dead didn't give me so much ill to speak of. And panning your spa in Arizona on her awful website because of a shade of orange on the curtains was petty as fuck."

"It was," the mayor of Miami agrees. Mom and I are in the family receiving line in my grandmother's carefully-cultivated tropical garden outside her South Beach fortress, and the mayor's just reached us to offer his condolences on my cousin's passing. "She once told me that my dog was ugly. Not surprised that she'd be just as mean to family."

His wife nods as she tugs on the collar of her black crepe dress. "She told me I needed a nose job. Also, is that Rafe's mistress lurking over by the bougainvillea? I'm sure Julienne would've given her a one-star review for her performance in bed."

"God bless you both, and don't ever change," Mom says. "What's in your heart is what matters."

We trade hugs, and they move on to the rest of my cousins and aunts and uncles.

"Julienne wrote on her blog that the sculpture I designed for the children's hospital was an eyesore," an artist I vaguely recognize murmurs. "May her judgmental and tasteless soul rest in peace."

"Amen," Mom agrees.

"Did you do the three dancing girls statue in the lobby?" I ask.

He nods.

"I love that! It's so bright and happy!"

"Hence the problem," his partner replies. "She called us just to tell us that her Instagram post tearing the sculpture to shreds got more likes than the number of people who'd otherwise see it in a year."

We all hug and they continue down the line.

I lean closer to Mom. "Julienne and Rafe didn't make many friends, did they?"

"Why make friends when you can live off trust funds and tear other people down?" Mom sips her drink and slides a glance at a waiter passing out elegant butterfly-shaped canapés, then leans forward to check out the head of the receiving line in the winding garden path.

The Dame, aka my grandmother, is in all black at the edge of the koi pond, standing stoically and welcoming the last of the mourners beside my dead cousin Julienne's in-laws.

Her mother-in-law was the only person other than Julienne's newborn baby to cry at the double funeral for my cousin and her husband. His father—aka The Creepy Asshole whom I'm keeping as much distance from as possible—kept checking his watch like he was going to miss a tee time.

And I'm very glad to have my bodyguard with me today.

Mom leans closer and lowers her voice. "I don't know what her will says about a guardian for the baby, but this might be the best thing to ever happen to him. Unless Rafe's parents get him, and then the world—and that child —are all doomed."

She has an unfortunate point. "Poor thing."

We both stare out over the flowers. I love bright and happy, but "celebrating the lives" of a serial cheater and his bitter wife feels so wrong. For so many reasons.

Mom takes another sip, then turns to me again. "You

have to wonder if she would've objected to the silver glitter casket. I thought she would've gone for gold."

Clearly, she's still not over Julienne's review of the first spa I designed for my grandmother's real estate empire. "It was platinum glitter."

"Platinum glitter while her husband is laid to rest in a casket that was shinier than a sports car. One star."

God, this is depressing. I *hate* depressing. "I don't like to one-star things, but I'm one-starring my boob sweat. Who approved a heat wave in October, and when do we get in the pool?"

"Never. Your grandmother planned this, not you. Remember?"

"I hate being overruled."

But my grandmother overrules everyone. On everything.

Mom sighs. But she doesn't fidget, because she *is* The Dame's daughter. So she's impeccably dressed in a svelte black Caroline Herrera that shows off her cleavage without being *too much*, her makeup perfect, her hair demure, her expression sad but not weepy.

I look just like her, except the part where her chicken legs are actually chicken legs, whereas mine are compressed since I'm six inches shorter than she is.

Damn paternal genes.

"I severely dislike funerals," she says. "Even though they were both horrible people, I'm still sad they're gone. All those years they could've found their souls on earth, and now they'll never get the chance to redeem themselves."

CRAZY FOR LOVING YOU

"But if you had to go, having horny dolphins chase your sailboat into the path of an oncoming pirate tourist ship is pretty epic."

"I will disown you if you die early on me in a freak accident involving horny anything and pirate anything else."

"Ditto. Also, I promise that when it's your time, I'll have you laid to rest in a dick casket, just to watch The Dame's eyeballs pop out of her head."

A smile teases her lips, and her blue eyes crinkle at the edges while she touches her phallic diamond earrings.

My mother loves penises. She's made a fortune in penis art since she divorced my father twenty-five years ago. Which is good, because The Dame disinherited her for marrying my father in the first place.

"For the lack of nice things said about Julienne and Rafe, there are a remarkable number of people here," she says.

"It's sweet of so many people to come for Grandma and the Rodericks." I'm well aware that most people are here only to schmooze with The Dame, or that the many enemies Julienne made with her snark blog wanted to be here to pan her funeral, or that Rafe's three mistresses are actually in mourning because none of them knew he was married and a dickhead and they all loved him in their own way.

Or that there would probably be more people here, except the Rodericks—Rafe's parents—don't have many friends in their social circle who would show up to a funeral.

Actually, they don't have many friends at all. Not of the *friendly* variety, anyway.

Probably because Anthony Roderick is a dick who tries to blackmail people into doing business with him.

Firsthand experience there, and even though it's been four years, the memory of him at Julienne's wedding, cornering me and leering and demanding that we *do a deal together since we're family now* still makes me shiver.

A local congressman steps up to us in line. "I got calls about Julienne and her opinion columns on a daily basis. My phones will be quieter with her gone."

"So eloquently put," Mom tells him.

"Thank you. My speechwriter and I worked on it for an hour last night."

He moves on, and Mom looks down the row again. "Thank *god*. Your grandmother's breaking rank. This must be about the last of them. How do you feel about politicians? The congressman is cute. You should ask him out."

We head for the nearest waiter, because *canapés*. Yum. "Too close to home."

"You and this ridiculous obsession with European men... Where did I go wrong?"

"Have *you* ever dated an Italian or a Spaniard?"

She frowns. "I don't think I have."

"Trust me. You should try it sometime."

"I *haven't* studied European penises up close..."

"Borrow my plane. Or take the yacht."

"Oh, a week on the yacht would be *lovely*. And inspiring. Can I bring a pool boy?"

"You know I'd be disappointed in you if you didn't."

"And then when I get back, we can talk about you calling the congressman."

"Mom."

"What? I have to *mom* you until you finally settle down."

We pass Alessandro, my bodyguard, who smirks at me.

I let him, because he's one of my favorite people in the world.

"I have too much living to do to settle down," I declare.

"Yes, yes, sow your wild oats. You're only young once. But, Daisy, you're in your mid-thirties now. You've been *living* like this for nearly half your life. And you're my only hope for grandchildren."

"I'm sure there's a grandmotherless family somewhere in Miami who would *love* to be adopted by you and your alimony checks, but you might have to hide your jewelry. It's *inappropriate*, Mother."

"*Daisy Imogen Carter-Kincaid.*"

I grin.

She tries not to grin back, but she fails, and instead sips her mai tai again to try to hide her amusement over my suggestion. We both know she's going to have her assistant look into a grandmotherless family as soon as this funeral party is over.

She makes enough money on her own that she can spare the alimony checks my father grumbles about writing every month. They might as well go toward spoiling surrogate grandchildren.

"I should ground you for insolence," she says.

"I'm due in Tokyo Tuesday for the final approval of Carter Towers' newest acquisition. And then Bali for a long weekend party with a rock band I can't name because of an NDA. So you can't ground me."

"Oh, Bali. I love Bali. Is this rock band party a K-Pop thing? Are you hooking up with one of them, or the whole band?"

I love-hate that she knows me so well. "Need to know. You don't need—actually, you don't *want* to know."

"Did you miss the part where I want grandchildren?"

I shake my head and turn back to glance at the crowd, and I suddenly feel like doing Jell-O shots and random acts of kindness.

No one's hanging out. Now that the receiving line's over, everyone's headed for the door.

So much for The Dame's plans for a celebration of life party.

Even the people who would usually schmooze and hint that they have a new charity we should donate to are running for the exits. So freaking sad.

I blame Anthony Roderick, because he's one of very few people in the world who has earned the distinct honor of going on my *assholes that I will never speak to again* list.

"How about a three-legged alligator grandson?" I offer Mom. "I always forget when it's my day to feed Steve at the enclave. He'd love you. He gets an extra gleam in his eye when he sees that much sparkle around the neck of the one tossing him a chicken."

"*Human* grandchildren."

"Hm. Maybe you should adopt another daughter. I always wanted a sister."

"I know, I know. You're busy being you. But my life is

so fulfilled by you. I just want you to feel the same joy that having children brings."

"Wow."

"Good, right? I had the congressman's speechwriter help me with that one too."

I crack up.

Mom cracks up.

And then we both sigh, because this really is the saddest funeral in the world.

As soon as we leave, I'm officially detouring on the way to the office. I feel like dropping little love bombs all over Miami.

Someone should be happy.

Might as well be people looking for burgers and donuts and for their parking meters to not expire.

"Your yacht's free for a week or two? You're sure?" Mom glances back at The Dame, who's also watching the masses flee her garden as she talks with Anthony Roderick.

I rarely feel sorry for my grandmother, but talking to Anthony Roderick is a fate I wouldn't wish on a flying cockroach. "Yes. Please take my yacht. It's feeling neglected."

"I *was* planning a trip to the Bahamas before Julienne's accident."

"Go. Use it. Escape. Have fun. Avoid horny dolphins and fake pirate ships."

She starts to hug me, but we both grimace, because it doesn't matter how many billions of dollars you have in the bank, you can't fight body odor in heat like this.

Freaking heat wave. Julienne would probably one-star her own funeral.

"You'll be okay? You won't be…sad?" Mom asks.

"I have my besties. And Tokyo and Bali. I'm good."

"No, honey, you're the *best*."

I smile at her.

And I get approximately eight hours to believe her.

Until *everything* changes.

2

Westley Jaeger, aka a recently retired, jaded military man determined to finally get the girl, even if she's not exactly the one of his dreams

BEACH BURGERS IS MORE crowded than usual tonight. The burgers are free today. Some rich local apparently did a random act of kindness and is paying, which we didn't know when we got here. There's barely standing room anywhere, but a table by the window opens up for Becca and me just as our number is called. I grab the tray of burgers and shakes and stuff a twenty into the tip jar while Becca stakes our claim.

The sun's sinking lower in the sky. Dolphins are playing in the bay. The temperature's dropping, with the heat forecasted to break tomorrow on the heels of thunderstorms overnight. Tiki music hums through the speakers. The scent of homemade French fries wafts through the air and mingles with the salty ocean breeze.

And tonight, I'm going to ask Becca *the question*.

We went to high school together in Chicago a lifetime ago. When I landed here in Miami after retirement this past June, and finally joined social media, I discovered she was living here too, divorced with two kids. I reached out, and we've been hanging out these past four months.

She has a funny laugh, her girls are great, and she's currently wiping the table with a disinfectant cloth from her stash in her bag.

Is she perfect?

No, but what woman is? What *person* is?

Thought I found perfection once before, and I couldn't have been more wrong.

But I'm pushing forty. Ready to move past the heart-break—and military commitment—that's hamstrung me the last several years, settle down, and live the rest of my life with what makes it worthwhile.

Family.

I grab extra napkins from the ketchup stand and weave through the beach bums and locals waiting in the rustic shack to the yellow-painted picnic table for two at the window, my heart ticking up a familiar rhythm.

Anticipation.

Except this isn't anticipation for a military mission, which is something that faded over the years too.

Now, it's anticipation for my *life*.

I set the tray on the table and climb onto the bench seat, my pulse steadily ramping up. Despite the view of the beach sunset, Becca's bent over her phone, her straw-berry blond hair lifting in the light breeze coming off the bay, her delicate fingers scrolling quickly across the screen. "Oh my god, West, did you hear about Judgy Julie?"

"Who?" I tell my heart to chill. Becca's a safe choice. Attractive. Stable. Probably doesn't want any more kids, and that's okay. Can't have everything in life.

"Judgy Julie. Julienne Carter-Roderick. The woman who one-starred you for refusing to take a wall out to put that giant marble fountain in her baby's nursery?"

"Ah. Right. Judgy Julie. She one-star her husband or something?" Guy gave me all the dicknugget vibes, even if he did overrule her on the fountain. Mental note: I will *not* be a dicknugget to Becca.

"She died."

I pause with a burger extended to her and tilt my good ear toward her. "She…died?"

Well, *fuck*.

How am I supposed to pop the question *now*?

Forge ahead, Marine! my balls bark at me, because they've been feeling neglected since I retired. *Don't pussy out now!*

"They both did. She and her husband. Apparently fairly tragically. Smells like karma. I didn't follow her— not after that horrible thing she said about your hammering skills not being able to arouse a gender-confused monkey, which was just rude—but I accidentally saw a review she posted of a baby sling last week where she tore it to shreds because it didn't make her baby feel like he was sleeping on a pillow of clouds and the fabric was a shade too teal for anyone to not want to puke after looking at it. Who says stuff like that?"

"Unhappy people."

She puts her phone down and takes the burger and drink. "I guess. She was just so *awful* to everyone. How long before she would've one-starred her own kid for being a kid, you know?"

Take charge and get her warmed up for the question, Marine! my nut sack orders. I clear my throat and unwrap my own burger. "Sunset's pretty."

Becca smiles. "Okay. Moving on. Got it. Do you know every time we've had burgers here, it's always been insanely crowded, and there's always been an open window seat?"

That's more like it. "Meant to be. Obviously."

Ooh-rah! You got this now! my balls cheer.

She bites into her burger.

And then she moans.

On a scale of *my leg just got blown off* to *porn star orgasm*, this moan ranks at a *this burger just made my panties wet*.

And I'm intrigued by Becca with wet panties. Let's be honest here. The thought of regular sex definitely plays into taking the leap back into real relationship waters for the first time in six years.

It's time. Time for the question.

I set my burger down.

Suck in a heavy breath.

And wait until she meets my eyes over her hamburger.

"Do you want to be my girlfriend?"

She coughs, her brown eyes go wide, and a hunk of cheeseburger flies out of her mouth and lands squarely on one of the extra napkins.

I quickly wrap it up and hand her the next napkin

while she thumps her chest and rasps out a wheezy breath.

"Gesundheit," I say while I reach around to pound her —gently—on the back.

She lunges for her milkshake and sucks the straw, making her cheeks hollow in.

"Water?" I ask when she comes up for air. I'm already halfway out of my seat to grab a cup from the soda fountain.

"*Jesus*, West, warn a girl before you make a joke," she finally says.

Aw, hell. My mother's a comedienne. I know the art of timing. I also know the art of bombing.

Becca freezes. "You...weren't joking."

And I thought it was hot working on that gym renovation without air conditioning this afternoon. I clear my throat. "About getting you a water? I never joke about water."

"About...the, erm, *dating* thing." She tries to smile again, but she looks more like she sucked down a raw oyster that's decided it wants to live and is clawing its way back up her throat while she pretends she's not going to puke.

The gentlemanly thing to do would be to brush it off.

Tell her I'm kidding. Laugh. Move on. That I'm following in my mother's footsteps.

Hell, the *saving face* thing to do is to laugh it off.

So I nod. Force a laugh. "Yeah. You got me. Sorry. Bad timing."

Her high cheekbones are going scarlet. She lifts the Beach Burger milkshake cup to her face like she can cool them off, and I know she doesn't believe me. "West, I—I don't know what to say."

Flex your muscles! Do a headstand! Save an old lady from choking! my balls bark at me. *Send her a dick pic! Show her what she's missing.*

Clearly, my balls aren't always that bright.

"That's not a yes." I swallow hard, because *fuck*, this hurts worse than that time O'Leary dropped a dumbbell on my foot right before a twenty-mile rucksack run.

This wasn't supposed to hurt. It's supposed to be logical.

We make good friends. I fix leaks under her sink. She cooks me dinner. We've both been burned by *love* before. Who wants *that* when you can just go for comfort and companionship?

She's shaking her head. "I just—I don't—*god*, this is so hard."

"You don't see me like that," I fill in for her. "It's okay. Bad joke."

"I—you—yes." She slumps back in her chair. "You're like—"

"A brother."

Her mouth flounders open for a second before she seals her lips shut.

She was going to say it.

She was going to say I'm like a brother to her.

Of fucking course she was. That's what I've been going for, isn't it?

"You're...very comfortable. And nice. And—very funny with jokes," she finishes lamely.

She looks like she wants a portal to hell to open up

and swallow her, because that would be less awkward than sitting here and telling me that I'm *comfortable*.

I could tell her about the time I nearly got blown to smithereens in Mosul. Or the time me and my buddies saved a dude who fell out of his raft on some nasty rapids. Or the time I let my commander talk to my mother.

But she's right.

"After the way you said your divorce went, I thought *comfortable* might be nice."

Her brows wrinkle. "Are *you* looking for just comfortable?"

Retreat! Retreat! my nuts yell. "Becca. We're not kids anymore. We've both been burned. And you keep saying you don't want to be alone the rest of your life. I don't either, but I can't see myself dating a twenty-something, and the dating pool isn't exactly full for people our age."

She starts to say something, cuts herself off, glancing sideways, and whispers something that I only catch because I've gotten fucking good at reading lips since that mortar round left me with eighty percent hearing loss in my right ear halfway through my career.

I just started dating someone.

Someone who isn't me.

Because she doesn't see me *like that*.

I have four sisters with zero filter when it comes to relationship advice. My parents taught me manners. The Marines taught me to be a man. And I suddenly feel like that awkward teenager on a string of bad dates again.

"Who is he?" I have lots of experience being a brother. I'll be her fucking *brother*.

Her cheeks turn into beets. "A dad I met at Mia's swim

meet. He—he was her fourth-grade teacher. That was the year—"

"You got divorced."

"He's a good guy. Also divorced. We just *clicked*. He coaches his son's little league team, which is why I hadn't seen him at swim meets until this weekend. The games always conflicted with swim practices. We're all going mini-golfing this weekend. It's not—I didn't do it to hurt you. I didn't realize you…thought this was going somewhere else."

"Not your fault. Forget I said anything."

Neither one of us will forget I said anything.

We make it through swallowing down burgers and shakes with stilted conversation that's making more bad memories surface.

A blind date to a funeral. The time my buddies put a laxative in my lunch and it kicked in right after I picked up my date for a drive up the California coast. That super fun date where we were playing sand volleyball and I accidentally gave her a black eye when we both dove for the ball at the same time and our heads collided.

I was thirty years old before I had a decent first date. It was with a single mother who was a couple years older. Just as jaded as I was, her because of her divorce, me because I'd never been good at *dating*. We traded horror stories, laughed ourselves sick, and I moved in with her and her kids six months later.

Lived with them for two years, hearing *I love you, but I'm never getting married again.*

Turned out, that meant *I don't love you as much as you love me.*

All four of my sisters are married. Living the dream, with kids and laughter and the good times and the bad times. Settled. *Happy*.

Is it so wrong to want that kind of life for myself now? I gave twenty years to Uncle Sam. Now I want some years for *me*.

Becca and I part in the parking lot. "Call you later," I tell her, though I think we both know I probably won't call her later.

Whoa, hotties in the sand volleyball pit, my nuts offer when I slump down onto the beach.

I look closer, realize the skimpy bikini crowd is probably just barely legal, and I take off for a walk on the shore while thunderclouds threaten to move in from the south.

I stroll past the condo I'm housesitting on the beach and break into a jog. My baby brother, who plays pro hockey, knows *people*. People with money who need nurseries re-done and beach houses babysat, though I have this suspicion he's actually playing older brother to *me* right now.

Arranging a place on the beach for me to chill at for the first six months after my time in the military. Introducing me to people who know people who need renovations done so that my business can take off.

Maybe he knows rich women who need a lube job, my nuts offer.

I tell them to shut the fuck up and ramp my jog into a full-on run. Might not be an active Marine anymore, but that doesn't mean I let myself get soft.

And I need to work out some *feelings*.

Fucking feelings.

Dating Becca was supposed to be about not *having* feelings.

Not feelings that could get hurt, anyway.

My sisters will undoubtedly tell me that's why it was doomed, but I like to think there's a woman out there somewhere who wants a companion with regular sex, but not the all-encompassing, obsessive, rainbows and chocolate flowers *love* that leads to heartbreak when it's over.

After a while, I turn around and head back. I'm almost breathing normally again when I hit my front door. Becca's long gone.

Probably off to see whoever it is she's dating.

"Mr. Westley Jaeger?" a guy in a suit asks as I trudge up the stairs of my temporary home. "Wonder West Construction?"

The hairs on the back of my neck stand up. Dudes in suits don't normally track me down. "Yeah?"

"Stanley Chihuahua. I represent Mrs. Imogen Carter and the Carter family. There's an issue with Julienne Carter-Roderick's will, and I need you to please come with me."

Julienne Carter-Roderick. Judgy Julie. What the hell? "What kind of issue?"

"Just a small note. I'm sure we can clear it up quickly."

"If she's saying I still owe her work because of that statue—"

"No, sir. All's well. Relatively speaking. You've been named as…well. Considering the sensitive nature of a will of this size and the relative fame of the recently deceased, I'd prefer to speak in private."

"You couldn't send a letter?" I don't know shit about

legal stuff beyond what my commander suggested I do for my own will back when I was a gunnery sergeant, but this feels off.

"There's a time factor involved. You can follow me in your own vehicle if you wish."

"To where?"

"Daisy Carter-Kincaid's house in Bluewater on Key Biscayne, sir."

Daisy Carter-Kincaid.

I know that name.

Why do I—aw, *hell*.

Daisy Carter-Kincaid is a rich party girl. Which probably means my baby brother—the hockey star who runs in high-profile social groups—is punking me.

Or coming through with that rich girl who needs a lube job! my nuts cheer.

They're hopeless.

"Daisy Carter-Kincaid's house," I repeat.

"Yes, sir."

I gesture him toward the row of beach houses. My baby brother knows things. And I'm pretty sure he's tricking me into going to a party.

Bring it on. "My truck's parked down the way. Let me get it, and I'll follow you."

3

West

ON THE DRIVE OUT to Key Biscayne, all the traffic lights turn green for me, nobody flips me off or cuts me off, the guard at the private Bluewater community entrance gate on Tiki Bar Drive is polite as a butterfly in his tropical floral print shirt, and even the eight-foot carved rooster just beyond the gate seems happy to see me.

I'm being escorted through a gorgeous private community that billionaires and superstars call home, at twilight, in a part of Miami that most people will never see other than in the spread of a magazine.

When my brother does something, he goes all in.

I have a moment of doubt, because sending a dude in a suit to pick me up isn't Tyler's style, but after driving past a bunch of pristine lawns with mansions tastefully tucked in beside palm trees, then across another bridge, and past three more mansions, the car in front of me finally pulls into a long, crushed seashell drive lined with Porsches, Teslas, Jaguars, and chromed-out Escalades, which *is* Ty's style.

This is definitely a party.

Hell, maybe *Mr. Chihuahua* is the "lawyer"'s stripper name, and Ty's signed me up to be his sidekick.

If so, he's getting mayonnaise in his stocking for Christmas.

Mr. Chihuahua leads me up to the porte-cochère of the massive, curved-front hacienda mansion and blocks two cars in, then gestures for me to do the same.

This porte-cochère?

It's really freaking cool. I've seen pictures of the house, because my sisters are all into the gossip rags and love texting me stuff, especially after Tyler got me set up to do that nursery renovation job for Julienne. Apparently she and Daisy are cousins, if I'm remembering all of my Daisy Carter-Kincaid trivia correctly.

I ignore most gossip—especially after some of the things Ty's been quoted as doing in magazines as his hockey career has taken off—but I couldn't ignore this house and its spread in *How The Rich Live* magazine.

Daisy has something like a half-dozen party lounges inside, all with different themes, from *Under the Sea* to a trampoline bar. Her guest suites are all named after tropical drinks, and rumor has it a certain rock legend and his wife asked if they could stay in the *Sex on the Beach* suite for an entire month while they tried to get pregnant, and when it didn't work the first month, they asked to stay another.

Her home office has a wall of frozen yogurt

dispensers. Her bedroom is the stuff of little girl princess dreams. She had her bathtub—a marble basin shaped like a rose—imported from Italy. And the whole house—the entire thing—is in the shape of a D with the copper roof modified to glitter and sparkle where it's not lined with solar panels, with a shooting star porte-cochère branching off the top.

Seriously.

The overhang shoots out to a star-shaped building that I assume is for security, though it's not manned right now.

Fuck yeah, we're partying tonight! my balls cheer.

I pretend they're talking to my bad ear. One-night stands were how I got through my last several years in the military, and I don't *want* to be that guy forever. I want stability. A home. A family.

I want what I thought I had before Sierra crushed my heart six years ago.

And how's that going for you, sucker? my nuts ask.

They might have a point. I might not *ever* get what I really want in life.

I take stock of everything from the security outpost to the tasteful tropical landscaping to the cars around us to the house with its massive double oak doors and arched windows following the curve of the building, because I haven't been out of the military long enough to lose that desire to have situational awareness at all times.

Mr. Chihuahua leaps out of his car and gestures for me to follow him. We don't head to the front door, but instead, steer around the curved side of the building along a path beneath palm trees and alongside hibiscus bushes, curiosity and suspicion growing with every step.

"Where are we going?" This doesn't feel like a party, and the music is fading as we walk.

"Pool house."

"Why?"

"Privacy."

"What—"

"Soon, Mr. Jaeger. I've been instructed to wait."

That's not ominous. *Fuck*. What the hell's going on?

Eventually, we reach a pool shaped like—

Huh.

That's a dick pool.

Daisy's initials are DICK—my sisters say her parents must've hated her—so I guess a dick pool makes sense. Definitely a cock-and-balls shape, with the balls as a hot tub. Another house's lights are just visible beyond the patio.

We skirt around the ball sack and a statue of a dude peeing and head to the small, brightly-painted pool house. It's about the size of a double-wide, except the front of the house is all glass, and inside, it feels like an exotic getaway with marble tile floors, a dolphin chandelier, a sleek bar along one wall, and tropical plants in every corner. Discreet signs point down a hallway to changing rooms and a restroom on one side and a spa on the other.

I do a double-take when I realize the arrows are actually crystal dicks.

Crystal?

Or diamond?

And is that a diamond-encrusted mosaic of a penis hanging on the wall?

This is nothing like the neighborhood pool my siblings

and I begged to go to every summer back home in Chicago. Not that I expected it to be, but I didn't expect so many penises either.

The subtle noise from the party is completely muted once the glass door slides shut behind us. "What—" I start again, but before I can finish, a colorful mass of a person tumbles into the room from one of the hallways. She's wearing stilettos, drink in hand, bringing a whirlwind of chaos with just her presence.

Her dress is a gold and white glittery number that barely covers her from boobs to thigh and shows off every curve. Her hair's neon red, tied in a tall ponytail on top of her head, and she's wearing a choker collar of diamonds that matches the dangly sparkles in her ears.

"Stanley! You brought me a stripper! You shouldn't have!"

He opens his mouth, but she holds up a finger. "Ah-ah, don't ruin the mood." She whips out a phone, hits the screen twice, and "Low Rider" fills the air. "Okay, big guy. Show me what you've got."

Comfortable. Becca said I was *comfortable*.

Can't wait to tell her *this* story. Though when I tell it, it'll involve tequila shots and falling in the pool and mistaking a blow-up doll for a drowning woman and getting crowned king of the dick pool.

Assuming I get to leave. This whole night is turning surreal. I don't like it.

Mr. Chihuahua sighs heavily. Glances at me. Back to her. Then to me again. "Five minutes, Mr. Jaeger. Please don't—don't let her scare you off. Mrs. Carter would be very put out."

The woman claps. "Oh, a stripper from Gramalicious? I didn't know she had it in her."

"Daisy?" I ask.

She grins and circles me, hips swaying, shoulders rolling to the music. It's hard to watch just her lips when she's a whirling blur of sensuality and outrageousness, so I don't catch everything she says over the music, but *she's* having a party whether the rest of us join in or not.

Her eyes sparkle as she twirls near me in that tight dress, her breasts jiggling just enough to be noticeable. "You gonna dance, or you just gonna stand there?"

My heart drums.

My fingers twitch.

Pure lust stirs low in my gut.

I don't know exactly why I'm here—being pranked into going to a party by my brother is feeling like a less and less likely option—but I haven't worked my ass off my entire life to not let loose and have a good time when the situation presents itself.

Especially tonight.

Don't know that I have *moves*—the last time I tried to impress a girl, I did it by throwing down in a chin-up contest on a rope, and yes, I won—but I close my eyes and let the music hit my veins.

Dancing isn't my thing.

Usually.

Tonight?

Tonight we're in straight *Fuck It-ville.*

"*Woo*, baby!" Daisy crows. "What's your name, sugarplum?"

"West." My voice comes out rough.

Jesus. I'm shaking my booty for *Daisy Carter-Kincaid*.

She circles me closer, one hand on her phone, the other holding her drink in that fancy martini glass. She's dancing, but not wobbling on those thin spikes under her heels. Her drink sloshes, but her eyes aren't bloodshot, and she's not slurring anything. "Where you from?"

"Everywhere."

The backs of her fingers brush my biceps, and her drink dribbles over the edge onto my skin. "I like everywhere. Where's your favorite?"

I'm not the partying-with-heiresses type. Whatever I'm here for, it's tonight, and tonight only. Probably no more than the next hour.

What the hell do I have to lose?

I stare straight into those lavender eyes, ignore the *warning, warning* buzzing at the back of my brain because *no one* has lavender eyes, which means she's hiding something, probably a lot of somethings.

But again—*fuck it*.

"My favorite?" I sway with her, squatting lower to be closer to her level. She's not at all as tall as you'd think she'd be from her reputation, but she's every bit as wild. "Right now, it's right here."

Her nose crinkles, and then her smile spreads wider. "Are you *flirting* with me, West from Everywhere?"

"Are you *dancing* with me, Daisy from Right Here?"

"What can I say? I love to dance." She winks. "*And* flirt. You gonna strip, or what?"

Once more—*fuck it*.

Why the hell *wouldn't* I strip?

I step back, pull my polo out of my jeans while I keep

doing my best to dance. You want a mountain of boulders moved, I'm your man. Need a makeshift linebacker in a pick-up game of football in the park, I'm the first guy you call. You want a striptease—can't say that's ever been my style.

But I'm doing this anyway. Slowly giving her a peek at my abs. Tugging my jeans down at one side, like I've seen on the cover of so many of my sisters' romance novels.

Her pupils go dark, and she keeps swaying to the music, tilting her head so her unnatural neon red ponytail swishes with the beat too.

"You strip often?" she breathes.

"Couple times a day."

"Where?"

"Usually my bathroom."

She tips her head back and laughs, and *fuck me*, that happy, rich laughter makes me want to get a hearing aid so I can soak in the sound fully in both ears. She's curvy and bold and bright, and she's rendered my balls mute.

"I think I like you, West from Everywhere," she says.

I don't let that go to my head—not the one on my shoulders anyway—because this has *first date* written on it, and first dates and I don't get along. "Let's leave it at that," I tell her.

She laughs again. Sips her drink. Nods to my stomach. "C'mon, then. Let's see what else you've got.

I'm about to whip the shirt over my head when a loud bang erupts behind us.

I spin and crouch, ready to face danger, and find myself eyeball to eyeball with—*fuck*.

Imogen Carter.

She's a crusty one. And meticulous to boot. Julienne Carter-Roderick might've officially been in charge of the nursery renovation, but her grandmother stopped by nearly every day to make sure the two-by-fours were straight enough and that none of my small crew were drinking.

Surprised the hell out of me when she hired me to fix a few windowpanes in her solarium after that one-star review Julienne gave me, but she did, and she was even crustier the week I was on her solarium job.

And that sour expression darkening her face is making even the dolphin chandelier above us wince and shrink back.

"Daisy, shut that music off before I have Pierson toss your phone into that abomination of a pool," she orders without taking her ice blue eyes off me. "Mr. Jaeger, I presume?"

I open my mouth to remind her we've met, then realize with people like this, it doesn't matter. She won't remember me.

I'm just the hired help.

Much like to the curvy, petite woman behind me, I'm just *the stripper*.

"Gram-gram!" Daisy kills the music and tucks her phone into her cleavage, though she's still swaying to the beat. "If I knew you wanted to party, I would've called up ol' Piersy and told him to find you some club clothes." She lifts her glass with a grin. "And did I tell you I closed the Milan deal last week? Summer in Italy, here we come. Woot! Also, a *stripper*? Nice, Gramalicious. I expected way less of you!"

"You're drunk," Imogen sniffs.

"Nope, just buzzed and happy." Daisy tosses herself sideways into one of the low sea blue chairs and drapes her bare, curvy legs over the armrest, which is shaped like a dolphin too, and reaches over her head to deposit the drink on the floor behind her.

Sweet Jesus, she's flexible.

Another noise has me whipping my head back toward Imogen, and this time, I don't miss the people behind her.

A tall, salt-and-pepper-haired man in a suit carrying Imogen's ivory purse. A brick shithouse with dark blond hair and a scowl who looks like a bodyguard. And Stanley Chihuahua, who's now carrying a baby carrier that's the source of the noise.

"Whatcha drinkin', Granny-boo?" Daisy asks. "Alessandro, get The Dame a cognac. She's about to stroke out. Then we can all take a nice, deep, cleansing Moon-breath and be happy again."

"How drunk is she?" Imogen asks the bodyguard who isn't moving to get the older woman a drink. Alessandro, I assume.

"She's not."

"You're completely certain?"

"Yes."

Daisy winks at me, like we're sharing a secret, except I don't know if it's that she's actually drunk and her bodyguard is lying, or that she's sober and just trying to get her grandmother's goat.

But I don't give two fucks about Daisy and goats.

I give two fucks about the kid in the carrier.

He's young. *Super* young. So little, his legs don't reach

the edge of the carrier, and he has little control over his hands as he waves them about, crying his lungs out.

Another lightheaded feeling washes over me as I realize who he is.

He has to be, doesn't he?

"Nothing better to do on the night we laid your cousin to rest than to throw a *party*?" Imogen scowls at Daisy, who rolls her eyes, grabs her drink, and sips off it upside down.

"Everyone mourns in their own way."

None of the adults move to comfort the baby.

The crying *orphan*.

Don't do it, Marine! my nut sack barks. *Retreat! Retreat!*

For being ignorant, randy suckers, they know me damn well.

Stanley Chihuahua grimaces at the carrier, puts it down, and steps a few feet away.

"Why am I here?" I interrupt as Daisy and her grandmother bicker.

They ignore me.

The baby wails harder.

And something deep in my heart twists.

I take three strides to the carrier and squat. No one tries to stop me, which pisses me off even more. I'm a fucking *stranger*. Unbuckling a baby. If there were strangers in my sisters' houses doing what I'm doing right now, I'd tackle the fuckers first and ask questions later.

There's an issue with Julienne Carter-Roderick's will. I need you to come with me. It's personal.

I'm starting to get a very, *very* bad feeling.

The baby's still so tiny I have to cradle his head as I put

him to my shoulder—next to my bad ear—and stand and bounce.

Imogen spears me a glance. Her lips pinch, but she doesn't tell me to unhand the kid.

Not that I would. Who would I hand him to? She's clearly not a baby person, or she'd be comforting him herself. Her lawyer and her purse carrier dude too.

"What am I doing here?" I press again while the little guy snuggles in deeper and his sobs slow.

Imogen ignores me.

These people are total assholes when it comes to answering questions.

But this baby is *not*. He smells like spit-up and pee, and he's so tiny my hand covers his entire back. His black hair is slick, like he's been sweating, and his tears are dripping onto my neck.

I'm the oldest of six. I have twelve nieces and nephews. I signed up for the Marines to take care of people.

This baby?

This baby needs someone to take care of him, and having him curl into me is sparking every protective instinct in my entire being.

None of them brought so much as a diaper bag, though, so I clearly *can't* take care of him any more than just holding him.

"Put that drink down," Imogen orders Daisy, who lifts a lazy brow that's also neon red.

"Gramsies, we all mourn in our own way. This is mine."

"Your time for *mourning* is over. Congratulations,

Daisy. You're Remington Nathaniel Roderick's new guardian."

Daisy blinks at her grandmother, then turns her lavender eyes to the lawyer, then me, then back to her grandmother.

While my hands tighten around the baby—is she fucking *kidding*?—Daisy busts out laughing. "That's a good one."

"I am regrettably not *joking*." Imogen Carter turns that glacial glare on me. "Mr. Jaeger, Julienne and Rafe named you as co-guardian."

I tilt my good ear toward her as my grip tightens even harder around the baby while my stomach goes bungee jumping to my toes. "Come again?"

"I *said*, Mr. Jaeger, that you and Daisy were named as co-guardians for my great-grandson. Whom you're currently holding."

Holy fuck.

My nuts are too in shock to offer up any commentary. There's a buzz in my ears—the good and the bad one— and I go momentarily light-headed while I, too, sink into a dolphin chair with the baby.

I'm definitely *not* here for a party.

4

Daisy

THIS IS NOT HAPPENING.

Except it is, and I need to call my support staff _immediately_ to get plans put in motion. Nannies. Trust funds. Roller coasters that need to be added to the neighborhood.

Fuck.

A _baby?_

We're in my office while my security team slowly kills the party, since word reached us that Anthony Roderick tried to sneak into the Bluewater enclave—undoubtedly looking for the baby, which he probably sees as _property_, since he's that kind of ass—and it's safer in my office than in the pool house because I have a tighter alarm system in here.

I should ping Cameron, Emily, and Luna—my three vagillionaire besties who live down the street in their own mansions with their boyfriends and fiancés—and let them know we might have a slight security situation brewing, except Luna and Beck's dog next door will bark if she feels the slightest bit of danger. Brutus, the community's free-range St. Bernard, would also bark if he saw anything suspicious, though who knows where Brutus is right now?

Hell, Steve the Alligator would probably bark at the Rodericks too. Steve can sense evil. I'm sure of it.

But on an actually-likely-to-happen note, Cam's fiancé, Jude, is basically *always* on high alert after the little security ordeal that brought him into her life. He notices even when the sea turtles change direction. And I suspect it bothers the shit out of him when I throw parties after everything Cam went through when they met, but generally, all I get is a text message.

You're not being stupid, are you?

Huh. Why *hasn't* he texted yet? Or Cam?

Oh.

Right.

Because they're probably having wild monkey sex.

Emily and Derek are probably having monkey sex too.

Actually, add Luna and Big Dick Beck to the monkey sex list as well.

I sigh, because I will most likely *not* be having wild monkey sex again anytime soon.

All I'll have is a memory of a striptease from the hot as fuck stranger who probably wouldn't be here if Gramalicious hadn't vetted him already, and who probably won't be here long, because *who stays to take care of a stranger's baby?*

He's feeding the baby right now. And he changed a diaper after Pierson, The Dame's butler, produced a bag of supplies, but *staying*? For the next eighteen years?

No way.

People don't do that.

But not only is he holding and feeding the baby, he's also engaged in the stare war to end all stare wars with my grandmother.

Usually challenging her only makes her paranormal undead powers stronger, but it seems that being challenged might also be strengthening *him*.

Whoa.

Just *whoa*.

I said sexy as fuck, right?

"Mr. Jaeger, my legal team has all the paperwork prepared for you to surrender custodial rights to Daisy," my grandmother says.

I need a paper bag. And that's *before* he growls a low, "No," at her.

She frowns and glowers, which is impressive.

Usually I'm the only one who can overcome the power of her Botox, but unlike me, Westley Jaeger hasn't made her a few billion dollars—I'm equally fucked the day my grandmother realizes I'm more lucky than brilliant, because I do love poking her—so he's really taking his life into his own hands.

"As you didn't appear to read the will in its entirety, allow me to sum it up for you," The Dame says dryly. "All of Rafe and Julienne's assets are to be liquidated with proceeds donated to the local chapter of Sea Stars Anonymous."

He stares blankly at her while I simultaneously try not to laugh and cry. "Are you for fucking real?" I ask.

Her face pinches again. "Yes, Daisy, I am *for fucking real*."

"Sea Stars Anonymous is a local charity group dedicated to helping people who believe they are reincarnated sea animals and want to return to their...previous manifestation," I tell West.

"I don't give two shi—craps where their stuff goes."

"Mr. Jaeger, just to clarify, Remington does not come with a trust fund, so if you're expecting some kind of financial windfall for—"

I suck in a breath and step back, bumping into one of my frozen yogurt dispensers and accidentally making it leak down my back.

But that face—the raw anger emanating from his blazing hot honey brown eyes— the way his nostrils flare, the way he bares his teeth—*hot as fuck* may not be a strong enough sentiment.

"Lady, I don't know what kind of selfish jackass you take me for, but you can shut your yap-hole right the hell now. This baby needs a family. His mother wanted it to be me. And if she's any indication of what money can do for a person, I'll be the best damn thing to ever happen to him. You want your lawyers to draw up papers having Party McDiamonds here surrender her rights to me, I'm good with that too. We clear?"

I need a fresh pair of panties. And also to realize I should probably be offended by *Party McDiamonds*, but I'm secretly very impressed with the nickname.

It's a new one.

The Dame squares off against him. "You're here *at my invitation*, Mr. Jaeger. Do *not* make me revoke it."

"I'm here at *his dead mother's* invitation. You go on and threaten whatever you need to threaten, but you can be one hundred percent fucking *certain* that when *my* lawyers look over that will and confirm for me that I'm this baby's legal guardian now, I'm taking him home, and I'm raising him right."

He's cradling the tiny bundle against his dark blue polo with one thick, corded forearm while a fire rages in his dark eyes, and is it possible for ovaries to melt? Because my mouth is dry and my knees are weak and I just had a flash of *something* that has nothing to do with my erogenous zones and everything to do with some deeper level of arousal than I've ever felt before.

Men with babies.

Men *who tell off my grandmother* with babies.

This is better than weekends in Bali with rock stars.

Oh, *god*.

My biological clock just gonged. Fuck.

Fuck.

"Where's his nanny?" I ask. I'm breathless and desperate, and I need to latch onto something solid and familiar.

Westley snorts like that's an inappropriate question.

"The nanny was fired the day before the accident for posting YouTube videos with him," The Dame informs me.

"Oh? Because Julienne didn't use him to help criticize baby wash and diaper cream *from the minute she brought him home from the hospital*."

"So glad to see you've found the silver lining for

Remington." Belatedly, I realize she hasn't started shapeshifting into a bull to ram a horn up West Jaeger's ass over his insolence. But before I can dwell on it, she adds, "As for you, you can consider this the next family test."

I suck in a sharp breath, because *no, she didn't.*

Except she did.

She just threatened to disinherit me if I don't raise Julienne's baby.

This whole inheriting-a-baby thing might have me teetering on the edge of a major fissure while an earthquake still rocks around me, but I'm not an asshole concerned about getting a couple hundred million bucks when The Dame kicks the bucket.

It's more that being disinherited means being fired from Carter International Properties.

It means *failing.*

I spent the first twenty-one years of my life being underestimated to the point that I didn't believe in myself. I *need* this job. I actually don't suck at it, and while I know my success is more because I have the Carter family name behind me than because I'm actually *good* at negotiating with people, she hasn't fired me yet.

Helping run a real estate empire? I can do that.

Raising Julienne's baby?

I. Am. So. Fucked.

"If you want to have your lawyers go ahead and draw up paperwork for Ms. Carter-Kincaid to surrender custodial rights to me, I'm happy to wait," Westley offers.

I straighten and shiver as a glop of frozen yogurt slides

down my ass. "The hell she will. How do I know *you'll* be a good guardian?"

He lifts a brow, then looks down at his arms, at the bundle of sleeping baby with a little milk dribbling out the corner of his mouth.

The utterly innocent bundle of *orphan* that I haven't touched yet, even though realizing he's completely alone in the world makes me want to smother him in my arms and hug him tight and promise him he'll be okay.

Oh my god.

I don't know if Julienne ever hugged him.

No wonder he's so comfortable in a stranger's arms. He just needs to be loved. That *is* all babies need, isn't it?

Or is it?

Fuck. I don't know the first thing about babies.

Fuckaroni.

I need Westley. I need him to teach me how to hold a baby and how to know when Remy's hungry and how to put him to sleep. Yes, *Remy*, because he's so tiny and innocent and a cute little name just fits him better.

Oh, double fuck with cheese and bacon on top.

I really *am* having maternal urges. And ridiculous notions about dark-eyed, overprotective strangers. I have a full staff who runs my house, and I'm *positive* any of them could teach me the same things this man holding the baby right now can.

Except those maternal urges to kiss Remy's little cheeks are getting mixed up with the *hello, hot single dad* vibes thumping in my ovaries, which I *do not* appreciate.

Mostly.

"Granny-kins, it's late, and tonight's been a real shit-show. I think it's time for you to hit the road." I smile, but *holy fucking shit*, how the hell am I going to do this *mothering* thing? "I got this."

I most definitely do not *got this*.

But I have to get my grandmother out of here before she catches on to how closely I might be veering into panic territory.

Imogen Carter, The Dame of the Carter family, *knows* things. And she's scowling at me like my position at Carter International Properties isn't the only thing in danger.

But it's the one thing she can take away that I care about. I can't lose my job.

I can't. My job is the only thing that I've ever been successful at that *matters*.

"*Go,*" I repeat.

"Stay home tomorrow. Bond with the baby and get help lined up," she orders me. "Mr. Jaeger, watch yourself."

While my grandmother leaves, Westley turns away from me, but not all the way, and I catch the big bad construction guy's face softening into a gentle smile.

Swoon.

No. *No.* Not swoon. Swoon is only for foreign hotties who believe me when I say my name is Melanie and that I get mistaken for Daisy Carter-Kincaid all the time. For men who know I'm a one-time deal. For men who can't just drive down to Miami, and yes, there was that one who *just drove down to Miami from California* a few years back, so no, I don't date Canadian or Mexican men either.

All of North America is out.

My security team agreed it was a good idea.

I knew when I found West in the pool house that he wasn't a stripper, but I also knew that whoever he was, he was there because The Dame had ordered him to be, much like she'd had my security team find me and inform me she was headed over and needed to talk.

And I knew it would irritate the shit out of her to walk in on me making out with whoever he was.

And now I have to pay for my sins.

So, so much.

5

West

IT'S LATE. My head hurts the way it normally does after an adrenaline crash. There's something orange dripping behind Daisy all over her marble floor and killing my curiosity about the wall of frozen yogurt in this bright, airy office—which I assume is her office because of the frozen yogurt wall and the distressed white desk at one end—and I don't have a fucking clue where this baby needs to sleep tonight.

Me? I'll be on the floor. Right next to him. For tonight, at least, while my temper cools and my injured pride heals. Nothing like being kicked with a dangled insta-family that'll be taken away soon enough by those lawyers Imogen Carter was talking about.

But this little guy has bigger problems than my temper and pride.

He's a fucking orphan. Without a bed. Probably have to sleep on—*christ*.

That round pink Persian-inspired rug in the center of the floor has a circle of penises woven into it. And the sunken white leather seating area around an indoor gas fireplace at the other end of the room has curved end tables decorated with jade stick figures doing each other in the butt.

My balls whimper. *Tonight could've gone soooo differently. Are we sure all's lost?*

"So. You're *not* a stripper," Daisy says with an easy, friendly, *trust me* smile that puts an ache back in my shoulders.

"No," I answer curtly.

"We could still play pretend."

I scowl.

She sighs, grabs a handful of napkins from a dispenser, and turns in a circle while she tries to wipe the orange frozen yogurt off the white and gold sparkle dress holding her tight, round ass. "Let's start over. Hi. I'm Daisy. Welcome to my house. Thanks for feeding the baby. Who are you and how did you know my cousin?"

I know how this ends. They have more money and access to better lawyers than I ever will. This kid isn't my insta-family, and my rapidly cooling temper is making me regret that ballsy move in telling off her grandmother. "Redid the kid's nursery. Never met her—Julienne— before the job. Haven't—didn't talk to her after."

"You're the guy she one-starred because you wouldn't take out a wall to put in a marble statue and fountain?"

I give a single nod, because I have no idea if it's actually *normal* for rich people to think taking out a fucking exterior wall—and raising a ceiling eight inches—in four days with a crew of two is *no big deal.*

"Don't take it personally. She gave my driveway one star because she would've picked starfish instead of crushed seashells, and she once one-starred my mom's boobs for being too boob-like. How'd you get the job?"

"My brother."

Her brows pull together briefly. "Wait. Tyler Jaeger? That asshole who knocked us out of the play-offs this spring with that buzzer beater?"

"You follow hockey."

"I follow a lot of things. How'd Tyler get you the job?"

"Knew somebody who knew somebody who said she couldn't get a contractor to take the job. Just retired from the Marines. Needed the work."

She rolls her eyes. "That makes unfortunate sense. Why did Julienne put you in her will?"

"No clue." I should put the baby down, but I don't want to. He's a tiny little thing. Can't be more than twelve, maybe fifteen pounds.

My parents' cat is bigger than this child.

More loved too. Not a single other person has tried to take him from me.

Daisy's face is morphing as I bounce in place with the sleeping baby, and I don't like it.

It's not *lust* exactly, but it's not *not lust* either. It's dark-eyed, heavy-lidded interest warring with body language that says *stay back, danger, danger,* and this isn't the first time that look has taken over her face tonight.

If life has taught me *anything* in twenty-plus years of

dating, and then reinforced it tonight, it's that dating single mothers doesn't work.

Time might heal all wounds, but the one poking me tonight needs more than six years, apparently.

"Why'd she name you as a guardian?" I ask Daisy.

"Either she had a sick sense of humor, or she thought she was just as immortal as The Dame and that it would never actually be an issue."

I lift a brow.

"Gramalicious. The Graminator. Gram-grams. Grammykins. My grandmother. Call her a Gramogenarian if you really want to get her panties in a twist. She says she's eighty-two, but I suspect she's actually the original Dracula."

My eyeball is twitching. If she keeps talking, it might never stop. "And you do...what, exactly, for your grandmother?"

"Apparently whatever she tells me to do."

She flashes a billion-dollar smile again, but I'm well aware that Imogen Carter just put a fuck-ton on her shoulders. The Carter family matriarch doesn't strike me as the type to trust anyone else to fill her lawn mower with gas, much less raise a child she has vested interest in.

"So I could google you, and that's what it'd say? *Daisy Carter-Kincaid is an heiress who asks how high when her grandmother says to jump?*"

"Oh, no. Google says I'm a partying heiress with a penchant for causing the occasional scene and getting into sticky situations."

"And your grandmother is trusting you with...the first in the next generation of the Carter family?"

"You're here too, Mr. Jaeger. My grandmother is doing what she legally needs to do to make sure Julienne and Rafe's final wishes are carried out."

"Before she removes me from the situation once the Rodericks are dealt with."

She winces. "You could take her a sacrifice of the still-beating heart of her enemy in a crystal goblet forged in the fires of hell, and she might go easy when she has her lawyers chew you up in court. But...do you actually *want* to raise a baby right now?"

"Do you?"

"Westley." She winks. "What kind of question is that? I have ovaries and mammary glands, don't I? *Obviously* I'd want to raise a baby *anytime*."

In other words, no. Possibly with a side of, *this is a conversation for not tonight.*

Am I going to raise this kid?

No.

But am I going to leave him with someone who doesn't have a fucking clue what she's doing?

Also no.

"Do you have a crib?" I ask.

Her whole face transforms into pure joy. "Yes! We just redid the butterfly lounge and turned it into this epic— oh. *Baby* crib. Not *party* crib. Sorry. No."

This is going to be the longest night in the history of long nights, and I once pulled a forty-eight-hour shift in the desert kicking in doors looking for a terrorist.

"Flat surface?" I ask. "For sleeping?"

She tosses the dirty napkins into a trash hole in the

white wall, then bites her lip while her darkening gaze travels down the length of my body again.

"Knock it off," I growl.

She doesn't flinch, which is probably a testament to how often she and her grandmother go at it. "Do you know much about babies? Like, does he need to sleep in a cage, or can he just sleep on a bed?"

"A *cage*?"

"That's what a crib is, right? A caged bed? So they can't...crawl away?"

"He's too little to crawl."

"You're sure?"

"He can't even lift his head by himself. I'm sure."

She eyeballs the baby. Then lifts her eyes to me again. "Why are you still here? Not that I'm not grateful for the help, but...you're not related to any of us. Julienne left you an asshole review for a new business. New, yes? And I doubt Rafe was any nicer. You know I can afford any help necessary so I can raise Remy on my own. You've also gotten a taste of what we both know my grandmother will throw at you to get you to leave, because she's very protective of family when they're still young enough to be molded into her next protégé. So...why not just bolt?"

"Because you don't have a fucking clue what you're doing."

She tips her head back and laughs. "Oh, Westley. You're adorable. And you've had quite the night. How about I take Remy upstairs to a cozy little corner of my room, and then we'll get you settled in one of my guest suites? Miami traffic sucks *all* hours of the day, and there's no need to travel home tired."

"No."

"No?"

"I sleep where Remy sleeps."

Her lips part like she's about to argue, but to my surprise, instead, she nods. "Thank you. It's kind of you to help."

I study her.

She stares right back.

And I have the oddest sensation that she's more grateful than she'll admit.

Retreat! Retreat! my nuts shout.

Because they know. They've seen this before.

Lady with a baby having a breakdown.

I tell my balls to knock it off. I'm older. I'm wiser. And I'm not falling for a hard-partying heiress just because she inherited an orphan who's going to need all the love he can get.

Yep.

That's my story. And if I repeat it enough, I might actually convince myself it's true.

6

Daisy

I GET West and Remy settled in the sitting room off my bedroom—hello, temptation—and then retreat.

I can't fully explain it, but I trust him.

Or possibly I'm just so relieved that I don't have to dive into this guardianship thing alone just yet, that I want to believe I can trust him.

Either way, my life as I knew it four hours ago is basically over, and I need to adapt. Fast.

I climb into bed with my laptop, and send a slew of emails to my staff, both at Carter International Properties and at home, about my schedule suddenly needing to be flexible for a little bit, all while listening to the muted sounds of West settling onto the couch in the room next door.

He's fascinating.

And by fascinating, I mean all of my erogenous zones

are pinging just from having him in my personal space. I want to know why he always tilts his left ear toward me when I'm talking. If he's a whiskey or a beer kind of guy. Or both. If his overprotective papa bear mode is just an adrenaline thing, or if there's more to his story. If he'll still be here in the morning. Why he's in Miami when his family is in Chicago—yes, *fine*, I googled his brother when I was supposed to be working, but who could resist?

The guy's basically playing hero tonight while I'm hiding in here trying not to hyperventilate at the idea of sudden motherhood.

And that whole *hero* thing—I don't trust *that* either.

Are people *really* that pure-intentioned?

Although, I don't have to wonder why I'm having erotic thoughts about him rubbing froyo all over my breasts.

That part's pretty obvious. He's six feet of overprotective muscle with a chiseled jaw shaded by dark stubble and a hint of a tattoo peeking out from beneath one of his sleeves. The guy could be on the cover of a romance novel.

I toss my laptop to the side and tiptoe to the door to the next room to peek in.

It takes a minute for my eyes to adjust enough to see that the baby's swaddled in a blanket and snoring softly on the floor, West just a few feet from him, long body stretched out, one arm under his head, his breath slow and even.

I don't actually believe he's sleeping. Even with the light so dim, I swear I can tell that he's too tense to be sleeping.

And he's positioned himself between Remy and the door to the hallway, so if anyone tries to come in in the middle of the night, they'll trip over him first.

Seriously.

What kind of guy would do this? Stay with a baby that isn't his, but still needs him?

I shake my head and chalk it all up to utter weirdness that'll make more sense in the morning, pull the door mostly shut, and head back to bed, stripping out of my shirt and panties. Why have nice bedding if you can't rub your whole body against it?

And then I slide under my soft, satiny sheets and flip off my light.

I'm mildly horny.

And I need to take the edge off.

A nice fantasy about Julio should do. He's a delectable beach bum I spent a night with in the Canary Islands a few months ago.

He also thinks my name is Sandi with an I, and he had quite the dirty-talking tongue on him.

I let myself imagine we'd met on a cobblestone road in Tuscany after highwaymen made off with my carriage and escort, leaving me naked and alone and vulnerable.

He'd whip off his shirt and wrap it about me, surrounding me with the scent of sun-dried cotton and salty seas, then heft me into his chiseled arms and carry me to the nearest tavern, where he'd spoon-feed me broth and murmur low in Italian about how he'll avenge my honor, and keep me safe until such a day as he's run his dagger through the hearts of every highwayman in Europe.

Possibly I've been reading too many historical romances.

But it's working.

My skin burns against my sheets, and I part my legs while I tease my nipples into hard nubs, ignoring the little detail in my fantasy that instead of a lean surfer's body with sun-kissed brown hair, all I can see is a thick-necked, dark-scruffed, brown-eyed warrior in a leather kilt.

My fingers drift over my breasts and down my soft belly as I smile and stifle a whimper. My pussy's aching. My clit is tingling. And I'm fantasizing about Westley Jaeger in gladiator gear, charging a raging bull trying to trample a baby, and holy fuck, *why are men with babies so fucking hot?*

I flick my clit to distract myself from remembering him pulling his shirt up, giving me a glimpse at a tattoo. At him staring my grandmother down like a warrior. At him bouncing Remy.

My head tilts back and I have to squeeze my lips tight together to keep from moaning.

I wonder if he's as good with his hands on a woman's body as he is with a baby.

No. No, Daisy.

Too close. He's off-limits. For so many reasons.

God, off-limits is *hot*.

I want off-limits. I want to be *bad*. I want—

A high-pitched wail suddenly erupts in the next room, and I yank my hand out of my chacha and fly off the bed.

I fling the door open to the sitting room, remember I'm naked as West looks up at me, and I screech.

He screeches.

CRAZY FOR LOVING YOU

Remy wails.

And I dive for cover under my vanity.

I'm good with nudity. My body's never going to earn me a strut down the catwalk during Fashion Week, but I know how to use it to maximum advantage.

Plus, I have these tits that just won't stop.

Also, *it's flipping dark*. No way he actually saw me.

So I don't know why I'm shrieking and hiding.

Okay, that's a lie. I totally know why I'm shrieking and hiding.

My grandmother would kill me if I tried to seduce West, which is actually the least of my concerns.

I do a lot of things she'd kill me for—I'm very good at walking that line between making her angry and making her head explode like a volcano before it reforms into a meaner version than before—but I make her enough money that she overlooks it. Mostly.

We both know I only make her a lot of money because people know if they don't deal with *me*, they'll deal with *her*. Without her name behind me, I'd need to get a door-to-door salesman mustache and the brown leather briefcase holding vacation timeshare brochures to make enough money to put food on my table.

And I don't mean food on the crystal Aisu table in my under-the-sea lounge downstairs either. I mean a wobbly Formica table that I pulled out of the trash after I get evicted from my fabulous D-shaped hacienda.

Fucking up Julienne's kid's life would never be over-lookable to The Dame.

Plus, West lives within driving distance of my house—obviously—and he knows my real name, which by default marks him off my list of *people I'd like to sleep with*. If co-inheriting my cousin's baby with him is complicated, getting physically involved would be catastrophic.

Sleeping with Westley Jaeger is completely and totally off the table.

All the tables.

There will be no nookie on the Aisu table or any of the other tables in this house.

Or anywhere in Bluewater.

So being naked around him probably should be too. And it's more expeditious to pretend I'm embarrassed to be naked than it is to stand there and tempt him with my goddessness while I tell him that we're not happening.

Yep.

That's my logic.

I drop my head to the floor and stifle a groan, and this one is definitely *not* a good groan.

He knocks at the door. "Do you have a rocking chair? Also, I'm not looking. Don't see a thing. I have four sisters. I'm an expert in not looking."

I scoot deeper under the vanity, which would be easier if I didn't have these melons on my chest getting in the way, and if I'd eaten a little less pasta the last four times I was in Italy this year.

And gelato.

I definitely should've eaten less—no, never mind.

I definitely should've eaten *more* gelato, because you only live once, and it's Italian gelato, and it's well worth the extra padding on my ass.

I should have some gelato delivered tomorrow.

Apparently along with a rocking chair. "I have a

mechanical unicorn that I can turn down the speed on?" I call back.

He mutters something under his breath.

Remy wails.

"Never mind," he says.

I almost offer to take Remy, but I've never actually held a baby before.

I've squealed over plenty. Made googoo eyes and baby-talked and booped their little noses and kissed their little heads.

But I haven't *held* a baby.

I need to.

Soon.

But as long as West's here, I don't have to, and so I'm putting it off until I'm well-rested.

Yep.

That's my story.

"Ten minutes," I call to him.

Maybe I can't hold a baby, but I can work miracles.

7

Daisy

FRIDAY MORNING, I'm yanked out of a dream by a loud, weird wailing in my ear. I'm disoriented and tangled in a sheet of doom that I apparently twisted myself into overnight, and as the remnants of the dream evaporate, I realize I'm not alone. I try to bolt upright, almost fall off the bed, and stick my head straight into the crotch of a tall, burly man who smells like baby powder and coffee.

There's a man.

Standing beside the gauzy curtains of my four-poster bed in my dollhouse bedroom.

And he's holding out a crying baby.

Oh, fuck.

I have a baby.

"He's been fed, changed, and burped," the tree trunk announces over the sound of the baby's cries. "Baby books say he needs tummy time, but no television. You're up, princess. Watch his head and neck. He's still too little to sit up on his own, and I need to get to work."

I blink away the crustiness in my eyes and try to make him come into focus. "Who are you?"

"Nobody important. Just a dude who watched a baby overnight."

Nobody important.

Not likely.

I know exactly who he is, and that dream that evaporated comes flying back into my head like a runaway locomotive.

Which is eerily symbolic of everything that was just going down in my dreams, which West was unfortunately starring in, this time in a train conductor uniform, which was sexier than you might think.

"You're...leaving?"

He sighs. "He's your cousin's kid. Not mine. There's not a single logical reason she'd put me in her will, and there's not a single logical reason for me to stay."

Panic swells under my breastbone and flops around like a grouper in the sand. "I don't know anything about babies," I blurt.

"You can afford help."

"But it takes time. There's a vetting process. I can't just hire the first nanny off the street." It's the rich kid version of street smarts. Don't hire anyone you haven't vetted, and make *everyone* sign an NDA.

Oh, fuck.

I didn't ask West to sign an NDA. I wonder if the Graminator did.

Probably.

I bat my eyelashes.

He rolls his eyes. "Four sisters. That doesn't work."

"I'll pay you."

"Don't insult me either."

The clock hands on the ivory wall across from my bed tell me it's almost eight AM.

Our little *incident* happened around three AM. I had him a rocking chair by three-fifteen—and I owe my housekeeper a case of strawberry Pocky to thank her for that, since it's Lucinda's favorite treat *ever*.

However, I don't think I'll be thanking anyone for the fantasy fuel that was listening to West sing Remy lullabies until around four.

He's cradling the baby one-armed and wearing the same clothes he arrived in—jeans and a blue polo—but his beard seems thicker and his eyes—which I swore were honey-brown last night but are now a deep-set green under his thick brows—are definitely more world-weary.

He works construction. Without air conditioning. Swinging a hammer in the Miami sun, wiping sweat off his forehead, bare-chested, and tipping his head back to enjoy a Diet Coke while the office ladies across the street gawk, and god, if I'm having bare-chested fantasies of a man holding a baby before coffee, then this co-parenting thing is an awful idea.

That's probably why Julienne did it.

Because she thought it would be hilarious to imagine me raising an infant with a retired Marine with the body of a god and the soul of a saint and the sense of humor of —well.

I'm not sure I've seen his sense of humor yet.

Unless this is it. *You're up, Daisy. I'm going to stand here and laugh my ass off while you try to figure out how to change a diaper.*

My phone rings somewhere amidst all the fluffy covers—my grandmother's ring tone, that Half-Cocked Heroes song about the devil calling—and Remy bursts into a harder wail.

West smirks. "Hands full today, Ms. Carter-Kincaid?"

"*Daisy*, if you please. Seeing me naked doesn't mean this has to get formal. Hand me that baby. We'll be fine." I double-check that I'm not naked and mentally high-five myself when I realize I'm wearing my oversize *Sober is a Four-Letter Word* T-shirt.

Present from Emily last Christmas.

I love my friends. They get me.

And since I'm decent, I throw the covers back, find my phone and silence it, and then peek over at Remy, ignoring that tempting scent of coffee lingering on the man holding the baby.

The baby.

Oh, the baby.

His skin is so smooth and soft-looking, his eyes mildly panicked like he knows his mama's gone, and his little hands are waving about like he's trying to grasp onto something but doesn't know how.

And I want to love him.

I want to love him and promise him he'll be fine and that I know what I'm doing, except I can't.

Who gives me a fucking baby?

West slowly transfers the infant to me, the back of his hand brushing the top of my arm and making me shiver, but he doesn't stop. It's like he has no idea that the mere thought of holding Remy is making me both freak out and go all twitterpated.

What if I drop him?

What if he's allergic to my soap?

What if he thinks my boobs have milk in them?

I sink back down onto my bed as the squirmy little human flings a dimpled hand at me.

He's light as a feather and seven gazillion times more fragile. But as soon as I have a firm grip on him, holding his sweaty little body against my breast, I start bouncing and whispering *shh* like it's the most natural thing in the world.

And he stops fussing. Stops crying.

Just snuggles in, a little bundle of pure innocence that has chosen *me*.

My breath catches, and I stare down so West can't see my face.

Babies?

So not in my life plan. I work hard so I can play hard. Make a deal in Madrid, then head to the Canary Islands for a wild three-day fling with a Spaniard. Start talks in Rio, then dash down to Antarctica for a South Pole polar plunge on a dare that costs some actor or Greek shipping magnate a hefty donation to charity and ends with a big, burly Viking warming me up in bed.

Coming home to the husband and three-point-two minions?

My genes aren't really built for the whole *solid family* thing.

I used to think it was the money, except it's not. Money's a symptom. Not the root cause.

We're a judgmental lot of assholes.

Performance determines worth.

And I never wanted a child to feel like an accomplishment.

Feel *accomplished*, yes.

Be someone else's accomplishment—like I am to my father—no.

And much as I love my mom, she, too, puts her self-worth directly in line with how well her art sells.

But holding this baby while he snuggles in close?

It's making me feel weird protective things that I was never supposed to feel but can't stop. Like I would move the entire fucking earth to keep him happy.

I wonder if Julienne felt those things about him, or if she was as screwed up as the rest of us?

West is watching me, something both soft and protective as hell flashing over his features, and my nipples pebble and remind me that I'm not wearing a bra under this shirt.

"Thank you for your help last night," I say quietly, my gaze darting down again.

"People should help people."

It's a simple sentiment, but it gives me more horny shivers in the vajayjay. My emotions are a wreck right now.

I don't like wrecked emotions, so I tell them to shape the fuck up.

"I don't know why Julienne tangled you up in this mess, but Remy and I will be fine."

I hope.

Even if I figure out how to take care of a baby, there's still the Rodericks to deal with. They'll undoubtedly challenge the will, which is dumb, because I don't think either of them cares about anything beyond money and stature.

Anthony Roderick would probably sell his wife for a million bucks and controlling share in a whiskey distillery, and Margot Roderick honestly believes neither her husband nor her son could do any wrong, when they're both what my mother would call *philandering assholes*.

Just thinking about them makes me want to buy out six florists today and make sure everyone all across Little Havana gets a free flower. It's how I get balance from the ugly parts of my life—by spreading love bombs across Miami.

"You're almost out of formula," West says gruffly.

Of fucking course I am. But I smile at him. "Got that covered."

I press a kiss to Remy's head because I need to look away from the man whose temper is rising so fast that he's making me sweat—who knew I was a sucker for the overprotective type?—and oh my god.

This baby.

He's so *sweet*.

He's cuddling closer and closer, smelling like peach fuzz and baby sweat, which shouldn't be addictive to sniff, except it is. And his hair—he has this thick black hair that's so fine and soft, it could probably be sold on the black market for a special new kind of cashmere.

Not that I'd do that to him.

But I know enough unscrupulous people who would.

My door bangs open.

West spins into a crouch, flinging himself between me and my visitors. "*Out!*" he orders Alessandro, who crosses his arms and lifts a brow.

I should be trying not to grin right now, but West just basically put his life on the line in issuing orders to my head of security without looking first.

Except having someone who's not paid to protect me put himself in the line of fire is volcanic on the hotness scale, and there's nothing funny about that.

"Your grandmother's on her way," Alessandro tells me.

He eyeballs West.

West eyeballs him right back.

"You staying?" Alessandro demands.

"Not really my place, is it?"

The two men continue to stare at each other, and something passes silently between them. I don't know what, but I know Alessandro is a better judge of character than any dog, and even Luna's Beck, who spends his whole life around dogs, agrees.

So when my head of security nods to West and holds out a fist for a bump, a puddle of warmth floods my chest.

A puddle of warmth that means absolutely nothing, because in the next breath, West is walking out the door.

"Hey, take my number," I call after him, making Remy squawk at the sudden noise.

He turns, and I catch the weirdest expression on his face. Like...hope? Or dread?

Or both?

"For attorneys." I wave a hand, realize I don't want to

PIPPA GRANT

take that hand off Remy, and quickly put it back. "And all that boring stuff."

"Got you covered," Alessandro says to me.

And then West is gone.

And I have this horrible suspicion I'm never going to see him again, which shouldn't be a bad thing—we *can't* date, for multiple reasons, and having him out of the way so no one is witness to me fucking up Remy is a *good* thing.

But I still feel the weirdest emptiness, an extra loneliness, at my temporary co-guardian doing exactly what my family wants him to do.

Leave.

It's right, but it's also so, so wrong.

8

West

I DON'T WANT to leave Daisy alone with Remy, because she has the same look on her face that Tyler had the day our first niece was born—the one that says *oh my god I have no idea what I'm doing holding this thing that's smaller than a football*.

But that baby is *hers* so much more than he can ever be *mine*. I have no blood claim. I didn't know his family. And it's not like I'm leaving him stranded at the steps of a firehouse and hoping he'll get adopted someday by a family who loves him.

This family has money. They have their own brand of loyalty. And it's none of my fucking business.

Alessandro walks me down a winding staircase, out through the D-shaped courtyard and past a D-shaped pool, and into a sitting room with another round sunken seating area with a gas fire pit in the middle, crystal penises decorating the end tables, and bright green plants placed about the room beneath the high ceiling. We walk through this room too, straight into a connected foyer with a curved glass staircase.

I pause at the doorway. "Can she handle this on her own?"

He studies me briefly, and I know he's not going to answer me. So it surprises me when he replies, "Doesn't matter. She will."

That's not ominous. Not at all. "There's no legit reason for me to stay."

"Just a legally binding will."

"You knew Julienne?"

"Unfortunately."

"She make her will while she was drunk?"

"Probably drew names out of a hat."

I look down at the textured white marble floor. All I need is one person to stand up and tell me this kid's parents had a solid reason for putting me in that will, and I'd stay.

I'd fight.

I could give him doting aunts. The best grandparents. An insane uncle—everyone needs an Uncle Tyler—and cousins and pool parties and root beer popsicles and birthday parties and lawn darts and a solid middle-class life full of fun and hard work.

But staying here is nothing more than a shortcut to another family I don't belong with.

Easier to walk away now than to stay, get attached, and complicate what's undoubtedly going to be a messy situation. "The Rodericks—they'll fight for the kid?"

CRAZY FOR LOVING YOU

I met Anthony Roderick once. Guy leered at his daughter-in-law like he wanted to take her to bed himself, slapped the housekeeper on the ass, and pissed in the bushes.

Not in that order.

I'd probably be in jail if I'd been any closer when the ass-slapping happened, but he was long gone by the time I made it out of the nursery. My Spanish wasn't good enough to understand the maid, but I knew the hand gesture. *Leave it be. It's fine.*

It wasn't fine.

"They'll try," Alessandro tells me. "They'll lose. We know people."

We know people.

See? The baby has Alessandro too. He doesn't need me. He'll never even remember me.

I hand him my card. "Either of them need anything, let me know."

He studies me again, and I get the feeling he's calling me a pansy-ass for leaving. Or possibly an idiot for thinking I could have anything Daisy Carter-Kincaid might need.

He opens the door, and a parrot squawks an obscenity at us from a perch near a window. "Get out of here, Frank," Alessandro says.

The parrot tells him to fuck off, then flutters away.

"We'll keep you on the guest list until the legal dust settles," he tells me.

I nod and head for my truck, parked in the same place I put it last night. Or fifty years ago. Feels that long.

"By the way, TMZ has a copy of the will and pictures of both of you."

My head whips up. "What?"

"Might want to keep your head down."

Fucker.

He grins.

I flip him off and head for my car.

In all the chaos, I forgot to tell my family.

My sister Keely reads TMZ religiously. I open my truck, climb in, and fire up my phone, which I shut down last night when the battery started getting low. I'm tired, and I don't want to deal with this. I got approximately forty-five minutes of sleep last night in the sprawling, sea-toned sitting room where the baby fussed and whimpered through the night, with the window open to let in the sea breeze and the sound of the bay outside.

Forty-five minutes of dream-filled sleep about getting summoned into that princess bedroom for a second chance at the striptease, followed by a booty call, courtesy of that flash of seeing Daisy naked at three AM.

She's wild and unpredictable and annoying and irresponsible and fucking *fascinating*.

And for two whole minutes, I thought we'd have some fun. Until *life* happened.

But life with Daisy isn't happening now. Because I've done the *date a single mother* thing one too many times.

No way I'm getting involved with a woman who just unexpectedly inherited a baby.

No matter what watching her face light up with joy and utter adoration at holding the baby did to that hollow in my chest.

My phone powers up, and a minute later, I get approximately six thousand message notifications. I scroll up, and start at the top of the family group text, and jump in apparently just in time.

Keely: WESTLEY MICHAEL JAEGER, YOU ARE IN SO MUCH TROUBLE WITH ME. A BABY? You inherited a BABY with a BILLIONAIRE HEIRESS PARTY GIRL and you let us find out from people.com? *angry emoji* *shocked emoji*

Mom: Keely, I told you, that article was about a different Westley Jaeger. Our West would've told us if he inherited a baby.

Britney: Mr. I'll Take Care Of This Myself? No, Mom, he wouldn't have.

Mom: He didn't even know that awful woman.

Keely: Yes, he did. Remember? "He strokes paint onto the wall like he's never satisfied a woman in his life and he probably stuffs his pants with ass padding to make it look that good."

Mom: Oh, THAT woman? THAT was the woman who left him a BABY? Honey. This is just Tyler setting up another prank.

Allie: God, Keely, did you memorize that review? And Tyler knows a lot of people, but even he can't hack people.com to put up a prank article about West.

Allie: Wait. Actually, he probably knows someone who could. Tyler, tell me you didn't set this up.

Tyler: I WISH I set it up. That's fucking epic. W, did someone else set this up? Who else knows you well enough to pull off the prank of the century?

Britney: West, we know you have your hands full, but if you don't answer in the next two minutes, we're organizing a convoy and charging Daisy Carter-Kincaid's mansion. *sword emoji* *dragon emoji* *knight emoji*

West: You can't teleport from Chicago, so don't threaten it. Yes, I inherited the 1-star lady's kid. No, I don't know why. Yes, with Daisy. No, you can't come see the house just because you want to. Sorry I didn't tell you—been a little busy the last twelve hours or so. Don't get excited—it won't stick.

Allie: West, I still have Liliana's high chair. Actually, it's the last baby thing I have left. Yours if you want it. I'll ship it, because you're my favorite big brother, and it's about time you settled down and gave Mom kids, considering how long you've already made her wait.

Keely: DO NOT GIVE AWAY YOUR LAST BABY ITEM OR YOU'LL GET PREGNANT AGAIN, YOU IDIOT. West, I'll buy you a fucking high chair. DO NOT TAKE ALLIE'S. Also, insensitive much? HELLO, THE SIERRA YEARS. If West wants a baby, I fully support him inheriting one of his own.

Britney: Not touching that Keely said the S-word, but hard agree on the high chair. Don't take Allie's. *pacifier emoji* *avocado emoji*

Allie: You guys, Oscar's fixed. More babies are NOT a concern. And avocado? WTF, Brit? I don't know what that means.

Allie: OH! Right. Avocado. Good baby food. I got it now.

Keely: *GIF of woman falling over laughing* You're all nuts, and DAISY CARTER-KINCAID CAN FUCKING

AFFORD A HIGH CHAIR. Can we get back to the important part here?

Britney: Keely's right, Allie. We should talk about the important part. Has Oscar had his semen tested to make sure it's swimmer-free? Not saying I know from personal experience how important that is, but *baby emoji* *baby emoji* *baby emoji*

Mom: OMD, you're pregnant with TRIPLETS?

Allie: Mom. It's O-M-G. Oh My Gosh. G. G. G.

Mom: I like D. It drives your father nuts when I say Oh My Dog. Back to the triplets. OMD, I'm CRYING. Four new grandbabies in one day.

Dad: I'm sitting next to goob reading these sexts too, May Ella. I can creed what you just let's go to bed.

Dad: Let's go to bed.

Dad: LET'S GO TO BED.

Dad: What the duck is wrong with my dingaling?

Dad: Dingaling.

Dad: GOOBERSNATCHER BRA BRA LIGHTWEIGHT, Tyler, QUIT MESSING WITH MY DINGAGLING SETTINGS.

Britney: NO! NO I AM NOT PREGNANT AGAIN. *profanity emoji* Jesus. I cut his fucking balls ALL THE WAY OFF after the twins happened. *eggplant emoji* And we get him tested every three weeks to make sure the snip-snip is still working. I just hit the emoji button too many times. Good DOG you people are crazy. *dog emoji* *eye roll emoji*

Tyler: High five, Dad. You keep sexting Mom. But leave us out of it.

West: Are you fuckers done?

Mom: Of course, honey. Though I am taking screenshots of all of this. I'm working on a new set for my show. Netflix asked for a second season. Their demographic testing shows I do well with the middle-aged set, which means I need more funny family stuff. Tyler, I also need you to show me how to do that intentional autocorrect thing with your father's phone.

Keely: And again, let's get back to West… *GIF of the three dudes from Three Men and a Baby* You okay, West? For real? They're not talking about taking the baby away from you, are they? Or would you rather not raise him? Either way, we support you.

Britney: God, yes. Let's talk about West AND THE REAL BABY. *baby emoji* See? ONE BABY. ONE BABY EMOJI. Not coming from my baby making loins. *pork-chop emoji* Also, ditto to Keely, West. However you want to play this, we have your back.

Tyler: You need a lawyer, West? I know a guy who knows a guy.

Keely: *GIF of someone popping gum and waiting for the story*

West: Yes. YES. I definitely need to talk to a lawyer. But I hope this lawyer's better than your last "I know a guy who knows a guy." He smelled like canned baloney and only won that case because the judge got tired of his burping.

Not true, but if there's one thing my family's good at, it's giving each other shit.

And given how many guys Tyler knows in the whole hockey league who've had to do paternity tests—which is somewhere between more guys than I knew in the

Marines who had to do paternity tests and the number of times I've already seen Daisy bounce up and down in excitement over something—I'm going to assume his lawyer contact is reasonably competent.

And probably expensive.

And very, very ironic.

The last time I tried parenting ended spectacularly horrifically.

But I had zero legal claim that time. I was just the boyfriend. Sierra didn't want to get married—said she'd done that once and wasn't doing it again. But when the military ordered me to move from South Carolina to California, I thought she'd change her mind.

That she'd realize I was worth moving for.

Except it turns out, she didn't love me *that* much.

I would've stayed just for her kids at that point. But she kicked me out. Told me to eat shit and die. And then hit on my best friend.

Wasn't in much of a place to be a solid father figure after that.

Probably could've stayed and fought for her, but at what ultimate price to her and her kids?

My phone dings, pulling me back to the present. Tyler's sending contact info for a local family law attorney.

Almost a father once with no legal claim.

Now, I have all the legal claim, but no *moral* reason to stay. "Just love him," I whisper to Daisy. "Love the *shit* out of him."

I had my doubts when I got here.

I had my doubts overnight.

But that soft but overwhelmed smile that crept over her face when she finally took the baby and looked down at him in her arms?

That's not something money can buy.

My gut says that kid's going to get the *only* thing I thought I could offer him.

And so I tell my family I'm bowing out—that it's for the best—put my truck in gear, and head back out the way I came.

Past all the mansions. A golf course. Condos. Palm trees. People in colorful clothes out for jogs or walks along the golf cart trails winding along the road. A group of ladies on a patio overlooking the miniature golf course, all gossiping and holding out their pinky fingers while they sip their coffee. Glimpsing a little row of shops beyond that carved rooster near the gate.

And I head back to what I'm supposed to be doing.

Getting my footing after the Marines. Fixing up an old gym. Living life on the beach.

And apparently *not* having a family anytime soon.

9

Daisy

IF IT WASN'T for Lucinda, I would be falling apart. But she bustles in two minutes after Alessandro escorted West out of my room, like she wasn't up mere hours ago hunting down a rocking chair in the middle of the night.

She holds the baby while I shower quickly, and when I'm ready to face the day, he's sleeping peacefully in a large basket lined with a soft but thin pillow.

And so I do what I do best—I dive into faking my way through this.

I call up a personal shopper I know, explain what I need, and she assures me she'll have a nursery arranged before dinnertime, complete with a wardrobe to get a Miami baby through the holidays. Then it's on to searching for nannies, which is new territory, but I've phone interviewed three nanny agencies before ten, and

77

have in-person meetings set with the executive directors of my two favorites.

My personal assistant shows up mid-morning with crates of diapers, wipes, and formula, and by the time I'm done interviewing the two nanny services, I feel like I have everything under control.

It helps that Lucinda's been playing babysitter.

She has four grandchildren and adores babies, but also loves giving them back to their parents at the end of her days with them.

Apparently it's the true joy of grandparenting. Or so she tells me.

In any case, by the time my doorbell chimes out its trumpet blast halfway through the afternoon, I'm on top of the world.

I am *rocking* this guardian thing.

But a few minutes later, the sour expression on my grandmother's face suggests she doesn't see it. She marches into my office, where I've finally sat down to catch up on work emails, and announces, "The Rodericks have formally filed a challenge to the will."

"Wow." I glance at my dick clock—one of my mom's pieces of art, which hangs proudly opposite the wall of windows overlooking the beach. Three PM. "Took longer than I thought it would."

"Where's Mr. Jaeger?"

"He left. I got this."

My grandmother peels her reading glasses off in that way that spells doom and tilts her chin down in a way that spells *you are so fucked, Daisy.*

"You do not *got this*," she informs me in that voice that

offers not even a sliver of a crack to weasel in an argument.

Like that's ever stopped me. "Pretty sure I do. Remy's sleeping. We have a nursery nearly all set up. Nannies lined up for interviews, and—"

"And you have a reputation that will *not* stand up in a court of family law."

"Gram-gram. No judge *anywhere* is going to look at Anthony and Margot Roderick and see anything but a man who'd sell his own wife for partial ownership of a whiskey distillery and a woman whose idea of charity is looking the other way when she sees someone carrying a no-name purse while dressed in knock-offs of last season's styles. We'll just have Derek massage my reputation, and—"

"And Westley Jaeger is a decorated retired Marine running his own business who makes you look more legitimate, no massaging required. Get him back."

I gape at her, because there's nothing else to do in this situation.

My grandmother *does not* invite non-family people to family events.

Specifically, to the *raising* of Carter family children. Control freak, thy name is *Imogen Carter*.

She lifts a silver brow. "I don't believe sitting there impersonating a guppy will produce the desired results."

"Grandma—"

"This is not up for debate. The tabloids are already reporting that you took Remington *to a party* last night after taking custody of him."

No point in arguing, because they'll say what they

want. It's a fact of being covered by the gossip sites. You get used to it. "And we have how many witnesses that will attest to that *not* being true?"

"*Partial* witnesses."

And again with the *no point in arguing*. One of the luxuries of being rich is that you can get away with so, *so* much.

Not that I do, for the record. I'm an heiress, not a troublemaker. "So we file restraining orders and make them look bad."

She sniffs like I've insulted her, and I realize her attorneys are already probably on it. Actually, she's probably also already talked to Emily's boyfriend, who runs a business cleaning up reputations. I like to say I've known him longer—he did some work for me after I was framed for shoplifting a few years ago—but after Emily's own desperate need for some reputation cleaning almost six months ago, she definitely knows him better.

And she's *far* more satisfied with his performance.

"Gram-gram. We're Carters. We'll get through this."

"We'll get through this far more efficiently with Mr. Jaeger's help. Get him back."

I don't often get headaches, but when I do, my grandmother is involved. "Give me one week, and I'll be the most picture-perfect guardian you've ever seen."

"Get him back by dinnertime, or you're disinherited."

This isn't the first time she's threatened to disinherit me, but I suspect it's about to be the last. The gig's up. She knows.

She knows I'm going to fuck this up. My heart is racing.

My throat is dry. And panic is making the tips of my fingers go numb.

"Mr. Jaeger has an extensive family and far more experience with children than you do. Get him back. Learn from him. Use him to re-cement your reputation now that your situation has changed. Also, I've canceled your trip to Japan."

"What?"

"Leaving the country without Remington so soon after taking custody of him is exactly the sort of behavior the Rodericks are expecting, and exactly the sort of behavior that suggests you don't put his interests first. God only knows why Julienne put *you* in her will, but until we've resolved the legal issues, your first and only job is being Remington's new mother."

I mentally curse in six different languages, but it doesn't help the gnawing fear now growing in my gut and the sudden realization that Bali isn't happening either. But I also jut my chin up, because if I've learned anything in working for my grandmother for well over a decade, it's that she actually respects a backbone. "I'm still coming to work next week."

"You're staying home."

"If West is here—" *Fuck*, what am I saying? That I'll go get him? I can't have him here. He'll see right through me in two seconds, and it won't be the Rodericks we're fighting.

It'll be the man who stood in this office last night and told my grandmother to gird her loins, because he was coming for her great grandbaby.

Is it possible to be utterly terrified and utterly turned on at the same time?

Because I think I'm there.

My grandmother watches me expectantly.

I swallow and start again. "If Mr. Jaeger is here, then Remy's covered, and there's no reason for me not to go to work. *Or*, I can take him to the daycare at the office."

"There's a large amount of uncertainty in your plans," she says dryly. "Get Mr. Jaeger back here by dinnertime and convinced to stay through the legal proceedings. Learn how to take care of Remington. And then perhaps we can discuss your return to the office."

"The Cairo deal—"

"I have it covered."

"And the Sydney spa—"

"Your employees will bring me up to speed."

Dammit.

And it's not just the projects. It's checking on Anita in accounts payable, whose daughter is undergoing chemo treatments. It's delivering cupcakes to human resources because Janette's boyfriend broke up with her, but she doesn't want to talk about it, so cupcakes are second best. It's catching up with Juan in hospitality to make sure he's taking his vacation time, because the guy's basically brilliant at his job, but he's prone to burnout if someone— namely, me—doesn't nag him to use his vacation days and escape and refresh.

Who's going to do all that while I'm out?

My grandmother rises. "Dinnertime, Daisy. Clock's ticking."

You wouldn't know she was eighty-two years old by the way she carries herself out of my office.

But it lends more weight to my theory that she's one of the undead.

Also, she doesn't realize it, but she *did* leave me with a large amount of wiggle room. She didn't specify which time zone for dinner, or even explicitly say *today's* dinnertime.

Still, I'm grateful for Alessandro always being able to read my mind when he pops his head into my office almost as soon as she's gone. "Problem?"

"We need to track down West Jaeger and beg him to move in for a while."

He smirks.

Not frowns. Not growls. Not cusses.

Alessandro once scared the piss out of a landscaper who was supposed to be here simply by raising an eyebrow. He's done the same to a few of my weekend flings. He vets every name on the guest list for every party or business meeting I have at home, and when he met Jude, Cameron's approved-by-the-government-at-levels-so-secret-we-shouldn't-even-know-he-exists fiancé, they had a staring match that lasted seventeen minutes without either of them blinking.

He doesn't like having new people around.

But at the mention of West moving in?

He's *smirking*.

I lift a brow—just like my grandmother would—and play it cool. "What?"

"You could tell her to pound sand."

I don't answer that.

Mostly because I don't have a good response.

So I do the only other thing I know to do. "And get me a bucketload of quarters. Like half a truck full. We're spreading some joy to some laundromats today, okay?"

He laughs and shakes his head. "Laundromats, huh?"

"Clean clothes make people happy. *Free* clean clothes make them happier."

He pats me on the shoulder. "You're gonna be just fine, Daisy. Both you *and* the little guy."

One can only hope.

10

West

I MANAGE to only think about everything that went down last night and into this morning approximately seven billion times while I'm working on the plumbing in the gym all day Friday. Blaring music helps. Watching YouTube videos of soldiers, sailors, airmen, and Marines having surprise homecomings helps. Texting a few old buddies about random bullshit helps too.

By the time I'm washing up in the now-running sinks in the locker room, I know I'm going to be okay. There's still legal crap to deal with—I need to get a copy of the will, but the attorney Ty recommended tells me it's pretty cut-and-dried to step down.

So I'm moving on.

In *all* aspects of my life.

I've just downloaded a dating app when my phone rings.

Becca?

Aw, *shit*. She probably reads TMZ too.

I almost let it go to voicemail, but I've never been a chickenshit. "Hello?"

"West! Hey! I just saw the weirdest news," she says way too brightly.

Mayday! Mayday! my balls shriek, because the last time I heard Becca that overtly and fakely happy was the night her ex-husband called to tell her his plans had changed, and he'd be taking their girls to his mother's house for a week, where she knew they'd be plied with cotton candy and daytime soap operas and get to listen in on screaming matches between the mother-in-law and her neighbor, who'd been fighting since approximately the dawn of time, though no one could remember why.

"Yeah?" I stroll through the gym, looking at the painted cinderblock walls, the boxes of weights and equipment ready to be unpacked next week. I'll have to hire short-term help to get it done, but I will, and then it's on to the next job.

Whatever that job is.

It'll land in my lap. Usually does.

"You inherited Judgy Julie's baby?" Becca half-whispers.

"I—yeah."

"I know you probably don't want to hear from me after last night, but I just thought if I could help out any—"

"No. Yeah. I mean, we're good. And sure. Help is good." *Fuck.* I can take down a man one-handed, but I can't tell a woman to fuck off.

Probably because I was an idiot. I still think *safe* relationships are best, but who am I to decide that for anyone else?

Or maybe this guy *is* her safe relationship, and I'm chopped liver.

In any case, I don't tell her I'm not hanging out day to day with Daisy, raising a new baby with an insta-family.

"Good. And yay! I love baby stuff. I mean, if you want help. You don't have to take it. If you don't want."

"Yeah. Thanks." Ambiguous is good, right?

"Of course! My pleasure. Seriously. I got the impression you're not at home, so I thought you might need some things dropped off?"

"I'm covered." Because I *am* about to head home. "But thank you."

"Hey, that's what friends are for. Oh, and I went through Julienne's blog when I heard, because I know you know a ton about kids, but I thought it might be helpful to have a list of the brands she used. I mean, babies are sensitive to changes with diapers and formula—assuming he wasn't breastfed—so I thought…"

"Yeah. Yeah, that's great. Thanks." *Why* can't I just tell her to buzz off?

"I'll text you the list. Or I can go get some for you? Whichever. Whatever's most helpful. And if you need a babysitter, you know where to find me. Or I could come to you. Just let me know."

"I—yeah. I'll let you know."

"I really value you as a friend, West, and I know you're probably going through some really weird stuff with the baby, so I just wanted you to know I'm here for you. Despite…last night being a little…unexpected."

"Yeah. We're good. Thanks, Becca."

"Okay. Good."

I thank her again, tell her the baby's crying, and hang up the phone. Then I lean against the nearest wall, drop my head back, and sigh.

I should've just told her I wasn't in the kid's life. But I couldn't bring myself to say it. *Yep, rejected by another family, thanks for asking.*

The whole fucking world is upside down.

"Problems?" Daisy asks.

I jump and turn, and there she is, in the gym's doorway in a bright yellow sleeveless one-piece jumper thing, pulling a stroller inside.

"No," I say curtly as my heart leaps and my balls perk up. *Friendly nooner? We're down!* "What can I do for you, Ms. Carter-Kincaid?"

"Ideally, or realistically?" She grins.

I don't.

And then she sighs. "You weren't nearly this kind of a killjoy when we both thought you were a stripper."

If only life could've stayed that simple. I'd still be hitting some dating apps today—women like Daisy don't see me as anything other than the same temporary distraction she would've been for me—but at least there would've been a happier end to a sucky night.

"Okay, Mr. Straight Shooter, here's the deal. Do you know anything about Anthony and Margot Roderick? Remy's paternal grandparents?"

I just watch her, waiting, because I know it won't take long for her to tell me what I already know.

Sure enough, not even three seconds pass before she's talking again. "They're basically dicks in human packaging, which means sometimes they get *feelings*. And currently, their feelings are hurt, as is their pride, so they're contesting Julienne's will. You'd think it would be a good thing that multiple family members would want the little guy, but the truth is way more complicated. Anthony Roderick thinks that having money means he should own everything he sees, and that blood means ownership, which means he thinks Remy here should be *his*, except he raised Rafe, who was a douche, and yes, I'm being polite because you shouldn't speak ill of the dead. But the point is, if Anthony Roderick raises this baby, he, too, will turn out to be a worm, which is totally preventable, because look at this sweet face. As for Margot, without Remy, she'll lose her will to live. Which in theory would mean that we should save her life by giving her the baby, except it's not Remy's responsibility to be someone's reason to live. It's his responsibility to be a fucking baby and grow up and test limits and be *himself*, rather than the mold of his dead father that his grandmother would want to turn him into. Except it's possible all she wants him for is a vial of blood so she can take his DNA to a mad scientist to have Rafe recreated."

I scowl, because this is ridiculous, except I don't miss that she said *we*.

Merely a legal formality, I tell myself. That's all she's here for. Expedited paperwork.

Also, did she even take a breath through all of that?

She tilts her head. "Dude. You don't have to *like* the truth for it to *be* the truth."

"So the grandparents weren't named in the will as guardians for a reason."

"They *did* get fifty dollars to buy themselves a few sacks of manure. Not sure if you read far enough to see that part."

"So you need paperwork," I supply.

Her brow furrows briefly, then her eyes fly wide. "Oh! No. Not at all. I mean, yes, my lawyers want you to sign a non-disclosure agreement about last night and everything I'm about to tell you—they get so pissed when I forget this stuff—but actually, I want you to move in with me."

Twenty years of military training is the only thing keeping me from choking on my own spit. Also, I don't believe for a second that she *forgets* non-disclosure agreements.

"I don't know if you follow the tabloids, but I tend to show up in them. A lot. Most of the time depicted as... well, actually, fairly accurately. I work hard, so why shouldn't I play hard too? But, as I'm sure you can imagine, it's not exactly the best look for the guardian of a baby, whereas—"

I cut her off with a low, growling grunt as I realize where she's going. "You need me to make you look good."

"I—yes." Her yellow outfit doesn't seem quite as bright when her shoulders slump. "I can make it as painless as possible. We have a helicopter so you can avoid Miami traffic to get as close to job sites as possible. I'll take overnight shifts with the baby. And my chef can make any food you need. I know you still have a month left for house-sitting on the beach, but I can have one of my staff take over and keep an eye on things. Also, I know a lot of people who—"

"How long?" Fuck. I just asked that. Also, she knows too damn much about me.

"Oh, not that long! I mean, what's a few months in the grand scheme of things? And you were going to need a new place to live soon anyway, so this way, you can just chill in one of my guest suites until you find a new place. I have plenty of room, plus a private beach, *plus* there's golf and watersports and the most amazing little village of shops in the Bluewater enclave. You'd have access to all of it."

"A few months." Nope. Not buying it.

She smiles, and I realize her eyes are blue today. A bright, sparkling, lively blue that makes me think of dancing Caribbean ocean waves. "*Maybe* a wee bit longer?"

"What kind of dirt do they have on you that you need a total and complete stranger's help to make you look like the better option?"

"I don't do anything I won't own in public. And even if I'd ever planned on having kids, I *still* wouldn't apologize for living the hell out of my life. But not instantly knowing how to do all this caretaking stuff doesn't mean I can't learn it. It just means I appear to have weaknesses and vulnerabilities in a court case until I *look* as competent as I feel. I know this is about as cluster-fucky as cluster-fucks can be, but I just need a little bit of temporary help. *Remy* needs a little bit of temporary help. And he's such a sweet little orphan baby."

That's the only argument she could make that will make me bend, and I think she knows it. Except there's that look again—that softness in her eyes that says she's not calling him a *sweet little orphan baby* to manipulate me, but because she feels it too.

That urge to protect and defend a helpless infant who's already lost both his parents.

I close my eyes and pinch the bridge of my nose, because I know what I'm going to say.

I don't *want* to say it. Saying it means getting attached.

But what's the alternative?

"I need to talk to my lawyer," I tell her gruffly.

She claps her hand. "I thought you might. I called him. He's outside."

I think I've just been outplayed.

And I'm afraid it won't be the last time.

11

Daisy

WHEN I WAS GROWING UP, no one ever accused me of being a genius. It was all *Daisy's so pretty* and *Daisy's so nice* and *I hope Daisy develops some marketable skills, because pretty and nice won't get her very far.*

Nice guys finish last, right?

Depends on what you consider *last*.

I'll never win awards for my charity work—not that I don't do it, I simply don't do it where everyone's watching. And why waste money on an award for giving money?

Just give more money to the people and causes that need it. Duh.

My grandmother sold her soul to stay immortal and at the helm of Carter International Properties for all eternity, so being CEO is off the table. Not that it was ever *on* the table. Some days, I really don't know why I'm still employed, but I keep doing my best, and encouraging the staff under me to do *their* best, and the pieces keep falling into place.

I'm no scientist, but I have a theory that when you treat people right and *care*, they'll bend over backward to do just about anything you ask. Which isn't why I give my staff extra days off, invite them to bring their kids to work, and throw not only a wicked awesome holiday party, but also untoppable Valentine's Day, Independence Day, and Talk Like A Pirate Day parties.

I also ask how Hussein in accounting is feeling after his accident. If Katya in legal is still having trouble with her ex. And if Jorge in marketing needs some extra time off since his mama has been sick back home.

Deep down, most people just want to be loved and appreciated and *seen*. So I give them what they need, and in return, they give me what I need, and we're all one big pile of happiness shining brighter than the Miami sun, with me standing between them and my grandmother.

Okay, maybe that's just me being a big pile of happiness. Since Thursday night, though, I've been standing on a pile of panic asking my staff for favors, alternated with begging Alessandro and Tiana, my personal assistant, to help me discreetly donate to college funds for orphaned kids and send shoes and toiletries to homeless shelters, that finally results in Lucinda shooing me outside late Saturday morning with orders to *let someone else take care of you.*

As if she hasn't been doing that anyway. But now, for the first time in thirty-six hours, I can actually take a full breath and relax. I'm sitting next to the sun-shielded cabana hut she set up for Remy by the pool inside my D-shaped courtyard, not to be confused with my dick pool on the outside of my own fortress, for the record.

That pool's there basically just to challenge my grandmother's Botox.

I know. *I know.* If I want her approval, I shouldn't bait her. But the Bluewater community is the *only* thing I have in my life that I've done on my own—Cameron, Emily, Luna and I designed and built it, *not* Carter International Properties—and I wanted a pool shaped like a dick.

So I have a dick pool.

I glance over at Remy, who's hangin' in a baby swing in the shade, fans blowing around him, bottles chilling in an ice bucket until he gets hungry, diapers stacked and ready for battle under the small changing table, while I sip a virgin piña colada and catch up on emails, checking in on my staff not just here in Miami, but also in New York and Atlanta, and I pretend everything's normal while I let the sunshine reassure me.

West is inside unpacking, which means I haven't been disinherited yet.

It also means I owe him favors basically for the rest of my life. I might be breathing easier at knowing that I can soak up all the baby knowledge I can get from him. But lucky for him, I have a *very* good idea of where to start with favors.

Alessandro got his hands on the background check and private investigator reports my grandmother had done before she brought Julienne's will to light, and I have a lead on West's maybe-girlfriend.

The thought both sours my stomach and gives me a

huge sense of relief, because if he has a girlfriend, then he's off-limits, and it doesn't matter how ovary-popping it is to watch him holding Remy or how I've noticed that he smells like sawdust and has rough fingers that send shivers across my skin every time we accidentally touch. There aren't many lines I won't cross, but cheating is a definite no-no.

The report doesn't definitively say she's his girlfriend, but it definitely says there's something there, and so I'm making it my mission to speed that process along.

I owe him, don't I?

And what's a better gift to give someone than love?

Just as I'm finishing up a text to Tiana with instructions on what I'd like to do, the door near my outdoor kitchen flings open, and three of my very favorite people in the entire universe tumble out onto the patio.

I leap up with a cheer, completely forgetting anything but the sight of these three women. "Yay! Friends!"

"Daisy! Oh, I'm so sorry." Luna reaches me first, wrapping her long, deeply tanned, slender arms around me. She's dressed in a bright sundress that reminds me of a party bar in Jamaica, and she smells like sunshine. "Why didn't you tell us about Julienne's funeral?"

"She and I weren't all that close. Actually, turns out, she wasn't really close to anyone. It's okay. Mom was there. You didn't need to witness all that awkwardness too."

"It was still a funeral. Do you need some dog hugs? Dog hugs make everything better. I can bring Penelope over."

"Oh my god, a baby," Cam whispers as she hugs both

of us tight. She's taller than Luna, with gorgeous, natural red hair that makes my extensions look the adorable kind of trashy, and in a business suit that's basically the opposite of my red bikini. And the huge opal surrounded by diamonds on her ring finger is also the opposite of everything I've ever thought I wanted in life. "You should've texted sooner! Do you know anything about raising babies? I don't know anything about babies. But there's *so* much stuff about raising babies on the internet. We're going to be fine."

"Have you talked to your lawyers yet? Wait. Of course you have. Does he have a trust fund? A college fund? An IRA?" Emily, the natural blonde of the group, and also closest to me in height, wraps her freakishly strong arms around all of us and squeezes us until we all squeak. She's business-casual and so genuinely gorgeous that flowers bow to her. "Derek's team's going to get what they can out of Julienne's house—the electronics, I mean—before anyone seals it up pending the auction, and they'll see if they can find anything about when Julienne and Rafe made their will. He's also working on a plan to make you look like an angel and the Rodericks look like unfit parents. I can't *believe* they're refuting the will. Did they honestly claim your grandmother forged it?"

"What else can we do? What do you need?" Cam asks.

I swallow hard as reality hits me in the face again. Playing babysitter for a couple days is one thing, but telling my three besties that I'm basically a mom now makes it more real. And being a mom to Remy makes Julienne being dead a little more real. No matter who you are, dying in your early thirties and leaving a baby behind *is* sad.

And not understanding why they thought *I* would make the best guardian to their child is even worse.

What if I screw it up?

And not for the sake of staying in my grandmother's good graces, but for Remy's sake?

"You guys are the best." I try to wrap my arms around them too, but I'm basically being straightjacketed by them, which is super comfortable and perfect and soothing. If I have to have a meltdown, having one while the three women who are the closest things I've ever had to real sisters squeeze the air out of me is exactly the time to do it.

I never had sisters until I had these three women, and I'll forever be grateful for the moment we met. And I'm so, so glad all three of them have found amazing men to share their lives with. I know they've all made good matches because I feel less like I'm losing each of them, and more like I've gained three brothers over the past six months.

"Remy's basically broke," I say, because answering questions is easy, whereas admitting I'm terrified parenting is the thing that's finally going to expose me as a total fraud to these women who mean so much to me is hard, "but he's got me, so no worries there. As for what I know about babies...I'm getting plenty of on-the-job training, and he's really pretty awesome."

"This baby is the luckiest baby in the world to have you," Luna tells me.

"In so many ways," Emily agrees.

"And us," Cam pipes up. "We're going to be the aunts he never knew he wanted. Dibs on the college fund!"

"I'm sure my grandma's taking care of the college fund and trust fund and IRA," I tell my friends. "Provided he doesn't fuck it up when he turns twenty-one, but she'd be over a hundred by then, so he might be spared the family test. Except for the part where she's part-vampire and basically immortal. So maybe I should do a college fund for him too."

Emily snorts in amusement.

"Vampire would explain a lot," Cam says, more to herself than to me. "I wonder if the mirror thing is true. That would be a simple way to conduct a test."

"What did your mom say about the baby?" Luna asks. She peers hesitantly toward the cabana hut, her voice dropping like she's afraid she'll wake him.

"She doesn't know yet. She's out of reach on my yacht."

That earns me a healthy side-eye from all three of them, but they don't press it.

"Will she try to move in?" Emily asks. "We can amend the community rules to dictate that anyone over thirty can't live with their parents. I don't think it would impact any other families in the neighborhood. And I'm already getting requests for another community forum since your note went out about increased security for the baby. But it *would* mean another association meeting…"

"Oh, psh. I'll hire stunt doubles for us," I assure her.

"I'm *not* letting a stunt double stand-in for me during negotiations."

We all crack up. Well, except Emily. Once a quarter, we have meetings with the Bluewater residents for them to air their complaints and make suggestions for improvements. As the community's management team, final decisions are in our hands, and we always send Emily in to negotiate terms of improvements.

She has a well-earned reputation for being tough but fair, and I always bring the alcoholic beverages because it makes watching the proceedings that much more fun.

Luna strokes my hair. "Your house isn't big enough to share with your mom? Your mom is awesome."

"She is," I agree. "But I still don't want her talking to Cristoff."

Emily's eyes go wide. She gets him half the week, and I get him the other half. Our chef is the most temperamental culinary genius I've ever met. I pay him exceptionally well, because I love food, and I especially love Cristoff's food, and I'm secretly entertained at how easy it is to make that vein in his forehead throb and then make it all better by tossing out a perfectly timed *By the way, Cristoff, I've never had better cinnamon pineapple risotto. One day you'll be immortalized with a statue in the Chef Hall of Fame. Magnifique!*

I like to think of it as my way of bringing balance to his life, because he wouldn't appreciate the compliment if he wasn't steaming hotter than a fresh-boiled lobster first.

"What's wrong with your mom talking to Cristoff?" Cam asks.

"The last time she talked to him, she made him so mad in four seconds flat that he only prepped me California rolls and avocado pasta for the next three weeks. Which was delicious, by the way, because it's Cristoff, but the point is, they can't exist in the same kitchen space if I want any variety in my menu."

"Wait, wasn't that the time he made me that amazing garlic-shallot-butternut squash ravioli with prawns in a cream sauce?" Emily asks.

"No, that was the time he gave you peanut butter sandwiches for a week. The ravioli was after one of my guests told him her chef did tuna steaks better, because her chef cooked them all the way through. So he was insulted, but mostly on behalf of the tuna instead of on his own behalf."

"Oh. Okay, yes, your mom definitely can't talk to Cristoff."

"Oh, no!" Luna suddenly says. "What are you going to do with the baby when you have to travel? Does he have a nanny? Will you take him along? What about…"

She trails off, and all three of my friends look at me.

Because *what do you do with a baby while you're having a hot weekend fling with an Italian stallion* is probably beyond what all three of them think is an appropriate thing to say out loud.

"What about what?" a now-familiar male voice asks behind them.

All three of my friends turn as one.

"Wow," Cam whispers.

"Hello, arm porn," Emily murmurs.

Luna pokes me. "Did you start dating American men again? Because that man right there would convince me to date American men again if I were you. Or at least to consider it."

"Where's the baby?" West asks.

"He's rockin' the pool life," I reply with a smile and a

gesture toward the baby cabana. "Water's perfect. Dive on in."

He's in jeans, tan work boots that I'd bet are steel-toed, and a Marines T-shirt that perfectly matches the scowl on his square jaw. To say he hasn't been in the best of moods since he agreed to move in would be an understatement. I'm telling myself that this isn't a mistake, that he'll cheer up soon, but I'm also getting nervous that I'm totally fucked.

Because he, too, could tell the courts I'm an unfit mother.

And then I'd lose *everything*.

"Did you put sunscreen on him?" he asks.

"Organic, baby-safe sunscreen, I hope," Luna pipes up.

"Who are you?" Emily rarely minces words. Also, don't get between her and the people she loves if you don't want to lose an appendage.

"Who are you?" West counters.

Emily slides me a look, her blond hair shimmering in the sunlight and making her look like a runway model while her sharp blue-gray eyes silently ask permission to practice her ninja-jiujitsu skills on him.

"So, that's the other part of my news," I say casually to my friends. "Westley Jaeger, meet Emily Stanton, Luna da Rosa, and Cameron Whitbury. Em trained our alligator to play fetch with men's balls, and Luna and Cam know how to dispose of a body, which is basically unnecessary when you consider the alligator."

"Was that a threat?"

"No, standard warning everyone gets when they visit Bluewater the first time. I couldn't possibly threaten you, given all that you're doing for my family." I smile easily at him to let him know I'm kidding, then turn to my friends. "Julienne and Rafe designated West here as Remy's co-guardian. Best I can tell, it was because Julienne liked how his ass filled out his jeans while he was remodeling the baby's nursery a few months ago."

"What are your intentions with this baby?" Emily asks.

West lifts a brow. "Are you related to Imogen Carter too?"

All four of us gasp, because *no one* insults my besties by implying that they, too, share blood with The Dame.

"We are *not* going to be friends," Luna murmurs.

"He's cranky. Took the night shift," I whisper, which is a better story than *he doesn't want to be here*. But I like him not wanting to be here. It puts a layer of protection between me and that undeniable attraction I have to the man who played along like he was a stripper before my grandmother dropped a bombshell on both of us the other night.

"My three friends here helped design and build the Bluewater community," I tell him as I sling my arms around Emily and Luna. "They all run billion-dollar corporations and are strong, powerful, sexy-ass mother-fucking women who are basically going to rule the world one day. Also known as Remy's de facto aunts, whom he'll probably love more than he loves me, which is saying something, because I'm kinda fabulous, but I'm going to have to learn to be a disciplinarian once he starts crawling and talking."

Bluewater was a dream come true for all of us. My friends wanted a warm, welcoming, *private* place to call home, and I wanted to be near the three women who understood completely how hard it is to navigate the world with the extra pressure of so many people wanting to see you fail, merely because you broke out of the mold they wanted to put you into.

Bonus that from the air, the enclave looks like a uterus, complete with fallopian tubes branching out to two ovaries. Emily, Luna, Cam, and I live on one. The marina's on the other ovary, at the end of the private airfield on the other fallopian tube.

There's a reason I call us Miami's vagillionaires.

Our community isn't just for us though. We wanted a safe haven for other people who need shelter from prying eyes and uplifting neighbors and who want to embrace the best part of life on the beach. We screen every applicant who wants to purchase property or a condo or open a shop, and we have a lengthy privacy agreement, which means now we have a robust, vibrant, diverse neighborhood with the most amazing people ever who don't just want to rub elbows with us, but who want to be a part of something bigger than themselves.

Remy's so lucky he gets to grow up here.

I can't wait to take him walking through the village to meet all the little shop owners and take him boating and out to feed Steve, the resident three-legged alligator, and *oh my god*, I'm basically a *mom* now.

West looks each of my friends up and down again, then his shoulders sag in defeat while he mutters something about sisters.

He has sisters. He told me so. Google confirmed it.

Google didn't tell me that he's an excellent oldest brother, but it didn't have to. I can *see* it.

I wonder how my life would've been different if I'd had an older brother like West?

Not that he feels *anything* like brotherly to me. He's entirely too potently sexy, even in his grumpy pants. Considering I'm the reason he's grumpy, I feel like I need to help him become *un*grumpy.

And lucky for him, I think I know exactly how to do that.

A noise from the baby cabana has all of us turning to look Remy's way. It's a yawn—I think—but it's a noisy yawn that probably means I need to figure out if that bottle warmer works the way Lucinda told me it does before she took off for the rest of the weekend.

"Is that the baby?"

"Can we look?"

"Have you held him? Have you *ever* held a baby? I don't think I've ever held a baby."

"Is it like taking care of a dog? Let them run loose, poop in the yard, and then put out some food on the floor?"

That was Luna.

And I think the question was enough to make West nearly stroke out.

I step over to the cabana and pull back the gauzy curtains. Remy waves his fists at me, his face screwed up like he either wants to yell, eat, or poop.

"Oh, those eyes," Emily, the skincare scientist, sighs.

"Look at his little gummy smile!" Cam, the aeronautical engineer genius, exclaims. "He doesn't have teeth!"

"What does he need?" Luna, the vegan lifestyle guru, half-reaches for him, then stops. "Does he need to like, go squat in the grass or something?"

West looks in too. "Why's he half-naked?"

"He likes it." Despite myself, I'm grinning all dopey too, because he *is* adorable with his gummy smile and perfect dark eyes, and all that wonder that says he can't wait until he's big enough to go conquer the whole damn world. "He might be planning on being a nudist. Which is awesome, if you ask me. He should definitely be comfortable in his own body. Maybe we should have nudist weekends, just for Remy."

Huh. West's eyes are back to being that honey-brown color.

The man with the magical color-changing eyes is giving me a take-no-bullshit look that probably served him well in the Marines, though it's definitely not intimidating to me.

If anything, it's making me *more* in favor of nudist weekends.

I could definitely be naked with this man. And I hate when naked and stress relief are a *bad* idea.

But is it?

Is it really?

Yes, Daisy, it's a bad idea. I make my inner voice sound like my grandmother, and it almost works to rein in those rampant hormones. *He has an almost-girlfriend, remember? He's off-limits.*

"If you want me to stay, you're going to have to change your tactics," he tells me.

"What right, exactly, *do* you have to this child?" Emily asks.

"It's all in the will." I wave my hand, not wanting him to go into too much detail. "Julienne and Rafe clearly knew what they were doing when they wrote it, even if none of the rest of us get it, so we're just figuring this out one day at a time. West comes from a good family, so it's not like I can object to one more person—or eighty more people—loving the baby. Do you remember May Ella Jaeger, the comedienne?"

"Who?" Luna asks.

"She has a special on Netflix!" Cam exclaims. "Jude and I started watching that the other night."

Emily glances at her. "Just started? It wasn't very good?"

Cam grins. "No, it was very good! We got distracted."

"Good for you," Luna cheers. "I love distracted."

"It definitely doesn't suck," Emily agrees with a love-sick smile of her own.

None of them seem to notice that West is going pink.

Maybe his mom embarrasses him?

Or maybe he's not comfortable hearing about my friends having gloriously active and satisfying sex lives.

While watching his mother's comedy special on Netflix.

"Anyway, May Ella Jaeger is West's mom," I say casually. "Which means he's hilarious too, of course."

My three friends turn and study him closer again.

He turns up the growly Marine face, and I suddenly feel the need to fan myself.

Grumpy doesn't usually do it for me, but I'm so damn

grateful that he's here, for so many reasons, and honestly, what kind of man agrees to move in and take care of a baby on a temporary basis that could be a *very* long temporary, when he has his own life to live?

The rare kind, that's who.

"*How* did you end up in the will again?" Emily repeats.

"They got drunk and drew names out of a hat," he deadpans like the good son of a comedienne that he is.

"I can see it," Cam says slowly. "Logical explanation."

Remy squeals again, and I slip into the cabana, which is nice and cool with the fans blowing over ice buckets. "Hey, there, you handsome devil. You ready for some yum-yum milky-milk? Yes? Yes, you are? Who's a good boy? Remy's a good boy."

"It *is* like having a dog!" Luna exclaims.

West mutters something again.

And I decide I'm doing it. I'm doing whatever I can to help the man out.

12

West

You CAN LEARN a lot by listening to four women talk.

And today, I've learned that Daisy has three solid friends who are just as terrifying as my sisters when they all get together.

That's a compliment, by the way. There's nothing more heartwarming than seeing women glare daggers of *we will go into Xena, Warrior Princess mode to protect our friend and this child at all costs.*

They don't need to worry about me. I'm just here as a temporary extra layer of protection between the baby and his evil grandparents.

I'm sitting in a chair across the pool, pretending to check email on my phone while soaking up this gorgeous Miami day, but I'm actually watching them as they all inspect the baby and gossip.

They're too far away to read their lips, but I can read body language.

Pretty sure their entire conversation is *reinforcements have arrived and you don't need that jarhead over there.*

I google each of them and confirm my suspicions.

They're actually *more* dangerous than my sisters. And their testimony in court should hold far more weight than my presence, except nearly all of them have had some recent questionable publicity.

Where money goes, scandal follows.

Alessandro drops into the pool chair beside me and stares across the sparkling blue pool water at the women. "You're actually sticking around? Without actual paperwork?"

Translation: these people can screw you at any moment. It's like he *knows*. Knows how much I don't want to get attached, but can't walk away, because Daisy's right.

This kid can't go to his grandparents. He deserves a fighting chance.

And I don't have another job lined up after the gym renovation is complete, nor do I have the beach house for much longer. I'd been thinking I'd move in with Becca, or at least closer to her, but clearly, that's not happening.

I nod briefly. "Yep."

I also know I'm an idiot for not having signed legal documents about what my rights are and aren't when all this is over. But any signed legal agreements between Daisy and me specifying that I'm out of the picture as soon as Remy's hers would basically eliminate the benefit of me being here to help her get him if anyone found them.

He nods with a short grunt.

Man-speak for *appreciate the help you're giving to the boss-lady, but you're still a moron under your dented armor.*

We both sit there for a few more minutes while the blonde—Emily Stanton, the billionaire skincare scientist —hands Remy back to Daisy. The women have been whispering for over an hour, taking turns fussing over the baby, but Emily's the only one who held him.

"You the kid's father?" Alessandro asks.

The question hits me out of left field and reminds me I'm in a completely different world. "What the *fuck?*"

He doesn't flinch. "Rafe Roderick was a cheating asshole. Julienne was no angel. Just because she wasn't a *known* cheat doesn't mean she didn't do it. Not judging. Just asking."

"You want a DNA test?"

His gaze flicks to the women, who are hugging Daisy like they're leaving, then back to me. "Crowd like this, DNA test will be the only reason you stick around any longer than it takes to get Anthony and Margot Roderick out of the picture."

"That's all I'm here for. Then I'm gone." My beef isn't actually with Daisy. She seems nice enough, if a little wild and unpredictable, and while the life she'll most likely give Remy isn't the one I'd pick for him, it won't be a *bad* life, and I don't think she'll raise him to be an asshole. Nor do I think it's ultimately my business.

Honestly, any other day, I'd let myself call her attractive.

But I'm not going there.

Not getting attached.

To either of them.

Alessandro's watching me. "So you're not trying to replace Sierra's kids with Remy. Baxter and Nina, right? Those were her kids?"

I shove to my feet, because *fuck.*

My family won't even say those names to me.

Somebody did his research. My jaw's clenching, and I want to hit him, but *that* won't help Remy either.

"Gentlemen, I'm hungry," Daisy calls. She's in a bikini that's barely holding in her breasts, with her smooth, soft belly and curvy hips and legs on full display. And now that her friends have departed, there's no distraction from looking at her. "Fish Tails for lunch. Twenty minutes. Let's go."

I eyeball her body again. There's no way she can get dressed *and* get a baby prepped to get out the door in twenty minutes.

"Are you seriously doubting my abilities already, Mr. Jaeger?" she calls playfully, like she can read my mind.

"Just thinking delivery would be easier."

"No way. I'm not staying cooped up in this house all day."

"This house is forty thousand square feet," I point out. Maybe not that big. But it's fucking *big*. "Go to a different room."

Alessandro smirks.

Daisy lifts her chest and puts her fists on her hips, drawing all of my attention to the sparkle in her belly button.

Hells, yeah! my balls cheer.

"Suit yourself if you want to stay," she says. "Remy and

I are going to lunch. And we're going to have a fabulous time introducing him to all the neighbors."

Fuck, she's hot, my left nut whispers.

My right nut bumps his fist.

And my brain engages on the words *introducing him to all the neighbors*. I don't know much about going out with celebrities and public figures—except my brother, who's large enough to take care of himself and not need a body-guard—but I have a feeling the baby's going to get mobbed.

And Alessandro's sigh reiterates the suspicion.

"Just you backing her up?" I ask him.

He shakes his head like I'm a moron.

Of course she'd have an entourage.

She doesn't need me.

But fuck it.

Why not go out to lunch?

See what this Bluewater community has to offer while I'm here. Who knows? Maybe I'll meet a rich single woman who just needs a little stress relief.

Probably not, but seriously—it's just lunch.

What's the worst that could happen?

13

Daisy

I HAD no idea that getting a mahi-mahi sandwich from Fish Tails, the Caribbean-themed seafood restaurant in Bluewater's private shopping village, could be such an epic ordeal.

Or that so much gear could fit in the back of my tricked-out VW Bug.

But here we are, not even *at* Fish Tails yet, with a diaper bag, a stroller, a baby carrier, a baby sling, and one very tight-lipped temporary co-guardian competing with Alessandro for Most Acutely Observant Dude With Muscles, all strolling down the plank sidewalks past Mrs. Chu's jewelry shop with the display of my mom's penis artwork in the picture window, dodging locals on golf carts and stopping to answer questions from other residents who saw the news in *People* or heard it from their neighbors and want to either offer their condolences, tell me they bought everything Julienne ever one-starred, or ask to see the baby.

Sometimes all three in one sentence.

My neighbors are awesome. Especially the Wealthy Widows. Nothing like gossipy, happy old ladies who have all the life experience I want to have one day, making suggestions on how best to care for a baby.

I am soaking it up.

"Are we eating today, or should we just go throw ourselves in Steve's lagoon to spare ourselves the pain of starving to death?" Alessandro mutters.

"I don't know who Steve is, but I'm betting we should go with him," West mutters back.

"You two are adorable," I tell them.

Also, I'm intentionally stalling, because Tiana texted back that my last-minute lunch plans required a wee bit more time to execute.

West is welcome. Even if he doesn't know it yet.

I smile at Mrs. Esteban, who's jogging in place beside us with ten-karat diamonds in her ears and glittering hand-weights gripped in each hand. "We'll catch up later," I tell her.

She nods. "Bring the little one by the gym sometime soon. We'll show him how to lift weights."

"Get him started right," I agree, even though I'm hardly known for working out right.

Emily always tells me I should take better care of my feet when I show up to do the elliptical in my stilettos.

But could I rock carrying a baby in stilettos if I didn't work out with them on?

I don't think so.

West suddenly freezes beside me as a strawberry blonde I don't recognize waves from the front of Fish Tails.

"Oh! Is that Becca?" I wave back at her while West turns a *what the hell have you done?* look at me.

I smile, because what I've done is a huge favor.

Not every temporary co-parent of mine is lucky enough to get the Daisy Carter-Kincaid matchmaking treatment. And today, we'll find out if she's worthy and smart enough to snag a man who'd take on a baby that supposedly isn't his, or if she doesn't deserve him.

My eye starts to twitch at the idea that she'd take him, but really, that would be for the best.

I'm not taking him. For one, he knows my real name and where I live. Plus, he's been very clear that he's only here as a short-term favor. And god knows getting laid is good for the soul. And the grumpies.

So maybe this favor isn't entirely for him. I'll make that up to him later too. If I need to.

"Don't be mad," I tell the glaring retired Marine. "My grandmother's background check on you was a little bit thorough. We went through and added all of your friends and family to the guest list, and when my assistant called Becca, she mentioned having diapers and formula as a baby gift, so we invited her to join us. Your family should feel free to drop by Miami anytime too. Cam really wants to meet your mom."

He doesn't answer me, but instead walks stiffly toward the woman and bends to give her an awkward peck on the cheek.

"Thanks. For the help," he grunts out like a caveman.

"Of course! That's what friends are for!" Her smile is awkwardly strained, and she keeps glancing toward me, then away, like staring at me straight-on might make her blind.

I make a quick wardrobe check.

Yep, I'm definitely wearing pants today. A skirt, actually—my favorite blue tropical print wrap skirt. I got it in a tourist shop in Antigua after my luggage fell overboard on the cruise down to the island—don't ask—and when my grandmother told me it made me look like a tourist whose better fashion sense got baked out by sunstroke, I decided it was a keeper.

Oh, and I'm wearing a white tank top too, so while I look awesome and am showing some cleavage, I'm not likely to cause permanent eye damage like the sun would.

"Becca?" I ask, sticking my hand out to shake. "Hi. I'm Daisy. West has told me *so much* about what an awesome friend you are." I tell the lie while beaming up at him and while she continues to stare at me star-struck, which is a little uncomfortable, because it's not like I've cured cancer or written an earworm song, which are both equally impressive accomplishments in my book.

Also, I'm rapidly getting the feeling that the note in Gram-gram's background check that West was dating Becca just might've been wrong.

Way wrong. "Oh! Looks like our table's ready. Care to join us?"

She babbles something that sounds like a *yes*, and West takes her by the shoulders and steers her into the cozy restaurant with its palm frond fans and Jimmy Buffet music playing in the background, dropping his hands back to his own pockets as soon as she's pointed in the right direction following the hostess.

They are *so* wrong together.

For one, she's wearing jean shorts and a buttoned-up sleeveless blouse, which is a perfectly acceptable Miami outfit, except for the part where West himself is so buttoned-up this morning that he needs someone more like Luna.

Free-spirited with a touch of a wild side. Luna also has a huge heart, which West probably also needs. Because don't we all? Not that you can judge a person's heart size by what their clothes say about their personality.

But I *can* judge compatibility by clothes. Usually.

And my matchmaker instincts—which are admittedly rusty, since I rarely put much time into matchmaking—say these two are *so* wrong, and that ship has sailed.

Dammit.

Maybe all isn't lost. Maybe I can salvage this for them. And then West will be happily dating someone, and I can mark him officially on my *off-limits* list for the most solid reason anyone ever goes on that list.

"You're evil," Alessandro murmurs to me.

"Just because I'm the byproduct of a messy divorce and have no use for commitment doesn't mean I believe *other* people shouldn't have love."

"I don't think what they have is love."

I sigh, because he's right, and now I'm going to go back to not having a solid excuse for telling myself West isn't hot as fuck.

He and Becca are doing a funky dance around the table, each one trying not to touch the other, or even look the other in the eye, as they pick seats at the window table shaped like a fish.

A grouper, specifically.

I asked Pixie, the owner, about which fish they were once, and I can totally see the resemblance now. Plus, it's a boxier fish, which works well for a table. So long as you don't bump your knee or elbow on the fins.

West ends up under the tail, with Becca on top of the tail, which leaves me with the head. Alessandro parks the stroller across from me and next to Becca, then surreptitiously slips into the vacant two-person table behind Becca where he can see the whole restaurant.

"Hush puppies?" I ask my companions. "Pixie makes the *best* hush puppies in the universe, and then she serves them with strawberry butter, which is basically like having an orgasm in your mouth."

Becca goes red.

West sighs. "Yeah. Hush puppies."

"They're out," Chipper Bergman says forlornly from the seat beside Alessandro. "I really wanted hush puppies, but they're out."

A perky teenager with braces bounces to our table with a bright grin. Her parents own a luxury condo across the golf course, and she works here all summer for a place to escape.

"Good news," she announces. "We found the batter. We're back in business. Hi, everyone. Welcome to Fish Tails! I'm Laney, and I'll be your server today. Hush puppies all around? And for you too, Mr. Bergman. I got you covered. You all need menus, or did Daisy already tell

119

you what's best? You should listen to her. She never picks wrong."

"Flattering, but also true. I recommend the seafood bucket for you, Becca. And West, definitely try the coconut-crusted swordfish with the mango salsa. Life-changing."

He snaps his gaze from roaming around the room and when it lands on me, his eyes narrow dangerously thin. Yes, yes, his life has *already* changed once in the past two days, but the more important part is, Becca should totally be salivating over him with narrowed eyes, because protective grumpy dudes with muscles are almost as sexy as dudes with babies, and West is a *protective grumpy dude with muscles AND a baby*.

But Becca isn't watching him. She's leaning over to peek at Remy.

I ignore my own disappointment and West's glare, and I ask for a mahi-mahi sandwich for myself, plus a pitcher of Pixie's famous mango sweet tea.

Neither West nor Becca object to my orders for them, so Laney bounces off after promising Chipper one last time that no, she's not kidding, there *is* more hush puppy batter in the kitchen.

"Of course there is," Becca says with a half-laugh, her gaze darting to West's chin.

I kick back in my chair with the front two legs off the ground. "So how do you two crazy kids know each other?"

"We went to high school together," Becca tells my left ear.

"In Chicago?"

Her brows furrow, and she finally makes eye contact. "You...really know a lot about West."

I wink at her. "Occupational hazard of getting in bed with someone."

West chokes on air.

"Figuratively speaking," I finish. "When you're born in the world I'm born in, you have to find out things about people. Sorry. Kind of. Also, I'm having complicated feelings about co-inheriting a baby with a guy whose brother plays for the Thrusters. Am I going to get in trouble if I admit I seriously hate them because they beat my home team so bad in the hockey playoffs that *I* woke up bruised the next day? *Rude.* How is Tyler, by the way? I could see myself liking him a lot if he got himself traded down here. He should do that."

Becca's still staring at me wide-eyed, and I realize she's not at all impressed by West's professional hockey-playing brother, but is still very impressed with me.

Maybe because I can spit out a lot of words without taking a breath.

"He's amused," West tells me.

"Oh, at the whole baby thing? That *is* funny. My cousin was a riot."

Becca's star-struck exterior finally cracks. "She *one-starred* West's job on her nursery. She wasn't funny."

"She one-starred a gallery opening for my mom's new jewelry line once. Mom put itching powder in her sheets in retribution. Now *that* was funny. Not the part where Julienne was dating a guy at the time who liked to secretly record sex tapes—hello, human decency and privacy laws —but definitely the part where Mom showed her actions have consequences. In the form of Julienne accidentally doing a sex tape where she couldn't get off because she was itching so bad. Or so I heard. I don't like watching people's private sex tapes."

Becca and West share a look, then Becca looks quickly away.

This isn't working. *Dammit.* Now West is going to think all of my favors suck just because this one went sideways.

"Your mom sounds...like she'll have fun being a grand-ma," Becca says while she lines up her wrapped silverware so it's even with one of the fish scales painted on the table.

"Oh, she will. If it were up to her, I'd have seventeen kids. How many do you guys want?" I pause three seconds, because I'm not actually an awful wingman, and add, "Each, I mean. Sorry. I worded that all wrong."

"I have the only two I'm *ever* having." Becca forces a laugh, but it doesn't quite erase the horror in her eyes, and now I have to find out what West's favorite food is and make sure it's brought in at least seven times a day. "What about you, Daisy?"

"Never gave it much thought. West? Your turn. Is Remy it, or do you want more one day?"

A muscle ticks in his jaw and he looks *me* dead in the eye.

Yep.

I owe him *big* time.

"Six," he says. "Be terrible to deprive Remy of the joy of siblings, wouldn't it?

"Oh, I don't know. I was an only child, and I turned out fine. But I guess it's a good thing I have a big house.

That way, we don't have to make it hard to share custody. Oh! I could even convert a couple of my lounges to schoolrooms, so we could hire private tutors for all of them, and then we'd never have to be separated."

I smile.

Becca's forced smile freezes awkwardly, and she looks at me, then West, then back to me, like it's dawning on her that *I* might want him around.

That's right, Becca. He's a catch. Open your eyes.

"You should've seen him singing Remy to sleep last night," I whisper to her. "Total dad porn material. Does he have tattoos? He won't show me."

"I—yes," she stutters.

"Mango sweet tea and hush puppies!" Laney announces.

"Oh, fabulous. Wait until you taste this. It's homemade and it'll ruin you for regular sweet tea forever. Right, Laney?"

"Yes, ma'am, it will."

She smiles and swings around to put a second basket of hush puppies on Chipper's table. I pour mango sweet teas all around and pass around the plates, then insist everyone try at least one hush puppy smothered all to hell with the strawberry butter.

Becca moans when she bites into it.

I moan louder.

West ducks his head over his plate and stares at it while he sucks his sweet tea through a straw. His ears have gone pink and it's only the fact that he looks utterly miserable that's keeping me from actually having fun right now.

Any woman who only wants a man after *another* woman shows interest in him isn't a woman that deserves a guy like West.

Like sixty percent of my good ideas, this one wasn't actually a good idea. Informative, but I really shouldn't have done it.

Alessandro sends me a warning glare, and it's not a *quit being a dick* look.

It's a *don't get more ideas* look.

Like I wouldn't be doing West a favor if I showed him that there are women in the world who would appreciate him.

"I could live on these hush puppies," I declare, and I pop the rest of mine into my mouth with another moan.

When I open my eyes, both West and Becca are staring at me, though West quickly goes back to scanning the restaurant like he's worried about rabid alligators invading and trying to eat us all.

I dab my lips with my napkin and smile at them. "Why eat if it's not an experience, right? So. Becca. You have two kids?"

"Yes!" She straightens with a smile like it's a relief to be back on neutral ground. "Two girls. Eleven and nine. Mia does swim team, and Izzy loves Tae Kwon Do. They're both huge readers, and Mia's in advanced math. She's so— oh, gosh, I could go on for hours."

"I get it. My mom used to brag about how many books I could balance on my head and how many minutes I could hold my breath underwater. Proud moms are good moms. Give it up, superstar!" I fist bump her while she goes back to slightly star struck, which is sad, because people should always tell moms they're doing an awesome job. "What do you do when you're not super-momming?"

"I'm a CPA with a firm downtown."

"I love accountants! I have three of them myself, and the business has an entire accounting department. They're awesome."

I've even partied with a few of them. But Becca doesn't strike me as the rainbow shots type of accountant.

And West *definitely* needs a rainbow shots kind of girl.

I have a sense about these things.

But while West sits there studying me like he's trying to figure out if I'm playing a game with his lady friend, she beams like I've just told her she's the new queen of Fish Tail-landia.

And I beam right back while I grab another hush puppy.

"Can I—is it okay if I hold the baby?" she asks. "I miss babies."

"Of course. He loves to be held. Especially by people who know how to hold babies."

West is still watching me.

And that's all he does until our food arrives.

He watches me charm the pants off his lady friend.

Figuratively, I mean. Unfortunately.

It's always more fun when clothes *actually* come off.

14

West

OUR FOOD HASN'T EVEN ARRIVED before I'm realizing that Daisy is perfectly competent at *anything* she wants to do.

From running a real estate empire to playing fucking *matchmaker* to learning everything she needs to know from someone who doesn't realize she doesn't know it.

Anyone walking by—and Becca herself—would see Daisy building Becca up like the best mom in the entire universe. *You hold him so well. Aw, is he looking at your necklace? Babies love shiny dangly things, don't they? When did your girls say their first words?*

She's making Becca's whole entire year. But she's also soaking in every word like Becca's offering a crash course on motherhood.

Which will be catastrophic if Daisy decides Becca needs to be her new best friend.

My nerves can tolerate a lot.

Having Daisy talk me up to Becca while pretending she's a ditz who misses social cues and needs motherhood advice?

It's worse than having my mother play matchmaker.

And she once asked a sold-out theater if there were any takers for her single military son, because she wanted grandbabies.

It got so many laughs it went in permanently and now everyone in the world with a Netflix account can soak up the glory of my mother's sense of humor about my single status.

Our food arrives. Becca keeps holding Remy and telling Daisy stories about raising her girls while she balances eating with jiggling him anytime he makes a little noise.

He's a funny kid.

Doesn't just sleep all the time. Sometimes he's looking around like he's not sure how he ended up in this weird world, or what it all means. Other times he has this almost-smile on his face that makes me think he knows something I don't.

He might only be two months old, but he already has a personality.

And if personality is genetic—I shoot another glance at Daisy when our food arrives—then he'll go places in the world.

Whether those places are good places or bad places, he'll undoubtedly jump in with both feet.

And there's a gnawing sensation in the pit of my

stomach that suggests overnight is all I needed to fall in love with the little guy.

To want to be here to see him grow up.

Fuck.

Just babysitting, I remind myself. I'm just here temporarily babysitting. I can care, but I need to be prepared to move on.

"I'm getting him the hugest library," Daisy tells Becca. "All the classics. Dr. Seuss. Baby Einstein. Phoebe Moon. Plus the rest of the bookstore. Have you seen our bookstore here in Bluewater? It's *so* cute. Oh! Isn't Pixie sweet? She gave you extra shrimp."

Becca's big red seafood bucket is overflowing with more shrimp, crawfish, and crab legs than two Marines could eat in an entire day, which is impressive, and it smells like melted butter topped with deliciousness and magic.

"I don't think extra shrimp was necessary," Becca says with a small laugh. "Wow. This is...huge."

Daisy winks and slides a glance my way. "I've said that a time or two lately. Want to try the mahi? It's delicious. Trade you a bite for a few shrimp."

They swap parts of their lunch like they're long-lost sisters, and Becca slides me a look as though she's wondering what Daisy's seen on me that's huge.

She hasn't mentioned her new boyfriend again.

And I don't give two fucks.

What the *hell* was I thinking? Becca isn't into me.

And honestly?

I wasn't really into her.

"How's your swordfish?" Daisy asks me. "Oh, lucky. I

didn't know it was sweet potato fries day. Pixie's sweet potato fries are the *best*." She plucks a fry off my plate and moans again.

Threesome! Threesome! Threesome! my nuts chant.

I need to get them a muzzle.

"West has the weirdest luck," Becca says while she tries to shell a shrimp one-handed. "He's the guy who'd take the scenic route to work one morning, get to the office, and find out there was a fifty-car pile-up on the interstate he usually takes. Or—he always gets window tables. *Always*." She points to the window beside us, overlooking a garden with lush plants and curving pathways. I don't know what's around the bend, but I suspect it's more million-dollar homes and golf cart trails.

My sisters wouldn't be able to stop gawking at anything here. Tyler would fit right in though.

"Let me take him so you can eat," I tell her, pointing to the baby.

"Oh! Right. Thank you."

I take Remy, who waves his arms like he's telling me a story, and let the women keep talking while I go back to watching the surroundings and bouncing twelve pounds of sweet baby.

Also, the swordfish is perfection.

Don't need to engage in the conversation going on around me, especially with a delicious meal to savor, and honestly, their words are flowing too fast for my one good ear to catch everything. Almost like being at home.

I take a bite of swordfish, make a face at Remy, who coos or tries to smile back, sweep a glance around the restaurant, then give a cursory study of the women.

And repeat.

Until I notice Daisy's lips are swelling.

Are they?

Or is this a trick of the light?

She frowns and touches two fingers to her bottom lip, like she's realizing something is off too.

"Whath appenin' to my lipsh?" she asks.

Red creeps up her neck, and she attacks it with her French manicured fingernails.

"Oh, fuck," I mutter. "Are you allergic to seafood?"

"My mom ith, but naw me. I'm thuperwoman." She tries to clear her throat.

Then tries again.

Alessandro tips his table lunging toward us. "Back," he barks.

All my instincts say I need to get her to Benedryl first, then epinephrine if that doesn't work, but I'm holding a baby, and Becca's shrieking and diving for cover while Alessandro leaps for Daisy.

Her whole face is mottled red now, and she's alternately scratching her skin and trying to talk.

"Hospital?" I say.

"Benedryl," Alessandro barks at a server, who shrieks, drops a full platter of fish sandwiches, and breaks into a run toward the kitchen.

I leap up, baby in hand, while everyone in the restaurant starts moving, craning necks, stepping out of their seats for closer looks, rising in the aisles.

"I have medical training," I tell Alessandro.

"I have medical training," he growls back.

"Maybe reminding her she was allergic to something before she ate it would've helped."

"Noth allergic," Daisy croaks out. "Aythe loths of frimp. Aww my wife."

"She's not allergic to anything." Alessandro's taking her pulse when the chef dashes out of the kitchen.

"Daisy," the perky lady with blue pigtails under her hairnet wails. "Your pretty face! What have I done to your pretty face?"

"It'll grow ba—aaa—ath."

"Benedryl!" the chef shrieks, shoving a box at Alessandro.

He rips the package in half, sending pill packs flying onto the neighboring tables, then pops one out and shoves it at Daisy. "Swallow. Then hospital. Now." He turns a glare on me. "Baby. Home. Now."

The blue-haired woman bursts into tears.

Remy bursts into tears.

Alessandro tosses Daisy over his shoulder, and stomps out of the restaurant through the growing crowd. I want to follow, but for what?

To be one more person slowing them down?

I'm not her relative. I shouldn't be *anything* to her.

Still, my heart's in my throat, and I can't tilt my good ear close enough to the door to hear what's being said out there along with seeing which direction they're going.

"That wasn't...normal," Becca says behind me. She's huffing like she leapfrogged the tables to get to us. "Should we go pay the bill?"

I nod, even though I don't want to go anywhere except wherever Daisy went, because christ on a cracker, if the

Benedryl doesn't work and she doesn't get to an emergency room fast enough—I shudder.

And then I feel movement under my left hand.

The hand holding Remy's butt.

And isn't that just about the most appropriate thing in the entire world?

15

West

BECCA OFFERS to drive me back to Daisy's house after I get Remy's diaper changed and attempt to pay the bill.

Pixie, the chef, refuses to let me, so I leave a nice tip on the table, and we quietly slip out the back toward the small parking lot where Becca's car is waiting. On the way, we pass a small, fenced-in lagoon with *Steve's House* on a sign. I stop and squint at the gator.

"Does that thing have a prosthetic leg?" I ask aloud.

"Mind your own fucking business!" the parrot from yesterday morning squawks at me.

Christ.

Was that really just yesterday morning?

"I guess we're not supposed to know," Becca says with a forced cheer. "Do you think Daisy will be okay?"

"Yeah. She'll be fine."

She better be fucking fine, because I'm about done with the emotional roller coaster.

"This works out well, since I have all the baby stuff," Becca offers. "I mean, the part where I'm giving you a ride. Not the part where Daisy had an allergic reaction."

"Yeah," I agree. I try to smile back at her, but it's hard to smile when you're gripping a phone so hard you can feel it in your molars. Not that I expect either of them to call me with an update, but I'd very much like to hear that Daisy's okay.

Becca looks away toward the parking lot.

We manage to get most everything crammed in the trunk of her Corolla—which is easier than it was to cram it into Daisy's Daisy Wagon—and we go out of our way to not accidentally touch while getting Remy's baby carrier strapped in well enough without the built-in base that hooks into the car's latch system. The entire ride to Daisy's mansion, the only thing we talk about is which street to turn on.

As soon as the porte-cochère comes into view around the bend, and then the house itself, Becca gawks with undisguised lust. "Wow."

She finds a *house* more sexually attractive than she finds *me*.

And I'm not as offended as I should be, but I still feel fucking awkward.

A woman I vaguely recognize—Daisy's personal assistant, I think—bustles out the front door when we stop under the porte-cochère. "Daisy will be a few hours," she tells me. "Which means you get to deal with Imogen. Congratulations and good luck."

"That sounded ominous," Becca says, but she's still gaping at the house.

"It was. Let me know what I owe you for the diapers and formula."

"Baby gift. I insist. Can I help you carry it all inside?"

"No." I wince, knowing I sound like an ass.

But I'm feeling like an ass.

I don't *want* to watch Becca *ooh* and *aah* over Daisy's house. Nor do I want her to get scrutinized by the devil woman who thinks I'm an inconvenience at best, and a pain in the ass to be disposed of at worst. "She's not a nice person. Imogen, I mean. I'll get you the tour another day."

She smiles again without meeting my eyes. "Sure. Great."

"I really appreciate the help." I'm a fucking retired Marine and I feel as smooth as a thirteen-year-old kid hiding from his sisters while drooling over the lingerie models in the JC Penney catalog.

"No problem. Thanks for lunch. It was fun. The first part, I mean."

Yeah.

The part where I wasn't talking and Daisy's face wasn't swelling like a red balloon.

I gesture to her trunk. "Could you…"

"Oh! Yes. Right. Sure. Of course. You bet."

Ten minutes later, one of the security guys from the house and I finally get everything dragged through the front door. Remy fell asleep in the car halfway through a bottle, so he's the easiest part.

The security guy is no help when we find Imogen

Carter pacing the sitting room just beyond the foyer though. Dude up and disappears.

And I'm left standing there staring at a wily old lady with calculating blue eyes who couldn't walk her ass thirty feet out the door to help drag in diapers and formula and baby gear.

It pisses me off even more than today already has.

I don't like being pissed.

I like being happy that I'm alive in a world that's not perfect, but does its best.

Yet since Thursday afternoon, very little is going smoothly.

I drop everything but the baby in a heap on the marble floor. Remy, I place down gently, since he's sleeping in his carrier.

"What?" I snap.

She draws her shoulders back and glares at me with the kind of glare that could explain the dinosaurs going extinct all those millions of years ago, if she'd been around back then. "I've signed Remington up for music lessons, and—"

"No."

"Mr. Jaeger—"

"He's *two fucking months old*. Music lessons can wait."

"You have a lot to learn about how children are raised in this family."

"*I'm* his family. *I* say what he does."

"*Daisy* is his family. You'd best learn your place."

Christ. This woman knows how to piss a person off. "My *place* is *right here*. If you ever want to see this child again, you're going to quit looking down your nose at me, quit issuing orders, and learn to say *please*. I don't know where the hell you came from, but where I come from, a person's character is determined by their actions, not their bank accounts. And I'm not raising a kid around people of questionable character who think *music lessons* are more important than making sure a kid knows he's loved and safe. Now, you can either pick up a box of diapers and help get it to Remy's room, or you can get the hell out of this house."

Huh.

She just grew two feet taller.

That's probably a bad sign.

Also a bad sign? That she can make me lose my temper with four words. There's something about her haughty insistence that the world bend to her just because she wants it to that sets off all of my triggers. Who is she, *really*, to think she can play god?

"*Mr. Jaeger*, you do *not* issue orders around here. Speak to me like that again, and *you* won't see this child again. *Ever*. Also, his name is *Remington*."

I fold my arms and glare at her.

She folds her arms and glares back.

Daisy's assistant is perched on the curved glass staircase behind us, leaning forward for a better angle on her phone.

Fuck. She's recording this.

"Now," I growl, "start over. Politely."

"I believe we've already covered who issues orders in this house."

"Daisy does. And since we got married over lunch, turns out, *I* do."

Fuck. *Fuck.* I don't know where the hell *that* came from, but it's stupidly satisfying to see her face drain of all the blood.

Maybe this is why Daisy likes chaos so much.

There's power in unpredictability when dealing with her grandmother.

"You did not," she breathes.

"Didn't we?"

She doesn't know if she should believe me.

Lying goes against everything I was taught growing up, and everything I learned as a Marine.

But nothing about the past few days has followed the rules of life.

"Help or get out," I growl.

"I'm not leaving until I speak with Daisy."

The assistant is still aiming her phone at all of us. Definitely recording this for YouTube.

"That'll be hard to do, since right after we said our vows, she had an allergic reaction to some shrimp," I tell Imogen. "If she doesn't make it, I'm the *only* hope you have of ever seeing this baby again."

"Tiana. Where is Daisy?" she barks.

The assistant shrugs. "Last I heard, getting admitted to the emergency room. Cell reception's spotty inside hospitals. And I didn't catch which one, but Alessandro assured me they had real doctors on staff."

"Daisy's not allergic to anything."

"She's allergic to something, and she's at the hospital."

Her neck swivels until she's aiming that apocalypse-inducing glare at me again. "You poisoned my granddaughter."

Christ. Am I in a soap opera now? "Did you actually see your other granddaughter's dead body, or is this all a conspiracy to ruin my life because I wouldn't put a fountain in her fucking nursery?"

She sucks in an audible breath, and I can't decide if I regret all those hours I spent listening to my sisters discuss *Pretty Is As Pretty Does*, that daytime show that my mom got them all addicted to, or if I'm having fun.

I'm probably not having fun if I have to question it.

She snaps her fingers, and a butler who was hiding behind a giant palm in the corner leaps to attention. "Yes, Mrs. Carter?"

"Pierson. Time to go." She spears me with one last glare. "The Rodericks have filed more legal paperwork suggesting that you're as unfit a parent as they claim Daisy is. Do *not* leave this house again until I say you can."

Definitely not happening.

I have jobs to finish.

A house to check on.

And some sanity to get in touch with.

But mostly, I need to make sure Daisy's okay.

And break the news to her that we're married.

Christ.

I don't know who I am today, but it's not the same person I was when I woke up yesterday.

16

Daisy

MY FACE IS the mushy part of an overripe seedless watermelon.

I know I'm only *pretty* because I'm rich. My eyes are too wide-set, my mouth too big, my nose too small, and my cheeks too round. I know this. I accept this. And because I have the personality to compensate for it, it never really bothers me.

Until times like today, when I feel utterly stupid for not seeing the warning signs sooner.

The last time I had shrimp, I caught a six-hour cold and thought I'd gotten stung by a honeybee on the lip when I wasn't watching my drink carefully out on my boat.

The time before that, I caught a rash on my face that I attributed to uneven sunscreen distribution.

But now, my entire body has revolted to let me know,

in no uncertain terms, that just like my mother, I've developed a shellfish allergy in adulthood.

"I'm not an adult," I whine to Alessandro while he drives us across the final bridge to my humble abode. "I'm a twelve-year-old with the mental capacity to handle business and the physical capacity to handle alcohol and this desperate need to know that Julienne's baby is okay. But I have at least seventy-three more years before I qualify as an adult. For the record."

He humors me with a grunt of agreement.

At least, I'm calling it agreement.

He'd probably call it frustration.

"Thank you for saving my life," I add. "And I'm still mad at you for not letting me go show Pixie that I'm *just fine*."

"Tiana took care of it."

We turn down my seashell drive, and I frown. My eyes are still a little blurry from all the swelling and tears, but there's definitely a big black truck parked under my porte-cochère. "Who's here? Is that *Becca*?"

"That's Mr. Jaeger's truck."

"Oh. Right." Relief I didn't know I needed floods through my limbs.

He's still here.

Probably with Remy.

I hop out of my car as soon as it slows to a roll.

"Stop," Alessandro orders. "You want a smashed nose to go with the rest of it?"

"I'm *fine*," I retort. "And I need to check on the baby."

I need to check on the baby.

Who am I?

141

It hasn't even been forty-eight hours, and I'm all...*motherly*.

I fling open the door, and seven cats shriek, meow, and dart at me.

"*Aaahh!*"

"*Mrow!*"

"*Meow!*"

"*Yaaaarrrooooo!*"

I gape at the tortoiseshell cat, because is he bungee jumping from the stairs or something?

But no.

He just has a weird meow.

"What the *fuck*?" Alessandro says behind me.

"Oh, shit, it's Saturday," I whisper.

"What's Saturday? Who authorized this? What the fuck's going on?"

I don't answer, but instead dash past my sunken sitting room and down the hall toward my lounges.

You can't keep a reputation for being an epic party-thrower without having themed lounges.

Plus, I get bored easily. And I like variety when I'm hosting friends.

Acquaintances.

Same thing.

Also, I wouldn't normally be upset about seven cats wandering around my house—we'd catch them all eventually, and if one got out, it would be *very* well cared for in Bluewater—except I don't know how cats are with babies.

Or how babies are with cats.

And if this didn't get cleared off my schedule, who else can sneak into my house?

Shit.

I need to get more responsible. *Now.*

"Is this like the exotic bird thing?" Alessandro says while I race toward the end of the curved hall.

"I told one of Luna and Beck's friends who runs a cat shelter that they could do a photo shoot. What better way to find the poor sweeties their forever homes than with professional photos of cats looking adorable?" I swing into the last room, my current favorite party room, which is basically one huge room of interconnected trampolines with ball pits lining the black walls, and instead of dozens of cats bouncing on trampolines, there's a single chubby calico meowing plaintively from the center trampoline while Luna's boyfriend, Beck, tries to crawl carefully out to get her.

And there's a photographer happily snapping away as the big blond bearded biker dude tries to not scare the single cat left on the trampoline.

I hold up a hand to stop Alessandro. The poor kitty looks terrified. If anyone can reach her, Beck can, but only if we don't scare the piss out of her first.

We back out of the room, because my face could scare a shapeshifting vampire wildebeest today.

"How many cats were coming today?" my bodyguard asks.

I shrug. "Somewhere between eight and thirty?"

"Fifteen," a breathless Tiana answers as she bustles in from the courtyard. I owe her overtime for coming in today. "We've caught one, if you count the one still in the trampoline room with Beck. I let them in because they were cleared by security."

143

I keep waiting for the day that they both get frustrated with me and leave, but so far, I have yet to drive them to drink or quit. It helps that when my grandmother insisted I hire a security team, I picked my own head bodyguard instead of letting her have a say.

"Cute idea to photo shoot them on trampolines," she adds. "They got some really adorable shots. At first. Until West decided to see what needed babyproofing around the house. He opened the door, and the cats took off."

"Where *is* West?"

She finally looks straight at me, gasps, and she stumbles back half a step. "Maybe you should go take a nap and let us deal with the cats."

I touch my face. "It's still bad, isn't it? Or is this because you don't want to tell me where West is?"

"He's around here somewhere. With the baby. Security's basically been trailing him to make sure he doesn't do anything stupid. And you probably shouldn't go near the photographer again if you don't want to end up in the *National Enquirer* with their proof that you're actually an alien. He might be cleared by security, but that picture would go for a fuck-ton of money. Also, your calendar's clear tomorrow. I can get you scheduled with Mirabella for a facial if you want."

"Is it that bad?"

"Yes."

Clearly, I don't pay her to lie to me. I wince, which makes my skin hurt. "You think it'll be better enough by tomorrow?"

"If not, Mirabella will know what to do. Even if it's to tell you to take a few more days off. Or Emily and Luna.

Someone. Somewhere. We'll make sure you have your game face back by Monday."

I don't need my game face.

I need to find West and the baby.

But they're not in any of the lounges. Nor in any of the sitting areas.

I cover the entire hump of the D of my house, all three levels.

The courtyard, where a cat has settled onto a floatie and is sunbathing in the center of my pool.

I head to my private wing, because I'm still in stilettos and I don't feel like stilettos when my face is sore and my hands are starting to shake from the amount of Benedryl and adrenaline still pumping through my system and this niggling fear over not being able to find West.

Why haven't I programmed his number into my phone yet?

Also, if I'm going to have to lead a search party to find Julienne's baby and my co-guardian, I want my face to match my clothes.

In other words, I'd like to be scary as hell when I find him, so he knows he damn well better *never* take that baby anywhere without telling me again.

What if he hopped a boat and they capsized too, just like Julienne and Rafe?

What if they went wandering through the enclave and didn't realize that *Steve's house* is for an alligator, not a dog, and tried to get into the fence to the lagoon to pet him?

I don't *think* Steve likes human as much as he's developed a taste for chicken since we adopted him and gave him his prosthetic leg, but I don't know that for *sure*, because I don't feed humans to the alligator.

I'm working myself into a panic as I race through changing into hot pink tiger-striped yoga pants and a unicorn tank top offering to bake you some *shut the fuck-upcakes*—it's battle armor—and then search my bedroom, home spa, closets, secret library, and office, just in case he's snooping.

But he's not.

He's *nowhere* in my private wing, not even in the rooftop gardens.

I spin in a slow circle, squinting in the sunshine at the palm trees dotting the landscape in Bluewater beyond my house, the roofs of the village, the condo buildings, the thickets of saw palmettos and hibiscus on the paths to Luna, Emily, and Cam's houses, and the bay, and as I'm finishing my circle, movement at my scrotum pool makes me pause.

There he is.

Pacing in front of the pool house, phone to his ear, which hopefully means Remy's with him in the building.

I head down the back staircase that leads to the shortcut to my second pool. West's voice travels down the short pathway, and I freeze.

"Yes. Daisy Carter-Kincaid. Yes. The heiress. No, I'm not some creeper trying to spy on her, I need to know if she's—*dammit.*"

There's a splash, and I peek around the corner to see waves rippling out in the center of my pool.

"Did you just chuck your phone in there?"

He jerks his head in my direction. Relief washes over

his face, his shoulders relax, and he starts to rub his eyebrow, then stops and growls. "I need your phone number. Now. Alessandro's too. And anyone else who keeps tabs on you. Except your grandmother. That woman can go the fuck to hell and show her horns where she belongs." He blows out a short breath. "Are you okay?"

I don't *take* orders.

I *give* orders.

But the concern laced into his tirade has me pulling out my phone. "Are you kidding? It'd take more than a couple little sea urchins to bring all of this fabulousness down. Gimme your digits. I'll text you."

He rattles off the number, and I send him a quick note with both Alessandro's and Tiana's numbers attached.

His phone dings, which means that wasn't his phone he sent flying into the pool.

I take a subtle glance to make sure he didn't chuck Remy into the water.

Definitely not a baby in there.

I stifle a snort as I realize it's one of my mom's crystal dicks. Probably shouldn't leave her artwork lying around the patio tables.

"How's the little pipe organ? He didn't get too nervous about Aunt Daisy being rushed to the hospital, did he?"

"He screamed in sympathy for hours."

Oh, sarcasm at its finest. That shouldn't be attractive, but it's making me a little hot under the collar.

Side effect of the Benedryl, undoubtedly.

"Is he inside?"

"Yes. Found a bed. He's happy."

"I should go hug him and promise him I'm gonna

147

make a full recovery. Except I don't want to scare the poor kid."

"Scare him how?"

"With my evil scar face."

His eyes narrow again while he studies me.

I get my picture taken a million times in a weekend when I'm out having fun. I get stared down in boardrooms on a regular basis. And I have to deal with my grandmother's scrutiny every waking minute of my life.

I get used to it.

But West studying the blotchy, saggy mess that's currently my face?

It's making me more self-conscious than that time an ass shot of me in a thong while I was on my period went around the internet.

Seventeen was a horrible age for wearing dresses that got caught in the wind.

And he's going to tell me I'm beautiful just the way I am, and I'm going to have to punch him, because he doesn't get to say nice things about me right now.

That would make me like him entirely too much when I might possibly already like him entirely too much simply for *being* here.

And also lose a little respect for him for lying to me.

I'm complicated like that.

"Probably a good idea to not let him see you right now," he finally says, "but if you think you get to have an allergic reaction to get out of overnight duty, you better be prepared to lose custody of the kid."

Oh, fuck.

He went and said the only thing *worse* than telling me I'm beautiful.

And I'm nothing if not impulsive.

Which is technically my excuse for what I do next, even if I would've done it anyway.

I'm impulsive like that.

17

West

ONE MINUTE, I'm insulting Daisy's appearance, and the next, she's leaping into the air, wrapping her arms and legs around me, and pressing a hard kiss to my lips.

My dazed brain registers plump breasts pressed to my chest, curvy thighs nestled against my cock, a luscious ass in my hands—because yes, of *course* I'm going to catch her —and the sweet Kool-Aid taste of her lips, and my balls whoop and holler and ask someone to hold their beer.

I'm not going to kiss her back—except suddenly I am, because even while being so pissed at her for everything from Becca to the allergic reaction, I'm so fucking grateful she's okay.

And now I'm slanting my lips against hers while relief courses through me that she's alive and kicking and breathing, while simultaneously being pissed as hell that *no one* in her household would tell me how she was doing.

CRAZY FOR LOVING YOU

I'm going to kiss her until she *never* leaves me hanging and uncertain while she's being rushed to an emergency room again.

That...made a lot more sense when my nuts said it.

She parts her lips and her tongue dives into my mouth and holy sweet fuck, is there *anything* she doesn't throw herself into full-throttle?

I'd be lying if I said it wasn't attractive as hell that she's leaping into this motherhood thing without an ounce of complaint. And I barely know her, except this whole co-guardianship thing—it's making me learn her *fast*.

That's what I'm talking about! my nuts crow. *Hump her! Hump her naked!*

Christ.

I can't make out with Daisy.

I'm only here to help her get custody of Remington. And apparently to piss her grandmother off. That strip-tease thing the other night was a joke from the universe that usually gives me window seats and green lights, and I need to remember my place.

My purpose.

Which is for a kid to get a good home with his family, *not* for me to have a weekend fling with a partying heiress who suddenly seems like so much more.

I wrench myself out of the kiss.

Wide, blood-shot eyes blink at me like she forgot where she was.

Or who she was kissing.

Impossible. We're experts and unforgettable, my balls tell me.

Fuckers need to *shut up*.

She blinks once more, then she smacks me lightly in the shoulder.

"Don't you *dare* use sarcasm to flirt with me again," she orders, but there's a twinkle in her eye that spells out *D-O-O-M*.

Specifically, mine.

She's still gripping my hips with her thighs like I'm the pole and she's the dancer, and it's affecting *my* pole.

Blue.

Her eyes are blue.

"I'm not flirting with you," I tell her.

"Yes, you are."

I have to clear my throat to get rid of that frog suddenly croaking inside it. "No, I'm not. By the way, I told your grandmother we got married."

"Did she have a stroke and die?"

"No."

"That's probably good, because a stroke or a heart attack would only make the dark powers inside her stronger. Also, you don't tell someone's grandmother you *got married* if you're not planning to flirt with them. And you should flirt with me. It would make Becca extremely jealous."

My jaw clenches, my ass bunches, and I'd curl my fingers into fists if they weren't already digging into Daisy's butt cheeks. "I don't want to flirt with Becca," I grit out.

She smiles. "And you're welcome for me helping you figure that out."

"Do not set me up with anyone *ever* again."

Her smile gets bigger.

Fuck, she's pretty when she smiles. Even with her face blotchy and shiny and still slightly swollen, and her eyes bloodshot, and her bright red hair lopsided and frizzy in its ponytail.

I'd blame sleep deprivation, but I got by just fine in my twenty sleep-deprived years in the military without fantasizing about any of the female Marines I occasionally came into contact with, which means whatever's going on here is bad. "You need to get off me."

"But we're married."

"That was a *story*."

"You don't strike me as the *story* type."

"I'm full of surprises."

"Or *maybe* my grandmother drove you to it, or *maybe* I'm rubbing off on you."

She's definitely rubbing *against* me. "If this temporary situation is going to work, we need boundaries."

"Ah, there's the Marine talking. I've been thinking. Normally, I don't get involved with locals—you'll understand when you meet my mother—but I think there's a reason people have so much sex when they have babies. It's a natural chill pill. So if you're not having sex with Becca, and I'm not having sex with anyone else in Miami, then we should work off some steam while we wait for the legal dust to settle."

"Did you just say *chill pill*?"

"I embrace all the happy words, hammer man. Doesn't matter what decade they were popular."

My sisters would love her.

Which is exactly what I've thought about every single woman I've ever dated.

And not a single one of those dates have ended well.

Some, in fact, have ended worse than others.

"You need to get off me," I repeat.

"So that's a no to working off steam?" She shrugs. "It's because of the face thing, isn't it? Give me ten minutes and my stylist, and you won't know what hit you."

"You're not the first woman to have an allergic reaction on a date with me. You won't be the last. Don't flatter yourself."

"Ah, so it *was* a date. And with two women, you player, you. So. Tell me more about this other time you were on a date and a woman had an allergic reaction?"

"Are you ever going to get down?"

"You have nice hands. I'm not inclined to make you remove them from my ass anytime soon."

I release her butt and lift my hands.

She doesn't move.

"West?"

I sigh. My sisters will *definitely* love her. "What?"

"Thank you for being here. It was a big comfort to know Remy was taken care of while I was battling for my life."

She leaps off me like she's a freaking gymnast who didn't just hide a truly sweet sentiment behind what I hope is a huge exaggeration, and turns and sashays her curvy ass to the pool house. "Is the howler in here? I need to see his cute face and snuggle him. Isn't that weird how he barely registered in my life forty-eight hours ago, and now I can't stop thinking about him?"

No.

It's not weird.

But her saying it is provoking the kind of reaction that means I need a cold shower.

I already knew I was getting attached to Remy.

I don't need my nuts suggesting we should get attached to Daisy too.

Even if watching her hold the baby is making my heart whisper that it might be too late anyway.

18

Daisy

WEST IS AVOIDING ME. He says he's baby-proofing and cat-hunting, but I know he's avoiding me. Since I got back from the hospital yesterday, we've spoken exactly thirty-four times, which is way less than I usually talk to houseguests.

Especially since he's refused to take the bait to talk about anything other than Remy.

But the baby gifts are starting to roll in, and he definitely needs to see the frog urinal that the prince of Stöl-land sent, so Sunday evening, while Cristoff is in the kitchen muttering to himself about not being able to use shellfish in my dishes anymore, I go searching out my co-guardian again.

But first, I strap Remy to my chest with the new baby backpack that came from a former boyfriend who loves to take six-week hikes through the mountain.

I'm well aware it's supposed to go on my back, but I don't like not having Remy in sight.

He's just so dang *cute*. And he *only* poops or cries when West is watching him, which means he's basically the world's best baby.

Three cats streak by as I make my way up the stairs to the guest wing of the house. I've named them Cotton Ball, Snickers, and Mr. Peabody, and I'm reasonably confident they'll be permanent fixtures here, along with Elvira, who's chilling in the pool on a unicorn floatie again.

"West?" I call as I make my way down the hallway and its row of arched windows overlooking the mangroves surrounding the hump in the D part of my house. "You up here?"

A muffled curse answers me from the Bahama Mama suite, so I backtrack to the mellow peach-and-yellow suite decorated with sunset pictures I've shot off my yacht in the Bahamas. Naturally.

The furniture is a vintage Queen Anne set that I had reupholstered with a pineapple patterned fabric, and the chandelier in the sitting room in here is my favorite—it's a blown glass oversized drink umbrella lined with color-changing LEDs that rotate from orange to yellow to pink to orange.

I spent a fuck-ton of money to win that at an auction a couple months ago, along with a jewel-encrusted giraffe that I keep in one of my lounges. My friends thought I was crazy, but they love that about me.

Even Remy stops to stare up at it when we walk in. "*Aaaooooo,*" he coos like the adorable perfect little baby that he is.

"*Aaaooo*," I agree.

He grins.

I grin back.

Like we're actually communicating.

"Fucking cat," West grunts deeper in the suite.

I follow his voice to the bedroom, where I find a picture-perfect view of his ass in black mesh shorts while he bends over and reaches under the bed.

"Get out here, you mangy beast," he says.

"*Aaaooooo*," Remy says again.

I coo back at him again and finagle us up onto the bed, then bounce.

"*Aaaah!*" West hollers.

A streak of black and white darts out of the room with a yowl, and my co-guardian sits back on his heels and gives me another of those looks he's gotten so good at.

This one's a green-eyed glare.

I am *fascinated* by his eyes. Mine change color because of my contacts—non-prescription, just for fun—but his, I'm certain, are a reflection of his mood.

On any other man I'd call them hazel with personality.

On him, they're magic.

"That cat is puking up hairballs up and down the hall," he informs me.

"Huh. We'll have to send him back."

He shoves his fists into his eye sockets. "That much puke means he's *sick*. He needs to see a vet."

I know, and I've already made a mental note to call the vet who sometimes checks in on Steve and ask for a house call. "You take me very seriously."

"You—you're wearing that backpack backwards."

"I like it better this way."

"I left you a schedule this morning. I'm busy until five, and you get the overnight shift."

"Why are you avoiding me?"

"It's called *alone time*, and some of us need it."

"Did you get a lot of alone time in the Marines?"

"Yes."

"Did you really go on a date with a woman once who only wanted to ask you to video call your brother? I swear Becca mentioned that yesterday."

He mutters something about being a martyr and hoping Julienne and Rafe are rotting in hell—at least, that's my interpretation—while he shoves to his feet and stalks toward the door.

Remy and I join him.

Cam, Emily, and Luna are all busy today either having sexytimes with their soulmates or saving the world at charity events. My housekeeper and personal assistant don't work on Sundays. Neither does the pool boy, who's actually a woman who runs Pool Boy Maintenance—she mostly hires eye candy to service rich cougars in the area, but I get her personally, since she's freaking awesome and can handle everything from unbalanced pool pH to rescuing armadillos that fall in the pool, which only happened that one time in the dick pool, but I was still grateful.

I could grab Alessandro and head to the village, but my face hasn't yet recovered from that theoretical boxing match with a lobster, so I'm homebound.

West turns into the Strawberry Daiquiri suite, which is his assigned bedroom suite for the duration of his stay. It doesn't look lived in *at all*, despite all the stuff he brought over yesterday.

Clearly his Marine training is still with him.

Or maybe he's plotting an escape from the room that Alessandro says has *Pepto Bismol-colored walls*.

Yes, yes, I should've given him the Piña Colada suite. It's much more masculine with its off-white walls and coconut chairs.

But that wouldn't have been as much fun as pushing his buttons.

You don't really know a person until you know them under stress. And since I'm going to be living with him for a while, I really should know how he handles stress.

It's for the good of the baby.

Seriously.

Also, I have a very good feel for when I've pushed someone too far after years of walking the line with my grandmother. Plus, knowing what stresses a person out helps me figure out how to do them favors that are better than arranging super-awkward group dates where I have allergic reactions to seafood.

So far, the only favor I can see that West needs is alone time, which isn't helping me figure out how to really pay him back at all.

"Can't you go read a book or something?" he says when we follow him into the suite.

"I can't read."

He swings around and looks me straight in the eye at that.

I blink coquettishly.

And his lips twitch.

Just the briefest amount, but I made the big bad Marine construction guy smile.

High fucking five to me.

I'll dance about this later. Right now, I'm not sure Remy's secure enough in this backwards backpack for me to risk it, which is unfortunate.

I love dancing.

"All these people are sending baby presents," I tell West. "I shouldn't open them alone."

"So call your grandmother."

He shoots. He scores. And I shudder before I catch on to the fact that he's razzing me right back.

"She says the Rodericks are claiming there's video evidence that Julienne and Rafe made their will while they were drunk, so their previous will should take precedence. They also claim I'm an unfit mother, and we'll probably be getting a call about a visit from social services as soon as the office opens tomorrow. Just so you're in the loop."

He studies me again the same way he did yesterday at the pool when I got back from my little field trip to the hospital. "What does their previous will say?"

"According to my grandmother, something about their future hypothetical children being raised by Benedictine monks in the Italian foothills."

His lips flatten for a moment before he lifts his head to the ceiling. "Why?" he mutters to himself. "*Why* do I keep falling for this?"

"Hate to break it to you, Westley, but that is literally what their previous will said. They made *it* while they were drunk on their honeymoon, which I know only because I keep security cameras on my yacht, which will actually make the Rodericks' legal challenge more difficult if both wills were made while drunk. Also, they stole-borrowed my yacht for their honeymoon. Google it. That's how Julienne became a trash blogger. She started by one-starring my ship for daring to—*gasp*—rock on the sea."

He's shaking his head and muttering again as he heads into the walk-in closet.

I follow, only to get treated to the sight of him pulling off his T-shirt.

"Whoa, baby, that is *epic*," I breathe.

He starts and turns around, and *hello*, even better.

"Do you have any concept of personal space?"

"Not really. That artwork is *amazing*. Phuket? Or Bora-Bora?" Amongst all the ink on his chest, I move to touch the beach bungalow-and-mountain landscape on one pec between a mermaid masthead over his shoulder and what appears to be an intricate string of thorns and roses curving around his shoulder blade, but he swats my hand away.

"Go away."

"I'll show you mine if you tell me."

"I don't want to see your ass."

I chuckle. "Aww, you know I have an ass on my ass! Westley Jaeger, have you been googling me?"

"I'm changing my pants."

"Do you have a tattoo on your ass too?"

"Don't say *ass* in front of the baby. Actually, you shouldn't cuss in front of the baby at all. They're very impressionable. And go away."

He's right. I should go away. If I tell myself we can be friends who keep in touch after Remy's guardianship is no longer in question, I'm lying, because I can't be friends with a hard-bodied, competent, half-cranky, half-resigned, all-saving-my-ass former military man, because he's too fucking attractive for me to *just* be friends with.

I know I don't need *feelings* about him.

Just *help*. Preferably with a side of mutual respect, since I know a thing or two firsthand about the awkwardness of having parents who hate each other, though hopefully all the legal baloney will be over with long before Remy can remember any of this.

But West doesn't like me, which is the other barrier to me being friends with him.

And that's probably my fault. "So what's the story with you and Becca? You like her, but you wouldn't look at her yesterday. Don't think a few little shrimp made me blind. I mean, it did, for about thirty minutes when I couldn't open my eyes, but before that."

He turns his back to me and drops his pants, white briefs and all, and my mouth goes dry.

He does not, in fact, have any tattoos on his ass.

But he *does* have two solid marble orbs that end in tree trunk thighs that could probably squat my entire house.

In my lifetime, I've seen a healthy share of asses. Athlete asses. Movie star asses. Asses from every continent on earth, of all shapes, sizes, and colors.

I could build an ass museum with all the asses I've seen.

But West Jaeger's ass tops them all.

The thick muscly types don't usually do it for me—I've

been in more of a mood for the slender starving rock star type lately—but I want to bend over and take a bite of one of those cheeks, and then trace every inch with both my tongue and my fingers.

Even more than all the ink on his back, his bare ass is pure erotic artwork.

That he's covering with board shorts.

I whimper.

He pulls a fresh white T-shirt over his dark, disheveled hair, and the tattoo disappears too.

But I know it's there.

And I won't forget anytime soon.

This is *not* good for my sanity. I shake my head as he bends over, grabs his dirty clothes, and places them carefully in a laundry hamper beneath the short row of folded and ironed jeans and T-shirts hanging on the lone rod in the closet.

He irons his jeans.

I'm simultaneously turned on and appalled, and I'm highly uncomfortable with both reactions.

"Going for a swim?" I manage to say nearly normally.

He grabs his phone off the end table in the sitting room and walks out without answering me.

Remy gurgles and coos.

"Agreed," I tell him. "We like hanging out with West, don't we?"

Remy smiles.

God, he's adorable.

It's seriously hard to believe he's a product of Julienne and Rafe.

"Wait up," I call to West. "I need your opinion on

whether the new speaker system for baby music should go in *this* nursery, or in the one closer to my bedroom. Or if I should just get a second one."

"Do you know why I gave you a schedule last night?"

Yay! He's talking to me again. "Because you can't shake your time in the military?"

"Because I need space from *you* if I'm going to stay here long enough for you to get full, uncontested custody of the baby."

"I'm sorry about yesterday," I say quietly. "I'm not hounding you about Becca because I want to be an ass. I just want to understand. You're doing me a huge favor, and I can't do you huge favors back if I don't know you well enough to know what kind of favors you like."

He studies me for a moment. "Thank you," he says gruffly before turning back down the hall.

Such a grumpy bear. He's so damn adorable. "It sucks that Julienne put you in this position, because you seem like one of the good guys who'd be a super amazing role model for Remy in a world where they're hard to find. Maybe we *should* get married."

That stops him short in the middle of the hallway, with the early evening light shafting through the arched windows and illuminating him like an avenging beach angel.

Oh, shi—shirt.

The one time he takes me seriously, it's about getting married.

"*Kidding.*" I laugh, which is easy, because I do this laugh seventeen times an hour when I'm partying with new acquaintances, which is basically every other weekend.

He slowly turns to face me again, still lit and glowing. "Why do you want this baby?"

Does he have to do that thing where he crosses his muscled arms over his chest while he interrogates me? Because I have a damn good air conditioning system, but I'm starting to sweat. "I—"

I have to stop and clear my throat. This is harder to say than *I'm sorry* was.

Why do I want Remy?

Because he's alone and helpless. Because he deserves a fucking awesome life. Because he's an orphan. Because he's my responsibility. Because my grandmother will disinherit me and yank away the only thing I've ever been marginally good at if I don't take on *this* challenge too.

But I can't say that.

"You're going to have to tell a judge," he points out. "So you might as well tell me."

"I don't know you well enough to trust you," I manage to say, just barely over a whisper.

"You've trusted me with your cousin's baby for the better part of the last two days."

"That's completely different than trusting you with *me*."

"Is that what you're going to tell Remy when he asks you personal questions? That he doesn't have the right to *know* you? How's he ever going to learn to have real relationships with other people when his mother figure won't let him in?"

Heat is creeping over my scalp and down my neck. I've been naked and felt less exposed than I do right now.

"I don't know what google told you about me, but it

only tells you what I *want* it to tell you. So go ahead. Judge me. Make assumptions. Draw your conclusions. Everyone does. Why shouldn't you too?"

"Going on the offensive only works if your offense is better than your defense."

I blink twice, because I'm not sure what he means, but I think he just called me out on avoiding the question.

Again.

"I'll never have a bigger bank account or house or legal team than you," he says, "but I also don't have family that threatens and bullies their way into being in charge. Don't know shit about raising kids firsthand, but I know they need unconditional love and a whole hell of a lot of work if they're going to grow up to not be shitheads."

Shit. Am I swooning? I think I'm swooning again. "Having money doesn't automatically make someone a shithead."

"No, but being related to your grandmother seems to."

I actually can't argue with him. Also, I swear the man is getting sexier by the millisecond.

And if that smirk as he turns and walks away again is any indication, he knows it.

19

West

CONFUCIUS ONCE SAID, *there's nothing like feeling like an asshole to encourage a guy to try to rescue an idiot cat from a swimming pool.*

So maybe I'm paraphrasing Confucius, but I do feel like an asshole for putting Daisy on the spot. It's not her fault I have a fucking hero complex. Not her fault her cousin married into a family of assholes and then named me in her will.

And it's not her fault I said *yes* when she asked me to come back.

That's all on me.

So I need to quit taking it all out on her and make the most of being here.

Nicely.

Also, this damn cat *does* need to be rescued from the

pool, since it stuck a claw through the pool floatie it's been chilling on since yesterday.

"C'mon, kitty kitty," I mutter. "You don't look like you can swim, so just let me grab you and get you to shore, okay?"

The gray tabby meow-squeals and prances in place on the deflating unicorn, which is not only wilting, but also taking on water, which the cat is freaking over.

Apparently it doesn't like getting its paws wet.

Or maybe it's terrified that whatever happened to the unicorn will happen to it.

But when I wade closer in the four-foot-deep water in the middle of the D-shaped pool in the courtyard, it arches its back and hisses, its tail going fluffier than my sister's Pomeranian at the height of summer humidity.

"All right, all right, I'll just pull you over to the side and you can climb off with your prissy little self."

Another three minutes, and it'll be swimming for it, but this one seems to have enough demon in it that it could probably levitate to shore. I should leave it to its own devices, but if it *can't* swim, I'll be the asshole who let a cat fall off a deflating unicorn and drown.

"Pussy problems?" a familiar voice calls.

My shoulders bunch, and I order them to relax. Me being an ass to her won't make any part of the next few weeks to months any easier.

"Where's the baby?" I try to keep my voice casual, but I don't know if I hit it.

"Steve's babysitting him."

I twist around, not sure I heard her right. "Steve—the *alligator?*"

PIPPA GRANT

She laughs, and *dammit*.

She's incapable of uttering a single true sentence, and here I am, wanting to actually laugh at both her audacity and the fact that I'm sixty percent tempted to believe her.

What the fuck is wrong with me?

"Relax, hammer man. Remy's napping. You should try it sometime. Does wonders for the grumpies. Aww, Elvira's unicorn popped. That's really sad."

Daisy plops down at the edge of the pool and dangles her feet in, watching me and the cat. While she was wearing the baby backpack backwards, all I could see was face and bare legs and tiger-striped toenails.

Now I get the full view of her in a tight pink tank top and short white shorts.

Her skin's still blotchy from yesterday's reaction, but her personality is back in order—not that it was missing long—so I'm not worried over residual side effects.

"You know how to catch a cat?" I ask her.

"I caught Twinkle Toes. The vet's coming over to check her out."

"You caught the cat?"

"I draped myself with a dead tuna fish and walked down the hall until she couldn't resist me anymore. Left it in your bed, by the way. Nothing better than waking up to tuna bed."

She grins and winks. It bothers me how much I feel at home right now, because my sisters and Tyler would say the same. And how much I'm not actually surprised that Daisy's taking care of the sick cat that I couldn't find.

My nuts start singing some Barry Manilow, because they're hopelessly falling for Daisy's breasts.

170

I remind my nuts that women like Barry White better, and they tell me I should pay better attention to who I'm flirting with. Or trying *not* to flirt with.

They might have a point.

I've nearly gotten the deflating unicorn to the opposite side of the pool with Demon Cat—aka Elvira, apparently —hissing and occasionally swatting at me from a distance. She's hissing and swatting at the water filling the floatie too.

"No reaction to having fish in your bed?" Daisy says.

"Only fair, since I put shrimp shells in your bed."

She sucks in half a breath before she leans back and laughs. "Westley Jaeger, you have a sense of humor."

I don't answer, because this seems like dangerous territory.

Where I'm *comfortable* to Becca, I'm apparently passing some kind of test with Daisy, who's simultaneously unreliable and dependable at the same time.

Which means she's faking one, and I don't like fake.

I like real.

I like rules.

I like order.

Therefore, I will *not* like Daisy Carter-Kincaid. I can be civil, but I don't have to like her.

Do what you want, but we like her, my balls inform me.

Traitors.

I get the floatie lined up with the edge of the patio, but the cat keeps creeping further back, trying to climb the unicorn head, which is the only part not actively under an inch of water.

"Go on, leap." I point to the fancy concrete surrounding the pool.

The cat hisses and swipes again, but it miscalculates, because it's a fucking cat, and gets its claw stuck in the unicorn's horn.

"Are you kidding me?" I mutter while it jerks its paw and tries to yank it out of the vinyl. But the bopping unicorn won't give it up, so now the cat appears to be boxing a deflating unicorn head.

Daisy tips her head back and laughs while whipping out a phone and pointing it at me.

"What do you people do for entertainment when I'm not around?" I jump out of the pool and drag the floatie out, but the damn cat is *still* fighting like it *wants* to stay in the pool and pulverize the unicorn. "What the fuck, cat? Let go. Be free. Stay out of the water."

It finally wrenches its claw loose, the momentum throwing it into the water.

I leap back in, but before I can reach it, it's scrambled out, a streak of soaking wet pussy flying into the land-scaping like someone just shot it out of the clown cannon my mom bitched about for two years when that one comedian got popular for using it to avenge people terri-fied of ventriloquists by launching puppets at every show.

She called it insulting the genre by splitting the fan base. *Mocking each other is why we can't have nice things. You can be funny without being mean.*

I hadn't understood, but eventually the cannon dude was arrested for tax fraud, so there's that.

But back to Daisy and the cat.

"Appreciate the help," I call to her.

She says something I don't hear clearly, so I tilt my good ear toward her. "Do I want to know?"

She sighs and splashes the water. "I said, my parents got divorced when I was seven."

"Because of a wet cat?"

"Basically. Several wet cats. In a manner of speaking."

I open my mouth.

Then close it.

"Yes, my father was the same kind of philandering asshole that Rafe was. Is. My father *is*. He's not dead. Not like Rafe. But he's still a cheater, and I have three ex-step-mothers happy to share stories, though after the first one, I never bothered to get to know them well enough to invite them over for story time. That would've been awkward."

Huh.

She's flustered.

I stand there watching her, testing a theory that she hates silence, and it's not three seconds before my patience is rewarded.

"I'm never having children, but I'm apparently having Remy, so you need to know that we will get along and never say bad things about each other in front of him, even though I don't know if you'll be around long enough for him to even remember this, or I will crush you in ways you had no idea you could be crushed, which will also make me very sad, because I don't *like* crushing people, but I'll do it to keep Remy from feeling like any more of a pawn than everyone's already treating him. Understood?"

That's reasonable. I don't think it's the full story on why she hasn't issued a single complaint about raising the baby beyond that first night, but it's a start.

Yeah! A start! my balls crow.

They're idiots.

So am I, because my place here isn't *real*. It's for show, for the lawyers and judges. Still, I don't look away from her. "Why do you call him Remy? Is that what Julienne called him?"

"No, she called him *Mington*."

I cross my arms. "Why do I even try with you?"

"Pinky swear. Here. Look." She bends over her phone, and a minute later, she flashes the screen at me across the pool. I hear muffled voices, and I can't see a damn thing on the screen, so I do something I'll probably regret, and I dive into the water to cross the pool.

Quicker than walking around.

Plus, I didn't go into the Marines because I wanted to be stuck on land forever.

I fucking love the water.

I surface, and she's frowning at me. It's a subtle frown, her brows barely pinched, her pink lips straighter than turned down, but it's definitely a frown.

She looks different without all her makeup on.

Like a real woman.

Not the one who's always on the magazines that my sisters keep when I'm visiting home. And not just because her skin is still blotchy in places.

But only a few places.

"Here. Look. Home videos from her private Instagram account."

"Private? Like where she said nice things about people?"

Daisy grimaces. "Sure. Let's go with that."

She lifts the phone again, and I lean closer to watch the video on the small screen.

The scent of coconut floods my nose as I get within sniffing distance of Daisy, and I suddenly need to know what Sierra is doing. How big Baxter and Nina are now. If she ever got remarried.

Noise off Daisy's phone reminds me to breathe, and there's another flash of weirdness in my chest as Julienne Carter-Roderick appears on the screen, stalking across the kitchen in her Coconut Grove mansion, wearing heels and a baby sling and talking to the camera. "Mington is three weeks old today, and he's brilliant, naturally. He said *Hello* in Mandarin this morning when I woke him up. That baby course in Italian clearly is a piece of shit, since it's teaching Mington to speak Mandarin, but at least he's learning to be quatralingualistic before he can crawl."

"Quatralingualistic?"

"She tried, poor thing. Her father—my uncle—abandoned her mother when she was two, and her mom never got over it, which meant the Graminator was basically the closest thing she had to a solid maternal role model. Nicely done with her yesterday, by the way. Tiana showed me the video last night. You're hot when you're all bossy and protective. And we *could* get married. That'd prove to the social workers that we're good for the baby."

I switch my attention from the video to her face.

She blinks innocently.

"If I'm not going to be an asshole, you need to not be an asshole."

"What? I've read a *ton* of romance novels on marriages of convenience, and it's not a bad idea."

She's honestly incapable of being serious for three fucking seconds. And I'm not nearly as annoyed by it as I should be. I stop when I realize I'm subconsciously leaning toward her, nearly smiling. "Do you flirt with everything that moves?"

"Basically. I hit on my friends all the time, but they all have boyfriends or fiancés now, so I have to find another object to practice on. And you, clearly, need to feel like you're attractive so you can find a higher caliber of crushes."

She gives me that grin again, shrugging her shoulders in a little *oopsie* move. "Sorry. I'm done. I swear. I just— you really *could* do better. Look at you. You deserve to have a woman who'll worship you the way Derek, Beck, and Jude worship Emily, Luna, and Cam, because I don't tolerate my friends being in relationships with people who don't deserve them."

"Just when I think we're making progress, you go and say something that makes me want to leave."

"West." She loops her arms around my neck, much like she leaped on me for that kiss that I can't erase off my lips, and she lowers her voice conspiratorially. "Friends watch out for friends. You'd tell me if I was dating someone horrifically wrong for me, wouldn't you?"

I study her blue eyes, then slowly nod. "Probably owe you that much."

She quirks another grin, and I realize she has tiny laugh lines at the corners of her eyes.

She really does laugh *all the time*. Because she's happy?

Or because she's faking it?

But her attention drops to my wet T-shirt, and an uncharacteristic seriousness touches her gaze. "You know what occurred to me yesterday, while I was at the emergency room?"

"That money can't buy your way out of allergies?"

She shakes her head. "You don't have Carter genes. Maybe Julienne *didn't* just draw names out of a hat. Maybe she looked at you, and how you told her off when she had her hissy fit about that wall and the fountain, and she realized she wanted her son to be raised by someone with the cojones to stand up to people. Like The Dame."

"I didn't tell her off."

"But you didn't tear the wall out either, did you?"

"She couldn't fire me if she wanted the nursery to get done. No one else would take the job."

Daisy tips her head back and laughs again, her arms still looped around my neck, and my cock twitches in interest.

Again.

Not. Good.

Let go and get down with your bad self, my nuts chide. *You're a grown-up. She's a grown-up. Do her and get her out of your system.*

I honestly don't know where I went wrong with my balls.

She looks back at me, still smiling, and swear to fuck, she's even prettier now than she is when she's wearing makeup. "Every single person in my family on my mother's side either does exactly what my grandmother tells them to do, or they do the exact opposite and think they're sticking it to her by disobeying, but not a single one of them is actually doing what they *want* to do. They're *all* being controlled by her to some degree."

"And you?"

She traces a finger down my neck. "I walk the line between doing what she wants and pissing her off. But only because I know her secret. She's actually the last living immortal Highlander, so even if I literally buried her, she'd rise again. Probably stronger this time. With a new shiny sword for—gah. Sorry. Wasn't supposed to let that part of the family legend slip out."

"You're terrible at avoiding questions." If she doesn't quit touching me, I'm going to kiss her again, and we'll both regret it.

No, check that.

I'll regret it. I will *definitely* regret it.

She grins, as if to reinforce the idea that she never regrets anything. "Of everything I've ever been accused of, that's a new one."

"What would you be if you could be anything?"

"Immortal like my grandmother, but more on the butterfly side than the orc side."

She's so—so—so fucking *infuriating*.

She wants my help, but she won't tell me why. She smiles, but I don't believe she's fully happy. She says she wants to be nice, but she runs one of the biggest real estate empires in the world.

You can't run an empire and be *nice*.

"Wow, you have really thick veins in your neck," she whispers.

She touches my neck again, and fuck.

I'm going to kiss her.

I'm going to kiss chaos. Disorder. Unpredictability.

Because *fuck it*.

If this is what life's throwing at me, why the hell shouldn't I take it?

20

Daisy

ONE MINUTE, I'm sitting on the edge of the pool, getting ready to kiss this delicious hunk of a man who's stepped up in a way no man has *ever* stepped up in my life, and the next, I'm three feet underwater.

I surge to the surface, ready to pounce, but West is already halfway across the pool.

"Oh, so *that's* how you want to play?" I call.

He tilts his ear toward me. "I don't know what your end game is, but you can't use your feminine wiles against me. I'm a highly trained military operative who can resist torture and interrogation with the best of them."

He's freaking hilarious.

And unexpectedly fun this afternoon.

And intent on resisting me, which makes him all that much more irresistible.

"Oh, you can, can you?" I reach under the water and

grab the bottom of my tank top to slowly peel it over my head.

Even from halfway across the pool, I can see his eyes dilate.

He's not immune to me.

Not in the least.

Is flirting with my co-guardian a bad idea?

Probably.

But do I love bad ideas?

Most definitely.

"Do your worst," he says.

The water's cool, but my skin's hot, and my competitive streak is bubbling to the surface. "I'm going to make you want to kiss me," I tell him.

"No, you're not."

I smile and fling my tank somewhere behind me.

A cat yowls, and then a streak of gray tabby shoots from the bushes to the outdoor kitchen at the top of my courtyard.

West wipes the water off his face. "You just hit the cat with your shirt."

"Without looking." I wiggle my brows. "You could be kissing that level of talent right now."

"I'm not kissing you."

"Not yet."

"You're insane."

"Westley. This is *not* how you win an argument with me." I reach behind my neck and untie my bikini top.

He freezes in the water. *Hard* freezes. "What are you doing?"

"Playing dirty."

"I have four sisters. I was flashed more times before I was eighteen than most men are in a lifetime. I'm immune."

"So you've never seen breasts you liked? You poor man. You really *didn't* get a good look at mine the other day."

"I've seen plenty of breasts I *liked*. I just don't need to see—*dammit*, Daisy."

I glide into the water toward where he's hiding in the deep end. "You changed in front of me. This is only fair."

"You *charged into my room naked*. We're even. And I wasn't trying to seduce you."

"I wrestle better in the water when I'm naked, and I owe you for dunking me."

He slices through the water, effortlessly avoiding me. "That was free of charge. No repayment necessary."

"I'm not one of those billionaires who uses her status to get things for free. I *need* to pay you back."

"Nope. I'm a giver. We're even at a karmic level."

"Am I really that unattractive?"

"Yes."

I laugh, because he's starting to smile, and I know he's lying.

"But you have a mediocre personality to compensate for your physical shortcomings," he adds, and that's it.

He could be the love child of Michael Phelps and Idris Elba—so basically a gorgeous fast swimmer—and I would still absolutely catch this man and dunk him right back.

I lunge for him, and he dives under the water, only to surface a moment later back in the shallow end of my awesome D pool.

"Time out," I call.

"Pussy," he calls back with a full shit-eating grin that makes the butterflies and geckos and probably even Steve the alligator, who can't see him, all faint with swooniness.

I'm torn between swooning and jumping him.

But first, I need to be more aerodynamic.

Aquadynamic?

Yeah.

Aquadynamic.

I reach under the water as my feet touch the bottom, and I wiggle out of my shorts. "You should probably strip too. Then you might stand a chance."

"You—"

He stops and shakes his head, and I send my shorts flying back over my shoulder.

No more cats yowl, but there's a crash and a crack, and West covers a grin with his hand. "You just murdered a pot of orchids."

"No, I gave them a new viewpoint. They were getting tired of just staring at the pool from the same angle day after day after—*aah*!"

He's like a fish.

One minute he's in the shallow end, then next he's halfway across the pool toward me.

And despite my bravado, there's nothing I can do to make my milk jugs aquadynamic.

And really, would I want to when a buff hottie like West is chasing me?

Still, I make a show of trying to swim away.

Friends can bang, right? We can bang out some stress, maybe have dinner together once or twice a week, and

183

then we'll be *much* more friendly while all the legal crap gets sorted.

He surfaces right next to me, and I shriek—for show, of course—and flap about helplessly trying half-heartedly to splash him.

"Daisy?" He shakes his head, treading water, droplets sluicing from his thick hair down his face, dripping off his nose, his eyes a mossy green that goes perfectly with the palm trees overhead.

"Yes, my scary captor? Do you need to impale me on your sword? Please?"

He sputters a laugh. "You don't quit, do you?"

"Quitters don't win. Oh, help. Help. I only have three fingers holding me up in this water that's trying to swallow me whole."

I don't thrash about and pretend I'm drowning, because that's one of my few other lines. *Don't cry wolf when it matters.*

He's studying me, and the smile is sliding off his face. That won't do.

"Oh, no. I'm being dragged down by the weight of my panties. You must take them off me. Please! Please help me, noble captor! I must get back to my baby!"

He doesn't smile this time.

I don't know what just went through his head, but whatever it was, it's changed something. He suddenly looks away.

"West?" I want to reach out and touch his face and turn it to me, but there's a *back off* shield going up in place again.

"The last time I got seriously involved with a woman,

she had kids, and I was left high and dry without *any* of them when she decided we were over. I'm not doing that again."

My heart twists, and another unfamiliar emotion drags at my stomach. "You can't judge all women by one who treated you poorly."

"Pretty sure I can judge you."

Ouch.

Also, probably fair.

He shoves away and dives back into the water.

I should slip out of the pool and let him enjoy some laps and some sun while Remy's sleeping, but I don't do the walk of shame.

Not after a one-night stand.

And not after sticking my foot in my mouth.

And not after accidentally pushing good men too far.

But where I'd usually do the walk of *I live the fuck out of my life, and I enjoy every minute*, instead, I stay in the pool, watching until he surfaces with his back to me.

"Maternal instincts," I blurt.

His shoulders bunch.

He's still in his white T-shirt, which is plastered to his body, not at all hiding the epic tattoos on his back. I want a closer look, to see what all he has inked there, but now's not the time.

"Of everyone in my family, I'm Remy's best shot at having the closest thing he'll ever have to a real mother, and I don't want to fuck him up. I want him to know where he came from without feeling obligated to repeat all of our mistakes. I want him to have a chance at growing up to be the best man he can be. I can't explain it any other way than to call it latent maternal instincts. That's why I want to be in his life. That's why I want to keep him. Because I look at him, and I see an innocent little creature who can be shaped and molded into something better than I am, and I want to be the person to help him get there. But I also don't know jack about how to turn a baby into a good person, whereas you—you just *ooze* good person, and I'm pretty sure I don't deserve to have a co-guardian like you, but for some reason, Julienne named you, and for some other reason, you're still here, and I—I'll quit being a flirty asshole. Sorry. I didn't realize…what you'd been through."

He hangs his head and rubs his temples, still without looking at me, and I know what he's thinking.

If you want him to have a chance, then you need to get the fuck out of his life, because you're just as screwed up as the rest of your family.

So maybe I can do the walk of shame.

That's what it feels like as I slip mostly naked out of the pool and head back into my house without looking back.

21

West

AFTER THE POOL INCIDENT, Daisy emails me with an updated proposed schedule for Remy that includes her taking the majority of the responsibility for him. She'd take it all, she says, but for the legal challenge sake, I need to actually show evidence of taking *some* responsibility for him. She ends with a brief apology for making me uncomfortable.

It's oddly *human*.

And I don't mean I don't think Daisy's human. I think she's the biggest kind of human—big personality, big bank account, big sex account.

Fuck.

She's like a female Tyler, except *bigger*.

And weirdly more professional.

Didn't see that coming. And I don't know if she's proving she can be professional, or if she had her assistant write it out for her, or if she's proving a point that she's not just a chaotic hornball.

But Monday morning, when I leave the Pepto Bismol room that I've been assigned and take Remy to her in her office, she's typing away at a computer in neon pink reading glasses that remind me of the 1960s. Her shoulders are bare, because she's in one of those shirts that has sleeves attached under her armpits. It's pink and skintight, but her cleavage is covered.

"Good morning! You're right on time." She lifts a small crystal bowl. "Frozen yogurt?"

"No. Thank you."

She peels off the reading glasses, tosses her bright, unnaturally red hair, and takes a bite while her eyes slide shut and a blissful smile slides over her lips. She visibly swallows. "Here if you ever want it." And then she rises to show off skintight, silver glitter pants. And when she crosses around her desk, my nuts start drooling.

Can we slather her in froyo and then fuck her while she's wearing those strappy stilettos? they want to know.

I tell them to shut the *fuck* up, because she's like this for everyone. Whether she knows she's capable of lifting a thousand flagpoles with one lick of her tongue on a frozen yogurt spoon, and if she does it on purpose for fun, I have no idea.

But my flagpole needs to stand at ease. "Diaper bag's packed with six bottles and enough diapers for an army."

"West! You didn't have to do that. Thank you. I'll make sure to return the favor. How is our little handsome man this morning?"

Remy yawns and waves a fist at her.

"Up at one and again at four," I report.

"Such a good boy." She bends over, giving me another whiff of coconut-scented Daisy, along with something fruity. She's a tropical bundle of chaos and unpredictability, but she's also something *more*.

The byproduct of a divorce that affected her more than she wants to admit, if that flash of panic and pain on her face yesterday afternoon was any indication.

Doesn't matter how much money a person has. Can't stop a heart from hurting.

She straightens and smiles at me. "I'll keep him until dinner, then you have him until bedtime, and I'll handle the overnight shift. I have three nannies coming in for interviews today, which will also help both of us get back to normal schedules."

I nod. And hesitate in handing him over, holding him close instead of moving toward her outstretched arms, because I don't like what I need to do today.

Namely, *leave*.

Not a good sign. *Don't get attached. Don't get attached. Don't get fucking attached, you idiot.*

"Yeah. I need to…" I trail off, gesturing to the door.

"Of course. Go on." She bends over him, trying to take him again, but once more, I can't quite let him go. "Aunt Daisy has this. Don't I, you adorable little heartbreaker?"

Remy coos at her.

"We're going to have so much fun! Tummy time and reading books and taking naps and eating bottles! And maybe we'll even go take a stroll through the village, but not eat any shrimp. Won't we? Yes, we will."

"Great. Thanks. Here." As I'm about to finally

surrender the baby, his lips part, then twist. His eyeballs cross, and a moment later, an unmistakable sound explodes from beneath his butt that I can feel clearly in the palm of my hand.

He shifts like he's really grinding into it, and another butt-plosion rockets against my hand.

Daisy freezes, but she also grins. "Let it all out, dude. Gas like that can't feel good. We all get it."

"He's not passing gas."

"We're all humans here. I pass gas. You pass gas. The baby can pass gas if he wants to pass gas. No judgment. This?" She circles her hand around her office, and I notice the paperweight on her desk is *also* a crystal penis. "This is a judgment-free zone."

I put my finger on the tip of my nose.

"Exactly," she declares. "Judgment-free zones are important."

"Not it," I reply.

"Not it?"

Shit. Now *I'm* being a shithead. But if she's serious—if she wants to raise this baby—then it's about time she gets a real taste for what she's in for. "He didn't pass gas, and I'm not it."

"What are you—" Her lip curls and her nose wrinkles as the scent of a baby's finest byproduct finally hits her.

I still haven't taken my finger off my nose, because this is a time-honored Jaeger tradition that started when my first niece was born thirteen years ago. "Like I said, *not it.*"

"Oh my god, what *is* that?" She flies to the window and flings it open, waving a hand as the cool breeze off the ocean rolls into the room.

"Apparently the kind of diaper you haven't had to change yet."

She's still fanning her nose, her eyes—which are a brilliant green today—wide and twitching at the edges. Either she's trying to force them into submission to telegraph that she has this under control, or the scent coming out of Remy's diaper is about to kill her.

"This explains everything." She inhales, coughs, and fans her face again. "He's the chosen one. He has the power. His butt is a bioweapon, and my grandmother wants to harness it for the power of taking over the world with her undead army."

Despite not wanting to, I grin. I can't *not*. She's hilarious. "My sisters tell me breastmilk poop is different than formula poop."

"Don't take this from me, Westley. He's the chosen one. His butt hath declared itself so. I bow before greatness. Remington Nathaniel Roderick, I am your humble servant. Please be kind and merciful, sir."

Utterly outrageous. I choke back a laugh. "Congratulations, Aunt Daisy. You're up."

She straightens and squares her bare shoulders. "Damn right. Hand him over."

In those stilettos, she's almost as high as my chest. There's no evidence of the lingering rash from her seafood reaction the other day, which either means she has killer makeup, or she has magic fast-healing skin.

She's also really fucking hot when she's marching into battle.

We'll slay for you, your holy sexiness, my balls crow.

She leans into me again, her hands brushing my arm

and chest. My cock twitches. My mouth goes dry. And no amount of foul diaper in the world could keep me from wanting to touch her cheeks to see if they're as soft as they look.

But she's off-limits. I told her so, and she's not trying to hit on me this morning, and the only reason she's next to me is to pick up Remy.

Whom she's pulling close despite the diaper that's overflowing. "Thank you. I've got him from here. See you around six."

Fuck.

I'm dismissed.

By a woman who's braving the diaper of doom, which is the last thing I'd expect from the Daisy Carter-Kincaid of the tabloids.

This woman—she has more layers than I want to admit. Than I *should* admit.

I brush a thumb over Remy's forehead. "Later, kiddo. Be good for Aunt Daisy."

Leaving is the hardest fucking thing I've ever done. But I have to.

Noooooo, my nuts wail as I head out to my truck. I need to get over and check on the beach house, plus grab a few more things before hitting the gym for what will likely be my last week on the job there.

My phone rings as I'm firing up the engine. I've been ignoring most of the family group texts—other than to reiterate that none of my family should fly down, that we need "time to adjust" before they invade—but I can't ignore phone calls.

And though there's over a decade between Tyler and me, he's still the only brother I have.

I answer through the truck's speaker system and hit the road. "What are you doing up this early?"

"Haven't been to bed yet," he replies happily. "Win like we did last night, it's party central all night long. Morning skate's gonna be a bitch."

I smile. Miss the little fucker. "What you get."

"Dude. Level with me. You okay?"

"Just fine."

"What's Becca think of all of this?"

My shoulders hitch, but I make them relax and wave to a lady out for a jog along the perfectly landscaped Bluewater golf cart trail. "Becca's dating someone."

There's a beat of silence. Doesn't take much to picture my little brother smothering a not-surprised laugh.

Our sisters like to tell me I'm romance novel fodder—*but, West, usually it's the GIRL who has all kinds of bad dates.*

"Ah, fuck her," Ty finally says. "Shit. *Shit.* West. Dude. Tell me you're not falling for Daisy. Don't go there, man. You know better. *Fuck.* We're not in Miami for another couple weeks. I can't come kick your ass. *Fuck.*"

"I'm not falling for Daisy." On purpose.

She's hard to *not* like. Even when I'm frustrated with her for any number of things, she's so—so—*fun.*

If there wasn't the complication of Remy, I could honestly see myself letting loose and having fun with her.

But ultimately, I want to settle down. She never will.

"Westley."

"I'm not falling for Daisy," I repeat. "The legal situation

—I shouldn't have ever been named in that will, and everyone knows it. But dude—that kid—his parents died. His paternal grandparents are nutcases who think he'd be a possession, not a person. His great-grandmother is—Daisy jokes she's an immortal dark being, which doesn't feel too far from the truth. Best I can tell, *she's* his most sane immediate relative. Daisy Carter-Kincaid. She's the sane one."

"Fuck."

"Yeah."

"Don't get attached, West. Don't do it. Actually, you know what? Walk away. Fucking walk away. People like Daisy—she can get all the help she needs. She doesn't have to break you in the process."

"She's not going to break me."

"You should've moved up here with me. The guys— lots of sisters. Lots of bunnies. We'd get you hooked up, find you a *normal* girl. Normal's basically overrated, but we'd get through the awkward first date, settle down, and have kids of your own. Get you past Sierra—"

"I'm fucking over Sierra."

"Mara," he tosses out.

"Didn't know she had a kid, only went out with her twice."

"Becca."

"Shut up."

"*Daisy.*"

"Not falling for Daisy. That would be crazy."

"Dude. I'm not saying abandon the kid, but I am saying you don't have to wear the weight of the world on your shoulders anymore. You're retired. You're single. Go have some fucking fun—with someone who's *not* Daisy, which is a fucking shame, because she's basically the most fun you can have legally outside of skydiving in go-karts—and don't apologize for it."

I'm gripping the steering wheel too tight. The ocean view, the palm trees, the Miami skyline—none of it is soothing and tropical and relaxing right now. "How do you know Daisy's fun?"

"I read the gossip rags. Berger got me hooked on them. Fucker's a celebrity gossip junkie. Also, Mom's booking a ticket to fly down."

"*No.*"

"You need *someone* there to protect you from yourself."

"I'm not getting attached."

"Sure. If you say so."

I'd be pissed that he's calling me a liar if I didn't know he was right. "And there's no reason for *Mom* to get attached. This legal stuff—"

"Go on and keep telling yourself that's your reason you don't want us there. But that's what family's for. For being there when the shit hits the fan."

"There's no shit. Swear to god, there's no shit. I've learned my lesson."

"Worried about you, bro."

"I'll be fine."

Except all day, while I'm working, I keep thinking about Remy.

His wide yawn. The way his dark eyes cross as he's falling asleep on a bottle. The way he shouts when he waves his fist in front of his face, like he's telling it to go somewhere but can't figure out where. Those moments when he stares into my eyes like he's trying to tell me something, and he wants me to confirm that he's right.

And then I think about Daisy.

Her legs wrapped around me. The smile on her face when she's talking to Remy or looking at him. Her confession about how she was raised, which was less about her parents and more about how it affected her.

What would a woman with as big a personality as Daisy's do if she believed in love?

I shake my head, because it doesn't matter.

What matters is that I'm effectively a temporary babysitter for a woman who's emotionally unavailable.

If I let myself believe anything more than that, I'm going to get burned.

22

Daisy

I AM in so over my head.

Remy cries for two hours straight after West leaves. He doesn't want a bottle. He doesn't want tummy time. He doesn't want to read a book or take a nap or rock or go in a baby carrier or the stroller or sit on my lap.

It's not until I change his diaper again and see the red marks on his little waist that I realize I wrapped his diaper too tight around him, and I break down in tears knowing that I hurt him, which makes him sob harder too.

We both get through it—him with a bottle, me with frozen yogurt since the baby books say you shouldn't drink while alone with a baby—and I manage to get a little work done, as well as interview three nannies, none of whom I like.

They're all perfectly lovely, but apparently I'm having

some control issues, and I'm not ready to trust anyone else with my baby if I don't click immediately.

Which is another conversation I need to have with myself. Or perhaps a therapist.

Remy and I also don't get out to stroll through the village and visit with Steve the Alligator and see people, because I'm weirdly too exhausted to contemplate packing up his stroller and how I'll handle it if he poops in public.

Also, he spends the *last* two hours of the evening fighting a bottle, then fighting a nap, and generally wailing his heart out. Lucinda comes in to check on us, points out that the nipple's plugged on the bottle, tells me I'm doing a good job, and disappears like perhaps my grandmother has threatened to fire her on my behalf if she doesn't make me learn this motherhood thing myself.

I'm going to freaking put a wooden stake through her heart and end this undead hypnotizer of the world thing she has going on.

When West gets back early evening, I somehow find it in me to force a smile and tell him we had the most fabulous day together, and wait until he sees what Remy picked out during our shopping spree.

Which didn't happen, but it's what West expects to hear, right?

Plus, it makes me sound like a vapid shopaholic with no redeeming qualities, which I'm sure helps him immensely since he's tilting his head the way he does when he's concentrating and looking at me like he's concerned about me as a person, and we can't have that. He and I need to get along on superficial terms.

Not on *Are you okay?* terms.

Are you okay? terms are dangerous for the heart. And connections. And he's made it clear I'm not welcome in the heart region.

Fine by me. I don't let anyone in my heart region either.

He was completely and totally right when he said we needed to not get involved, and I owe him this much.

Besides, I have a bigger issue to worry about.

Namely, how the *fuck* I'm going to actually do this mothering thing.

As soon as West and Remy disappear, I fly up the stairs to my room and change into body armor.

Also known as my ivory business suit.

I *hate* the ivory business suit. It's so...so...so much like what The Dame wears every day.

But it's necessary. So are the pearls. The diamond brooch from my paternal great-grandmother. The panty-hose. *Pantyhose.* I'm wearing fucking *pantyhose* and the boring-ass please-don't-ever-fuck-me pumps.

Seriously.

They're more effective than a chastity belt.

I also call Emily and beg her for Derek to do my hair. She declines—politely, which of course I expected, since Derek only does *her* hair—but she also gets me an emergency last-minute appointment with Maxim, her other favorite stylist who's actually a real stylist, and not just a trained-at-home dude who uses his skills to seduce his woman.

My friends' significant others are all super hot in super weird ways that I never would've expected, and I love them all, which I can do, because it's friend-love, and not *love*-love.

I take a selfie and send it to Cam—queen of the business suit, whose ass I will never be able to compete with—and she assures me that once I've had my hair done, I'll look so professional that even the professionalist professional wouldn't realize my favorite pastime is doing body shots off baseball players.

I text Luna just because there's something about her that always makes me feel one with the earth, and I need to borrow some of her pure, awesome Luna energy.

And two hours after I hand off Remy, I'm strolling across the velvet carpet lining the marble floor of the high-windowed gallery in The Dame's castle—I mean *home*—toward her office in the east wing. Framed paintings of flamingoes, monkeys, crocodiles, and poodles—don't ask—line the opposite wall and watch me like they know I'm a total poser.

You only have money because you have your family name behind you, the flamingo mocks.

You're going to fail this baby test, the poodle sniffs.

And here I thought I got lots of sleep last night.

Maybe that's the problem. Maybe I need *less* sleep so the animals in the portraits won't talk to me anymore.

I knock once at the massive double doors then twist the wrought-iron handle. "Evening, Grammykins. We need to talk."

Except my grandmother isn't in her office.

"Miss Daisy?" One of her security team peeks into the room behind me, and I school my features behind one of my normal smiles, like everything's just fine.

"Barry. Hi. How's the baby?"

His dark face splits in a grin, and he whips out his phone to flip through a slideshow of the second most adorable baby on the planet.

"Aww, look at those curls! Mimi recovering okay?"

"She's amazing."

"I'm so glad to hear it. Do you happen to know where my grandmother is?"

"On her way to Japan, Miss Daisy."

Oh, *fuck*. I forgot about Japan.

And there goes a mini panic attack in my stomach. It feels like there's a jousting match going on between my liver and my appendix.

I should be on that plane to Japan, because I can't even change a diaper and feed a bottle right.

How the fuck can I raise a baby?

Barry smiles knowingly. "That lack of sleep gets you every time, doesn't it? They're worth it though." He claps a meaty hand to my shoulder and squeezes, and for a split second, I want to ask if he wants two babies.

Which *of course* I won't. Because there's another entirely different swell of panic rising at the thought of not seeing that gummy smile ever again.

I'm a total mess.

And I need people. And work. And for someone else to hire a nanny. And preferably for me to not have to have West around to witness my complete and utter failure at this motherhood thing.

Because I realized something today.

My grandmother didn't call me to chew me out about West telling her we were married.

He's my grandmother's spy.

I smile at the security guard. "Thanks, Barry. You let me know if the Gramigenarian isn't paying you enough." I wink, he chuckles, and tells me to take my time and snag a nap here before I go home if I need it.

I might actually need it, but more, I need to talk to my grandmother.

It's a long drive back to my house. Alessandro, who normally keeps his cool during everything, flips off three drivers and cuts six more off in the horrible Miami traffic, like maybe he's channeling my mood. He tells me he's not getting the spy vibes off West, but he could be wrong. But finally, with just barely enough time before I'm due for my next shift with Remy—god help me—we get back to my house.

I dash to my office, double-check my game face, then I dial my grandmother's number for a video chat.

She answers on the seventh ring. She's in her private jet, and she has the pursed-lip look of annoyance that should warn me not to push my luck.

"Where's Remington?"

"With West. You know. Your favorite grandson."

"Were I to get to *choose* my grandchildren, Mr. Jaeger would not be my first choice."

"No? Because you didn't have a fit about him telling you we got married."

"I don't *have fits.*"

I study her closely.

She studies me right back.

Something *wrong* is going on here. My grandmother doesn't get attached to people outside the family—not people she hasn't hand-picked herself, anyway—but while she was frosty as Antarctica in that video Tiana showed me of West facing her down the day I had my allergic reaction, she also hasn't ordered him out of my life.

My grandmother is freaking *playing* me.

And he probably *is* a spy. "Sure. Anyway, I'm calling to let you know I'm going back to work tomorrow." I have to. I *need* to. I can't work from home and do my job effectively, and more, I can't work here alone all day with a non-verbal dictator who's adorable and fascinating and perfect, but a dictator nonetheless.

"No."

"Granerella. What kind of example are we setting if women can't work with babies? I can take Remington with me. There's a daycare center two floors beneath my office. And it's not like I'm breastfeeding or recovering from childbirth. I'm *perfectly* capable of doing my job and raising a baby too."

I'm actually not, but I'm not about to admit that to her.

I get things done because people think I know what I'm talking about.

I don't.

I'm a total and complete fraud. I barely graduated high school. I only graduated college because my father made friends with half my professors and bribed them. And my grandmother only hired me into the family business because of a massive risk I took that could've fallen apart at any second, but didn't, mostly because she put her stamp of approval on it, thus negating any reason for anyone to fear I was bullshitting them.

And now, she's studying me like I've actually made a solid point.

So I do what I always do, and I forge ahead. "The sooner we can demonstrate that I'm balancing a career with being a good mother to Remington, the more likely it is all the Rodericks' legal challenges will go up in flames. Plus, Carter International Properties will be seen as a leader in the changing world of working mothers. I mean, I can't promise you the cover of *Time* again, but..."

She leans back like she wants to cross her arms and glower at me, but her pupils dilate, and I know I've got her.

She fucking *loves* being on magazine covers.

"You're not traveling overseas for business anytime soon," she informs me.

Dammit. That's the other thing I miss. But I've been weirdly too busy to think about the mini-vacation in Bali that I can't make anymore either, which is also a sign that my life is way out of whack. "Babies can travel."

"I sincerely doubt any judge will approve Remington leaving the country when his guardianship is in question."

Oh. Fuck.

Didn't think about that.

"How many private detectives do you have working on digging up blackmail dirt to get the Rodericks to back off? They'll be done within a week."

"They will *never* back off."

I bite my tongue, because *Oh. Right. Because you wouldn't either* is probably not the best thing to say right now.

Also, I sort of might have missed mentioning that part

to West, and thank fuck he's not standing in my doorway overhearing this conversation right now.

"You have a home office," she adds. "Use it."

"I have a personal connection to my staff, and they're more motivated when they see me."

That, I know is true. I haven't actually done the dealing in my grandmother's real estate company in several years. Instead, I've empowered the people who work for me to do it in her name, and I just give them what they need to succeed.

Whether that's a wall of frozen yogurt in the break room for morale, an ear to listen while they vent about a coworker or a project hitch, or a suggestion of which part of the real estate world we should conquer next— expanding from just office buildings to hotels, spas, and wineries was my idea, but implemented by my staff until they needed someone at the VP level to sign off—I've basically been the person making sure they all have what they need to get their jobs done.

She frowns deeper. "Two days a week in the office to start. Otherwise, you're *at your house*. No parties. No more *animal photo shoots*, and no questionable activities *of any kind*. Nothing to give the Rodericks any firepower or any *hint* of a suggestion that you're doing anything beyond balancing motherhood and a day job. And do *not* endanger Mr. Jaeger's position in your household. He's currently the only thing making you look legitimate."

I. Am. So. Fucked.

No small part of me wants to flip her off and walk out the door.

But…working for Carter International Properties isn't just a job.

It's the first thing I've ever been *proud* of.

I love having fun. Love partying. Love meeting new people. Love shopping and yachting and skydiving and skiing. But watching my employees utterly light up when a deal they've worked so hard on all falls into place? Being there when they tour a new hotel under construction and see firsthand what their hard work is leading to?

That's a part of my life I can't see giving up either.

And it's not like I can just walk into another real estate office and offer to be a vice president.

Who would take me seriously?

No one.

"Fine," I agree. "Two days a week. But just so you know, I'll be back to five days a week *and* traveling within a month. The Rodericks are going *down*. And I'm going to rock motherhood like it's never been rocked before."

"No pictures with Remington on the internet either, Daisy. He's the next generation in this family. Always remember that."

I rarely wonder why my mother gave my grandmother the bird, walked away from her own inheritance, and went into penis art. It's pretty fucking obvious.

Right now, I'm tempted to flip her the bird myself.

But seeing as I can't even change a diaper right, I'm in no position to pack Remy up and jet off to a private island where he can grow up wild and free to be whatever he wants.

I hang up with the Graminator just as West knocks at my office door. "Ready? He needs a bath."

Fuuuuuuck. "Are you my grandmother's spy?"

He pins me with a look that says I've lost my marbles, and possibly that he's insulted to boot. "Your grand-mother is the Antichrist."

"She likes you."

"I'm not into cougars. Especially the undead ones."

It's not often I try not to laugh, but I have this horrible feeling that letting him see how amused I am by his joke is a terrible idea. I can't see him working for my grand-mother either, but I do honestly believe she likes him, which is the most disconcerting thought I've had in my entire life.

"You okay?" West asks.

I reach for Remy, who's squirming and making that pinched-up face that suggests he's not happy about some-thing, and it's now my job to determine exactly how to make him happy.

I want to make you happy, baby Remy. I do...

I just don't know how.

"Totally fine," I tell West. "Just missed this little guy."

It's the weirdest truth. I *did* miss him.

And I don't know how I'm going to get through taking care of him all night tonight, but I'll make it or fake it.

It's what I do.

23

West

FOR THE REST of the week, I only see Daisy at designated handoff times, which are usually first thing in the morning or right after office hours.

She doesn't send Remy through any of her staff, but instead, delivers him to me herself with updates about how fussy he's been, how much formula he's had, when he last napped, and what new legal proceedings the Rodericks have started.

By mid-week, I start to understand how she's so successful. There's not a single handoff where I don't feel like I'm not getting the better end of the deal—even the handoff late Friday where she informs me that social services wants to schedule an appointment to make sure we're providing a safe, healthy environment for Remy— and she does it all with a smile that makes me feel like I've just been blessed by the sun.

I finish the gym renovation job, and I try to not obsess over the fact that I cannot shake the image of her pulling off her wet tank top in the pool, while reminding myself that keeping things platonic between us is best for the baby.

And for me.

And for her.

I have no idea if she obsesses over me while she's there, because I can't read minds, and even if I could, I don't see her enough to try brain-reading.

That's what we're doing.

We're living together, but separately, because she asked me to be here to lend credibility to her mothering skills.

It's fucked up, but we're falling into a routine, all while I remind myself not to get attached and somehow miss her all at the same time.

My family texts every day for updates. Becca texts once to ask if there's anything else she can drop off for us.

The Graminator—yes, I've started calling her that too —drops by late Friday. Or so I'm told by the housekeeper. Imogen Carter apparently doesn't want to see me any more than I want to see her, and the more I think about it, the weirder I feel about Daisy's assertion that Imogen likes me.

Or her accusation that I'd actually work for her grandmother.

I'm ignoring that and concentrating on what I need to do for Remy first. I swear he changes every day. He's smiling more. Cooing more. Pooping more.

His legs are losing that bow-legged look that my

sisters tell me is a side effect of being folded up in the womb for so many months before birth, and his thighs are starting to chunk out.

His hair is thinning in back, where he lays on his head for fourteen hours a day.

Daisy took him to the doctor after finding his medical records and discovering he was overdue for his two-month checkup.

And shots.

Fuck, that was a long night.

Hell, it's a long *week*, and I'm not even doing most of the parenting.

Daisy is.

Which is also dangerously attractive.

Who would've thought a partying heiress would take so well to instant motherhood?

But she does. And I'm just going about my life trying to be nothing more than a guy enjoying a different beach house.

I wake up Sunday morning to thunder outside and a perfunctory knock at the door.

Shit.

I overslept. And I told Daisy I'd take Remy this morning because she has a *date*.

The thought makes me growl way more than I have any right to as I leap up, quickly straightening the covers because old habits die hard, and I've made my bed every day of my adult life. Basic training drilled it into me. Retirement doesn't mean I can let it go.

But instead of Daisy, three men I recognize by reputation and folklore walk into my bedroom.

The shortest of the three—who's still nearly as tall as I am—is carrying Remy.

At least, I hope that's Remy, and not *another* child I've unknowingly temporarily inherited.

"Ah, good. You're up," he says with hints of a clipped British accent.

"That's good?" the blond tree trunk with a military buzz cut says.

"*Not* good," the blond tree trunk with the thick beard says. "I wanted to have the honors."

"Gentlemen, we're giving him the benefit of the doubt for the moment. Also—" the dark-haired one holds the baby out to me.

I reach for him automatically, and all three men put their fingers to their noses.

"Forking shirt," I mutter, because I'm trying to cuss less around Remy.

"He soiled himself *after* we relieved Daisy of him," the ringleader says. "In case you're tempted to blame her. Derek Price. Pleasure to meet you. Finally."

"I'd shake, but my hands are full," I say dryly.

"Not as full as they're about to be," Beard says. "Beck Mason."

Beck—he's the one who works with animals. "The cats?"

"All Daisy's now."

"I've noticed." The gray tabby—Elvira—sleeps on my bed most nights.

"You say that like it's a bad thing."

"Not at all. I love having cats watch me shower and trip me on my way to take a piss." That's Twinkle Toes.

The previously puking cat that Daisy's housekeeper tells me is now on a special sensitive stomach diet.

"Weird, but if that's what you like," Mysterious Military Man says. "Jude Ellis. Don't piss me off."

I carry Remy to the changing table in the next room. Even though this is *temporary*, it's set up like it's permanent. Crib, changing table, baby swing, play mat—twin to everything Daisy has in her quarters.

I tell myself it's where the nanny will eventually go, because I need to remind myself I'm temporary. A few months, Daisy says. Maybe shorter if she gets enough positive press about what a great guardian she's become.

The men all follow me into the baby's room.

"I have four sisters," I tell them. "Go on. Get the inquisition over with so we can go have a beer."

"No inquisition," Derek assures me. "We've already checked your background thoroughly."

"And tailed you to work," Jude adds.

"And interrogated the cats about how you act when no one's watching," Beck chimes in. He doesn't blink.

Or crack a grin.

But he does crack a knuckle.

I have a moment of honestly believing he can communicate with felines. And I don't trust Twinkle Toes to not tell lies about me.

Shit.

I need more sleep. I haven't even been pulling most of the overnighters, but I still need more sleep.

"What can I do for you three this morning?" I ask while I prep for diaper duty.

"We merely wanted to get to know you better, since it appears you'll be in Daisy's life for a while," Derek says.

Clearly the smooth-talker of the group, and this story-line of *you'll be in Daisy's life for a while* is making my shoulders hitch. Every day, I get a little more attached.

Every day, I start to believe a little more that Daisy *wants* help.

From *me*.

Even when she's being perfectly cheerful and profes-sional—not a word I would've pinned to her that first night, or even the second—there's this *look* in her eyes.

Like she's not entirely certain she's doing it right.

"You know Daisy well?" I ask.

"Helped her out of a jam a few years back. Jude and Beck are newer friends, but it doesn't take long to fall in love with Daisy."

"Your ladies know you're interested in their friend?"

"She's like a sister," Beck informs me.

"Sometimes annoying, sometimes awesome, always lovable," Jude agrees.

"Unless she's skinny-dipping."

"In Cam's pool."

"Caught her in Luna's too."

"I found her in Emily's shower," Derek says.

All three of us look at him.

"She was taking photos of the showerheads to show a contractor at some condo complex what sort of fixtures she wanted. Emily has such exquisite taste in showers. And showerheads. And showering companions."

"Are you talking about yourself, or about watching Emily shower with Daisy?" A week of diaper duty has made me a pro, so I'm already picking Remy up off the table as I ask the question.

Self-preservation.

None of them will punch me for the question if I'm holding a baby.

But all three of them pause thoughtfully, as though it wouldn't surprise them to find Daisy showering with any of their girlfriends, and they're not opposed to the idea of watching.

"You all have issues," I tell them.

All three crack grins.

"You might be okay," Beck says.

"More okay if you get us tickets to the Florida-Thrusters game," Derek muses.

"Hockey tickets? That's your price?"

"That and a cheeseburger," Beck agrees.

"And a full run-down of your intentions toward Daisy," Jude adds.

"I intend to be a good co-guardian to Remy. Period. Dot. End of story." At least, as much as I can say of the story. Not really my place to rat her out to her friends if they want to believe I'm the kind of guy who'd stick around for eighteen years for a kid that I don't actually have a legit claim to.

Except I'm starting to think I would.

Derek cocks a brow at me. "Fairly boring story."

"She not pretty enough for you?" Beck asks.

Jude folds his arms over his chest. "You believe all that crap about her reputation?"

I shrug. "Don't care what she does, unless it impacts Remy."

At least, in an ideal world I wouldn't care.

The truth is more complicated, and it involves asking these three the secret handshake to getting in on scaring the fuck out of anyone who'd look at her wrong.

I'm no slouch. I still work out, because I'm not old until Tyler can out-bench me, and I refuse to get old for at least forty more years.

But I'm also not stupid, nor am I the biggest guy in the room. Both Beck and Jude have some inches and some girth on me.

In height and muscles.

My cock can hold its own here, I'm positive.

Point is, I could probably not embarrass myself in an arm-wrestling match with any of them individually—including Derek—and I could handle any of Daisy's potential boyfriends just as well as they could, but four of us teaming up would weed out the real jackasses quick.

And my blood pressure is hitting the roof at the idea of *any* jackass coming near Daisy.

And by *jackass*, I basically mean anyone who has any intentions of getting her into bed for any reason.

Male.

Female.

Rich.

Poor.

Secretly a serial killer.

Volunteers for Doctors Without Borders or the Peace Corps.

All jackasses who better not lay a fucking finger on her.

Shit.

I have a problem. I know better than to have a problem, but I'm definitely developing a problem.

All three of my morning guests grin at me.

"This will be so fun to watch," Jude says.

Beck nods in agreement.

"Gentlemen. You know Daisy doesn't date. Don't torture the poor man with making him think he has a chance."

"You're so fucked," Remy tells me.

Okay, not really.

But he does give a loud coo that ends in a grin that's nearly identical to the three loony lovebirds cheering for my demise.

A crack of thunder rumbles across the ground outside.

"Look, here's the deal," Derek says. "We're actually here to offer you our friendship, because of the four women who built this community, well...we've already gotten the best three. And we're sorry you got the leftovers."

"*What?*"

"Daisy's no Luna," Beck says.

"Or Cam," Jude agrees. "And you're not even getting to sample Crazy Daisy in the sheets, so—"

Baby or not, I have one hand wrapped around the giant's neck while I shove him against the nearest wall. "Do not. *Ever.* Say that again," I growl.

He grins again.

Beck snort-chuckles.

Derek smooth-chuckles.

"Yep, he's clear," Jude declares. "We can be friends. And he's fucked."

He grabs my hand off his neck and twists my wrist until it almost snaps.

"*Forked*," I correct, and I sweep his feet out from under him, laying him out flat on the ground. "Don't say *fuck* in front of the baby, and don't *forking* make me take you down again. Ooh-rah."

These assholes are all *still* grinning.

Jude leaps back to his feet and Beck shakes his head at all of us.

Derek claps me on the shoulder. "Good luck with the baby today. We'll be at Emily's house. Cristoff's been leaving her shrimp and crab dishes all week since he can't leave them here for Daisy. Might be enough for you if you get bored and lonely."

Well, fuck.

That's actually a damn good offer.

"Poker?" I ask.

"And beer," Beck says. "And cheeseburgers."

"We can play for this." Derek holds up a wallet, and —*dammit*.

Fucker lifted my wallet.

Jude grabs him by the collar and lifts. "Give it back."

"You know I do this to all my friends."

Now it's Beck's turn to clap me on the shoulder. "Welcome to the club, man. Welcome to the club."

24

Daisy

MORDECAI'S IS BLURRY.

Or maybe that's my eyes making the dimly-lit bistro seem fuzzy and glowy around the edges as Emily, Cam, and Luna steer me to our usual booth in the back. Normally it's shaped like a horseshoe.

The booth, I mean. Not the whole bistro.

Today, the horseshoe is a big blob that either looks like half a heart or a cocoon where I could happily curl up and pull a Sleeping Beauty, depending on which eye I use to look at it out of.

"Am I wearing clothes?" I whisper to Luna while I scoot in deep so I can make sweet, sweet love—in the form of sleep—to the soft cushion.

I think I whisper, anyway, but Lady Raquel, our favorite server for Drag Queen Brunch, whips around and looks me over. Today, she's in a sequined white jumpsuit and matching white platform boots, à la The King of Rock 'n Roll, with her hair in a blue Marge Simpson 'do that looks utterly fabulous on her. Rhinestones sparkle in both her ears and nose, and I suddenly want to hug her, but I can't, because she has at least nine inches on me and my head would basically turn into a shelf for her fabulous boobs if I did.

Plus, there's a table between us.

"Girl, you're a mess," she says. "A fabulous mess—love that sequin tank, darling—but you know better than to drink the cheap stuff before brunch. Sit your tush down, and I'll cover up that Fireball with a bloody margamosa that'll put your whole world to rights."

"I don't know what a bloody margamosa is, but I want seven," I tell her.

"She'll have pancakes," Cam interrupts.

"Alcohol," I whine. "I want to part-eye."

"Part...eye?" Emily repeats.

"I'm too tired to say *part-ee*."

"Oh, honey." Luna pets my hair, which I may or may not have combed. I can't remember. All I remember is Remy crying because I forgot to put the powdered formula in the bottle before I fed it to him, so he just got a bunch of water, which is apparently really bad for babies since they don't know when to stop drinking water, or so said one of those parenting books, but I can't remember if it was the parenting book I believe or the parenting book that's full of bullshit.

I can't remember if I'm being a bullshit parent.

"Is it...that bad?" Emily asks.

"I am so tired I confused Lichtenstein with Frankenstein during a telecon and I couldn't understand why we were talking about building a city center inside a fictional monster. I am so tired that I called Alessandro to have him order a chocolate-covered strawberry basket for himself for his birthday, instead of calling Tiana like I should've. I am so tired that *I tried to brush my teeth with diaper cream this morning.* Ladies. *Ladies.* I think—I think my TPE is drying up."

"Your *TPE*?" Emily asks.

"Tight pussy energy."

Luna winks at me. "Or maybe your TPE has never encountered this kind of big dick energy."

"Fascinating," Cam murmurs.

"What?" I ask.

"TPE plus BDE divided by forced cohabitation to the co-parenting power...I'm pretty sure the solution to that equation is an explosion."

"A *big* explosion," Luna agrees.

"This has *nothing* to do with the size of West's dick energy. It's all about *parenting.* I'm tired. *So* tired."

"Is he not pulling his weight?" Cam demands. "Do I need to go talk to him? Do I need to call *Jude* to talk to him? Jude is super scary when he wants to be. He could make West piss himself. That'd serve him right for making you so tired."

"No, no, he's taken as many shite nifts—night shifts— as I have, but...like...having a baby is *stressful.* And not in a ruling the world kind of stressful, but in a...this little *thing* that can't communicate but has *needs* has to have those needs met *every hour of the day* even when I don't know what those needs are and when he's not with me, I'm thinking about him, and when he *is* with me, I'm thinking about him, and every minute that I'm thinking about him, I'm also wondering if West is judging me for being a horrible parent and if I'm going to utterly flunk this parenting test and if my grandmother will disown me and if I'll end up living in a cardboard regatta boat in the Everglades while panhandling with the crocodiles and pythons and raising the next Tarzan the Everglade Jungle Man. Is that a napkin or a pillow? I need a pillow. And for Anthony and Margot Roderick to disappear and drop this ridiculous challenge to the will. And for our meeting with the social worker to go amazingly well. And a pancake. Cam. How did you know pancakes sound sooooo good right now?"

"Can I *oh, honey* her again, or is that too much?" Luna whispers.

"Shh!" Emily hisses, and I bolt straight upright and open my eyelids as far as they'll go, because I know that *shh*.

That *shh* means my second favorite part of Drag Queen Brunch has arrived in the form of four romance authors that we low-key stalk here every month.

Related: I have a secret library full of all of their books, though I prefer to listen on audiobook, because I can do that on a plane, or in the car, or in the shower, or while I'm pretending to be on a conference call when my grandmother pays her weekly visits to my office.

Also related: my grandmother thinks I'm working on a deal in Monaco with a man named Salvio who's having personal problems, but that's actually part of the one author's long-running series that *I cannot get enough of.*

Plus, Teddy Hamilton narrates the books, and his voice is *to die for*.

"Did you meet your deadline?" the one in the taco shirt asks the one with the big blue glasses.

"I said fuck it, wrote three blow jobs, and called it a day," she replies.

"Speaking of saying fuck it," the one in the stained unicorn shirt and sloppy half-bun says while they scoot into the booth beside us, "my third-grader asked me the other day if a cunt is the same thing as a vagina."

The other three romance authors that we eavesdrop on at Drag Queen Brunch for the last forever all suck in shocked breaths.

My three friends and I all suck in shocked breaths.

Even me.

And I'm hard to shock.

But I'm suddenly seeing my future.

Remy, sitting down to dinner, asking if his penis is normal and what he's supposed to do if it stands up in the middle of him giving a presentation on elephants in sixth-grade science class.

I somehow don't think *own it, big guy* will be the right answer.

The woman in the *Coffee is the answer* T-shirt leans forward and grips unicorn author's hand. "Did you tell him the truth?"

"I told him to go ask his father," she wails. "I write romance novels, but I can't talk to my children about vaginas!"

"You should say *vagina* ten times a day until the word loses its mystique," the author in the blue glasses says.

"And then take him out to tacos for the talk-o," the fourth author chimes in.

"Penis," I whisper to myself. "Testicle. Balls."

Wait.

I don't have this problem. There's very little I won't say. I can even say—well, something that's not appropriate even for me at Drag Queen Brunch.

"Shh," Cam whispers. "I feel like I need to take notes. In case Jude and I ever have babies."

"I don't care about Salvio in book five anymore," I announce. "I need life advice. I need *parenting* advice."

Three sets of hands grab me before I can slide under the table and attack the authors.

"Daisy! If you go over there, you'll scare them away, and our men can only work so fast at stalking to find out where they go instead, since it's technically illegal," Emily hisses. "We can handle this. We're the vagillion-aires, remember? We'll get you through Remy's baby years."

"I don't know what Julienne was thinking when she wrote her will. And *there were witnesses*. She and Rafe *had* to at least be able to *fake* being sober. No one leaves me a baby. An eleven-year-old who can brush his own teeth and whose biggest problem is deciding which flowers to send his—no, probably not an eleven-year-old. Okay. People can leave me teenagers who need spectacular life advice—huh. No. Probably not that either. Wait. I've got it. People can leave me twenty-eight-year-olds who need dating advice and some coaxing to get out, party a little, try the go-karts, and definitely go skinny-dipping with a woman in The Dame's pool."

Emily laughs. "You're going to be fine, Daisy. You love people. He's a people. He's just a small people."

"I cracked my egg baby in health class in high school. Plus, I'm a little inappropriate for the under-twenty-five set, you know? But I feel this...connection with him. Like he needs me, except I'm terrified I'm going to break him and I don't think a baby can live off hugs for his entire life. Like, I need to feed him and wash him and teach him to talk."

And not fuck up so badly that my grandmother takes him from me, fires me, and disowns me.

I'm not actually kidding that the thought of losing Remy is more important to me than the thought of being disinherited.

I'm starting to feel like *someone* to the little guy, but...it could all go away.

In an instant.

"I read somewhere when I was researching the effects of high-speed travel on humans that babies are more durable than we think," Cam offers. "But you're still not supposed to drop them on their heads."

"That makes sense."

"It's just like taking care of a dog," Luna says. "Put out food and water, pet them some, toss them a ball, make sure they get plenty of time to do their business in the yard, and they'll grow to love you unconditionally."

"So that's where my parents went wrong."

Oh, hell.

And now I'm fighting a smile as my three friends crack up at the idea of raising Remy the Dog Man.

Because they're right.

We're going to get through this. They have my back, and they will, even after West leaves.

My heart rolls over and pangs, because despite how little I've seen him this last week, I *like* him. And not in a *we should have a weekend fling in Bermuda* kind of way.

But in a *he could be one of my closest friends*, if I knew how to be real friends with anyone other than these three, kind of way.

"Maybe you and Beck should wait a few years before kids," Emily says to Luna, and we all erupt in giggles again.

"Oh! Oh, you guys! I have pictures. Do you want to see pictures?" I dive for my purse, my exhaustion forgotten as I remember the best part of parenting.

The baby smiles.

And Remy has the *cutest* baby smile.

I'm flashing photos on my phone when Lady Raquel returns with a round of pink drinks in margarita glasses. "Food coloring," she whispers with a wink. "The name and the disguise make tequila in the morning more acceptable. Oooh! Baby! And who is that *handsome* hunk of a man?"

"I really need to see Jude holding a baby like that," Cam sighs dreamily.

"Total ovary-melter," Emily agrees. "When Derek plays with his nieces and nephews, I can barely stop myself from jumping his bones right there."

"That's how I feel about Beck and the dogs." Luna's smile is so sappy and sweet that she manages to outshine Cam and Emily together, which is an impressive feat.

It's not often I feel lonely with my friends, but they all have their someones.

And I have a baby I barely feel competent with, a social worker coming soon to make sure he's safe since the Rodericks are calling both me and West unfit parents, pressure from my grandmother because Remy is all she has left of Julienne—yes, she's obnoxious, but she *does* care in her own way—and a very familiar tingling in my cooch and nips every time West knocks on my door with Remy for a handoff.

"West preps the diaper bag every morning," I blurt. "And he leaves little notes about milestones and Remy's mood and how many times he was up overnight on his nights, and I feel like I'm missing half of Remy's life and I want to ask him if we can do more stuff *together*, but I don't know how to be a normal person who has a guy as a friend." I leave out the part about our agreement that he's temporary.

"You don't be *friends* with men who look like that. Not unless you're getting benefits," Lady Raquel says sagely.

All four of the romance authors are leaning toward us.

"Plot twist," coffee lady whispers.

"Total blow job in waiting," Blue Glasses says loudly.

Taco author nudges her. "Shh!"

"Thank god I'm not alone," the unicorn says. "Lady Raquel! We need some of those pink drinks."

"For inspiration," the taco author agrees as she pulls out a laptop.

"Maybe you *should* try the blow job," Luna tells me. "Could a blow job ever make anything worse?"

"It never has before." We clink glasses.

And I remember that I've promised West I'll quit hitting on him, and just how screwed both Remy and I will be if he decides we're not worth it.

And what's keeping him here?

Really?

A promise he made to a woman who didn't deserve it.

I owe him what he's asked for.

"How's Derek coming with Julienne's computer?" I whisper to Emily.

"They've been through every electronic device they could find at the house, and there's no video evidence of Julienne and Rafe making their will. But they did find emails dated about six weeks ago with correspondence to their attorneys that clearly spelled out they wanted you and West Jaeger to be co-guardians. Hang in there. He's digging deeper into the Rodericks' past too. He's confident they'll find something useful for court."

"Thanks."

"Hey. Chin up. It'll be okay." She squeezes my hand. "We've seen each other through way worse than this. You and Remy are going to be just fine, very soon."

I hope she's right.

But for the first time in my life, I'm actually worried that I'm going to fail at something that *matters*.

25

West

THURSDAY NIGHT, I hit every red light and traffic jam and rude driver in Miami on my way back to Bluewater from a small job in Coral Gables, which I was late to since Daisy's replacement house sitter for me found a leak in the bathroom sink of the beach house, and I had to fix that first thing this morning. The weather reports suggest a late-season tropical storm is forming in the Atlantic. And Becca is asking if she and the girls can come bring the baby a present this weekend, since diapers and formula don't really count.

I weave through the picturesque Bluewater streets, trading waves with residents out for walks with their dogs or switching out the chalkboard signs outside their shops. Everything's bright and colorful and happy here, but I'm so run down, I can't appreciate it.

Despite how familiar all the faces have become, from the women Daisy calls the Wealthy Widows, to Frank the cussing parrot and Steve the three-legged alligator, to her best friends' boyfriends and fiancé, this isn't *my* world.

It's *Daisy's*, and I'm just trespassing temporarily until she's overcome the legal challenges presented so she can keep Remy.

And getting more and more attached to the little guy every day.

He found his hands this week. Spent *hours* watching himself flex his fists, then more hours trying to grab a parrot hanging on the play mat someone sent as a gift.

Overall, he's a happy kid. And I fucking miss him.

When I finally pull up to the D mansion, the sky is fading from dusky rose to deep purple over the palm trees. I was supposed to get Remy thirty minutes ago, and my phone has been blowing up in my cupholder the entire ride.

I'm already late, so I check the messages I've missed.

Mom: Westley, enough is enough. I'm booking a flight to come see you.
Tyler: Aw, Ma, you just want to soak up the Miami rays and have an excuse to hang around long enough to see me play there weekend after next, don't you?
Allie: Yeah, she wants to be there to hug you and tell you it's okay when you wipe out and lose.
Keely: Solid burn!
Britney: Nice, but not productive. West, Mom's right. You can't treat this like it's Sierra Part Two and you're trying

not to get attached. You legally inherited a baby. You're retired and not moving. And even if god forbid something awful happens, WE'RE YOUR FUCKING FAMILY and you don't have to protect us. It's OUR job to protect YOU.

Tyler: Wow. That was deep.

Mom: I also read that Daisy Carter-Kincaid was caught getting trashed at a brunch the other day.

Dad: I want to lick your pussy.

Dad: Tyler is my favorite child.

Dad: I AM GOING TO BANANA-RAMA-JAM-JAM YOU, Tyler is my favorite child.

Allie: NICE on the text replacement prank, Mom.

Mom: I have no idea what you're talking about. Tyler's always reprogramming your father's phone, not me. Westley, where are you? Do I need to call?

Britney: He's probably stuck in Miami traffic. Or dead. Their drivers are worse than Chicago drivers.

Mom: *gif of angry yelling cartoon mom*

Dad: *gif of Tyler tripping and sliding on the ice into Ares Berger's ass*

Britney: *gif of woman spitting drink*

Allie: *gif of baby falling over laughing*

Keely: *eye roll emoji* I'm calling *dragon emoji* and we're booking tickets, because while you yahoos are having fun, WEST IS DEALING WITH A SERIOUS BABY ISSUE, and SOMEONE needs to be there for him.

Mom: *gif of a chastised woman*

Britney: *gif of cute cat asking for forgiveness*

Allie: *gif of embarrassed dog saying sorry*

Dad: *gif of an iguana farting in a bathtub*

Dad: Whoops. That was supposed to be I AM NOT

WORTHY TO LICK THE FEET OF THE GREAT MAY
ELLA JAEGER.
Dad: I AM NOT WORTHY TO LICK THE FEET OF
THE GREAT MAY ELLA JAEGER.
Dad: *middle finger emoji*

The texts stop, and I realize I'm sitting here half-smiling at my insane family, despite not wanting the reminder of Sierra nor all of them to come meet a baby that won't be in my life long. But Keely's threat to call The Dragon, aka Staci, our non-texting sister, means things are serious.

I shoot them a quick message telling them I haven't died in Miami traffic, and that they should hold off on making plans until after the social worker comes to check us out next week. Who knows if Daisy will still need me after that?

Odds are good it'll go amazing, because Daisy's rocking this parenting thing, and the social worker will tell the judge that the will should stand as is.

And then I'll be gone.

My stomach dips.

After another quick text to Daisy telling her I got stuck in traffic and I'm on my way, I climb out of my truck and trudge up to the now-familiar huge oak double doors. I barely notice the curved glass staircase, the slate floor, the four cats that dash out to check on me, and the arched windows that I pass on my way to my bedroom.

But I notice what's waiting for me in the sitting room.

Daisy, leaning back in the round hot pink chair that vaguely resembles a strawberry, her feet propped up on the glass coffee table next to her phone, Remy resting against her thighs while he holds her thumbs and she covers his face with his fists, then pulls them away, whispering, "*Peekaboo!*" and making him giggle, which in turn makes her giggle.

Over. And over. And over.

Her hair's light purple now. And shorter. And hanging loose around her face, which is only lightly covered with makeup. Mascara and lipstick and nothing else.

She's in red stilettos, leopard-print leggings and a black tank top that don't go at all with Remy's little sailor outfit, and everything about this picture is so fucking *natural* that the damn muscle in my chest that I've been keeping cooped up gives a big, loud, powerful thump.

I never thought I'd see the day when I'd call purple hair and leopard print leggings *natural*, but on Daisy, they are.

That's who she is.

Bright.

Unpredictable.

Crazy.

And just so *Daisy*.

I swallow hard, because I can't deny it anymore.

She's not a vapid party girl.

She's a smart businesswoman who works hard and plays hard and *loves* hard, no matter the wild front she puts out to the world. There's no faking that shine in her eyes when Remy giggles. It's the same shine I've seen time and again on my sisters' faces when they've brought home all their babies—the biological and the adopted.

Love isn't about blood.

And blood isn't always about love.

But Daisy—she loves that baby. Not because she has to. But because how could she not?

Hell, who am I kidding?

I don't recognize the glow because of my *sisters*. I recognize the glow because of *me*. *I'm* fucking glowing just watching the two of them. Standing here grinning like a sap. Getting a little choked up when she pulls his fists to her lips and kisses them.

Yeah.

I'm a little attached.

"Who's the most perfect baby in the whole wide world?" she coos.

Remy shouts a big ol' "*Aaaaooooooaa!*"

"That's right. My Remy's the very most perfect baby in the whole world."

My eyes get hot.

She doesn't need me. She's got this.

Fuck.

"Oh, hey, West. You wanna try some three-way peekaboo? You're going to lose, just so you know, because Remy is the peekaboo *champion*. I already ordered his trophy too, so you basically have to lose, because I'm not redoing it to put your name on it."

I clear my throat. "Sorry I'm late. Traffic."

"Ha! So you admit Miami drivers aren't all angels. *Finally*, he sees the light. Miami drivers are shirt-heads, aren't they, little man? Yes, they are. Yes, they are. *Peekaboo!*"

Remy squeals.

Daisy laughs.

And my heart twists and soars at the same time.

This is a dangerous, dangerous path. But it's not one I can resist.

It's not one I've ever been able to resist. "You mind sitting here another few minutes while I grab a shower?"

"Stealing a few more minutes with the most perfect baby in the whole wide world? Torture. Utter torture."

She boops Remy on the nose, he coos, and she laughs again. "Go on, stinky butt. You're polluting the air."

Her smile is the last thing I see before I step out of the sitting room, and it's making me hard as rebar.

I tell myself it's just a side effect of seeing a woman with a baby—clearly, they're my kryptonite—but when I step in the shower, I'm not picturing Daisy with Remy.

I'm picturing Daisy in the pool. Tossing her swimsuit top onto the cat. Draping her arms around me. Gripping my hips with her thighs.

Christ.

She's snuck into my brain, and I don't know how to get her out.

We can't get involved, because when it ends—and it will, because I'm rules and straight lines, and she's chaos and heart-shaped bubbles floating in the sky—I'll be facing the same path I've walked too painfully before.

I can walk away from a woman.

I can't walk away from a kid. Not again. Kids don't deserve to pay the price for adults not being able to work shit out.

That's why I avoided Becca's kids before asking her if we could date. So none of us would get attached.

I don't miss Sierra. Time heals wounds, and in retrospect, it's easy to see where the cracks were in our relationship. But her kids?

There's still a hole there.

Nina would've graduated eighth grade this past May.

Baxter's probably taking his ACTs and SATs and talking about where to go to college.

And it's none of my fucking business anymore, because all I was, was the man who dated their mother for two years. It didn't matter how many times I picked them up from school. How many band concerts I went to. How many lines I helped rehearse for the school play.

I wasn't their father.

I was the guy who got orders across the country, and the guy who didn't mean enough to their mother to justify uprooting everyone to go with me.

Or even enough to wait for me.

I was the one who left.

My boner's creeping away on its own, which is good, because Daisy's the kind who'd pop into the shower here, and the last thing I need is her catching me rubbing one out.

She'd think I was thinking about her.

She'd be right.

And we'd be headed for disaster.

But there has to be a happy medium. A place where we can be *friends*, without being anything more.

And since I told her to back the fuck off, it's up to me to set the stage to get us there.

Can't hurt.

Especially with a social worker coming next week to make sure we're good parent material.

Yep. We can be friends.

We *should* be friends.

This attraction? It's a fluke because of stress, and the fact that Daisy *is* an attractive woman. It'll pass.

And if it doesn't, I'm still a Marine at heart.

I'll fucking *make* it pass.

26

Daisy

REMY'S GNAWING on a board book and looking sleepy when West emerges from the bathroom in gray sweat-pants and a black Marines T-shirt that's hugging his chest in all the right places.

I stifle a sigh that he's so intent on having nothing to do with me, because we really could both use some frus-tration relief, and he's sexy as fuck basically twenty-four hours a day.

"You had dinner?" he asks gruffly.

My mood goes from sad panda to leaping llama in a flash. "Just cotton candy and the crushed dreams of ever getting enough sleep again." And a donut from Carbs 'n Coffee, because today was my monthly buy-everyone's-coffee-and-donuts day, which didn't feel like enough, so I also sent sub sandwich platters to all of Miami's elemen-tary schools for the teacher lounges.

His lips quirk again in more of a smile than I've seen since he moved in. "I had road exhaust and a pack of peanuts."

"Cristoff left egg rolls and chicken bacon avocado paninis in the fridge."

His nose wrinkles. "Got any bread?"

"Probably. Alessandro is a total bread freak and I have to keep him fed if I want to stay safe."

"Peanut butter?"

"Hello, peanut butter of the month club subscription."

"Potato chips?"

"Westley Jaeger, you need to stop talking dirty to me if you're not interested."

He drops his head with a wry grin. "Fair enough. I'm gonna go fix something. Welcome to join me if you want."

"So very kind of you to think of the poor starving heiress putting a temporary roof over your head. I accept." I lift Remy and kiss his cheek. "C'mon, little man. Let's go torture you with all the food you can't eat yet."

He whimpers when I take the book away, but I pop a pacifier in his mouth, and he settles in with a hand resting on my boob and his forehead pressed to my neck as I stand.

West's eyes pinch like he's in pain, but he turns and opens the door, gesturing us out, and whatever was there a minute ago is gone. "Lead on. Watch out for the cats."

Lead I do.

With an extra swing in my hips, while I toss questions back to him about how work's going, if he's explored Bluewater at all, and how bad Derek, Jude, and Beck's inquisition was of him on Sunday while I was off brunching and breaking down.

Which I don't add, by the way, because he doesn't need to know that. Plus, I feel like I'm getting my feet back under me, like I *can* do this.

I'm not surprised when he gives me short answers and turns the questions back to me. "Take over the world at work yet?" he asks while he picks through my peanut butter collection in my bright, cheery kitchen. He's standing under copper pots and pans hanging from the ceiling over the white marble island, making quick work of dismissing the fancier peanut butters I've laid out for the simpler organic crunchy versions.

He does the same with the bread, passing over the rosemary focaccia in favor of cracked wheat—which even I'll admit makes sense—but when he pops open a bag of Lays and crumbles the plain potato chips over the layer of peanut butter on the bread, my eyes go wide.

"What are you doing?"

"Making the best peanut butter sandwich in the universe."

"That—that—that's *sacrilege*."

"Thank you. By the way, major points to you for having Lays. I thought you'd have gold-crusted organic potato chips made of rare exotic potatoes."

"Original is best." Remy fusses on my shoulder, so I rise and bounce him until he drifts back to sleep. "And I'm serious. You can't do that to a peanut butter and jelly sandwich."

"Peanut butter and honey." He lifts a jar of local honey too. "Can, did, and would do it again. The rule-breaker objects to rule-breaking? What's going on here, Ms. Carter-Kincaid? Are you *secretly craving order?* Say it isn't so."

He's *laughing* at me now, which I'll allow, because he's fucking gorgeous when he lets that smile loose.

Eyes crinkling. They're honey-brown tonight, and if licking eyeballs was a thing, I'd be tempted. All of his dark stubble parts to reveal straight white teeth. Even his damp hair seems happy. And when he's smiling, his shoulders relax, his grip on the peanut butter knife loosens, and I get a glimpse at the man he could be if he'd let go of whatever it is that's keeping him from embracing the beauty of the unexpected.

"Fine," I declare. "I'll try your monstrosity, but I won't like it."

"Bet you one overnight shift you'll never eat peanut butter sandwiches without chips in them again."

"You're on."

I hold out my free hand, and when he takes it to shake, a warm zing slides from my fingers to my elbows.

Zings are bad news.

Not when I'm overseas, I mean. Zings signify solid potential for a fun fling when I'm at least two thousand miles from home, operating under a fake name with no chance of my mother getting ideas or my date getting attached.

But I can't fling with West. Pretty sure he's an all-or-nothing man, and we need to get along for the social worker next week. Or at least prove we're independently capable of caring for a baby, along with not being dysfunctional when we're together.

Especially since this is temporary.

I drop his hand and grab one of his peanut butter abominations.

I know, I know. *Daisy, you'll do anything! What's wrong with a peanut butter-potato chip sandwich?*

I don't like my food to touch. Okay?

Gravy goes on potatoes and porterhouse, but not on the green beans.

I chomp into the crime against peanut butter—I mean, the sandwich—fully intending to hate it, except...

Huh.

The salt and the honey work well together.

And the crunch is—it's like crunchy peanut butter, except...dammit.

Except *better*.

I narrow my eyes.

He smiles broader. My heart pounds a little faster. And I decide that if a pout will make him smile even bigger, then I'll do it.

"I suppose it's edible," I sniff. "But it's no fluffernutter, bacon, and Nutella sandwich."

If he smiles any harder, he's going to break his cheeks.

I flip my phone out of my cleavage and snap a pic before it disappears. "Ha! Gotcha being happy."

"Victories are always worth celebrating."

He doesn't try to wrestle my phone away to delete the photo, but instead digs into his own sandwich.

His eyes slide closed, and a different smile flits across his face.

I wonder if that's what he looks like as he's drifting off

to sleep after a sweaty romp in the sheets. Happy. Glowing. Satiated.

I set the phone aside and grab a carrot stick from the vegetable tray we found in the fridge, chomp into it, and promptly inhale too quickly and choke.

And not like fake-choke either.

I'm talking carrot lodged in my throat, dripping carrot crumbles into my lungs while I try to pound myself on the breast bone without hitting the baby.

Oh, god.

I'm going to die.

I'm going to choke on a carrot and die before I get to see Remy grow up. He'll have to live with the heartbreak of knowing that every woman who ever tried to love him died too soon.

One killed by horny dolphins.

The other felled by a vegetable.

I try to cough, and I can't.

My head is getting hot.

My face is swelling.

It's like the shrimp, but worse. Sixty zillion times worse.

I'll be the vagillionaire heiress taken down by a carrot stick.

My lungs burn. My knees shake. Oh, *fuck*, I'm going to drop the baby.

I am.

I'm dropping the baby.

I try to tell West to catch him, but I can't see past the haze of panic, and I can't talk, and I—

Something hard jolts my ribs once, twice, and on the third thrust, a half-eaten carrot flies out of my mouth.

I gasp and hunch forward while the island countertop swims back into focus.

My eyes are wet, my limbs are shaking, and there's a solid arm still wrapped around my waist.

"Daisy? Fuck. *Fork.* Say something." A large, solid, warm hand rubs my back while I wheeze. "Are you okay?"

"Remy," I gasp out.

The hand stops.

The arm tenses.

Oh, *god*.

I dropped the baby and killed him.

I choked on a carrot, and that sweet, innocent little bundle of smiles and baby poop is the one who paid the ultimate price.

I dropped him on his head. I silenced him forever.

I have blood on my hands.

My wheeze turns into a sob, and I spin away from West, who shouldn't touch me, because I'm a murderer.

My pulse ramps up so hot and hard that I go light-headed and a scream forms deep inside my head, hollering just like Remy, like that precious little boy who will never scream again, because he's—he's—he's—

Squirming on the island in front of me.

Wailing.

Flinging his hands around, his face beet red, his legs kicking one of his tiny socks right off.

"You didn't die," I gasp. I grab him and kiss his cheeks and lift him to look at him again while he squirms and wails and my eyes go hot and overflow. "I didn't drop you.

Oh my god, I thought I dropped you. I'm so sorry, baby. I'll never choke on anything again. I'll quit eating, and I'll never choke on anything ever, *ever* again, and I won't leave you, and I won't ever let anything bad happen."

I can't stop crying.

The tears have started, and they won't stop, and I'm standing in my kitchen making promises to my little orphan boy that *I can't keep.*

I *can't* promise him nothing bad will ever happen. That he'll always be safe. That I'll always be here.

"I'm sorry," I choke out. "I'm so sorry, sweet boy."

Two massive arms encircle us both, and I don't deserve them.

I don't deserve West's warmth. I don't deserve Remy's smiles. I don't deserve peanut butter and potato chip sandwiches.

I'm a selfish asshole who parties too hard and pretends I don't do terrible things in business because I do it with a smile and promise people they'll be better off after they turn their buildings and land over to me, even if it's not always as true as I want it to be.

And I do it all to make my grandmother happy, when the truth is, I can't.

No one can make her happy.

Because you *can't* make another person happy any more than I can promise Remy that I can see into the future to where we're all one big happy family without problems or pain or conflict.

"Shh," West says. "You're okay, Daisy. Remy's okay. You're both okay."

"Please don't leave me," I whimper. "I can't do this on

my own. I can't. I'll gut my pool house and build you whatever you want out there if you don't want to live here in my house with us, but please, please don't leave me to do this parenting thing alone. I can't. *I can't.* And I can't tell my grandmother, or she'll take Remy from me too, and I—"

"Daisy—"

"*Please.*"

Warm lips brush my hair. "Okay," he whispers.

I shouldn't trust him. I've been burned by people I know a lot better, a lot harder.

But all he's done is everything he never should've been asked to do.

I'll make this up to him.

I will.

I'm Daisy Imogen fucking Carter-Kincaid. I can do anything.

Apparently except parent a baby by myself without trying to self-destruct.

27

West

THE REST of dinner is simultaneously more awkward than my failed date with Becca and almost as comfortable as a family picnic back home in Chicago, all while I do my fucking best to ignore that voice in my head whispering that there's more to Daisy Carter-Kincaid than maybe even she knows.

And that I am truly in over my head.

"Movie dates or beach dates?" she asks.

"No," I reply, which sends her into a fit of giggles that ends with her coughing and me going tense and then her pointing to the bread.

"More abomination sandwiches!" she orders.

"Maybe you should drink some water instead." Bantering is so much easier than letting myself think about the panic in her voice when she thought she dropped the baby.

She's got him.

She does.

She just needs the confidence to believe it, which is the last thing I ever would've thought someone like Daisy could need.

But it's all making sense. Big on the outside to shield the scared on the inside.

"Quit being bossy and answer the questions," she orders. "I'm profiling you so I know how to rebuild the pool house."

"You don't have to rebuild your pool house."

"My pool house is my *sanctuary*. I go there when I'm tired of people, which, as I'm sure you can imagine, only *rarely* happens, but when it does, I *need* it. So I have to rebuild it so I don't invade your space when you're having private time with Mr. Pokey."

See?

Awkward and comfortable.

All at the same time.

"You get tired of people?" I ask while I start making her another sandwich. On the second, I made the mistake of asking where she put all the food she was eating, and she grabbed her boobs, and I got a boner, which is another reason I'm happy to keep making her sandwiches.

It keeps the island between us as a boner-deterrent. And also to keep me from reaching for her to pull her into a hug, just because I think she needs it.

But she's pretending she doesn't, so I'll pretend she doesn't too.

She eyes me suspiciously, like she's not sure she should say what's on her mind, and then just blurts it all out. "I *love* chocolate milk, but even I can't drink it thirty-six hours a day, fourteen days a week. And there are different brands of chocolate milk, and some I can drink more than others."

"Huh. Would've pegged you for the tequila type over the chocolate milk type."

"I chase my chocolate milk with tequila."

"That's disgusting. Carrot?"

I hold up a carrot stick, and she chucks her metal water bottle at me.

With the lid off.

I duck easily, because she has awful aim, but I still get splashed with a flying arc of liquid when the bottle clangs to the tile floor behind me. "Are you *insane?*"

She grins. "I didn't have to miss. Maybe tomorrow for dinner, you should wear a white T-shirt."

"Daisy…"

"I've been stifling myself for *ten days* for you. I think I've earned that one."

I can't really argue.

"In fact, I think I should get an inappropriate comment to you at least once a day," she continues playfully. "If you weren't so uptight, I could *fully* be myself. I'm censoring big-time here. So yes, you owe me *one moment* of being myself in an entire twenty-four-hour period."

"That…makes unfortunate sense," I concede, though it doesn't feel like a concession, and I'm actually smiling to myself at the thought of everything she might come up with.

"When were you involved with that woman with kids again? Doesn't Becca have kids? Is that your type?"

My shoulders hitch. "That wasn't you censoring your-self. Again."

"I'll tell you why I only date foreign men if you tell me why you only date single mothers. Is it your swimmers? Did they all go belly-up? Accident in the Marines or something? Were you sick as a kid?"

I fold my arms over the wet spot on my T-shirt and try to glare at her, but it's harder than it would've been before she choked.

She sighs and rolls her eyes. "Fine. I only date foreign men because my father is terrified of flying."

"*What?*"

"Also because they don't usually recognize me and they tolerate my romantic ADD so much better."

"You're making awful generalizations about people right now."

"And it *sounds* so much more exotic to say I spent the weekend with a Greek god than it does to say I spent the weekend with a farmer in Iowa."

She's so full of shit. "If you're not a big enough person to confess to having commitment issues, just say so."

Her cheeks go bright pink, and there's that over-whelming urge to hug her again. But it's accompanied by a need to google a therapist for her.

"Fine." She throws her hands up. "I'm not a big enough person to confess to having commitment issues."

I bite into a carrot and chew it slowly, watching the blush fade behind a growing scowl, like I'm intentionally showing her how to eat a carrot without choking and she doesn't appreciate it.

This *is* so much like being home. And I'm also relieved

her embarrassment is fading. She's welcome, though I'll probably never tell her so.

I swallow and go back to fixing her sandwich. "Single mothers are the only people I've ever survived a first date with."

"Oh, please."

"High school prom. I asked my little sister's best friend. Year younger than me. Cute. Nice ass. She asked if we could double-date with another one of her friends. Turned out her *friend* was the girl who stole her boyfriend, who was the fourth person in our party, and she spent the *entire night* trying to make him jealous with me while her *friend* tried to talk me into slipping out the back door for a quickie."

"High school doesn't count."

"Two years into the Marines. Met a woman at the gym. Asked her out. She said she'd only say yes if I could out-bench her. So we start benching, and she's keeping up rep-for-rep, up to like one-fifty—"

"Hate to tell you, but that's a sign she didn't actually *want* to go out with you."

"Yeah. Figured that out when I crashed at two-thirty and she kept going to two-fifty, then told me to try again when I grew a pair. She'd just been dumped by a guy who was on the bodybuilding circuit, who she trained with for like three years before that. Went on to be a pro wrestler and married this guy who looks like Santa Claus."

"*No.*"

"Yep."

"Talk about opposites attracting."

I nod while she steals my root beer glass and tips it to her lips.

"Her wrestler name was The Mrs. Clausinator," I add casually.

Daisy spews root beer out her nose.

And I mentally thank my mother for teaching me the art of timing.

"A while later," I continue, refusing to be embarrassed, because my family has already helpfully relived these moments for me enough that I don't care anymore, "my buddies set me up with a drag queen."

Her scowl is instant behind the napkin she's wiping her face with. "That's not funny."

"It was awkward for a few minutes, but we ended up shutting down the county fair, shoving our faces with funnel cake and winning this giant stuffed sloth in the ring toss. Had a fucking awesome time. Good lady. Still keep in touch—she's a paralegal for a human rights attorney in LA now, still does drag shows on the weekends, and I kicked my buddies' asses from here to Saskatchewan for embarrassing her."

She's eyeballing me like she's not certain that was enough punishment, and that's exactly the problem.

She cares about so much more than just herself. But she gets painted as nothing more than a fun-loving waste of oxygen.

"Why do you always tilt your head like that when you're listening to someone?" she asks.

Huh. Didn't realize I was doing it again.

I tap my right ear. "Mostly deaf. Too close to an improvised explosive one time in Kabul."

Her frown isn't going away. "Is that your worst injury? From the Marines?"

"Pretty much."

"You have nightmares?"

"Used to. Rarer now."

"Therapy?"

"Yep."

"Ever consider a hearing aid?"

"That would be admitting it's a problem, and it's not." I pass her another sandwich. "Why do you work for your grandmother?"

And there goes the battle armor. It's subtle, but her blue eyes shift from the color of the sky to the color of flame, and the ever-present smile goes brittle at the edges. "Why wouldn't I?"

I gesture to the gourmet kitchen that opens to an outdoor kitchen by her pool, and by extension, the massive mansion we're standing in. "You could afford to quit. Must like the job."

"It keeps me entertained."

"Not like partying in Rio would."

"Gotta pay for my lifestyle somehow. Working for Gramalicious means a big payday for little work."

I snort, because I don't believe for a minute that she doesn't work hard.

Imogen Carter has disinherited too many people to play favorites for a hard-partying granddaughter who doesn't actually do anything at the office.

She grins behind her sandwich. "Fine. I like my job. It's fun, it's different every day, and I get to meet people all over the world and travel to fabulous places. When I first started, I'd make deals because I was in all these meetings with men who never realized how easy it was to manipulate them with my clothing and a well-timed lipstick application."

A red haze creeps into my vision.

She pats my fist, which is clenching the knife so tight I could probably melt the metal. "Cool your jets, Super West. I got bored with that after a year or two and started using genuine business tactics, much to my grandmother's horror, because it slowed down the speed of acquisitions for a while. I *do* have a college degree in psychology. I know a few tricks *other* than pulling my blouse down and crossing my legs."

Christ, now I'm picturing her giving out blow jobs for business deals. "Not helping."

"Your sisters must love-hate you."

A week ago, this conversation would've ended with me demanding to know if she took anything seriously.

Pretty sure we've covered that though, and I don't have a single doubt that she takes Remy seriously as a heart attack. And that she'd do anything for him, and not just because she has the money to afford the world, but because she *loves* him. He's sleeping happily in a baby swing by the arched windows overlooking the gently-lit courtyard, completely oblivious to how freaked out she was just an hour ago.

"Tell you a secret?" she says softly.

I tap my right ear. "Tell this one. I won't hear it."

That smile. *Fuck.*

Yeah! Ooh-rah! Commence with the fucking! my balls cheer.

Swear to god, I'm not related to them.

"Whenever someone in my family turns twenty-one, The Dame gives us a million dollars. Do something good with it, she gives you a job. Fuck—*fork* it up, and she disinherits you."

"That's insane."

"It's also why she's basically disinherited eighty percent of her descendants. My cousin William tripled his million at the slots in Vegas, and she shut him down *hard*. Gambling isn't the way to ensure the family business survives the next generation."

"What'd you do?"

She clearly survived.

And if the way she's shifting on her seat is any indication, she doesn't actually want to talk about it. "I spent a quarter of it on initiation fees to the Sandbar Club, and—"

"I'm sorry, *what*?"

She smiles, and it's full of mischief. "It's an exclusive club for Miami's richest businessmen."

"Business...men?"

"Formerly all men, yes. I spent a week playing spy on some of its rumored members, dropping hints in various places that Carter International Properties was expanding into hotels, but looking for partners in the venture, and then I applied for the club. I might've also gotten chummy with the membership chairman's wife, who didn't know he was sleeping with his secretary, but he knew I knew, so..."

"You cheated your way into an exclusive club of assholes."

"Basically. Yes. And then I convinced ten members to

give me a million dollars each as buy-in for the Mermaid Grand Resort."

"I know that name."

"All-inclusive resorts in the Caribbean."

"Ah. Allie. My sister. She went to one for her ten-year anniversary."

"I'll have to thank her for her patronage." She winks at me. "It didn't exist when I was twenty-one. But I marched into The Dame's office and dropped ten checks on her desk, told her I was buying oceanfront property in the Dominican Republic to open an all-inclusive resort, and she was either with me, or she was against me. Now, we have sixteen properties, and we're expanding to add four more in the next year. I passed The Dame's test. And every year, she buys out one more of the original investors, because they're idiots who thought that handing a twenty-one-year-old party girl a check for a million bucks was a good idea."

"Why not open it yourself? You did all the work."

She rolls her eyes. "Every last one of those men would've sued me to get their money back the minute they found out I was in charge. *I* don't make money. My grandmother's name makes money."

"Alessandro says you make your grandmother's money."

"He's biased. Without the Carter family name behind me…" She trails off with a shrug.

Like she honestly thinks she couldn't do it on her own.

I don't know much about the business of running an empire, but I know that anytime I walk into her office to trade off Remy, she's on the phone or on her computer.

She makes phone calls to Japan in the middle of the night —*yeah, he was up at three, but I was up anyway to talk to Tokyo*—and the days she's gone to her office, she's taken night duty before and after since she's gone from seven AM to nine PM.

Daisy's no lazy slouch.

She works hard.

And she's turning a sly grin my way. "Sort of like how you wouldn't be nearly as hot without the Jaeger name behind you. Be honest. How many women mistake you for Tyler and just drop their panties right there?"

And there's the distraction. "Is your grandmother crashing the visit with the social worker next week?"

"She'll try. I suspect Alessandro will be doing a periodic security exercise that involves locking the house down about the time we get the call that she's at the Bluewater gate though."

"Or you could tell her to stay the fuck away."

"I don't like my life to be miserable, and I'd really like to not be disinherited. *Party girl* isn't an official title anywhere else in the world."

I shake my head and screw the lid onto the peanut butter jar. Family's complicated. Mine are all relatively normal—yeah, Mom goes on tour and uses all of us as fodder for her stand-up routine, and my sisters all have their quirks, and Tyler's a special case all by himself—but none of us are so intimidated by any of the rest of us that we avoid conflict at all costs.

Except Daisy *doesn't* avoid conflict with her grandmother.

Not all the time.

Just selectively.

"You completely avoided my question about why you date single mothers," she says through a mouthful of peanut butter and chip sandwich.

"Don't think so."

"You deflected."

"Says the master deflector."

"Am I technically a single mother now?"

"You're complicated."

She snort-laughs, and my heart stops for a half a second. We don't need choking part two tonight.

Or ever.

"That," she tells me after she steals another drink of my root beer, "was the most accurate thing you've ever said. High five, big guy. Nailed it."

I oblige the high five.

And twenty minutes later, when she yawns and stretches, I reluctantly shoo her out of the kitchen and take over Remy duties.

She's a mess. Nothing at all like the women I'm usually attracted to. But every little nuance I discover in her personality makes me want to know more.

And I can say *as friends* all I want, but I've never been good at lying to myself.

28

Daisy

UNLIKE MY HIGHLY ORGANIZED vagillionaire friends, most mornings, I hit the snooze button until I can't any longer, which inevitably results in me rushing through a shower, ignoring the clothes Tiana laid out for me the night before and grabbing something brighter or darker or shorter or longer depending on my mood. I spend thirty minutes too long on hair and makeup, which means Alessandro, Tiana, and I roll through Carbs 'n Coffee on our way to the office for me to scarf down fried deliciousness and caffeine before I wreak havoc on the world.

At least, ideally, that would be my usual morning.

There's a lot less havoc-wreaking and a lot more fire-extinguishing—of the metaphorical variety—now that I'm a responsible businessperson. I haven't actually wreaked regular havoc in *years*, and now, as Remy's primary caretaker, I'm even less inclined to leap up and light the world on fire.

The *good* kind of fire, naturally.

But this morning, I get up before my alarm goes off, because there's a ball of anxiety that's making sleep impossible. I need to be on my A-game for the social worker—especially since the Rodericks are now claiming I keep rabid animals on-site and that Remy's in immediate danger—so I surf the internet for random Go Fund Mes to donate a few million dollars to, then treat myself to some pampering before I have to be *on* for the day.

I'm stretched out in my zero-gravity water chamber in the home spa off my bedroom, cucumbers on my aching eyes, eucalyptus candles burning, audiobook playing softly. Technically, I should be meditating or soaking up the peace and tranquility of being in a sensory deprivation chamber, but I'm actually hanging on to every word of *Fake Royal Bride*, this awesome romantic comedy written by the coffee author from Drag Queen Brunch. I snagged the audiobook as soon as I overheard that it was available with Teddy Hamilton narrating, because I clearly have a problem.

Two, actually, because I suddenly realize I'm not alone.

I lift the lid and bolt upright, tossing the cucumbers aside and making salt water slosh onto the floor while Teddy narrates Rock Ludlow dirty-talking the innocent princess on their fake wedding night. "Who's there?"

"No one who's planning on saying *that* to you," comes a familiar voice from the bedroom as Rock asks if he can lick the princess's pussy. "Can you shut that off? We have a problem."

It takes me a minute of fumbling to shut off Teddy's voice and the princess suggesting she needs Rock to stroke his hard member while he eats her out, which would normally be fine, but West and I have been getting along *amazingly* well since the choking incident a week ago, sharing breakfast and dinner most days, and we even hung out together at the pool half the weekend, where I flirted with him without *overtly* flirting with him, and I think he actually flirted *back*. So I don't want him to think that all I *ever* think about is sex.

Plus, he said the word *problem*.

"What? What is it?" I throw on a sparkly unicorn robe for his sake and dart into my bedroom. "Is Remy sick? Did the social worker get here early? Oh my god, the cats ate his face. *Did the cats eat his face?*"

West lifts a single brow, telegraphing that I've clearly lost my mind, and holds his phone out to me.

Headlines assault my eyeballs.

Playgirl Heiress Drops Baby On Head!

Daisy Carter-Kincaid's Nanny Tells All!

The DICK's New Marine Boy-Toy Actually A Woman!

"*This* is the problem?" I ask. "Tabloid stories?"

"They have pictures of my family."

He's not breathing fire out his nose or stomping his foot like an angry bull, but I realize this calm façade is exactly that—a façade.

His magic eyes are the color of pissed-off headstrong alpha male with all protective instincts activated, and it's making that omnipresent pull in my nether regions stronger this morning.

I'm debating between reminding him that his mom *is* a

CRAZY FOR LOVING YOU

celebrity—anyone with a Netflix show qualifies in my book—and offering him use of my legal team when he continues.

"*Bad* pictures."

And now I'm intrigued. "Like snorting coke with drug lords bad, or like this kind of bad?" I half-close one eye, tilt my head, and stick my tongue out and try to lick my nose while scrunching one cheek and shoving a finger into my ear.

When I blink back to normal, he's closed his eyes and is taking a long, deep breath.

Huh.

He's not wearing a shirt.

That's *lovely*. And it's a testament to how good of a friend and mother I am that I didn't notice before now.

Okay, I'm lying.

I noticed.

I just didn't get a chance to look closely at all the intricate inkwork until he closed his eyes.

"The second," he grits out.

Is he—oh. My.

He *is*.

He's sporting morning wood in those gray sweatpants while fuming about tabloid stories.

Despite my best bad photo face.

Or because of it?

The many facets of Westley Jaeger are *fascinating*.

I snap my focus back to his face before he opens his eyes and claims this is my one chance to hit on him today. "Where's Remy?"

"Having breakfast with Alessandro."

I fling open my balcony doors and step outside to drop into the fluffy butter-yellow love seat by the wide window overlooking Biscayne Bay and tuck my legs underneath me, then pat the cushion beside me where I'd normally stretch my legs out. The ever-present sound of rolling waves greets me like an old friend, as does the scent of salt water and flowers. We're due for a nasty storm tonight—borderline tropical strength—and the wind's heavier, the sky darker than normal. "Sit. Relax. I can solve this."

He follows me out. "I'm not having Remy grow up with his pictures plastered all the fuck over trash rags."

If he doesn't stop talking, I'm not going to stop swooning. "*Sit.*"

He glares, but he sits. Glances around quickly. His eyes linger on my bed just inside the door, with the covers tossed willy-nilly everywhere behind the gauzy bed curtains because I am *so* not a make-your-bed type person.

Which probably annoys the hell out of him, except when he snaps his face back to the bay, there's something more intriguing than irritation in the way his Adam's apple bobs.

I shift on the love seat until I'm right next to him, then go up on my knees and settle my hands on his shoulders. "*Relax.* Being pissed never solved anything." I knead my thumbs into the tight muscles, which tighten even harder before he gives up and lets his shoulders slump.

"You shouldn't do that," he says gruffly.

"I shouldn't help you relax before the social worker gets here? Because angry bull in a china shop is *exactly* the attitude you want her to see, right?"

"They have a picture of you in the ER from your shrimp reaction too."

"Like anyone in the world *hasn't* seen me in a bad picture. Please. I own the hell out of the shitty photos. They're my gift to the people in the world who are having a craptastic day."

He doesn't reply.

Possibly because I'm digging my thumbs into a huge ball of tension behind his right shoulder blade.

"I'm calling and making you an appointment with Tiny as soon as you concede that I'm right and everything is going to be fine," I inform him.

"Tiny?"

"My massage therapist. She's six feet of pure magic when it comes to working out kinks."

"I'm not using your massage therapist."

"Shh. Trust me. It'll change your life."

"My life's changed enough lately. And those pictures of you in the ER are going to be used to call into question how sober you were and if you put Remy in danger."

"Westley. Quit being more difficult than you have to be. The ER drew blood. I can prove it was an allergic reaction, which could happen to any parent." Oh, god. It could, couldn't it? Will we lose Remy because I'm allergic to shellfish?

Wait. No. That doesn't make sense. If being allergic disqualified you as a parent, then my mom couldn't be a parent either.

Except her allergy developed as an adult too.

Fuck. *Fucksticks*.

Okay. Not going to worry about it.

I knead deeper, because his head is lolling to one side, and *one* of us needs to be relaxed in a couple hours.

It clearly won't be me. "And I'm on baby duty tonight. Tiny can be here anytime I ask her to. And it's not like you have plans after work, so *take the fucking massage and say thank you*."

"Is this supposed to be making me relax?"

"Don't even pretend it's not working. I can feel your rock muscles becoming merely bouncy ball muscles. I might not be as strong as Tiny, but I have magic fingers, and you can't deny it. You want more. You know you do."

"Not even seven AM, and you've hit your one come-on for the day."

Dammit. "That was *not* a come-on. That was an opportunity of a lifetime. Do you know how many people Tiny can see in a day? Six. Maybe eight if she skips her workout routine and tosses back a double Red Bull. Which means you're like eight out of the three hundred million people in the country who could see Tiny today. You're blessed, Westley. Still waiting on that thank you."

"Do you *ever* stay focused?"

"Nope." And that's exactly why no one ever thought I'd succeed.

Showed them, didn't I?

Here I am. Succeeding. Behind my grandmother's name. Panicking over raising my cousin's baby. Going to the office every day because I'm better at faking business than I am at faking mothering.

Hashtag success.

The social worker lady is going to see right through me and *we are doomed*.

I wasn't actually kidding about living in a cardboard box out in the Everglades, and it's not because I don't own my house outright—I do—and it's not because I didn't put a clause in my contract giving me twenty-five percent share in every property I help my grandmother develop—I did.

It's because I'll be mortified when people discover the truth about me.

West tilts his head back to look at me, and I dig a thumb deeper into that tight muscle in his shoulder.

He grunts, and his eyes slide closed. "Social...worker... need...talk..."

"Step one: relax. Step two: conquer the world. Or the social worker. Whatever."

That earns me a smile. And it's one of those I-don't-want-to-be-smiling-but-can't-help-it smiles that makes my heart give a big ol' fist pump. He lets his head fall forward again while I attack all the tension he's carrying, and I smile to myself.

I'll win him over. Sooner or later. Probably sooner, because I'm irresistible when I want to be.

I *like* having him around. And not just because he's good with Remy.

He's good with *me*.

It's weird.

What's weirder is that I like it. I don't actually *want* him to leave.

Ever.

Which is an extra weird feeling to have when I consider that we haven't slept together.

Not that I don't *want* to. My vibrator and my fingers

have gotten quite the workouts lately with West's face and body as inspiration. Not that I'll tell him that, because I save my one inappropriate comment every day for things that I suspect will amuse him.

The guy needs to relax more.

"Believe it or not, I have an entire wardrobe appropriate for meeting social workers," I tell him, which helps calm me down too. "I also have a script Emily's Derek wrote for me back before he was Emily's Derek, when he was just a guy I hired to make me look good after I got framed for shoplifting—which I was cleared of, by the way, so that shouldn't be a problem today. I also know how to paint the paparazzi as the bad guys. Plus, we have you with your impeccable credentials. No one's taking Remy from us today."

No one's taking Remy from *me* today. Another day, possibly, but not today.

West, though? They'd never take him from West.

He's a solid, dependable dreamboat, and I'm honestly starting to wonder if my grandmother's plan isn't to pay *him* to raise Remy, because he's the only reason I'm semi-competent at taking care of the baby myself.

Either he's inspiring me to not want to fail, or he's inadvertently teaching me something.

"Daisy?" he says on a sigh.

I knead deeper and wish I wasn't getting a lady hard-on from touching his bare skin. "Yes?"

"That feels amazing. Thank you."

"It's my pleasure."

He tilts his head back to look at me again. "You're not who I thought you'd be."

"Aha! He admits he thought about me."

"*After* I met you."

"Wouldn't it have been boring to inherit a baby with anyone else?"

His eyes are twinkling in the soft dawn light, pure green mischief, and *oh my god*, mischievous West is *everything*.

"I don't know. I might've preferred inheriting a baby with a Kardashian." He smiles at me, tilting his head back so I'm looking at him upside down.

I mock gasp. "Are you saying I'm not outrageous and outspoken enough for you? That's it. Neighborhood pool party tonight. Come naked except diamonds covering the jewels and bits."

He hasn't shaved since he got here, and his beard is thick and dark, and I can't resist stroking the rough growth. Holding his head so it's nestled against my breasts.

Have I *ever* had a guy friend?

I don't think I have. And I like it.

And I don't.

I don't want to be his *friend*. I want to kiss him. I want to explore every inch of his body, trace his tattoos and caress the ridges of his muscles. I want to strip him out of his sweatpants and straddle him and ride him until we both fall off the cliff into satisfied oblivion.

I drop my hands and start to move, because I promised I'd respect his boundaries.

I fucking *hate* boundaries.

But I'll do this for him, because he's done so much for me, and my family, and I owe it to him to not push.

Except when I start to shift away, he reaches behind us and settles his hands on my head, then tilts his face, and suddenly his lips are brushing mine, tasting like coffee and temptation, his rough beard tickling the sensitive skin around my mouth and sending my nerve endings into hyperdrive, and all of my good intentions fly out the window.

This.

This kiss is *everything* I shouldn't want and can't have, but fuck if I can stop myself.

I slide a hand down his chest, and a low growl rumbles deep under my fingers before he pushes deeper into the kiss.

Lips parting.

Tongue tasting.

His mouth claiming me like I'm a gold-dusted caramel pistachio truffle that needs to be savored.

I don't glide into kisses.

I leap headfirst into the deep end without actually verifying it's the deep end, because I'm into kissing because I like kissing, but more because I want the grand finale.

I want to toss my clothes over the balcony and get hot and sweaty and see how many different paths I can take to the land of the grand O.

But normally, I'm seizing the moment before the moment ends. Before my weekend is over, before the party breaks up, before I have to go back to my normal life.

West *is* my new normal.

He's *every* moment.

And this kiss—it's different but *perfect*.

It's a *hello, so that's who you are.*

It's a *nice to meet you.*

It's a *yes, actually, I do like you and I could spend all morning kissing you from every angle to learn what you like and what you don't.*

And right now, he seems to like pulling me into his lap so we can tackle this kiss head-on.

Best way to tackle a problem, if you ask me. And it's definitely a problem that I haven't yet been able to test for myself exactly what these bulgy biceps feel like.

"We—should—" he starts.

He's going to say *stop*, and I don't want him to, so I rock in his lap against the hard ridge pressing into my hip.

Seriously, just look at us getting along so well right now.

We should kiss all the time.

His grip tightens on my thigh, and I slip my tongue into his mouth, gliding against his while he groans and matches me stroke for stroke.

A seagull swoops by with a cry that sounds like *warning, warning!*, but I ignore it, because who wants a seagull warning when I'm practically naked and he's showing off his morning salute and he's kissing me like he would've died if I'd died choking on that carrot last week?

He wrenches back. "*Daisy.*"

Fuck.

I sigh and drop my forehead to his shoulder.

His nice, round, solid, dependable, highly-lickable shoulder that I *can't* bite right now, because I know that tone.

It's the *we can't do this* tone.

"See?" I say, pretending I'm not breathless and sorely disappointed in places I don't get disappointed—like that little muscle in my chest. "Every morning is better when we get along. Go on. Get dressed. We're gonna knock that social worker's socks off so she'll go tell the Rodericks to pound sand and get the fuck out of the court system."

Belatedly, I remember that getting out of the court system means *he leaves*. I plant a kiss on his neck as I slide off his lap, because I can't help myself, and I don't want to think about him leaving. "Meet you in the salon in twenty!"

It's rare that I *want* to find my sanity. I prefer life without it.

What's life without the fun?

But *fun* isn't all I have to live for anymore. I have to be a responsible, dependable person, and it's not even that I can't parent Remy alone.

My grandmother could cut me off tomorrow, and I could give away ninety percent of my bank account and still die a rich woman. I can afford all the help in the world.

But money can't buy what I want from West more and more every day.

He's figuring out my secrets. He's seen me choking, having allergic reactions, and falling in love with a baby.

He's seeing *me*.

And he's staying.

I can't deny Remy the opportunity to have that kind of dependable, family-is-what-you-make-it, people-are-more-than-their-accomplishments-and-bank-balance example in his life.

Life isn't simple. It's complicated and messy. No matter how much I try to believe that it's just a big party with a side of hard work to make the partying possible, there's still heartbreak and tough times and loneliness.

All three of my very best friends in the entire universe have gone through hell this year. And all three of them have come out on top, and in love with amazing men to boot.

But I don't do love.

It lies. It cheats. And it hurts.

So West and me?

We're going to be friends. Hopefully friends who are close enough that he'll agree to still be part of Remy's life after all the legal challenges are over.

Part of *my* life.

But only as friends. And that little voice inside me asking for more can shut the fuck up.

29

West

I DON'T KNOW what happened in Daisy's room this morning with that kiss, but I know it won't be the last time.

Watching her panic last week, worrying she'd hurt Remy—she wasn't faking.

She loves him.

And that changed everything.

This past week, waking up in her house, seeing her every day, *talking* to her every day, joking with her, just hanging out with her—it's been a glimpse at a woman I very much want to know more.

Falling for her now would be like falling into the same trap all over again. Single mother. Kid who doesn't have another solid father figure. Circumstances that make it seem right.

And then it all gets blown to fucking hell.

Even knowing how this will end can't stop me from going in though. I don't know if she needs me, but I believe she wants me, and there's more power in *want* than in *need*. I've never been someone's *choice*. I've been their convenience.

And I know that's how we started. She said as much. She needs me to make her look good.

Except she doesn't, and *nothing* about this last week has been about putting on a show.

It's just been two people coming to appreciate each other's quirks, strengths, and shortcomings.

It's the kind of comfort I've been craving.

And the only thing missing is more of that kissing, which I shouldn't do, but I can't help myself.

I want her. Plain and simple.

But first, I *need* to convince the social worker that Daisy's a solid parent to Remy. Because once she doesn't *need* me, then we can both acknowledge what we actually *want*.

I'm pacing in the parlor at five minutes to ten, with two cats pacing behind me but no Daisy or Remy in sight yet. The room is at the center of the curve in the D, with party rooms off the wings on either side and a wall of windows overlooking the courtyard pool. A round indoor gas fireplace is inset in the center, with tropical plants decorating every nook and cranny around some fancy-ass furniture.

Basically, it's a nightmare for a mobile baby.

Fire. Poisonous plants. Bookshelves not screwed to the walls and decorated with glass and stoneware artwork that could cause a head injury.

There's nothing childproofed in here at all—right down to me not knowing exactly how many cats we still have in the house, although the food bowls in the kitchen are always empty when I get up each morning, and this is where we'll be convincing a state official that we can be good parents.

Not a problem, I tell myself. I'm a fucking *handyman*. I can fix this.

I eyeball the sunken couches and built-in gas firepit again.

Probably. I can *probably* fix this.

"Oh, wow, you look like a groomsman," Daisy says suddenly.

I turn to the sound of her voice, and *what the ever-loving fuck?*

She's in a fifties housewife dress, right down to the pantyhose with a seam up the back and discreet low-heeled shoes. Her purple hair is gone, and instead, it's brown and tied back in a simple bun. Her makeup is light and tasteful, and she's sweeping into the room with Remy in one arm and a stack of books tucked under the other.

I swipe my hand over my eyes and look up at the ceiling two stories above, hoping to find some answers to this insane one-eighty in her appearance, but instead, I realize the chandelier overhead is shaped like a dick.

It's a dick with dick pendants hanging from it.

And…an artistic spurt coming out the tip.

My jaw unhinges and my nuts crack up.

I've been here how many weeks and never noticed this before?

"Huh. Hope the social worker lady has a sense of

humor," Daisy says cheerfully. "Can't argue that if we talk about body parts more often, they lose their stigma though, don't you think?"

The clicking of her shoes against the Italian marble floor stops beside me. "Though the glitter spurt is probably unnecessary. Tiana, could you send me a note to update the chandelier?"

"About time," Daisy's assistant murmurs.

I take one more deep breath, then look down at her. "What did you do?"

She grins. "It's a wig. And I watched one of Luna's YouTube tutorials on putting on a business face. Like you can talk. Hello, handsome in a suit. Could you roll up your sleeves though? You have such nice forearms. It's a shame to cover them up."

Her cleavage is fully covered by the pink gingham dress, which goes all the way to her neck and flares down below her knees. She's wearing a light white cardigan over the whole ensemble, and I don't like it.

It's not *Daisy*.

Trumpets blare like a royal assembly is announcing the arrival of a king in a cartoon movie, and Daisy twirls toward the door. "Oh, good. She's here."

"What was that?" I ask.

"Doorbell," Alessandro supplies with a grunt. "Stay," he orders Daisy.

She rolls her eyes—which are a soft brown now, matching her hair and making her seem as tame and harmless as a country mouse.

"I would've had Cristoff prepare lunch, but I didn't

want to look like I was bribing her," she murmurs to me. "I'm not offering mimosas either. You're welcome."

"I hate your hair," I tell her. "And your eyes."

"But you like the pantyhose, don't you?" She grins, which is the only thing authentic about her, and turns her leg to show off the seam. "Admit it. You're having house-wife fantasies right now."

"I'm having a heart attack at the idea of Remy finding the controllers for that fireplace."

She looks at the built-in fireplace, surrounded by a round couch inset in the floor as well, and frowns, then frowns at the baby, who scrunches up his face and lets loose in his diaper with a grunt that's drowned out by the trumpet in his butt that could out-trumpet her doorbell.

"Ms. Louise Anacosta," Alessandro announces.

Daisy and I both look up at the very stern woman in a business suit so buttoned-up she makes Daisy's house-dress look like a Playboy Bunny outfit.

"Oh, forking shirt," Daisy whispers through a smile.

"Ms. Carter-Kincaid?" Tall, Skinny, and Scary says as she descends the two steps to the sunken sitting room. "And Mr. Jaeger?"

I suddenly like Daisy's eyes more, because hers look like chocolate, whereas Ms. Anacosta's brown eyes look like judgmental holes to the hellmouth.

This is going to be fun.

I step forward. "Westley Jaeger. Nice to meet you."

"You're the appointed guardian unrelated to the child?"

"Yes, ma'am."

"And how did you come to be named in the deceased's will?"

"Made a good impression when I remodeled their nursery for them, I suppose."

Daisy slides to my side. "Hi, Louise. I'm Daisy. Remy's mother was my cousin."

"I'm aware of your relation to the deceased," Louise replies in a way that makes me wonder if she ever got one-starred by Julienne for anything.

But Daisy doesn't let the cold answer deter her. "Welcome, and thank you for coming."

Remy screws his face up again and grunts while he adds to the mess in his diaper.

Louise peers down at him over her half-moon glasses, and she smiles. "Well, you certainly *sound* healthy."

She's a completely different woman when she smiles, and I let out a breath I didn't know I was holding. "I'll get him," I tell Daisy.

"Oh, no need. We set up a changing station in the corner." She smiles brighter at Louise. "Water? Soda? Lemonade?

And the stiff, judgmental state official comes back. She taps a pen against the clipboard in her hand. "No, thank you."

Daisy strolls easily to the sideboard at the edge of the room beside the windows, and my eyes almost fall out of my head.

Furniture isn't my strong suit—I prefer tearing down walls and putting them back up to decorating—but I don't think that thing was built as a baby changing station. It's too carved, too polished, and too *billionaire*.

Daisy whips a changing mat out of the top drawer, then wipes and a fresh diaper from the next drawer down.

"You change diapers yourself?" Louise asks.

"Few times a day on workdays, few more on the weekend," Daisy replies cheerfully. "We've gotten good at this in the last couple weeks, haven't we, Remy? Yes, we have. Yes, we have." She boops him on the nose, and he screams bloody murder like she poked him in the eyeball.

"Hates being dirty," I say quickly.

"Abhors it," Daisy agrees, though pink's rising in her cheeks, and she's not wearing enough makeup to hide it.

"Do you frequently change him on antique furniture without straps?" Louise asks.

"You'd be amazed what you can convert into a changing table. It's so far to his room, and who wants to stew in his own poop any longer than necessary?"

Remy screams.

Daisy makes quick work of unbuttoning his dinosaur-themed onesie—he, at least, is dressed like a modern baby. She peels back the diaper, wipe in hand, as Louise steps closer to supervise, and—

And Remy wasn't done.

An arc of liquid shoots out, spraying both Daisy and Louise.

Daisy shrieks and covers him back up with the dirty diaper.

Louise coughs and steps back, right onto Elvira, who yowls and takes a flying leap across the room, skirting the inset couches, landing in the middle of the fireplace—which is off, thank god—and then flying down a hall.

Six other cats shoot out from beneath furniture and out of the corners and yowl and hiss as they follow Elvira.

Louise stares off down the hallway, baby pee soaking her gray business jacket, her lips parted. "How many animals reside in this house?"

"About one for every five thousand square feet," Daisy replies, but it's not as quick and easy.

"I've got him," I tell her, nudging her aside.

She whips two extra wipes out of the pack and turns to hand one to Louise, keeping one hand on Remy. "Healthy kidneys. Bet that's not the first time a kid's gotten you on the job, is it?"

"Not in the least," Louise agrees dryly.

"He's never done that before," Daisy hisses to me. Her pulse is fluttering madly in her throat, butterfly wings in that hollow that I'd like to kiss and calm.

"I've gotten nailed by every one of my nephews at least six times each," I murmur back.

"And you weren't going to tell me?"

I grin.

Because no, I wasn't going to tell her.

I might be boring, and I might want to kiss her again, but that doesn't mean I can't be funny. And I'm amused as hell.

"I am so mad at you right now," Daisy says under her breath.

But her lips are tipped up in a familiar curve, and I have zero doubt she's both impressed and plotting revenge.

I can't wait.

"Go on. Get cleaned up." This time, she lets me nudge

her out of the way, and she takes a wet wipe for the streak that arced from her shoulder to her belly, and while I tackle the diaper, she stands just inside my peripheral vision and strokes her boobs.

Dammit. That's not at *all* making my cock notice. Or my balls offer up some randy suggestions. And think about her in my lap. Stroking her tongue against mine.

While I'm supposed to be playing the role of *good parent figure.*

Not *horny asshole who wants to jump the heiress.*

"Can I show you the house, Louise?" Daisy says brightly.

"That would be—"

"Daisy! *Daisy!* Oh, my poor baby, I'm here! Everything's fine! Mama's here now!"

I jerk my head up.

Remy screams.

Daisy mutters something I don't catch with my bad ear, but it's clearly a complex profanity.

Louise's eyes flare wide as she turns toward Daisy's unexpected guest—a tall, busty blonde in a shrink-wrapped neon green dress and heels up to a normal woman's knees. Her eyes are familiar. So are her lips. And her nose.

"Why didn't you radio the yacht? I would've been here in an *instant.*" She has at least eight inches on Daisy, which I assume means four or five when they're both barefoot, and she grabs Daisy and smushes her face to her breasts. "I never prepared you for motherhood. I'm a failure, and now I've set *you* up for failure."

"Mom. Stop. You're not a failure."

"Daisy's not failing," I add.

"I certainly hope that's true," Louise says.

Daisy's mom looks up and frowns. "Daisy. Did you replace Tiana? And who's this handsome drink of water?"

Louise frowns deeper. "I'm Louise Anacosta, Department of Children and Family Services, and I'll thank you to *not* call me a handsome drink of water."

I'd think Louise had a wicked sense of humor, but she doesn't crack a smile while she delivers the line.

Daisy's gaze flies to mine, and I have to look away, because *I'm* going to crack a smile if I don't, but in the process, I make eye contact with her mom.

"Oh! The stranger. You're the stranger Julienne named in her will. Oh, that poor baby. Are you pinching him? Is that why he's crying?"

And no more smiles. "He's hungry." Or possibly stressed at all the changes in his life and at Daisy being stressed and me being stressed and two more strangers waltzing in the door. "Daisy—"

"Helene," Louise interrupts. "Helene Carter-Kincaid, yes? You're concerned about your daughter and this man being caretakers for this child?"

She finally seems to realize she needs to shut up.

At least for half a second.

"Well, they certainly can't be worse than his biological parents were. Can you imagine having your childhood one-starred by your mother while your father sleeps with half the neighborhood? Don't believe all those stories you see about Daisy in the news. She's the most loyal, loving, amazing woman in the world, and I've never seen her fail when she's given a task. All of my insecurities about her parenting skills are a reflection of my own insecurities and failures, but she'll be fine. I don't know anything about *him*, but I imagine that's what your background checks are for. How did you get put in that will again?"

"That's a question for another day." If Daisy gets any perkier, she's going to topple over and land on her face in a pile of reality. "Mom, I need to give Louise a tour of the house. Can you please go find Tiana and ask her if she'll meet me in the situation room at two?"

Helene's lips purse like she suspects this is code for *go away*. And then she pulls back and sneezes.

"Oh, and I got a cat…" Daisy adds.

Helene sneezes again.

"Or seven…" Daisy murmurs.

"No! Bad dog!" Alessandro yells.

I whip my head toward the shout, one hand on Remy, and then I'm shoving him at Daisy and leaping between her and our *new* guest.

A dog.

A St. Bernard, to be precise, who's sprinting full-steam after Mr. Peabody.

"Brutus! No!" Daisy cries.

"Oh my god, the baby!" Helene yells.

Brutus—apparently—leaps over the couch, hot on Mr. Peabody's heels. They make the furniture slide. They scramble over the fireplace with a bang. They dart down the hallway, Alessandro in hot pursuit, while cats from all over stream into the room, yowling and hissing, tails poofed, backs arched, and they, too, make a mad rush down the hallway toward the lounges.

"Ms. Carter-Kincaid, *what is going on in here?*" Louise demands.

"Neighbor's dog—" she starts.

But she doesn't finish.

Because Elvira—the demonic, unicorn floatie-hating, tripping-a-man-on-his-way-to-the-bathroom cat—has decided to make a grand re-entrance.

From the balcony at the top of the stairs.

Straight onto the penis chandelier.

"My art!" Helene shrieks.

"Elvira, *no!*" Daisy yells.

"*WWWAAAAAAAHHHHHH,*" Remy adds.

But it's no use.

Elvira leaps.

And misses.

And lands within a centimeter of a panicked Louise.

That's it.

We're completely fucked.

And that's before a dude wearing seventeen gold chains, low-slung pants, and a sideways ballcap strolls in.

"Yo. D. We still on for my kids to paint your tramp room?"

"*Who is that?*" Louise shrieks.

"Lil Nutt Sacc," Daisy whispers as a flock of teenagers filter in behind the hip hop mogul. "*Mother. What did you do?*

Helene's shoulders inch as high as her wince. "I didn't know today was a bad day for art class."

Louise freezes.

She's covered in cat hair. Possibly got cat piss on herself too, to go with the baby piss.

"Lil Nutt Sacc?" she repeats.

"Who's asking?" the hip hop mogul says with a jerk of his chin.

Three cats race back in, but Louise doesn't seem to notice.

She's gaping.

He squints at her. "Aw, man, *Lou Lou-licious*? Dog, get *out*. Whatcha doin' here? How do you know D? Give it up, girl."

My jaw hits the floor.

Daisy's mouth is a perfect O.

And Helene's eyes are darting between the social worker and Lil Nutt like she's watching tennis as they approach each other for a chest bump.

"You know Daisy?" Louise asks him.

"Hells, yeah. Lets my kids come artify her fancy party lounges. Feeds 'em pizza. Good people. And her mom's hot too."

Daisy sinks to the nearest sofa, Remy clutched to her chest.

I wordlessly sit down next to her.

"We have lost all control," I mutter.

"That might not be a bad thing," she mutters back.

It's bad.

It's *always* bad.

Question is, will it be bad enough for us to watch this woman walk away with our baby today?

30

Daisy

FOR THE SECOND time in four hours, I collapse onto the low couch in the center of my parlor and drop my head back to stare at my mom's chandelier, which has a layer of cat hair sticking to it now. "So, that went well."

West settles in next to me, and for once, I don't know exactly what I'm supposed to offer him.

If we were at a club or a bar, I'd have a double-shot of whiskey put on my tab for him. Or possibly a double shot of whiskey for everyone in the bar.

But I don't think he's the type to drink his troubles away.

If I was out of the country, I'd head to the nearest beach or winery or club, put on a different wig, tell my bodyguard to call me Liza, and I'd hook up with whoever looked the most fun.

Except that doesn't even seem appealing right now.

I think I've been ruined for one-night stands and weekend flings.

And I don't know that I'm sad about it.

"They're not looking for perfection, Daisy," West says quietly. "You did great."

"Of course I did. I always do great." I have a house with more potential dangers for a child than a nuclear waste facility. The world thinks I'm an airheaded party girl. My cats got drunk on the organic catnip Luna sent over and went on a rampage after the neighborhood's free-range St. Bernard—who is the *laziest fucking dog on the planet* when he's not being a total sweetheart—decided he wanted a little pussy.

And I'm letting my family down.

Remy. My mom. My grandma. My dead cousin, who might've been awful, but who didn't deserve to die so young and tragically.

"You did." West brushes my hair back with a gentle hand, and my wig falls off and topples to the floor behind me.

He snortles.

It's adorable.

"Quit laughing, Mr. Suit. *You* dressed up for this too."

"Is that a Halloween costume, or do you parade around Miami like a fifties housewife just for fun some days, handing out chocolate chip cookies to all the neighbors?"

I freeze.

I did, indeed, provide pizza lunch for Lil Nutt Sacc and his class of future artists. But I don't talk about buying all of Miami Beach's lunches at Beach Burgers, or filling up the parking meters all along Ocean Drive and all the side streets so that no one has to pay, or randomly—and anonymously—having Carbs 'n Coffee deliver donuts to all the local hospitals' staff once a month.

And actually—I *did* buy this dress for Halloween, and then also use it to hand out cookies once.

At a bar, not in a neighborhood, but close enough.

"Daisy?" West says.

"Did you always know you wanted to be a Marine, or was that what you just settled on when you didn't know what else to be after high school?"

He settles an arm along the back of the sofa, close enough that I can tell myself he's wrapping an arm around my shoulders.

I mean, if that's what I wanted to believe.

"I…don't know." He's staring at the fireplace.

I'm staring at him.

"I'm the oldest of six. Always had a lot of responsibility. Dad's a retired carpenter. Mom worked long, weird hours, and her stand-up career didn't take off until I was in high school, so I always knew it would be the military or student loans for college. Taking care of me. Taking care of my sisters and Ty—it's what I always did. When the Marine recruiter came and talked…I guess it just clicked. Felt right. Never gave it much thought after that."

"Is that why you date single mothers? Because they need to be taken care of?"

"No."

He's lying. Or maybe he thinks he's telling the truth. He'd probably tell me single mothers are strong and more capable than he'll ever be, but that doesn't mean he doesn't want to take care of them, whether he realizes it or not.

I shift on the seat, pulling my knees up until they're resting on his thighs. "Who takes care of you?"

The corner of his lips hitches up. "I'm a simple guy. Don't need much taking care of."

"*Everyone* needs taking care of *sometime*. No man is a bubble."

"You mean an island?"

"No. Islands are awesome. Sand. Palm trees. The beach. A lifetime supply of chocolate, peanut butter, and books in the secret hideaway you find when you start exploring..."

He barks out a laugh and shakes his head. "And a bubble is just a lone pocket of air trapped inside a cage of soap water?"

"Exactly. You're one smart cookie, Westley Jaeger."

He tilts his head to study me, and my breath whooshes out of me. *Hazel*. He has magic, color-changing *hazel* eyes that have seen more of the world than I have.

Maybe he hasn't been as many places.

But he's seen *more*. Bad stuff that would reduce me to a crumpled mass of helplessness. Can't be a Marine in this day and age and *not* have experienced bad things.

And he *doesn't* have anyone taking care of him. He does it himself, because he doesn't think he needs anyone.

His family must want to throttle him on a regular basis.

But this is their lucky day.

Because I, Daisy Imogen Carter-Kincaid, am going to take care of this man.

"You're going to take Remy from me one day, aren't you?" he says quietly.

A lump rolls up from the bottom of my neck to the top of my throat like it's chasing Indiana Jones, and I have to swallow hard to get it back down.

Westley Jaeger's body and mind might be made of steel, but his heart is cotton candy.

Cotton candy that he's freely given to a baby that, by all rights, never should've been his, but is now firmly settled in his heart.

I shake my head and draw an X over my own heart. "No. Never."

His eyes narrow slightly, his lips part, and I hear the question that he doesn't voice.

Even when whatever this is between us fizzles out?

It's a legit question.

I don't date.

But then, I've never had a Westley in my life.

I honestly can't imagine my life without him now though.

"Long term, I'm not in your grandmother's plans," he reminds me.

He's not wrong, and we both know it. She likes him short-term because he gives me credibility. Like he did today, talking about his time in the service, his experience with his sisters, his brother, his nieces and nephews, talking about how well I'm doing with the baby despite not having a lot of practice.

What mother does before her first kid? he'd asked.

My grandmother was correct to fight to keep him here

right now. But she's wrong if she thinks there's a day coming when West *shouldn't* be in Remy's life.

"I will fight her tooth and nail," I whisper. "And she might be immortal, but I have a way bigger army."

He doesn't crack a grin. Like he knows I'm serious.

My grandmother is in peak shape for an eighty-two-year-old woman. Her mind's sharp. Her body's strong. She gives zero fucks and feeds off of fear, which is relatively abundant when she's around. It's an endless source of energy.

She could *honestly* live past one hundred.

But my friends outnumber hers a thousand to one.

A lick of power rolls through my belly as the full impact of *having friends* sets my nerves humming.

I can stand up to my grandmother. And I will land on my feet.

No, check that.

I can fucking *soar*.

West is still studying me, but he's not in growly overprotective Marine mode.

No, this is something else.

It's white-hot attraction mixed with…pride?

"You *do* have the bigger army," he murmurs. "But having a Marine Corps is better."

I slide a hand over his stomach and lean closer. "Maybe I should have both."

His lips are mere inches away. My mother will be upstairs with Remy for the next fourteen years. The doors are all locked and guarded.

I can kiss this man for the rest of the day if I want, and no one will disturb us.

There's no shame in being caught doing what comes naturally, but this—this isn't just raw, carnal pleasure to be had.

This is *more*.

He's not asking for just my body. He's asking for *me*.

And I don't want just *his* body.

I want this strong, capable, dependable man who asks for so little for himself to know that there's someone in this world who will put *him* first.

"What are we doing, Daisy?"

"Shh. You have a little something…" I brush a thumb over his lower lip. "Right here."

There's that half-grin again. "No, I don't."

"You're about to."

He doesn't stop me.

He probably should. This is me, diving into the deep end with both feet like I usually do.

Except when my lips brush his, and his fingers wrap around the back of my head, and his heart leaps beneath my hand, I know *this* is the deep end I've been looking for my entire life.

His short beard scratches the delicate skin around my mouth, lighting up my nerve endings. His lips part, brushing open-mouth kisses to my own parted lips, and I'm not melting.

I'm toasting like a marshmallow. Hot and sticky and pliable.

Knowing I'm in danger of going up in flames, and not caring a bit, because *oh my god*, his mouth.

And his hands.

And his—"Well. *Someone* is certainly happy to see you, Daisy."

We fly apart. West leaps off the sofa. I flail my arms, uncertain what to do with them. *"Mom. Where's Remy?"*

"Sleeping. Your grandmother's on her way." She turns to West, who's not pacing, but looks like he wants to be slipping into the dark corners of the room. Outside, lightning flashes.

Stupid tropical storm.

"What are your intentions toward my daughter?" Mom demands.

"Mom."

West silences me with a hand on my shoulder. "Oh, you know. The usual. Pretend I like her. Take naked pictures. Post them online. Sue her for emotional distress when people call me an asshole online. Use the proceeds to buy a hot air balloon and an amusement park. Then pursue my porn star career."

I gape at him.

Mom can't stop blinking. Her jaw's unhinged.

"And *this* is why I don't date," I mutter.

"Don't worry, baby. I'll leave room in the budget for Remy to have lots of funnel cake for breakfast. And nannies with hooters the size of small houses." He pats my shoulder and straightens again, spearing my speechless mother with a glare I wouldn't want to be on the receiving end of. "Any other questions?"

I snort.

It's not a delicate snort.

It's a full-on, *I should not be laughing at this* snort.

But despite the growly voice, I don't think West is

truly offended. There's this *fuck, yeah, I can have fun too* twinkle in his eye that makes me want to jump him.

He's not *just* a responsibility-first military man.

He's hiding some *fun* under that exterior.

Thunder rolls through the house.

"If your grandmother gets stuck here during the storm, I *will* utilize military training to get Remy to safety," West adds.

Hello, hot flash in the chacha. "Will you take me with you?"

"Only if you leave everything but that leopard print thong bikini behind."

Oh, fuck.

I know he's joking just to horrify my mother some more, but I don't actually *have* a leopard print thong bikini. And I think I need to rectify that. Stat.

"Oh my god, Daisy. He's the man-you," my mother gasps.

"See?" he growls. "Things can *always* get worse."

He turns on his heel with military precision—which is also hot as fuck—and strolls to the staircase while my mother gapes wide-eyed at his back.

"*Mother*," I hiss. "*Apologize.*"

"He just *sassed* me."

"Because you *interrupted* us and then questioned his honor."

Her eyes light up, and she rubs her hands together in glee, and I realize I've made a very big, very bad, very fatal mistake.

And now my mother thinks we're getting married.

Not *now*.

But eventually. When I fall so hard I can't see my life without West in it.

And she thinks I don't know what she's thinking.

But I do.

And I need a paper bag.

Because for once, she might actually be psychic.

Psychic.

"Oh my god," I gasp, and I lunge for my phone.

It's all suddenly crystal clear.

I just need a few hours to prove it.

31

West

THE STORM'S ROLLING in hard and heavy tonight, and I'm mentally going through the condo renovation I'm helping a buddy with. Pretty sure I remembered to seal all the windows, but I'll need to go check it out in the morning after the storm passes.

I've barricaded myself and Remy in the Pepto Bismol room—the one Daisy called the *Strawberry Daiquiri* suite— and I'm debating texting her to ask if the community has bad weather sirens—and which room is safest in a tornado—when there's a knock at the door.

I watch, and the lock unlocks, the door cracks open, and I catch sight of a blue eye and dangling purple hair. "Come quick. My grandmother's in the shower and my mother's having a video call with a gallery up in Atlanta."

Fuck. Her grandmother *is* stuck here.

I need to prepare some contingency plans. "Go where?"

"My wing. Security's better there."

"Tornado shelter?"

"I have four. My staff will keep us separate from Mom and the Graminator if anything worse develops, but the weather reports say the storm's weakening fast."

I'm not actually surprised Daisy checked the weather.

But I am worried about how much I want to go with her. *Without* Remy. And there's not much about my sleep shorts that'll hide how I'm feeling.

But I grab the sleeping baby and a book and follow her down the hallway, watching her hips swing in those pink velour pants and that strip of skin low on her back flash beneath her short black T-shirt. Our window to sneak out of here is short.

And I have to get my cock under control.

"Sorry about my mom," she whispers. "You were awesome. And I told my grandmother you know what her Achilles' heel is, so she should leave you alone lest you turn her to a pile of dust and ash. Also, I found something. You should probably see it."

Remy half-coos in his sleep.

Daisy picks up the pace, and soon we're rounding the top of the D and coming to a stop at the wall at the end of the corridor.

Logically, I know her bedroom is on the other side of that wall.

Practically, we're at a dead end.

She flashes a grin back at me. "Want to see something cool?"

Without waiting for an answer, she leans into the corner.

There's a subtle click, and a secret door opens.

"Okay, yeah, that's cool." I follow her inside, but we're not in her bedroom. We're in a massive library.

Rather than the typical billionaire home library with dark shelves and leather-bound books and priceless artwork, though, Daisy's library has watercolors I don't recognize and white shelves filled with worn paperbacks. These books have been *read*. And loved. I angle closer, looking at the titles.

Romance novels.

My sisters are going to love her.

If she's serious. If she'll let me stay in Remy's life.

If this *thing* I'm feeling is mutual.

I'm attached, and I don't want to get *unattached*. And legally speaking, I don't *have* to.

I *can* be a part of Remy's life. Forever.

"Have you read all of these?" I ask.

"All but those." She points to the shelves around the white marble fireplace. "I spend a lot of time on airplanes, and sometimes I can't sleep after business calls around the world in the middle of the night, so I...anyway. It's my little secret."

"That you read romance novels?"

"That I *read*." She grins and winks, but I don't believe for a second that she hasn't been impacted by people's opinions of her.

I turn away from the shelves and take stock of the rest of the room, because the idea of Daisy as a secret romantic who spends hours in here, reading and dreaming of finding her Prince Charming is too much to handle tonight.

I've hoped before.

Hoped, and loved, and lost.

With women who weren't the fascinating, intricate puzzle that is Daisy Imogen Carter-Kincaid.

The rest of her library is exquisite. Pine wood flooring. Overstuffed chairs the color of the ocean. A fresco ceiling painted with a young girl dancing with unicorns. Daisies worked into the wide plaster trim along the ceiling and around the doorways. Little touches of femininity every-where, from the heart-shaped sconces on the plaster wall to the delicate pink glass flowers on the white marble fireplace mantle.

No windows here—and I wonder if there's another hidden door that leads outside somewhere.

"Why do people in south Florida need fireplaces?" I ask.

"Sometimes it gets below sixty." She tiptoes beside me on bare feet. "Here. Let me have this little guy. I need snuggles."

I could give her snuggles.

I'd *like* to give her snuggles. Naked snuggles on that fuzzy white rug in front of the fireplace. With my cock rocking against her pussy.

I clear my throat and hand her the baby, who curls into her chest and sighs happily while she smiles softly at him.

Seriously.

Easiest baby *ever*. Even with all of the movement, he's stayed asleep.

CRAZY FOR LOVING YOU

He'll be up again and hungry in an hour or two, but for now, he's blissed out and happy.

"Sit." Daisy waves at one of the chairs in front of the fireplace.

I oblige, and I have to concentrate hard on not appreciating the curve of her breasts and hips in that get-up.

She grabs her phone from a decorative table near the door, then crosses back to me. Instead of taking the other seat, she settles into my lap while thunder rolls outside.

My arms go around her, my nuts cheer, and when she looks at me, I want to kiss her.

"Hi," I say softly.

She shifts Remy across her breasts and presses a kiss to my cheek. "Good evening, my gallant chair. I need to show you something."

"I'd be a lot happier about that sentiment if you weren't holding a baby."

"Westley Jaeger, are you thinking dirty thoughts about me?"

"Only some are dirty."

She smiles, and it's brighter and more dazzling than lightning on the ocean, and an order of magnitude more dangerous. "Here. You need to watch this."

She shifts in my lap, swipes her thumb over the phone, and stops on a video in her text messages, which she enlarges to the full screen. She hits play, then hands me the phone to hold while we both watch.

It's dim, like it's being shot at night, with little specks of light floating across the screen.

"What is this?" I ask.

"*Shh.*"

A shadow moves into the frame, and I realize I'm staring at—oh, fuck.

Seriously?

It's a crystal ball.

"Ah, yes. Julienne. I knew you'd be coming. Your husband has been unfaithful again." The first voice is low and raspy, and it makes my hairs stand on end.

"Doesn't take a psychic to read the gossip pages, Becky. I'm well aware of what he's been doing while *I'm growing our baby.*"

Hearing Julienne's voice puts a hitch in my shoulders. Daisy shivers, and I pull her closer. She's soft and curvy and fits perfectly, and I don't want to move. Don't want to watch the rest of this video either, because the creepy-crawlies dancing up my spine are warning me that whatever it is, it'll change everything.

"You're concerned about your safety," Becky the psychic says.

The shadow that I assume is Julienne's nods. "I think my mother-in-law is trying to kill me."

What?

Daisy puts a hand to my chest. "Shh," she says again.

Becky the Psychic leans over the ball. "She's very attached to her son."

"She hates me. She's so jealous. She always wanted to be famous, and now I am, *and* I get half of Rafe's trust fund if I can prove he's cheating, and she's still *nothing.* But when we went to her house last night for dinner, she was acting...*strange.* Like, she usually at least pretends to like me, but she was all, *you won't be my problem much longer.* What does that even *mean?*"

"I see darkness in your future, my child."

"No fucking *duh*, there's darkness. Divorce and scandal and when she left her phone out, I checked the last text messages because she's a *moron* and doesn't know to erase text alerts, and she's been talking with someone called *Bob* about peanuts and hospitals. *I'm going to the hospital to have a baby in two weeks.* And she doesn't know a *Bob*. That's *clearly* a code name so we don't know he's a hit man. I think she's going to slip peanut dust into my food after I give birth. *She's going to knock me off.*"

"She's off her rocker," I whisper.

"You *are* in danger," Becky intones. "*Grave* danger. But not from the corners you suspect."

Julienne shrieks. "What? *What? Both* of my in-laws want to kill me?"

"You have enemies, my child. More enemies than you know. And they come soon. You must put your house in order. Reconcile with your husband. It is the only path to eternal peace."

Daisy's not the only one with a shiver now. *Eternal peace* is a fuck-ton more ominous considering both Julienne and Rafe are *dead* now.

"That's insane," I mutter.

"You mean freaky," Daisy whispers. "Shh!"

"My house in order," Julienne is saying. "Oh. My. God. Becky. *My in-laws get my house if I die.* I mean, Rafe gets it first, and then—oh my god. Oh my god. What if they're going to kill *him* too? What if they've realized he's a huge disappointment and they want to murder us *both* to take the baby and try for a better son?"

"You *must* get your house in order," Becky repeats.

"Yes. Yes. Anthony and Margot aren't getting shit from me. She said my hair looked *awful*. Can you believe her nerve?"

"That should be stupidly funny," Daisy whispers. "One star for her hair."

"The stars have written your destiny, Julienne. You *must* correct your wrongs."

"I'm not dying today, bitch. Forget it. But I'm fixing my will. And I'm making Rafe fix his too, and then I'm shoving it in their faces when I catch them and their hit man. But—but *who*? Fuck. I'm not leaving anything to my grandmother. She's such a haughty asshole."

"This is insane," I mutter. I can't stop saying it, because it keeps getting stranger and stranger.

"I see—I see a man," Becky suddenly gasps. It's an overdramatic kind of gasp, the kind that normal people don't make, the kind that makes me ask who believes this shit, and I almost shut the phone off, but Daisy swats my finger away when I try.

"A man? For me?" Julienne asks. "Should I leave Rafe?"

"A man...you can trust... He's tall. Dark. Handsome... Have you met anyone new lately, Julienne? Has someone tall, dark, and handsome come into your life?"

"*Oh my god*, my general contractor. For the baby's room. He's *totally* tall, dark, and handsome."

Oh, fuck me. No.

No.

"Yes. Yes!" Becky the Psychic says. "And his name... His name starts with...a...a B? No, a...a T? No, I see...a J?

Julienne gasps.

"Yes! I see a J!" Becky says.

"His last name?" Julienne whispers.

"This is *forking* insane," I say, stronger.

"It explains everything," Daisy replies while Julienne shrieks my name.

"Should I leave Rafe for Westley?" Julienne breathes.

My nuts, the randy suckers without any taste, retreat so far into my abdomen that they bruise my stomach on their way to hiding behind my lungs. She's dead. She's not coming after them. And they're still in hiding.

"No, you *must* stick by your husband to survive," Madame Becky says.

"So name Westley as my baby's guardian if Anthony and Margot take us both out." Julienne's leaning forward like she believes every bit of insanity that she's spewing. "He can take my son away. Keep him safe from them."

"And...I see a woman..."

"Probably a lot of them, with the way he looks," Julienne whispers.

"She's...blond. No, brunette. No...*purple*. Purple? Surely not—"

"Daisy!" Julienne shrieks.

Another full-body shiver hits me, because this *cannot* be real. "You have got to be shirting me."

"My cousin Daisy!" Julienne shrieks again. "She never wears the same hair two weeks in a row!"

"She's a scam artist," I say to Daisy while panic swells up in my veins. This is what they need. This video is all they'll need to one day prove I shouldn't be in Remy's life. Julienne let a psychic tell her who to put in her will. That's why I'm here. "She guesses until she's close enough for her *clients* to reach their own conclusion."

She kills the video. "Julienne thought of you during a psychic reading when she thought her mother-in-law was plotting to kill her with peanuts."

"She was allergic?"

"*Highly*. But West—she *knew* you'd be good for her baby. Better than anyone she's related to."

She still took parenting advice from a scam artist.

"Where'd you find this?"

She tosses her phone onto the other chair and shifts deeper into my arms. Remy's little eyes have closed. He's breathing through his mouth and drooling on her chest. "Julienne one-starred Madame Becky the week Remy was born."

"You read her blog?"

"Not on purpose. I was—" She cuts herself off, and the pieces tumble into place.

"You looked up what formula and diapers he was used to." Of course she did. Daisy isn't stupid. Never has been. And she knew she needed to figure out how to take care of a baby.

"I remembered this afternoon, and on a whim, I reached out to ask Madame Becky if she knew anything— and not about my future, just about Julienne's last weeks —and she sent me the video."

"She videotapes her readings?"

"Just some. She's running a how-to fortune teller course soon."

"You think Margot Roderick would've poisoned her if —if the dolphins hadn't gotten to her first?"

"No idea. But I sent the video to our attorneys. It might not prove Julienne was right in the head, but it'll prove she wasn't drunk and she most definitely did *not* want the Rodericks to raise her son. Plus, she still had to convince Rafe, so it's not like the will was impulsive. She named both of us on purpose. And now we know why."

"I'm here because she was a paranoid nutjob."

"No, nuts would kill her. She was more of a paranoid banana-job."

I smile, but I don't feel it. This is it. She brought me here to say goodbye. "Point is...I'm not his family, and I shouldn't have been in that will."

"Westley, you are more *family* than anyone I've ever known."

"You've never even seen me with mine."

"Yes, I have."

"No, you—"

"*Family* is what you *make* it. Tell me you didn't have your Marines family. Go on. Tell me you didn't have brothers and sisters in the Corps."

I open my mouth.

Then shut it.

Because of course I'm not going to tell her I didn't— *don't* still have family in the Corps.

"You didn't have to stay. You *chose* to. That makes you more family to Remy than even I am," she whispers. "I *had* to step up. You didn't. And if you hadn't been there that first night—maybe that psychic knew what she was talking about."

"You believe in psychics?"

"I believe in you."

Of all the women in the world, I never expected *this* one to be the one to bring me fully to my knees. But here we are. With her holding the only bit of evidence she needs to kick me out of her posh life and back to where I belong.

And instead, she's opening the door wider.

Inviting me in.

"Daisy—"

"Do you still want to stay? I wouldn't blame you if—"

I silence her with a kiss.

I don't know if she's offering me herself as well as Remy. I don't know how long she'll let me be the man who holds her and kisses her. I don't even know if she wants to kiss *me*, or if she just likes kissing.

But her free hand is curling into the fabric of my shirt and she's parting her lips and stroking her tongue against mine and making soft, needy whimpers in the back of her throat that are making me feel like the only man in the world who can give her what she needs.

And I'm ready. Willing. Able.

Whatever she wants.

Whatever she needs.

For as long as she wants me.

That's my boy! my nuts yell.

And suddenly I'm chuckling into the best kiss I've ever had in my entire life.

"Are you laughing at my technique, Mr. Jaeger?" she whispers.

"No. You—you're—you make me lightheaded. I like it."

Her eyes are dancing, teasing, but there's a vulnerability lurking too.

Like she knows we can't just be a one-night stand. There's Remy to think about. Our futures. Intertwined.

CRAZY FOR LOVING YOU

Of fucking course I'm not walking away from this kid. He's snuck into my heart.

Daisy can give him a good life. A solid life, with opportunities I couldn't begin to imagine.

But I can give him a boisterous, loud, joyful *family*. Cousins. Aunts. Uncles.

All those things that can't be measured on a profit and loss balance sheet.

Daisy brushes her fingers down my beard. "You're not kissing me just because I'm a single mom, are you?"

"I'm kissing you because you're so much more."

Her brow furrows, and her gaze drops. "I'm not. I fake my way through everything," she whispers.

Whoa, my nuts say. *She fakes it? Fuck! Give the woman a real fucking orgasm, Marine!*

"I mean—not *that*." She squirms and climbs off my lap. "I mean I'm only successful in business because people like me."

Regroup! Regroup! my balls shriek. *Regroup and go after that nooky!*

Insensitive fuckers.

But in this case, I don't think they're wrong.

Daisy needs some TLC. And it's time I give it to her.

32

Daisy

So there I was. Sitting right in West's lap. Kissing the hell out of him. Feeling that thick ridge under my thigh. Knowing I was going to get some tonight.

And now I've completely and totally killed the mood.

Because he thinks I'm something I'm not.

A month ago, I wouldn't have cared. I would've lured him downstairs to my office, smothered us both with froyo, and weathered this storm with some good old-fashioned monkey sex all night.

But I can't let him think I'm something I'm not. He's in this for the long haul, and we *can't* co-parent Remy if I'm not honest with him.

"Daisy." He grips my shoulders gently, stopping me from my retreat into my bedroom. "Being a people person is a skill. And you're not faking your way through taking care of Remy."

Oh, god, he has no idea. Do I love the little guy? With all my heart. But can I do this? I honest to god don't know. I'm going to fuck him up so bad. "I am. I'm totally faking it."

"That kid *adores* you. Babies see through fake."

"But he's so *easy*. It's not *me*. It's *him*. I'm not looking for pity here. I have a good life. There are seven and a half billion people on earth, and I have more than all but like a thousand of them. But I'm not a *good person*. My friend Emily? She helps minimize the appearance of scar tissue on people who need it. Cam runs a foundation that funds scholarships for kids and so much more. Luna's a freaking charity goddess *and* an earth savior to boot. Her boyfriend Big Dick Beck saves innocent dogs. And what do I do? I tell Carbs 'n Coffee to put everyone's bill on my tab some random day. That's—that's—"

"Incredibly thoughtful."

"So *small* compared to what I *could* do." My chest is warming even as I have to stop myself from banging my head against the nearest bookcase, because it's *not enough*.

"It's not small to make someone's day. And getting up to the counter to order a burger and finding out—"

I suck in a breath, and he freezes.

I didn't say *burgers*. I said *donuts*.

"You did that at Beach Burgers," he says quietly. "The day we inherited Remy."

"Maybe," I mutter, and I hope I'm talking to his bad ear.

No such luck though.

"Never saw a tip jar so full as it was that night." His voice is a quiet, soothing rumble. "There's a ripple effect.

You do something nice for someone, they're inspired to do something nice for someone else. You didn't just buy a few hundred burgers, Daisy. You reminded a few hundred people of the power of *joy*."

"I was buying happier feelings," I blurt. "The funeral— it was awful. *No one* was sad they were gone. I didn't do it for the people getting free burgers. I did it to make myself feel better."

"You did it for both."

"Does it really count as a random act of kindness if I'm doing it so someone misses me when I'm gone?"

"Who knew it was you?"

I mumble an answer, lower this time.

"Little louder for the good ear, Daisy." He grips my shoulders firmer and turns me around. I want to bury my head over Remy, but I make myself meet his gaze.

"I said, *no one*. I mean, Tiana and Alessandro know, and the manager at Beach Burgers, but he also knows I won't do it again if he lets it slip that it's me, and his staff makes *such* good money on those days when I—I mean, I got a free burger out of it myself, and—"

"Why are you minimizing your impact in the world?"

"Because it's not about *them*. It's about making *me* feel good. And that's just as selfish and stupid as my grand-mother diving into a pile of cash in her version of an adult ball pit room in her fortress. I'm a horrible, awful, selfish asshole who only wants to have fun."

He gapes at me like I've just sprouted some of my mom's artwork out of my ears. Like he's seeing me for the first time.

Like it all makes sense now.

I'm an alien in a human body, incapable of this *love* thing people speak of.

"Have you had so little love in your life that you don't know how valuable you are? And I'm not talking about your bank account, Daisy. I'm talking about *this*."

His hand settles high on my breast, next to Remy's little head, as close as he can get to my heart.

"I don't have one of *those*," I tell him. "I can't. I'm a Carter. We get them traded in for mechanical banks when we're born."

He doesn't roll his eyes or grit his teeth, which is almost worse.

Instead, he cups my head. Smooths my hair back. Steps closer. "You could make yourself feel good in so many other ways. Drugs. Alcohol. Sex. But you choose to do it with random acts of kindness. And taking care of a baby that isn't yours. And making the world a better place. How often do you get drunk? *Really* drunk? Because I've been here close to a month, and I haven't seen it. Haven't flown in any men from Europe or Australia to scratch an itch either. You could've been just like your cousin, tearing down everything and everyone publicly, but you don't. You let three dozen kids into your house to paint your walls with artwork most of the world would've called graffiti. You think to buy coffee and donuts for other people. You're not a selfish asshole. You're a good person with a big heart and a shitty family if they've never told you how amazing you are."

"You shouldn't put me on a pedestal. I'm going to let you down."

"People fuck up, Daisy. It's what makes us human. Hell,

I'm gonna let you down too. But you know what? *I'll forgive you.* We'll learn. We'll move on. And we'll be *fine.*"

Oh, fuck.

Oh, fuck on a roller coaster. Actually—fucking on a roller coaster could be fun. Except not when my heart's about to fully unleash itself and take off on the joy ride of its life.

Is it possible to fall in love with a man when you're not watching? Because I'm fairly certain I am head over heels in love with this man standing here telling me *I matter.*

Not for my name.

Not for my bank account.

But for every *little* thing I've ever done in my life.

This man—he'd treat me like a queen even if I were broke and living in that box in the Everglades. *He* could sue *me* for full custody, but he believes in me.

I suck in a big breath and turn back to the wall, hit the secret lever, and slip through to my bedroom.

Set the window and door alarms while West sighs heavily behind me.

I know that sigh.

It's the sigh of a man who knows that he's had his last moment with Daisy Carter-Kincaid.

In West's case, he's wrong.

So wrong.

I kiss Remy softly on the head and gently put him in the bassinet in the corner of my room that he's outgrowing too quickly, then turn back to the secret door to my library, still open.

"West?"

He looks up from running a hand through his thick hair. "Hm?"

"I'm going to jump your bones."

His eyes flare wide, and then a slow smile creeps over his face while I stalk to him. "Are you?"

"I am."

"Tonight?"

"Right now."

He gestures to my body. "While you're wearing that?"

The shirt peels off in a flash, and that thick ridge I felt beneath me while I was in his lap on the chair leaps to attention, tenting his black shorts. "Better?"

"Fuck, Daisy," he whispers hoarsely. His gaze jumps from my eyes to my bare breasts and back again.

"Not your first glimpse, Mr. Jaeger," I remind him as I slip my arms around his shoulders and arch my back, putting my belly against his hard-on. "But if you want me to put it back on—"

A groan rumbles low in his throat, and he bends to capture my mouth while his hands slide up my sides to cup my breasts.

I shudder and press myself into his touch, because *god*, his hands are so perfect.

Rough skin. Firm touch. Dexterous thumbs.

He circles my nipples, and the sensation of another human being doing for me what I've had to do for myself for too long sends a jolt of lust pulsing between my thighs, and I'm suddenly climbing him like a monkey. "More," I tell him. "Touch me *more*."

He turns, carrying me while I dive deeper into this kiss, squeezing my thighs around him and rocking against his solid erection, his hands going to my ass, fingertips gripping my hamstrings *so* close to my core, digging in at the tops of my inner thighs, and I nearly spontaneously combust, because I love being touched.

Love it.

Love connecting. Love feeling. Love bliss.

But there's a responsibility to *this* touch.

Giving myself to West isn't about feeling good for an hour. It's about letting him in.

He's here.

In a room that not even Cam, Luna, and Emily have been in.

He knows I'm not perfect.

He knows so many of my secrets.

I want to know all of his.

And I want him to know they're safe with me.

He drops to one knee, and I whimper when our bodies disconnect. "What—" I start, and then he's lying me back on the fuzzy rug in front of my fireplace.

Thunder rumbles deep and low and long outside, reverberating through the walls while West slides down my body and sucks one pebbled nipple into his mouth.

"Oh, *yes*." Fireworks explode in my soul. I gasp and grip his hair, holding him while he licks and sucks and nips at first one breast, then the other. I'm soaking through my pants, and my clit is hot and desperate. "Yes, yes, *yes*," I chant while he feasts on my breasts and explores my ribs and my stomach with his hands. I hook my ankles around his back, and he suddenly chuckles.

"Not going anywhere, Daisy." He strokes a hand down my thigh and makes every nerve ending in my body stand up and beg for his touch. "I've been fantasizing about touching you for—well, it feels like years."

"I can't let you go," I confess softly.

I can't.

This isn't a fast boom-bang-bye.

This is *West*.

He's been my rock.

And I want to be his rock. I *want* to be the person he calls when he has a problem. I *want* to be the voice he needs to hear before he goes to sleep at night. I want to be the last naked body he wants to see for the rest of his life.

Oh, god.

I want him to love me as much as I love him.

The realization swells out of my chest and makes my arms and legs tingle.

It's too big.

Too much.

And yet so *right*.

He's studying me with dark eyes ringed in emerald. "You want me."

"I don't understand how any woman *couldn't*."

A wry smile darkens his face. "I'm very boring."

"You are *not*." I shove his shoulder until he rolls off me, and I follow him so I'm on top, tugging his shirt off.

He dutifully lifts his arms. "I am."

And as soon as he's tangled with his arms stuck in his shirt over his head, I scoot back down so I'm straddling that glorious hard-on and cradle it between my thighs while I lick a trail around the outline of his tattoos.

"*Fuck*, Daisy," he gasps.

"You are *not* boring. You're *hilarious*."

"You're—*christ*, that feels so good—the only—*oh, fuck yes*—person who thinks—*so.*"

"Huh. I'm the smart one for once."

"You've always been—" he cuts himself off with a strangled moan.

Probably because I pinch his nipples and rock against his erection and lick his hot, flat stomach with its gorgeous artwork. We need to lose our pants. And then I need to suck on his cock until he can't remember his own name, and then I'm going to treat him to a full striptease that'll have him hard again in two minutes.

I'm going to make love to this man all night long.

"Westley?" I whisper as I lick my way up his throat.

"Yes?"

"You make me feel alive."

He catches my face before I can attack his mouth again. "You have more *life* in your pinky than most people have in their entire families."

"But you make my *heart* feel alive."

The words slip out before I can stop them.

And I don't think I would've stopped them even if I could.

Not when it makes that soft smile creep over his lips while he lifts his head to rub his nose against mine. "You make me feel not boring."

"I drive you crazy."

He pumps his hips against mine. "You do."

We're both laughing as I claim his mouth again, because I'll continue to drive him crazy, and he'll continue to tolerate me stoically, but I have this feeling he hasn't had *fun* in his life in too long.

Oldest child. Marine. Dating single mothers.

He *needs* me. Because I don't *need* him. Not to be a second adult in the house. Not to take overnight duty. Not to fix a squeaky hinge or chase cats out of pools.

I just *want* him.

So bad I almost can't breathe at the thought of him *not* being here.

His tongue delves deeper into my mouth, his hands roaming while I stroke his beard, then his neck, and lower.

I need him out of his shorts.

Outside in the rain.

Dancing in the ocean.

Playing unicorn jousting in my pool.

Fixing me peanut butter and potato chip sandwiches.

Oh, god, I am *so* in love with this man.

His hands slip under my pants, and he freezes for half a second.

I smile into his kiss. "Whoops. Forgot to do laundry."

"You did not."

"Okay, I didn't. Are you horrified?"

His fingers drift lower, down my crack, exposing my ass until he's stroking a finger along my seam. "So fucking turned on," he growls.

I whimper as his finger dips into my channel, because *yes*.

"So wet," he murmurs, holding my gaze captive and fucking me with his finger. "Christ, you feel like heaven. Do you taste as good?"

I jerk against his hand, my breath ragged, my heart

completely obliterated. "Maybe if you're good, you can find out later."

He grins. "I can be good."

"Wait. Maybe if you're *bad*, you can find out later. *Ohmygod, don't stop.*"

"This?" he asks, pulling his finger all the way out.

I whimper. "*Yes.*"

"Now?" He traces my ass with both hands while I rub myself shamelessly over the steel rod still behind too many layers of fabric. "Maybe I want you to stroke me first before I give you any more."

"You—distracted me."

"With this?" he slides a finger inside me again, and I moan.

"*Yes.*"

"I can't seem to help myself. Such a sweet, hot pussy."

Westley Jaeger. Dirty-talker. I did *not* see that coming, but I probably should've.

And it takes an act of heroic strength, but after shamelessly thrusting into his touch three more times, I wiggle out of his reach and down his body to peel his shorts back.

"You—" he starts, but I bend and lick at the tip of his magnificent cock, and whatever he was going to say is lost in a rumble of thunder that's either him groaning, or the storm outside, and I'm not sure which.

So I lick again, sliding my lips around his head while I use both fists to grip his length.

And that's *definitely* West making those rumbling noises.

I suck on his tip, and he fists my hair in his hands,

grunting and swearing while I tease his head, then take him all the way to the back of my throat.

He's big. And thick. And so hard.

And I'm getting hotter in the pussy with how good he tastes.

"Daisy," he rasps.

I hum against his dick, and he swears again.

And suddenly I'm being lifted off him. He rolls, and I'm trapped beneath him.

"I wasn't done," I tell him.

"I almost was."

"And the problem with that is...?"

He ducks his head into my shoulder, hiding another of those smiles. "I want to be good for you. And it's...been a while."

"If you think this is the only time I'm getting you naked in the next forever, you are *sadly* mistaken."

His eyes meet mine again, and there it is again.

That whisper.

That promise.

This one's different.

"Are we going to fight for who's on top?" I ask. "Because you should know I will *always* win."

He presses a kiss to my neck and slides a hand over my breast, then down to dip into my waistband. "Do you?"

His fingers find my pussy again, and my tongue forgets how to make words.

"Condom?" he asks.

I point to the statue of a dog beside the fireplace.

I think.

He's finger-fucking me again, and I can't be held

responsible for where I point when my eyes are crossed and all the blood is flowing to my clit.

He nips at my ear, and suddenly I'm coming all over his fingers, my body clenching tight while his brows go up and his eyes go dark as midnight.

"Christ, Daisy, you're—"

"Oh my god, *I'm coming!*" I yelp.

And I can't stop myself, because he's pressing *right there*, that magic spot inside my pussy that's making me spasm harder and higher than I've ever gone.

It's blinding hot and I can't feel my toes, but I know they're curling while I pull my knees to my chest and let it all wash over me with West coaxing me until I'm boneless.

And that's how I feel about him.

Boneless. Unable to resist him.

And completely fulfilled yet still wanting *more*.

I don't know if I'll ever get enough of him.

But I'll be perfectly content to spend the next forever trying.

33

West

THERE'S nothing more gorgeous than watching a woman transform during an orgasm, but Daisy—she's *more.*

She throws herself into everything completely.

Even now, in the midst of a post-climax glow, she's reaching for that weird dog statue.

"Because you're so very talented with your fingers," she declares as she slides the dog to one side and pulls a strip of condoms from behind it, "you get to choose. Blow job? Or your very impressive cock in my pussy?"

Either way, I don't see myself lasting long.

Not with that mouth.

A cry suddenly accompanies a roll of thunder, and the lights flicker.

Daisy freezes.

I freeze.

And Remy wails again.

"Oh, no, he didn't," she whispers.

I sigh and drop my forehead to her shoulder. "I'll get him."

"No, you won't. We're both going to hold our breath for five minutes, and if that doesn't work, then I'll get him."

Nooooooo, my balls wail.

"You can't hold your breath for five minutes," I tell her.

"Don't test me."

I'm smiling as I push up. "Five minutes, and I'll have him back to sleep."

Two hours later, though, Remy is still up, happily cooing away.

"Go to sleep," I whisper to him.

He grins and squeals at me.

Like he knows he's being a little cockblocker.

Daisy's passed out on her bed, because my bedtime story for Remy an hour ago worked on her.

We're never, ever, ever getting nooky again, my balls sigh.

They might be right.

Considering we spend the rest of the night awake, by the time morning rolls around, I can't even think of getting it up without groaning at the energy it would require for my body to function.

The storm's slowly abating about dawn, and Remy's *finally* fallen asleep when Daisy stirs on the bed. She's still topless, lying sideways with her soft pants on, and she blinks twice before her sleepy gaze lands on me.

And that little smile turning up the corners of her lips —it melts me.

Completely.

And utterly.

I'm done.

Gone in a way I've never felt.

"Ohmygod, *why did you let me fall asleep?*" She leaps off the bed without a hint of self-consciousness.

I put a finger to my lips, then point at Remy, who needs to be moved, but *fuck*, if I move him, I swear he'll wake up.

"West." She shakes her head, then wraps an arm around my ears and pulls my head to her bare breast. "You crazy man. You should've woken me up."

"One of us needs sleep."

"Your turn. Bed. Go."

"Rough night."

"You are in *so much trouble* for not waking me up. Hand me the baby. And go to sleep. Now. Before I call my mother and grandmother in here to visit."

The semi-hard-on that I apparently *do* still have in me shrinks back.

"C'mon, Mr. I Can Do Everything. You can *go to bed.*"

She pulls Remy out of my arms, and he fusses, but not for long.

She freezes. "Oh, god. This is totally inappropriate, isn't it?"

I study her, bare-chested, with a baby tucked against her skin, then gesture to my own bare chest. "Babies like skin. Helps them bond."

Fuck, she's gorgeous.

She cuts off my view by pointing to the bed again.

I rise, but I grab her hand and pull her along with me.

Because if I have to sleep, I want a pillow.

A Daisy pillow.

She wordlessly climbs onto the bed with me, one-handedly fluffs a pillow, and then lets me wrap my arms around her legs while she sits with Remy.

And then Daisy—party heiress Daisy—sings me pop songs until I fall asleep.

34

Daisy

REMY IS IN A *MOOD*.

I don't know if it's the change in atmospheric pressure after the storm, or having my grandmother on the premises, or realizing that my mother is easily manipulated, but he won't sleep more than fifteen minutes at a stretch.

Grandma Helene claims to be up to the task of making him happy, and she makes it a solid two hours before marching into my office, where I'm arguing with The Dame about a prospective new development in Australia.

"He doesn't want food. His diaper's clean. I gave him a bath, which he hated. Reading to him is like having a demon sprout off his forehead and spew terror all over everywhere. He screamed so loud that he scared the cat. And *don't* ask which one. All of them. Just assume he scared all of them. *I've lost my touch with babies.* Daisy. *How did this happen?* It was just yesterday that you were a baby, and now I can't soothe this one."

My office door opens, and a dark-haired older woman I've only seen on Netflix strolls in. "That's because he needs his *other* grandma," she announces.

Oh.

My.

God.

I had this woman's son's dick in my mouth just a few hours ago.

"He knows who'd fly through a tropical storm to get here, doesn't he?" she coos at Remy, who momentarily stops screaming to look at her.

"Who are you?" Gramalicious demands, rising to her full five-foot-one-inch height, since being immortal doesn't exclude her from the effects of gravity.

"Oh. *Oh!* Are you Westley's mother?" Mom's whole face lights up. "We have *so* much to talk about. Like how wonderful your son is. And how much you're going to adore Daisy. And how quickly we're going to get you away from *my* mother, because that's in everyone's best interest. Are you hungry? Thirsty? You want some frozen yogurt?" She points to my wall. "Daisy. What flavors do you have this week? The coconut is the *best*, especially if you swirl it with the chocolate."

May Ella Jaeger finally looks up from making faces at Remy to glance at my wall of froyo.

"I'll take chocolate," a voice says behind her.

"Coconut for me," another voice says.

"Get out of the way, you Amazonian. You and your big head are blocking my view."

Three—no, *four* other women tumble into my office, with Alessandro on their heels.

"They were on the list," he says with the same level of exasperation generally reserved for venting after The Dame leaves.

All five of the Jaeger women speak at once.

And I start grinning.

Because *god*, I've missed having people in my house.

"Australia can wait, Grammykins," I say.

"It *cannot*—"

"It's a bad investment. It can." I twirl out of my seat—I'm not behind my desk, because my grandmother commandeered it this morning—and cross the floor to West's family. "Hi. I'm Daisy. And I can't wait to meet all of you."

"Oh my god, she's *real*," the shortest one says. We're about eye level.

"Of course she's real," the one with blond highlights replies.

"I can't tell if she's slept with him yet," the one with West's hazel eyes says.

"She's not sleeping with *West*," the one with the darkest hair and plain chocolate eyes replies. "He's all business first. Probably hasn't even noticed her since she's competing with this adorable little bundle of fluff. Hi, you cranky little cranky-pants. You need hugs from Aunt Allie, don't you?"

"Watch out, Allie. They're contagious," hazel eyes says.

"For the last time, *Oscar is fixed*."

"Who are these people?" my grandmother demands.

"Family." I'm grinning as I shoo them all out of the

office. "There's more froyo in the kitchen. Peanut butter and potato chip sandwiches, anyone?"

"Daisy Imogen—" my grandmother starts again.

"I've got her," Alessandro says with a sigh.

"You know you're my favorite."

"Next week's my anniversary."

"And you know you're getting a good raise even if you don't deal with her." I peck him on the cheek and gesture for West's family to follow me to the kitchen, where we find the man himself hunched over a massive plate of cheesy scrambled eggs.

His dark hair is sticking up at odd angles. There are dark circles under his eyes. And even his shoulders look tired.

But he still leaps to his feet, fully wide awake, as soon as we parade in. "Oh, fuck," he mutters.

"Go back to bed." I go up on tiptoe and kiss his cheek too. "I've got 'em."

"But—they're—fuck," he finishes again.

"Westley. That's no way to greet your mother." His mom's eyes are twinkling like flying down to Miami where her son inherited a baby with *me* is just another day in the life, and she can't wait to whip out his baby pictures and swap embarrassing tales with my mom.

"I was talking about *them*." He gestures with his fork to his sisters, who are all pretending to be talking to the baby in my mom's arms while they eyeball all of us.

"They were worried about you."

He cocks an eyebrow. "They wanted to meet Daisy."

"That too," the short one says. "Initial indications are

that we could get along, but so far, I've only been *promised* frozen yogurt."

"My grandmother's in my office," I murmur to him. "But all is not lost. I keep spare tubs in the freezer."

"That freezer?" he points to my built-in Subzero.

"Nope. This one." I pull open a cabinet under the island, which is half-stocked with pre-mixed frozen margaritas, and half-stocked with froyo.

Remy starts crying all over again.

And West's sisters step up to the challenge.

"Does he have gas?"

"Does he need to poop?"

"One time, Mia screamed for six hours because she'd gotten a hair tied around her toe."

"The twins used to take turns screaming like that. They'd feed off each other. Be glad you only have one."

"My oldest used to scream anytime we held her facing outward."

"*My* oldest would scream anytime we held him facing *inward*."

"Babies are so complicated.

"And different."

"He's probably freaking out because there are seventeen million new people in here."

"How much is he eating every day? Is he having a growth spurt?"

"Which kid was it who had their teeth come in at two months?"

"Oh, look, he's lifting his head!"

West looks at them.

Looks at me.

Shakes his head with a half-smile. "You love this."

"They're. So. Awesome."

He bends over, grabs a container of froyo, and finds a spoon. "They're all yours. Come find me later."

I lift a brow.

He just chuckles and keeps going.

He pauses to hug each of them, kisses each of them on the tops of their heads. But when he heads for the door, none of his family stops him.

They notice he's going.

But his sisters trade grins that say they understand.

"Long night?" his mom asks me. She has a way of wording the question that makes me think she's talking about more than just Remy not sleeping.

"The longest," I reply. And I think I'm getting red in the cheeks.

Which makes *my* mom grin so big, her cheeks are about to crack.

And the weird thing is, I don't think I mind that she's hearing wedding bells.

Not one bit.

35

West

THE NOISE from the kitchen has barely faded down the hallway when I run into someone who makes me appreciate my family on a level I never would've thought possible.

"Mr. Jaeger," Imogen Carter sniffs.

"Mrs. Carter." If she were my grandmother just being a butthead, I'd call her Satan and move on. But I think she honestly expects the world to bend to her, and I'm not in a mood to fight.

Besides, she can make Daisy's life hell.

I'd like to avoid that.

Alessandro's behind her, and he shoots me a look that simultaneously calls me a chicken and thanks me for not being a dick.

I'm gearing up for a fight when she steps calmly around me. "Have a nice day, Mr. Jaeger."

That was...weird.

I cut a look to Alessandro, but he seems just as perplexed as I am that she didn't take the opportunity to tell me she's signed Remy up for ballroom dancing lessons.

A chill washes over me.

She doesn't think I'll be here long. I'm no longer her *problem*.

Fuck.

I believe Daisy when she says she'll stand up to her grandmother, but Imogen's hardly powerless.

My breathing is fast and choppy, and I remind myself I'm here to take it one day at a time. One fucking *minute* at a time if I need to.

We'll be fine.

Daisy and I will be fine, and Remy will be fine, and everything, right now, in this moment, is good.

That's good enough.

I need to get out to my job site, but I don't want to.

I want to go sit by the pool.

Cannonball into it.

Race my sisters on unicorn rafts.

And have *fun*. Not in a who-can-do-the-most-push-ups way. But in a *this is my family and they're awesome* kind of way.

One margarita into my mom, and she'll be busting out the jokes like she's on a stage. One margarita into Allie, and she'll start confessing to all the things she made Keely take the fall for in high school.

And I can laugh at them instead of telling them they're

being ridiculous and immature, because life's about more than just following the rules.

What the fuck has following the rules ever gotten for my heart?

I almost turn around to go grab Daisy, toss her over my shoulder, and then dash out to the pool to leap in with both of us, but there's no need.

She's sneaking up behind me and grabbing my hand as I pause at the bottom of the stairs. "Come here," she whispers.

I don't know where we're going.

I don't care.

Five minutes ago, she was watching my family like she was in heaven and couldn't wait to get to know everyone and would be opening up the pool and the bar and ordering in everyone's favorite foods and six dozen of her other friends for a massive *Welcome to Miami* party.

And now she's here.

With me.

Just the two of us.

While double the grandmas and quadruple the aunts stand between Remy and Imogen Carter.

"They wore you out already?" I ask her while she drags me down the hallway toward her lounges.

"Are you kidding? *Never.* It's a personal goal to always be the last partier standing. I haven't even gotten started yet. Don't warn them, by the way. I need to know what your family is *actually* made of, so I know when to go easy."

"Daisy—"

"And I mean that in the *sisterly* way. Not the *I never lose* kind of way. But *you*, my hot hunky co-parent, have gotten the short end of the stick, and I am determined to correct that *immediately*."

Hells to the YEAH! my balls roar.

I tell them not to get too excited.

But she's *here*. When she could be with a half-dozen other people, soaking in all those vibes her extroverted personality needs.

She turns into the trampoline room, drags me inside with her, throws the doors shut, and then releases my hand to shove a chair under the door handle.

She frowns. "Think that'll hold them out?"

"The lock might."

"*Oh!* Right."

She moves the chair away, twists the lock on the door-knob, and then turns.

And leaps.

That's Daisy.

I'm laughing as I catch her.

"To the ball pits!" she orders while she peppers my cheeks with kisses.

This is the weirdest of her lounges. Four steps lead up to a massive floor of linked trampolines, with ball pits lining the walls that were black two days ago, but are now painted with everything from seventies-style flowers and sayings to sparkly bling to penises.

I choke on a laugh, step onto the trampoline, and almost drop her.

She twists around, grins at the wall of dicks, and then shimmies down. "You know what? Better idea. Race you to the ball pit!"

She takes off, bouncing like a madwoman, and I follow.

Fuck, this is fun. "What's in the ball pits?"

"Your special surprise."

"Which ball pit?"

"This one—no! That one!"

I feel like a teenager. Racing across a trampoline to catch a bright, happy, hilarious beam of sunshine in a short, tight, giraffe-hide-patterned skirt and a tan, expensive-looking tank top. Her light purple hair is hanging loose, her makeup is light, and her feet are bare.

And my heart is carefree as a birthday balloon.

"What about *this* one?" I ask as I snag her around the waist.

She shrieks with laughter, tries to leap away, and instead takes both of us down.

We bounce, bumping hips, and soon she's rolled so she's straddling me while the stretchy material beneath us makes everything unstable and crazy and perfect.

"How about *this* one?" she says, bending to brush her lips against mine.

"I've been misled, madame. I demand a ball pit."

She laughs again.

And I take advantage of the moment to kiss her.

Holding her face to mine, inhaling that laughter, swiping my tongue over her lower lip, biting softly, exploring, tracing, just *living*.

Tomorrow doesn't matter.

Yesterday doesn't matter.

Just this—kissing Daisy. On a trampoline. While she dives headfirst into kissing me back with those plump lips and quick tongue and eager hands stroking down my chest and pushing my shirt up.

Her hips roll over mine, rubbing my aching cock, and I groan into her mouth.

I've been perpetually aroused since the moment I got here, and I don't have a fucking condom.

"No frowny faces," she informs me as she pulls out of the kiss and rises up to strip out of her shirt.

She's wearing a teeny tiny black lace bra that makes my cock strain harder between her thighs. I trace the cups over the swell of her breasts and sit up to suck at her nipples through the thin fabric.

"Oh, god, West," she gasps. "That feels so good. But no. Bad boy. This is for *you*."

"Then you shouldn't offer such delectable treats."

She shimmies out of reach, sending both of us bouncing again, and I put a hand to her head to keep us from knocking noggins and giving each other concussions.

There's a devious glint in her eyes, though. "That's right. You just hold on right there."

"Hold on to—"

She slides the rest of the way down my bouncing body, slips a hand into my sweatpants, and frees my erection. The cool air hits it, then the heat of her fist, and then—oh, *fuck*, yes.

Then her mouth.

She kisses my tip, swirls her tongue around my head, and sucks my cock all the way to the back of her throat, her wet, hot mouth fucking *heaven*.

"Daisy," I gasp.

She presses on the trampoline on either side of my hips, and rides with me while I bounce.

I start to protest, but then she cups my tight balls while she pulls off my cock, swirls her tongue around my head again, and then sucks me back down, and I can't speak.

I can just feel. The thick, heavy sensation in my cock warning me that I can't hold out. The *warning, warning* buzzing in the fuzzy recesses of my brain, declaring that *this is not a safe place to get a blow job*, but it's drowned out by the sight of those blue, *blue* eyes boring into mine.

Sit back and enjoy this, Marine.

I don't know if that's Daisy or my balls talking, but *christ*, her mouth—and her tongue suckling the underside of my dick—and her *joy*, her spirit, her determination to make *me* feel good—fuck.

Fuck.

"Daisy—I can't—I'm gonna—"

There's a glint in her eyes, and she sucks me harder, and suddenly I'm coming down her throat in a white-hot flash of sensation that makes my fingers and toes tingle and my legs and stomach tighten and my heart swell.

So much—*so* much sensation. Physical. Emotional. Spiritual.

She strokes my legs while she sucks down my climax, and my heart waves a white flag.

We're done.

We surrender.

There have been no women before Daisy Carter-Kincaid, and there will be no women after who have or will *ever* completely capture me, body, heart, and soul.

My body goes limp, and she slides off my cock with a

337

soft *pop*, then kisses my tip and tucks me back into my pants.

"You are *so* fucking hot," she whispers as she crawls back on top of me, the world tilting and rolling as the trampoline adjusts beneath us.

"I don't—think—you can—talk," I pant.

She grins, squeezing her arms together to make her cleavage more pronounced, and *fuck*, I'm getting hard again.

How does she *do* that?

I trace the line between her breasts. "You know you don't need to put these on display to be sexy and gorgeous. It's all in *here*." I brush a thumb over her heart, then her temple.

Her eyes go shiny, and she blinks quickly. "*Dammit*, West. You're ruining my sex goddess high."

I roll and pin her beneath me on the trampoline. "Sex goddesses can feel with their hearts and minds too."

She squirms, and I start to lift off her, but she grabs me around the ribs and holds me tight. "My fucking skirt is too tight to wrap my legs around you," she grumbles.

"I could help with that."

One brow arches. "Westley Jaeger, are you offering to rip my skirt off me?"

"Maybe. If the lady says one nice thing about herself first."

"I have a killer rack *and* I give one hell of a blow job. Your turn. Go caveman on this damn skirt."

"Something nice about your personality," I correct.

She heaves an exaggerated sigh. "This is pointless."

I nip at her ear, and she hums happily. "More of that if you say something nice about yourself," I whisper.

"But *why*?"

"Because you're amazing, and I don't think you know it."

She eyes me warily. Like she doesn't like that we're heading into personal territory.

But I don't just want her body. I want her mind. And her heart. And I want her to know she can trust me with *all* of her. That I'm safe.

I won't hurt her.

Something flickers in those blue eyes, and then the willpower and determination kick in. Like this is one more challenge.

And she's up for it.

"I sometimes anonymously donate dog food to shelters," she says softly.

"Human shelters?"

Her eyes flare wide for half a second.

I grin.

She cracks up. "You—*you*—"

I rock until she releases me, then leap off her and take off on the trampoline. "You know someone who thinks of the baby first after she chokes on a carrot is a person with a big heart, right?" I call while she chases after me.

"Sheer terror of the torture my grandmother the vampire would inflict if I screwed up her plans for the next host body she plans to inhabit."

"She tries to control you because she knows you're bigger and better than she is."

"Boob envy. *How are you all the way over there*? Get back

here! I have a condom and I have every intention of using it!"

"No more of my cock until you say three nice things about your personality."

Fuck, this is fun.

I dive off the trampoline and into one of the ball pits, and Daisy shrieks and comes bouncing after me, her breasts barely contained in that little black bra, her legs constricted by the skirt, but her cheeks are flushed and she's laughing as she leaps like she's drunk and finally lands in the massive ball pit with me.

"I have an awful singing voice but I sing anyway because it gives me joy, and I want other people with bad singing voices to know it's okay," she says.

I'm wading through the balls, diving like I'm in a pool, pretending I'm running from her. "Fine. We can count that one," I concede with a grin.

"For that one, you should strip out of your shirt, because that was *very* big of me to admit. Most people think I think I could be the next Taylor Swift if I'd just take the time to get into a studio."

"You're too old to be the next Taylor Swift."

Her eyes flare again, and then she falls over backward in the balls, laughing. "Oh my god, West. Just when I think you're all honey drops and powdered sugar, you show your minty saltwater taffy side."

"I'm only ninety-eight percent saint. But I suppose I can give you this." I stand up straight, swing my hips like I'm dancing to bad music on a porn video, and make a show of lifting my shirt until I whip it the rest of the way off, swing it like a lasso over my head, and toss it to her.

CRAZY FOR LOVING YOU

Just like I wanted to the night we met.

She snags it and pulls it to her nose, and *fuck*, I'm full-mast again.

Her eyes go dark as she watches me. "I speak six languages," she says. "But I'm self-taught, and I don't actually trust myself to not accidentally tell someone I went down on his mother last night, so I only practice on staff I occasionally hire for part-time jobs to do my translations for me."

I'm simultaneously aroused and heartbroken for her lack of confidence. "Which six?"

"English, pig Latin, pirate—"

I make a flying leap for her in the pit, and she shrieks, but she doesn't move.

"Which six?" I repeat, trying to get a hold of her in the ball pit, which keeps shifting around us and making us both sink deeper inside it.

"English, French, German, Italian, Spanish, and Japanese." She frowns while blue and yellow and red balls start to swallow her face, and then switches rapid-fire into several different accents. "I've also mastered pretending to be British, sometimes Canadian, eh, and g'day, mate, Australian is my favorite. Look at that. I'm holding your blue balls in my hands, eh?"

"You're incredible. And also disappearing."

She laughs, and I keep trying to grab her while we sink deeper and deeper into the cool, dark depths of the ball pit.

Her arm hooks around mine, and I realize we've hit the bottom.

"And I would do literally *anything* for Cam, Emily, and

my Moon," she whispers. "Bluewater is the only community I've ever developed outside my family's properties, and it was *so* much fun. I wouldn't have done it without them. So that's not a nice thing about me. It's a nice thing about them."

"You go out of your way to make other people happy and to make them feel good about themselves."

"Completely self-serving."

"Liar."

"Okay, *fine*. I'm compensating for the ugly. Because people deserve joy with their trials. Happy now?"

"Almost."

I can't see her clearly—the light's dim at the bottom of a ball pit, but I find her nose with mine, and then I angle in for a kiss.

And she lets me.

It's not an *I want to rip your clothes off* kiss.

It's an *I love you* kiss.

The words scare me. I used them liberally in my younger years, and I always got burned. But Daisy—she's so fucking easy to love.

Her big parts and her hidden parts.

"West?" she whispers.

"Hmm?"

"I'm very naked in here."

I stroke a hand down her body, balls all around us, and holy fuck, she is.

Butt naked.

I press a trail of kisses to her jaw. "Where did that skirt go?"

"Oh, someone will find it eventually next time I have a

party. We'll call it a souvenir."

"The fuck they will. It's *mine*."

She strokes a hand down my neck. Then my back. And lower, until she's tugging my pants down again. "I like being yours."

"You're going to destroy me. You know that?"

"Never. You're too special." Her hand finds my cock, and she squeezes and strokes once, and I groan in sheer pleasure from having her hands on me. "I'm going to take care of you, Westley Jaeger. You wait and see."

She strokes me again, and my head brushes the soft skin on her lower belly, those damn plastic balls filtering between us, and then her other hand joins in, except—

"Fuck, yes," I groan while she slides a condom down my length.

"I didn't lose the important part," she says, all cocky self-assurance that makes me laugh.

And then I'm sliding into her hot, slick pussy, and she's gasping and chanting *yes, more, there*, and nothing —*nothing*—has ever felt as right as making love to Daisy in the middle of a ball pit.

I start to laugh while I pump into her, because *I'm making love to a woman in a fucking ball pit*.

"West," she whispers, arching into me while I thrust.

"We're crazy, you know that?"

"You're the only man I've ever seduced in my ball pit," she informs me. "Or on my trampoline. Or...in my home."

I meet her eyes in the low light, with a fucking yellow ball between our cheeks and I realize she feels it too.

The *I love you* that we're both too scared to say.

"My nuts and I are highly honored," I tell her.

And then we're both laughing again, and I thrust deeper inside of her until we're not laughing anymore, until we're two people chasing mutual pleasure, except I'm *positive* this gorgeous, amazing woman panting and writhing beneath me is holding out until *I* get off first.

"Daisy—"

"Oh my god, *look at this place!*" my sister Allie suddenly shrieks somewhere above us.

"Love the walls," Staci says dryly.

I freeze.

Daisy freezes.

And then she squeezes my dick with her inner walls, and *fuck*, I'm gonna come.

Again.

I pull back slowly, then push inside her while my sisters squawk about above us.

If they jump in this pit, I'm going to dismember each and every one of them.

Daisy flexes her channel around me again as I bury myself fully within her, and *oh, fucking glory*, she's so tight and hot and perfect.

"One more," she whispers desperately. "Just one more, West. One more."

I reach between us as I pull out, find her clit, and flick it as I drive in, and she bites my shoulder while she clenches tight and hot and hard, and suddenly I'm coming too, stifling my groans in the crook of her neck while we climax together, hidden under layers and layers of balls, finally, *finally* feeling like I'm *home*.

Where my heart belongs.

With this hilariously fun, unpredictable, chaotic

woman who's hiding more love under all her layers than anyone I've ever known, while my family tries their best to wreak more havoc above us.

Daisy snort-laughs into my shoulder.

And I crack up too, despite all the overwhelming sensations that are just *too* much around my dick right now.

Dude, get us a cigarette, my nuts say. *And then one of those Costco-sized boxes of condoms. Or maybe four. You know. A week's supply.*

"Hold on," I whisper to Daisy. "I'll get rid of them."

"Don't move," she whispers back. "I'm not done soaking in the feel of you."

I kiss her shoulder. Her jaw.

An errant ball pit ball when I try to reach her cheek. "Dammit."

She giggles.

I stifle another snort of laughter.

"Why are those balls moving?" Keely suddenly says.

"Oh, shit, I have to pee," Allie replies. "Is there a bathroom in here? Fucking childbirth."

"Wait. Why *are* those balls moving?" Staci says.

"It's the alligator," I call. "Get out."

"*West is getting nooky in the ball pit!*" Keely shrieks.

"I am *not* going in there," Brit says. "*Gross.*"

"He's not getting nooky," Staci tells them all. "He's probably trying to find a place to hide to get some sleep."

"I love your sisters," Daisy whispers.

"I'm about to love horrifying them by standing up naked," I murmur back.

"West? *Are* you getting nooky?" Allie asks.

"You could jump in and find out for yourself," I call.

There's a beat of silence.

And then a rustle of bodies moving.

I tense, because I don't actually trust my sisters to *not* jump in here. But the door slams, and when all is silent for another full minute, during which Daisy runs her hands over my chest, my shoulders, my face—I finally breathe a sigh of relief.

And go back to the kissing.

Because I am *never* going to get enough of kissing Daisy.

36

Daisy

WEST'S FAMILY is *the best ever*.

We spend two days hanging out and getting to know each other and wrangling the cats and playing in the pool. Between our moms and his sisters, Remy is spoiled rotten while both West and I manage to get caught up on work some too.

And also sneak away to bang at every opportunity.

We're very busy, but in the best way.

I've set a goal, which I emailed him about in detail, about the way we're going to christen every single room in my house.

And it turns out, he's very good with executing a plan. Which doesn't surprise me in the least.

This whole *being in a relationship* thing is new.

And *awesome*.

Finding new ways to make West smile is the best. He's

not the grumpy, straight-laced Marine all the time. Turns out, he's fucking amazing at relaxing. And tolerating all the shit his sisters give him. And giving it right back.

And he's always aware of exactly when I need something.

It's a skill I'm studying closely so I can figure out how to turn it on him.

Late Friday, my grandmother calls—which is eight million times better than her stopping by—to tell me Margot Roderick has been arrested.

I'm still sitting at my desk in my office, staring at my phone in shock while Elvira makes herself at home on my dick rug, when West pops his head in. He's gotten a haircut, but it's not military short—just trimmed up—and it shows off the silver strands I've started to notice more and more amidst all the dark brown.

I love them.

They're more evidence that he's seen enough of life that he knows what he's getting into with me.

"Daisy?"

That's all he says—just my name—but it's everything.

Are you okay? What do you need? What can I do?

He doesn't *need* to do anything—this is the kind of news I could handle on my own *just fine*, because I'm an independent woman, except I don't *want* to handle it on my own.

I *want* to decompress about it with someone.

"Froyo run?" I ask.

His face scrunches into one of those *don't bullshit me* faces, but he still strolls over to my wall of frozen yogurt, grabs two cups, and fills them both before crossing to my desk and setting them both in front of me.

My windows are open, and there's an ocean breeze rolling in. The sun's starting a slow descent in the late afternoon sky.

And all is right in the world.

I mean, as right as it *can* be right now.

He drops into the seat across from my desk, a dainty, round ivory spinny chair that his large, masculine frame should look ridiculous in, but he blends in everywhere from the pool to my bed to sitting under my mom's dick art, so I shouldn't be surprised he looks right here.

I take a slow bite of caramel froyo—I swear, he always knows exactly what I'm in the mood for—and then I burst into tears, which startles the cat so badly she darts out of the room.

"Margot hired a hitman to take out Julienne," I sob.

West's eyes go wide, and then he's one big blur of motion, leaping across my desk, clearing the froyo without any danger of sending it flying, lifting me out of my chair, and pulling me close, my ear to his heart, his lips pressing kisses to my crown.

"Ah, Daisy," he whispers.

"She's—in jail—and I—" I stop, hiccup, and don't even try to continue.

There was so much more my grandmother said.

Restraining order filings.

Lawsuits.

Private eye reports on Anthony Roderick.

But it all comes down to one thing: Remy's safe.

Margot's in jail.

Anthony's being investigated for tax fraud, and all appearances are that he's fled the country.

My grandmother's family lawyers filed to have the Rodericks' challenge to the will dismissed, but it's a mere technicality.

Remy's safe, and he's *ours*.

And the emotions are too big for me to handle on my own. The relief. The joy. The love.

"I'm okay," I babble to West's chest. "It's all—it's—"

"Too much," he finishes.

I nod and reach for my phone and open my email. The full message from The Dame is on top, so I click it open and pass it to him.

The details—I don't want to think about the details.

I want to go hug Remy. And my mom. And West's sisters and his mom. And then go tell Luna and Cam and Emily. And throw a party. And hug and kiss Remy.

But more, I want to stay right here.

Snuggled up to West.

Except maybe naked.

Out on the beach.

Yes.

"You read this?" he asks me softly.

I freeze. "Oh, fuck. Did she say we have to get rid of you now? She's such an asshole. Ignore her. I'll handle her. She tries to get rid of my mom and my Uncle Jethro at least three times a year too."

He chuckles. "I don't care if she doesn't like me. So long as *you* do."

"I *love* you." I gasp and slap a hand over my mouth, because I wasn't supposed to tell him like that.

There were supposed to be candles. Flowers. Peanut butter and potato chip sandwiches. Vanilla froyo, which is his favorite, sometimes with a light layer of rainbow sprinkles.

And me in a hot pink teddy.

His arms tighten around me. "I love you too, Daisy," he whispers. "And it scares the fuck out of me, because love's never been kind, but I can't help myself. You're so damn easy to love."

I blink up at him, and he's watching me with the most serious expression I've seen since the night I asked him to come back and help me with Remy.

He's offering me his whole heart.

That whole, perfect, bruised but still beating, gentle giant heart.

I touch his cheek. Smooth his brow. Let my fingers trace his lips. "I don't deserve you."

"Yes, you do."

"I love you," I whisper again. "I don't deserve you, but I love you."

His smile is everything.

Everything.

And I can't resist kissing that smile until I'm breathless and hungry and pulling him to the floor beneath my desk to love him the way he deserves.

Forever.

It's always been for other people.

But only because I hadn't yet met my West.

37

West

THE ONLY THING better than watching my baby brother kill it on the ice on a Saturday night?

Having my family—and Daisy's chosen family of her billionaire besties and their boyfriends—with me while we cheer and holler and raise the fucking roof in the arena while he does it.

The Miami-based half of our crowd cheers for the home team too, but they also join us in celebrating Ty's goal in the third period.

Remy's not a fan of all the yelling, but he loves the attention that comes from getting passed around the box to everyone who'll hold him, from my sisters to Daisy's friends' boyfriends.

For someone as popular as she is, Daisy's not on her phone often. Usually just an hour a night, catching up before bedtime, unless it's her mom or her three best friends texting, which she'll answer immediately.

Or me, when I'm out on my job site, I've discovered.

But she keeps sneaking it out during the game.

"What are you doing?" I finally ask.

She grins. "What I do best, Westley. You just wait and see."

And see I do.

Once we're back home, after the game, she disappears into her closet and returns a minute later in a little glitter bikini that matches her sparkly gold hair this week.

She shoves my board shorts at me.

"Do I *really* need these?" I ask with a brow wiggle.

"You do if you don't want to flash your whole family." She winks. "Party's in five."

"Wait—*whole* family?"

"*Whole* family. And a few more friends too."

I drop trou and fling my shirt off.

Daisy's eyes go dark.

And we're fifteen minutes late to the party.

We hit the pool hand-in-hand, Daisy carrying Remy and both of us wearing *I refuse to feel guilty for why I'm late* grins on our faces.

But it's not just family.

It's a whole freaking *party*.

"Westley!" Tyler crows from the edge of the pool.

Three of his teammates rush him—Zeus and Ares Berger, two massive brutes, along with Nick Murphy, the team's goalie—and they toss him in.

Then they trade glances, and the loudest Berger twin

yells, "Cannonball!" and all three go flying into the pool, followed by a guy I've seen in the neighborhood.

My sisters shriek and dive for cover.

Their husbands and kids—the ones old enough to be awake—are all laughing and diving in too. So's my dad, who flew down this morning to join us.

Six cats yowl and dart out from their hiding spots in the bushes around the pool.

There's tropical island music playing.

Burgers grilling, courtesy of Derek.

Beck and Jude are hanging with him in the outdoor kitchen, both with beers.

One of Daisy's security guys is manning a bar.

My mom's riding the mechanical unicorn that I thought Daisy was kidding about, while Cam stands to the side and hits buttons on her phone, making the unicorn go slower or faster while Mom yells to Allie to *get it all on film!*

The cats are all prowling about, sniffing curiously and then dodging back inside through the cat doors Daisy had me install throughout the complex.

"Westley!" Tyler crows again. He climbs out of the pool, dripping wet, and smothers me in a hug that ends with some pumping on my back that makes me realize I need to get back to the gym.

Little fucker's gonna be able to beat me in arm-wrestling too soon.

"Fatherhood looks good on you, dude," he says.

"Wet looks good on you," I reply.

He lets out a war cry, bends, grabs me in a fireman

hold, and the next thing I know, I'm going into the pool too.

That's fine.

I'll let him have this one.

"Tyler Jaeger!" Daisy exclaims as I'm coming up for air. She's handed Remy off to one of my sisters, and I have no doubt the kid's going to be passed around from person to person all night long. "You beat my team."

He grins. "Daisy Carter-Kincaid. I did. And I'd do it a —*aaah!*"

She gets him by the ear, twists, and shoves him into the pool. Then she dusts her hands. "Got him for you, baby," she calls to me. "Clear out, Berger boys! *Cannonball!*"

"She's so fucking awesome," Zeus Berger says behind me while Daisy makes an Olympics-worthy splash.

Ares Berger, equally large as his twin, is grinning and shaking his head.

"Your wife know you're looking at another woman?" Nick Murphy, the Thrusters' goalie, says.

"You kidding? She thinks Daisy's awesome too. Gives good advice on shoes."

Ares dunks him.

Then dunks Nick.

Then Tyler.

Then the dark-haired, familiar dude whose chin seems to be sparkling.

I hold out a fist. "Nice."

He dunks me too.

I surface with a sputtering laugh.

The crowd's growing, with more people from the

neighborhood coming in. I don't recognize everyone, but I'm sure Daisy does. I get a glimpse of Remy, currently being held by Beck while Luna melts into a pile of lust and adoration beside him.

"*Unicorn jousting!*" Zeus suddenly hollers. "I got the shortest kid on my team. Ares. Take the other short one. Show 'em how twins do it."

They bump fists and take off for my twin nieces, who are floating in miniature unicorns.

Daisy surfaces next to me and wraps her arms around my waist. "C'mon. Introduce me formally to that brother of yours. I want to know if he's as cool as your sisters."

"As cool as?" Ty puts a hand to his heart. "I'm so much fucking *cooler*."

"Until you can ride the mechanical unicorn as well as Mom, you'll never be cooler," Staci pipes up from her spot at the edge of the pool, where she's twirling her youngest in a floatie too. "West, you need a nanny? We can relocate permanently to the Piña Colada suite."

"That one's caused six accidental pregnancies," Daisy tells her.

"*Dammit*," she mutters.

Keely cackles.

Tyler pumps a fist. "Way to *go*, Javi, my man!"

My brother-in-law flashes a thumbs-up from across the pool, where he has their second-youngest and is teaching him how to swim.

"More grandbabieeeeees!" Mom crows before she goes flying off the bucking unicorn and lands with a perfect tuck-and-roll on the mats surrounding it.

"Got it!" Allie replies with a laugh.

"Your family is so awesome," Daisy sighs happily.

"Suspiciously so." Emily plops down next to Staci. "Do you all *really* get along all the time?"

"Only when Brit's not stealing my hairspray," Staci replies.

Luna sits on her other side, hair braided down her back, bangles covering her slender wrists. "Which one of you watches *Bachelor in Miami*? Daisy said someone does."

My sisters all gather around Daisy's friends, everyone chatting while the Berger twins and Nick Murphy and Ty climb up onto unicorn rafts and each grab one of my nieces or nephews for a squeal-fest of unicorn jousting.

Derek serves up burgers.

Helene sits in one of the pool chairs with a plate of street tacos. "Daisy, I don't know when Cristoff started making these, but I demand them *every week*."

"Costco," Daisy calls.

Every one of my sisters gasps.

"You replaced Cristoff with a chef named *Costco?*" Helene asks her daughter.

Daisy grins. "Sure, Mom. Let's go with that."

"You shop at Costco?" Staci whispers.

"Street tacos and wine. Fuck, yeah."

"I love you," Brit breathes.

"Make way, peasants!" Zeus yells. "Horse with a sword, coming through!"

My niece Mia squeals in delight. Some of the older nieces and nephews leap into the pool to try to knock Tyler off his raft. Elvira circles the pool like she's thinking of claiming another floatie for herself.

And I wrap my arms around Daisy's shoulders and

lean against the wall of the pool while she leans against me.

Family.

Fun.

Friendship.

This is what I want every day for the rest of my life.

Remy growing up surrounded by love and happiness and having no boundaries on how far he can go. Waking up every morning in Daisy's bed.

Mom pops up behind us and sits at the edge of the pool along with the rest of the line. "Where's the baby?"

"Somewhere. We should get him to bed." I peer around the pool area, looking for him.

"Spoilsport. We have to go home on Monday. And when will I see him again?"

"Anytime you want, say the word, and we'll send a plane," Daisy tells her.

Mom bursts into tears.

"Dammit, Daisy," Allie says, and she bursts into tears too.

"Whoa," Zeus says.

"Retreat!" Murphy yells.

"Not again," Oscar and Javi both groan together.

"What? *What?*" Daisy spins and stares at me. "What did I do?"

"Welcome to the happy tears." I shrug. "It's a Jaeger thing. Once one starts, they all start."

"Oh, god. I think I might cry too," she whispers.

"This is beautiful." Luna wipes her eyes. "I love happiness."

"Daisy, how strong is the chlorine in this pool?" Emily asks. She, too, appears to be on the verge of crying.

"Group hug!" Daisy yells.

My mom and sisters cry harder.

Daisy bursts into tears.

All of the hockey players paddle for the deep end.

Except Tyler, who falls off his raft laughing. I catch his eye, and I almost double over too.

I love these women.

All of them.

Even when they drive me nuts, they're all heart.

And they're all climbing into the pool for one big group hug. With Daisy at the center.

Finally getting all the love she deserves.

I sweep another look around, peering for whoever has Remy, and I spot Helene instead, who's also wiping her eyes, and I watch her lips. "I couldn't give her this kind of family," she says quietly. "I wanted to, but...it turns out, I have very poor taste in men. I could never spot the monogamous ones."

"You did something right, or she wouldn't be who she is."

I push out of the pool, because I can't see Remy.

None of my sisters have him.

None of the billionaires.

None of their significant others.

Where the fuck is my baby?

Alessandro meets my eye, sweeps a look around the pool, frowns, and disappears into Daisy's private wing of the house, lifting a walkie-talkie to his mouth.

My veins ice over.

I don't stop to towel off, but instead head toward where Alessandro just disappeared, eyes roaming, looking, watching.

"You see the baby?" I ask Jude as I pass him.

He makes a sweep of the patio, then leaps to his feet. "Somebody put him to bed?"

Beck and Derek join us as the bartender touches his earpiece and looks straight at me.

My heart leaps into mission mode, except this isn't *get the job done.*

This is *what the fuck?*

I turn and scan the party on the deck again, this time catching Daisy's eye in the pool.

Her smile freezes, and suddenly, she turns in a circle.

Then another circle.

There's no baby down here.

There's no baby down here.

She goes white as a ghost.

She knows too.

Alessandro steps out of her door. "Sleeping?" I ask him.

He shakes his head tightly and says something else into his walkie-talkie.

Maybe Alessandro overlooked him. Maybe someone in my family put him in the crib in the Strawberry Daiquiri suite. Maybe one of the hockey players Daisy invited wanted baby snuggles inside. Maybe one of my older nieces or nephews wanted a few minutes alone with him.

He's safe.

Margot Roderick is in jail, being held without bond.

Anthony Roderick is supposedly out of the country.

Supposedly.

It's not enough.

It's not enough, and after stopping the party and searching everywhere, it's clear.

Remy's gone.

I swore I'd protect him, and *he's gone.*

38

Daisy

I CAN'T DIAL my phone. I can't send a text. I can't stop shaking.

"It was just friends and family at the party," I tell the police officer for the sixth time. "I swear I knew everyone here."

Alessandro and West are talking to another officer. They're calm. Collected.

Except for that flutter in West's neck.

He's freaking the fuck out.

As he should.

And it's my fault. *All* my fault. How old am I? How long have I lived with people who would use their money to buy anything and everything, from call girls to favors from tax officials to *fucking hit men?*

Of course Remy's *not here*.

I threw a party, because that's all I do. I throw parties. I make people like me. And it distracted all of us to the point that we gave the Rodericks the perfect opportunity to sneak in.

"They paid a kidnapper," I whisper. "They paid a kidnapper, and he probably has Remy halfway around the world by now."

None of the men in the room—not the officers, not West, not Alessandro, and not Jude, who's in the corner waiting for orders on how to help—contradict me.

"We shut down the roads," Alessandro tells me. "He couldn't have been gone more than fifteen minutes before we noticed."

"Cam activated Bluewater's SOS system," Jude tells me. "We're accounting for every boat in the marina and every plane at the landing strip."

"Shutting down the causeway too," one of the officers tells me. "They can't get back to the mainland without a vehicle search."

My little baby.

He's so helpless. And little. And *alone*.

"I shouldn't have taken him to the party."

I barely whisper it, but suddenly West is there, wrapping me in his arms. "Daisy—"

"*No*." I shake free. "I know better. *I know better*. There's never *safe* when there's money involved. Money can buy *anything*, and I put him in the middle of dozens of people and let my guard down."

"We *both* knew better. This isn't on you."

"Where are we looking? Where can I help? Get me a flashlight. I'm going out. Have you searched the beaches?

363

The pool houses? What are we doing standing here talking?"

"We need to be with you if the kidnapper calls—" the officer starts.

"This kidnapper doesn't want *money*. He wants *Remy*." I fly into motion, because I can't stand still.

Remy's out there somewhere.

He's out there, and *I have to find him.*

Not for Julienne.

Not for my grandmother.

For *me*.

He's *mine*. Mine to love. Mine to raise. Mine to save.

I don't care how he came to be here in my life. Or how much sleep I lose, or how many dirty diapers I have to change, because that gummy smile—that sweet, innocent adoration, that happy coo, his chubby little face when he's falling asleep on a bottle, the way I swear he's trying to tell me stories every morning—he's become my everything.

I can't imagine a day without him.

West falls into step next to me as I head for my shoe closet. "I'll go with you."

And there's the other half of my everything.

The one I've let down so very, very badly.

It was bound to happen sooner or later, wasn't it?

"No," I say. "We split up. We cover more ground that way."

"Or whoever took Remy gets you too."

"Buddy system," Jude agrees.

"Where's Cam?"

"With all your parents."

I shove my feet into my favorite stilettos, then

remember how my last trip through the sand on stilettos went, and I mutter to myself and grab my black-and-white checked Sketchers instead.

"I'm hitting the beach," I tell them.

West and Jude share a look, and West falls into step on my heels. "Daisy—"

"Don't. Don't try to make me feel better."

My pulse is on hyperdrive. I can't feel my feet.

And I can't stop wondering if Remy's crying. If he knows what's going on. If he's scared.

I take the back staircase and land on the beach, scanning the horizon for ship lights. Boat lights. I've docked right up on this beach in a dinghy before. It's possible. Which means anyone could've been hiding in the mangroves between our properties, just waiting for a chance to sneak in.

West doesn't speak while we go up and down the beach. Around the paths between my house, Luna's house, Cam's house, and Emily's house, and repeat. Checking bushes. Flashing lights into the mangroves.

Searching.

Fruitlessly.

His phone dings.

My phone dings.

Always the same.

No news. You?

From Cam and Jude. Derek and Emily. Luna and Beck. All of their security. West's family. Residents in Bluewater who woke up at the SOS.

Tyler and his teammates join in too—they're not flying

home until morning, and all of them claim they don't need sleep.

They're as bad as I am.

Around two AM, though, I finally break.

I've lost my baby.

I drop to the ground in the sand behind my pool house and I let the sobs overtake me.

West sits next to me, and even though I know he's hurting too, that he's panicked too, that I promised him I'd never hurt him, that I'd take care of him, I let him take care of me.

This is what I do.

I let people down.

I play a good game. I pretend I'm worthy. I pretend I can do it.

But when push comes to shove, I can't keep up.

His phone dings.

My phone dings.

I ignore it, because I know what it says.

No news. You?

Maybe, *You need to keep your energy up. Stop by my house for kombucha.* Because that's so Luna. Thinking of getting us strength in every holistic way possible.

"Daisy," West chokes out. "He's safe."

My head whips up so fast I almost crack my skull into his face. "What?"

"He's safe." He turns his phone so I can see, and there he is.

Remy.

Wearing the sailor pajamas I put him in before bed. Screaming himself red in the face. Clutched in Beck's arms.

I leap to my feet, relief and dread coursing through my veins.

Relief, because *he's safe*.

Dread, because I know what I have to do to make sure he stays that way.

"Where?"

West grabs my hand and tugs me up the beach to the back of my pool house. "The marina. Hiding in a boat. They're on the way. Suspect in custody."

The next ten minutes are the longest ten minutes of my life. I can't get through my house fast enough. It's too big. Too much.

Too unnecessary.

I burst out the front door, and I head down my driveway, West right beside me, even though it hurts to have him here, because I don't deserve him either.

I can't drive. I can barely walk straight. But I keep going until the flash of headlights shines over me. I squint, watching as Cam's souped-up golf cart slows, then stops. Jude's driving.

And Cam—

She's in the passenger seat. With Remy cradled in her arms.

"Oh my god, he's safe," I gasp.

"He's safe," Cam confirms, handing me the sleeping bundle. "He liked the ride."

She wraps her arms around me and Remy. "It's okay, Daisy. It's okay."

A Range Rover stops behind the cart, and more of my friends and half of West's family descend on us. Police cruisers follow.

I squeeze Remy tight and lean into Cam while West strokes my hair, letting all the sobs fall out while I soak in every second—every *millisecond*—of this moment.

Holding my little boy. The one who was never supposed to be mine, but who stole my heart, completely, with that gummy smile and pure, simple acceptance.

"I'll do better," I whisper. "I swear I'll do better."

I will. I know *exactly* how I'll do better.

And it's going to hurt like hell.

But for Remy's sake, I have to.

39

West

RELIEF ISN'T the right word.

Even though he was only missing for three, maybe four hours, having Remy home feels like having my whole fucking life saved. Like I've stood on the edge of the cliff, on crumbling rocks that could truly destroy me the way Sierra couldn't, the way Becca couldn't, the way losing most of my hearing in my right ear couldn't, and staring into true, bleak, empty desolation.

This baby might not have been born mine, but he's mine in every way that counts.

He's mine in my *heart*.

Just like the woman standing guard at his crib.

"Daisy. Go to bed. I'll keep watch."

I can hear the exhaustion in my own voice, but I know that's not why she shakes her head.

She feels the responsibility every bit as much as I do.

The guilt.

The remnants of the fear.

The knowledge that if we hadn't realized he was gone as fast as we did, tonight could've ended very, *very* differently.

I won't convince her to go to bed.

And so I do the next best thing, and I wrap my arms around her, and I stand there with her.

For the rest of the night.

Keeping watch.

I think Daisy might actually fall asleep on her feet for a while, but when the first light of dawn breaks through her gauzy curtains, she straightens and pulls back with a look of sheer determination on her face that makes my heart stop.

And not in a good way.

"Daisy?"

"I need to shower. And get to work. Can you—can you not let him out of your sight?" Her voice cracks.

"It's Sunday."

"Please."

"Daisy—"

"Please."

No, my heart screams.

Because I know this look. This is the look of a woman pulling away.

"This wasn't your fault," I tell her as she walks to the bathroom.

"I know."

"Daisy—"

"I know, West. I know. I'm not the psycho who plotted

to murder her own daughter-in-law, and I'm not the psycho asshole who paid someone to kidnap a baby as a *life prize*. I know, okay? I know."

I let her go, because I don't have any more good arguments to keep her.

And half an hour later, when she emerges from the bathroom, and I'm feeding Remy a bottle in the rocking chair, she kisses me softly on the cheek, then kisses him seven times on his head and cheeks.

And it feels like a fucking goodbye.

I tell myself it's not.

That she needs time to process.

Hell, *I* need time to process.

Sleep would help.

Her, I mean. I don't need sleep. I'm a fucking Marine.

A *retired* Marine whose mother isn't even the fussiest person to fuss over me this morning when Remy and I make our way to the kitchen for breakfast.

No, that designation goes to Helene.

She looks like she hasn't slept either, and she insists on making me an omelet, then plain scrambled eggs when the omelet turns out like shit, and then asks for my to-go order from Carbs 'n Coffee since she actually can't cook.

Her words.

My sisters won't give me enough space.

And I'm okay with that this morning.

We video chat with Tyler, who's on a plane back to Virginia. All of his teammates—*all* of them—insist on seeing Remy for themselves, which results in all of my nieces and nephews insisting on talking to all the hockey players, and Daisy's kitchen turns into one big massive pit of noise that I love as much as I hate.

We spend almost all day in there.

And because I'm not a fool, I give her space.

Daisy's not in the house. Helene says she went to her office.

She hugs me.

A lot.

I tell myself that's not a sign, but come on.

I've done this dance before.

I know when a woman's gotten skittish.

But I don't know how to fix this. Promise Daisy it'll never happen again? I can't. Neither of us can physically keep an eye on Remy twenty-four hours a day.

I can call in friends, but she has a seven-person security team here already.

We can't post a guard on him his entire life.

He needs freedom. Room to grow. To explore.

And he can't get that so long as the Rodericks are a threat. The police confirmed that the kidnapper named Anthony Roderick as the man who hired him. Anthony Roderick, the asshole who once made Daisy so uncomfortable—she hasn't told me *that* story yet—that he was already on the list of people not allowed in Bluewater. Anthony Roderick, who's a free man, hiding somewhere that the law can't reach him.

Which means the only thing I can do is end the threat.

I know how to end a threat.

I've been ending threats for twenty years.

Daisy's friends drop by mid-afternoon with their

boyfriends, and while they all coo and fuss over the baby —yes, *all* of them—I jerk my head at Jude.

He and I have a few things in common.

"Plan?" he says without preamble when we step to the side of the sunken sitting room.

"Getting there. I'm not having my kid grow up in danger from nutjobs."

"I'm in."

He pulls out a phone and texts someone.

On one of the couches, Derek looks up from the baby, checks his phone, then nods to Jude.

Fuckers.

"Cut me out and I'll disassemble Cam's golf cart," I mutter to him.

"You know I'd feed your balls to Steve if you so much as try."

"Have to catch me first."

Keely leaps over to me and tackles me with a hug before Jude can answer. "I don't want to go tomorrow. I miss you, you big overbearing monkey."

"Hey, don't insult monkeys," Staci calls.

Remy erupts in a wail.

And *that's my boy.*

My eyes get hot.

We almost lost him last night. I didn't even *know* him a few weeks ago, and my world would've fallen apart if he hadn't been found. He's not just my responsibility.

He's a bright spot in my life.

Which isn't that much of a surprise—I could tell myself all I wanted that I wouldn't get attached, but I knew it was a lie.

"Quit pinching him and hand him over," I tell Brit.

Her finger flies to her nose.

My sisters all follow suit immediately, then my mom, and my dad. My brothers-in-law. Even my youngest nieces and nephews.

And I don't care if I have to change a messy diaper.

I'd do anything for this kid.

Anything.

I take him upstairs—to Daisy's room, not the guest room, because until she tells me we're done, I'm carrying on like normal. And our *normal* is me in her bedroom.

Hell, even *after* she tells me we're done, I'm carrying on like normal.

I won't give up on her.

And that's exactly what I'm telling myself when I leave her private wing and head back downstairs, carrying a fussy Remy who's probably ready for a bottle.

But I don't make it to the kitchen.

Because Alessandro corners me. "She wants to see you in her office."

I square my shoulders.

Ignore the look of pity on his face.

And head in to let her do her worst.

40

Daisy

When West walks in with Remy, I almost break.

The man's face is set fierce and determined, like he knows what's coming, and he's prepared to fight me the whole time.

He's carrying the baby face-out, and that little face twists in a smile and almost breaks me.

But I have to do what's best for him.

For both of them.

"Have a seat." I point to the ivory chairs opposite my desk and push up my reading glasses, which aren't actually reading glasses, but I feel like a badass with eye protection when I'm wearing them.

He ignores my directive. "You don't have to do this."

I could waste time quibbling with him over what *this* is, but the sooner I rip off the Band-Aid, the better. So instead, I push a small stack of paperwork across my desk toward him. "I've signed away all my custodial rights to Remy. He's yours. Free and clear."

He sucks in a breath and drops to the chair, and I have to look away. "*What?*"

"My lifestyle doesn't lend itself to motherhood."

"Bullshit."

"If it's not late-night parties, it's traveling around the globe for work. You've connected with him. You love him. He loves you. You're what's best for him. I've started paperwork for a trust fund so you're not financially inconvenienced—"

"I don't want your fucking money. If you're scared, just say you're scared."

"I'm being practical. He deserves to grow up outside the spotlight. Without all those extra pressures that could turn him into everything his mother was. And I can't escape it. *This is my life*, with parties and people and dangers. I can pretend it's not. I can try to fit into something different for a while. But I can't stand being cooped up here. Not all day, every day. I need to be out in the world. With people. And I can't be what he needs while I'm living the life I always wanted."

God, my heart hurts. And I hate lying to West, but I know if I told him the truth—that I'm a fucked-up basket case who will one day leave Remy a fucked-up basket case too—he'd try to convince me that I'm wrong.

That he can fix me.

That we can manage the attention.

That we can keep Remy safe.

The *only* thing that will keep Remy safe is me removing myself from the situation so that West can take him somewhere far, far from here, and raise him quietly with lots of family around.

And I only partially mean physically safe.

Mostly, I mean safe from the influence of my grandmother that I'll inadvertently pass on to him, despite what I plan to do next.

I could move halfway around the globe, change my name, change my face, change my hair, my boobs, *everything*, and I'd still be 25% Imogen Carter.

And that's too much to inflict on one more generation.

Remy needs to be free.

West's gaze bores into me with the force of a million sea-green ocean tides.

"Go ahead and rip them up," I tell him with a nod at the paperwork. "I have the original and twenty-eight more copies. And I'm not changing my mind."

Dammit, I hate it when my voice cracks.

"Tell me you don't love him."

"I love him with every fiber of my being." And there goes the stinging in my eyes. "And that's why I have to let him go."

I rise. My knees wobble. My heart cracks open and spills out rotten rainbow sprinkles that are infected with a double dose of cynicism and hopelessness.

If I'm one-quarter Imogen Carter, I'm also fifty percent *cheating bastard*—and I do mean *bastard* in all the ways one can mean *bastard*—and that's nothing to be proud of either.

I've never let a man into my heart the way I've let West in, because my genes are corrupt.

Watching him walk away will hurt every bit as much as letting Remy go.

But I can't be what he needs either.

We're in this honeymoon phase. I'm playing at having a family. But I'll get bored. He'll get tired of my constant need for new entertainment. At me wanting to go out at night.

Just because I've felt more like staying in with him lately doesn't mean it'll last.

It's better to let him go now.

Before either of us get more attached.

"Now, if you'll excuse me, I have an appointment in Brazil that I need to leave for. Feel free to stay as long as you need. I'll be gone at least two weeks."

"Why are you doing this to yourself?"

His voice is hoarse, and I want to stop and fling myself at him and promise him promises that I can't keep.

Because any other man would ask *why are you doing this to me?*

But not West.

Even while I'm throwing daggers at him, he's asking why I'm hurting myself.

"Life's complicated, Mr. Jaeger."

And I'm going to lose all of my willpower to do what's best for both of them if I don't leave.

Right now.

41

Daisy

"FOR THE RECORD, I am formally opposed to every bit of this course of action," Tiana informs me as she follows me out the side door of my mansion to my waiting Daisy Wagon.

"Noted."

I'm in big Tiffany sunglasses. Bright yellow Versace dress. Stilettos. Diamonds. My hair swept up like Jackie O. Lips red. Lashes thick and dark. Eyes smoky.

I'm dressed to fucking crush the world, and all I really want to do is curl up in my bed and eat froyo until I cry myself out.

Girls like me don't get the man, the babies, the white picket fence.

We get the parties. The superficial. The mansion on the beach and the reputation for being the *nice* person among the rich assholes.

Fuck that.

I don't want it anymore.

I step into my Beetle, cross my legs, and look away from my house. "Alessandro, take me to The Dame's house."

He meets Tiana's gaze in the rearview mirror, then shifts his attention to me. "Don't think that's such a good idea."

"Any other day, your opinion counts. Today, I want you to drive me to my grandmother's fucking compound."

It's a quiet hour drive to South Beach after that, full of shitty drivers, horns honking, stop-and-go traffic, and more indigestion than I'd wish on three-quarters of my worst enemies.

Anthony Roderick can have six times this amount of indigestion. And jock itch to boot. And all his nose and pubic hairs plucked out by a monkey with a rusty pair of pliers. And lice in his ear hairs.

We pull up to The Dame's hacienda, and I don't wait for Pierson to greet me at the door.

I also don't wait to be told where to find my grandmother.

I know.

And I'm not surprised to find her working in her office.

"You didn't call me to tell me Remington was missing," she says.

No *hello*.

No *are you okay?*

Just *you did it wrong, Daisy.*

"I quit."

Her eyes flare wide and her mouth forms a silent *O*.

"Also, I surrendered all parental and guardian rights to Remy. He's one hundred percent Mr. Jaeger's son now."

God, my heart.

But I won't subject either one of them to *this* anymore.

Or myself.

And I won't use them as a crutch either.

I won't let them be my *easy* family. The one that Julienne's will *gave* me. They deserve more than me being there simply because they're convenient, and they deserve better than *me*. The me I am today, anyway.

Even if I feel like there are icy daggers shredding into my chest and pecking away at my newly exposed heart.

Maybe I'll never build skyscrapers in Hong Kong again. Maybe my line of spas for Carter International Properties will all close because the curtains are mango instead of cerulean.

Or whatever.

But *I am not worthless*.

And I won't sit here and let her make me think I am for one more minute.

The Dame rises to her full height.

If she were truly an immortal highland vampire dragon, she'd spit fire out her nostrils and crack open her old lady shell to reveal her true form, an armor-plated flying cockroach.

"Daisy," she whispers. "Oh my god, *Daisy*."

My knees wobble, because she's not breathing fire or using her powers of mind control to bend me double in pain.

Instead, she seems utterly gobsmacked.

In a lesser woman, I'd call her stricken.

"Go ahead," I say, my voice quivering. "Disinherit me. *I don't care.*"

She slowly shakes her head, eyes still wide. "You—Daisy—I could never actually—" She swallows, and all of her armor *does* crack.

But it's not a beast who emerges.

It's a broken, old, sad woman. "I've hurt you."

"You've hurt a lot of people."

"I—I merely wanted you to calm down. Not—"

I freeze. *"You plagiarized Julienne's will?"*

"No! No. Of course not. That would be ridiculous. But when she told me she was naming you and Mr. Jaeger—"

"You knew Margot Roderick wanted to kill her?"

The Dame actually blanches. "She was so prone to exaggeration...and making enemies..."

I turn around and march toward the door. I don't want to hear any more.

"I've always been so proud of you," she says quietly behind me.

That should mean something. It should be everything I've worked my ass off for since I was twenty-one years old.

But what kind of a victory is it when I don't *want* it anymore?

"Daisy. Stop," she says. "You don't have to quit."

I ignore her.

I don't remember what my employment agreement said. Probably something about indentured servitude for life in exchange for that twenty-five percent cut I asked for. Or something about losing a share in the company if I quit before a hundred and fifty years.

But I don't care.

I have Bluewater. That's *mine*. Mine, and Emily's, and Luna's, and Cam's. She can't take that from us.

I have my pool.

I have my yacht.

I have my mom.

I have my friends, who will undoubtedly tell me I'm a moron for sending West away, but I had to.

For his own good. For *Remy's* own good.

I step back out into the sunshine, and I wait for the freedom to wash over me.

It doesn't come.

Not *washing*, anyway.

But the tears do.

A month ago, I would've drowned myself in tequila and techno music at a club on the beach.

Today, I just want to go home.

Tiana and Alessandro surround me with a huge hug.

"I love you guys," I whisper.

"We know. And we love you too."

And that's all it takes to finally break me.

Just a little bit of love.

This love, I might deserve.

But West's?

He can do so much better.

42

Daisy

Four days after the Weekend of Horror, as I'm officially calling it, I'm camped out in my pool house, contemplating not much of anything at all, because I am slobber-faced drunk.

I could go fry in the sun on a float in my pool, but I don't want to.

I want to lay here.

On the cool tile floor.

With my boobs squished under me and a glass of something pink and beautiful just out of reach, even with the straw teasing me mere inches away.

I'm trying to extend my lips to reach it when the door slides open and the most fabulous pair of shoes *ever* stop just behind the glass.

Those fabulous shoes are followed by another pair of fabulous shoes, and one set of adorable bare feet.

"Oh, honey," a soft voice says.

"I told you we should've come yesterday."

"Her mom said she was fine."

"Her mom was mistaken. Or possibly in denial. Did you see how puffy her eyes were? She's just as upset as Daisy is. Maybe more so."

"Oga aye," I sigh against the floor.

I have no idea what it means, but it's the sounds my mouth wants to make.

"Should we take her to the gym?"

"I don't think she can walk on those shoes, much less work out in them today."

"Maybe dunk her in the pool?"

"Jude's just outside. If she starts to drown, he'll leap in after her."

"No pool," I say. "Sun bad. Water bad. Want tequila."

Emily's face swims into view as she squats in front of me. She's so pretty. I want to be pretty like Emily. "You need an intervention."

"Can you do it while I'm sleeping?"

"Daisy, you poor thing." Luna's flowy, flowery skirt flares out on the ground beside my head, and she strokes my hair, which might be dangerous, since it's entirely possible Steve has crawled in there to bask in the glorious filth of my 'do. "Is this your first heartbreak?"

"Have to have a heart for it to break."

"Definitely time for the pool," Cam says.

They're joking, so I ignore them.

Except suddenly my arms and legs are being lifted, my skin is *snick!*-ing off the ground, and any hopes of getting that straw disappear.

The sun is bright.

And the water is a huge wake-up.

I sputter, my head spins, and I flail around for half a second before I surface. I'm still in my yellow Versace dress from four days ago. And I have half a mind to sink back into the water and let it carry all my troubles away.

"I miss my baby," I whisper, and then I don't know where my eyes start and the water ends, or something like that, because my eyeballs are leaking again.

"Well, duh. You love him."

All three of my friends settle in at the edge of my pool, peeling off shoes and dropping their toes in the water.

Even Cam, who's impeccably dressed in a business suit.

My friends are the best.

Except for the part where they're making me cry.

Apparently I have a touch of the dramatic in me.

"Just because they were easy to love doesn't mean they're supposed to be *mine* to love," I wail. I fling myself backward, but I don't sink, because I have two giant life rafts permanently attached to my chest.

"That's a good sign you're a very good fit," Luna says. "When you don't think you should fit, but you can't help yourself, and you can't see your life without them ever again."

"But it's hard." It is—it's both easy and so, *so* hard. "And he's *gone*." I made Tiana tell me when she checked on me yesterday.

One of the times, anyway.

Apparently quitting my job doesn't mean my personal staff will quit me.

My friends are oddly silent, and hope makes my heart leap. I tilt my head to look at them. "Is he still here? Are *they* still here?"

They share one of those *should we tell her?* looks, and Emily finally meets my eyes. "No. West and Remy aren't here."

Ah, tears again.

"Why, exactly, did you send them away again?" Cam asks.

"I don't know how to do family, and I don't want to fuck either of them up." I clap a hand over my mouth.

I hate when the truth slips out.

"Excuse me, and what are we?" Luna asks.

"Chopped liver, obviously." Emily smirks.

Cam heaves a melodramatic sigh. "Or dead tuna in her bed. Something she doesn't want but can't get rid of."

"That's not—you're not—*ugh*."

"I get it, Daisy," Emily says softly. "Believe me, I do. But the thing is…you're better than you give yourself credit for. You're not your grandmother. You're a kickass—"

"Big-hearted," Luna interrupts.

"Brilliant," Cam adds.

"Fucking *vagillionaire* who's basically the biggest-hearted egg in the ovary at the top of this fallopian tube."

"I'm a *faaaaake*," I wail.

"Your entire department at Carter International walked off the job this week," Emily says casually.

That has me scrambling for my feet, belatedly realizing I'm still in my stilettos, and wondering if that'll leave a mark on the bottom of my dick pool. "What?"

"Yeah. They all said they won't work directly for your grandmother."

"Or any other dickstool she wants to replace you with." Luna winks at me. "They only want to work for *you*."

Oh, god.

Oh, god.

Everything is falling apart. "Those people need that money to pay their mortgages. And for insulin for their kids. And—"

And my three friends are sharing another look.

"*What?*"

Luna slides into the pool, dress and all, and grabs me in a hug. "Peopling is your superpower, Daisy. You're like, *The Motivator*. People want to work for you."

Cam taps her finger to her lips like she's thinking. "And if peopling is your superpower...huh. One might even deduce that *having family* and *loving someone* is a natural extension of that."

I freeze so hard the pool water gets frosty around me. "Of course I love West and Remy," I whisper. "That's *why* I sent them away."

Except what was it West said?

I'll screw up, Daisy. You'll screw up. But we'll forgive each other.

Forgiveness isn't something my family does.

But that doesn't mean *I* can't.

"What do I do?" I ask my friends. "How do I fix this?"

"Step one is a hostile takeover at Carter International." Cam rubs her hands together in glee.

Emily's eyes light up. "*Yes!* I'd be shocked if Tiana

388

hasn't been fielding calls from the board all week, which is good. She's badass too. Probably negotiating you a higher salary."

"I don't need more fucking money, *I need my family back.*"

"Oh, that." Cam grins.

Emily grins bigger.

Luna squeezes me tight. "That's my girl! But if you do get a higher salary, we have a few ideas of some things you can do with the extra money."

"School supplies across America," Cam says. "Teachers post their wishlists online. You could fulfill every one of their wishes."

Emily nods. "Facials for the elderly. They deserve pampering too."

"I mean, so do dogs," Luna adds. "But since you already have dogs covered, I propose adding ice cream and frozen yogurt to your free-food-for-a-day rotation."

I splash them all. "You guys know about that?"

"We know lots of things." Luna squeezes me tighter. "And you're going to be okay, Daisy. You'll get through this."

"I fucked up so bad."

"We all do sometimes."

"You ready to fix it?" Cam asks.

Am I? *Can* I?

"Signing over guardianship to West was the right thing to do," I say slowly. "He's so—so dependable. And solid. But fun. With *so* much love to give. I know he'll treat Remy right. The way—"

The way he treated me.

Like I matter.

My hands are starting to shake. "I promised him I'd take care of him. And I thought I *was* taking care of him by stepping back. But now...I don't know."

"You need a cheeseburger," Luna says sagely.

"And a solid round of kickboxing," Emily adds.

Cam nods. "While jamming out to eighties music."

A party with my best friends.

That *does* sound better than wallowing in my lady cave for the next three years.

"But you have to shower first," Luna tells me. "And then we'll help you find your footing again. Promise."

43

West

I MISS BEING ON MISSIONS, but right now, creeping through the sand, approaching a beach hut just after sunset entirely too close to Miami, getting ready to serve justice to an asshole of the nth degree, my heart isn't in it.

My heart's back in Miami. My *entire* heart.

I make eye contact with Jude.

He nods, and we split up. Him to the back. Me to the front. We're both unarmed, but we're plenty dangerous without traditional weapons.

I crouch in position between the door and the open window, waiting.

Doesn't take long.

"Hey, ugly motherfucker," Jude says inside. "It's justice time."

"What—who—*fuck!*"

Footsteps on the wood floor.

The bang of the door flying open.

A man darting out.

And I leap.

Takes me all of a half-second to have Anthony Roderick's face shoved in the sand while I wrap his wrists. He's gasping and spitting when I lift him and shove a gag in his mouth.

Jude joins me as I'm tossing the fucker over my shoulder. Doesn't ask if this is him. Doesn't have to. We've both been staring at his picture nonstop for days, and much as I swore I'd forget the one day I met him in person, back when I was doing Remy's first nursery, I didn't.

"Remember me?" I growl low. "You paid to have someone kidnap my son. And now you're going to pay."

He screams in terror, but it's muffled behind the gag.

And I don't feel a lick of remorse.

Thinks his money can buy his way out of trouble. That he's above the law. Sitting here on a fucking *beach*, in a country that doesn't give two shits that he's here and wouldn't extradite him even if they knew, probably cooking up another scheme to kidnap my boy and whisk him away here.

Am I breaking some kind of law?

Probably.

Do I care?

Not. One. Fucking. Bit.

Daisy won't rest until this asshole is completely neutralized. *I* won't fucking rest until this asshole is completely neutralized.

So we're neutralizing him.

And yes.

My son.

In all the ways that count.

Our helicopter is at a makeshift landing zone three hundred yards away in a small clearing in the jungle. Jude leaps into the cockpit and starts the rotors.

I dump Anthony Roderick into the man-sized trunk behind the two seats.

And we lift off, heading over the Straights back to Florida, in a helicopter courtesy of Miami's best vagillion-aires, our flight very courteously being ignored by local air traffic controllers.

Guess it's true.

Money *can* buy anything.

Even justice, occasionally.

The ride isn't long, or high, and I climb in back to give Roderick some fresh air after we've sufficiently scared the fuck out of him.

He's pale as a ghost.

Goes paler when I strap headphones onto his ears and let him know much dirt Derek's company dug up on him and sent over to the FBI.

Funny, the things Derek Price can find. Usually he cleans up people's reputations. But being around people who need cleaning means he knows a thing or two about dirt.

I like the guy.

We land at the private Bluewater airstrip, and my nerves kick into high gear. My balls tell them to stand down, but it doesn't help.

And no, I'm not nervous about the fact that I just kidnapped a criminal from a country without an extradition treaty. Nor am I nervous about dropping the fucker with a guy Jude knows who doesn't ask any questions about where we found him, but who we can trust to make sure the asshole gets where he needs to be.

Jude drives me back to where I need to be. He offers a fist bump before I get out. "Nice job out there."

"*Ooh-rah*. Where'd you learn to fly a helicopter?"

He grins. "Same place I learned to kick old ladies' asses in shuffleboard."

The liar follows me into the house—habit, probably.

It's been ten days since Remy's attempted kidnapping. Ten days too long to do what I need to do *right now*.

But we both need to see that Remy's still safe.

And he is. Comfortably swinging and sleeping in the bright living room while Becca plays Angry Birds on her phone next to him.

She jumps up when we enter, her gaze going to me, then up, up, up to Jude. "Hey! You're back. That was…quick."

"Just lunch," Jude says. "Windows locked?"

"Yes. Everyone's safe."

He nods, and without another word, turns and leaves.

"Thanks," I say to Becca.

"Of course. Anytime." She gnaws on her lower lip while I head over to kiss Remy. "Did you really go to lunch?"

"Yep." Yesterday. To plot out today after we got intel on where Roderick was hiding.

"You just seem…different. Not…like you just got back from lunch."

"Never know when a lunch is going to change your

life." I pull Remy out of his travel swing. He fusses and yawns, but he and I have somewhere to be.

"You're really good with him."

"He makes it easy. Thanks again for watching him. Catch you later?"

"Yeah." I thank her once more before I grab Remy's diaper bag and travel swing. This feels like goodbye.

In a *good* way.

I load Remy into my car, and we hit the road.

Miami drivers are insane today, but I have precious cargo, so we take our time, which only makes my heart pump faster and the doubts and fears whisper louder. I distract myself by talking to Remy, who's strapped in tight. He coos in response, and *fuck*, I love that kid.

He's a lot of work. But he smiles when I walk in the door. The way he pumps his legs when he's hungry—so fucking adorable. He's getting better at holding his head up. And rocking him to sleep every night puts me more at peace than I've been in forever.

Except for that little hole in my heart where Daisy still belongs.

Once we get across the causeway, I turn the radio on to try to calm my nerves, but instead, the first thing I hear is two deejays talking about an anonymous donor who arranged catering for a full early Thanksgiving feast at all the Coast Guard stations around Miami.

Dessert included.

Of course.

I reach the Bluewater gate, and the guard holds up a hand. My heart stops in time with my truck.

"You got that baby?" he asks.

"Yes," I say slowly.

He peeks in the back, and a grin as wide as the sea spreads over his face. "Miss that little fella. He's getting big. You should come by more often."

He waves me through, and I head into Daisy's enclave. There are people playing tennis near the condo buildings. The Wealthy Widows are sipping something on the tropical miniature golf course's clubhouse patio. Frank the parrot flies by overhead, and I can only imagine what's coming out of his little beak.

The shops in the village are busy but not crowded, with a few putting out early Christmas lights, and people wave as we drive by.

It's so *Daisy*.

Happy and a little wild, but also full of heart.

We pull down her long, empty driveway, and I wonder if I've gotten the wrong intel. If she's *not* actually home. I know she quit her job. I know Imogen Carter's on the verge of being overthrown at her own company by her board, and that Daisy's being begged to go back. Even temporarily to oversee a smooth transition. And I've been led to believe that despite telling her yacht captain to take the boat to sea to make it look like she's left town, she's actually home.

I've barely parked before Alessandro steps out the door.

"You call first?" he asks.

I shake my head.

He grins. "Knew I liked you. She's at the dick pool. How's the little slugger?"

Remy smiles and waves from his carrier.

"Good to hear it, my man." Alessandro boops his nose. "You keep growing, and don't let Aunt Daisy pull any bull-shirt, you hear me?"

Well over a month ago, I walked this same path around Daisy's house to her pool. But I don't feel anything like that dude expecting to find out that my brother set me up for a party.

I snort softly to myself.

Feels like a lifetime ago.

Voices carry down the path as I approach the pool, and one in particular stands out.

Loud. Boisterous. Happy.

Am I wrong?

Does she *not* need me?

"Yes! I want to pay for everyone's pizza all night at all six of your locations. And can I have ten of those deliv-ered to an address in Oak Park?"

My heart starts pumping again.

More than pumping.

It's throbbing and glowing and telling my nuts to come out of hiding.

Oak Park.

I haven't heard of an Oak Park neighborhood in Miami, but my parents live in Oak Park in Chicago.

"Shouldn't you at least make sure they're home before you order them pizza?" another female voice says. Emily, I think.

"That would take half the fun out of it. Hush," Luna replies with a laugh.

"Just how good *is* Chicago pizza? Do I need to fuel up the jet?" Cam asks.

My heart stutters to a stop, and my eyes burn.

She is.

She's ordering pizza for my family. And all of Chicago. Expanding her random acts of kindness around the world.

Remy coos loudly, and all the voices stop as we peek around the corner of the path and step out into the pool area.

All four of Miami's strongest, smartest, hottest billionaires turn and look at us.

Cam reacts first. She leaps up. "Yep. I need to get that jet ready."

Emily next. "I could go for pizza."

"Is it vegan?" Luna pretends to be confused when Cameron and Emily grab her and head toward the souped-up, aerodynamic golf cart around the side of the pool house, but she winks at me before they load up and take off.

Daisy's staring at me like she can't decide if she wants to throw her phone at me, or hang up and jump me.

"Tiana?"

Her assistant darts out of the pool house. "Got your credit card. I'll take care of it. Whoops, have to go see what Alessandro wants."

Daisy's eyes are blue today.

And her hair's brown.

And she's wearing a sparkly top that reminds me of my nieces' favorite pillows, with the sequins that flip one way to reveal a different picture or a sassy saying, and I wonder what Daisy's shirt would say if I flipped her sequins.

Undoubtedly something very *Daisy*.

Fuck, I've missed her.

Her eyes dart from mine to Remy's carrier, going shiny as she sits there, just staring from her lounge chair at the edge of the pool.

"I—" I start.

She leaps to her feet. "Oh my god, is he sick? Does he need a kidney transplant?"

"What?"

Her eyes snap to mine, and all the laughter and smiles of a minute ago have faded behind fear. Regret. Shame.

I take two steps, but she holds out a hand to stop me. "I...didn't expect you."

"I know. We just—"

"I'm not ready," she whispers.

My heart stops. Again. "Remy's safe," I tell her. "Anthony Roderick's in custody. And even if he wasn't, he wouldn't—I made sure he's never coming near us again."

Her eyes go shiny. "Thank you."

"Officially, I have no idea what you're thanking me for," I add. Awkwardly. Naturally, because here we are, building up to our next first date.

I hope.

Her lips wobble like she's torn between laughing and crying. "Officially noted. But I'm still not ready. I haven't finished—" she sucks in a big breath and looks away "—working on me."

"Daisy, you're fucking perfect just the way you are. You don't have to—"

"I still love you," she blurts. "Shit. *Shirt*. Wait. Hold on. I have a speech."

"Daisy—"

"I was supposed to come to *you*. When I finally deserved you. I was an idiot, and I was afraid to love you. And I was afraid if I let you any closer, you'd see what a useless mess of a human I am. But I'm working on it. I'm figuring out who I'm supposed to be, and what I'm supposed to do, so that I can deserve you without relying on you to be the best part of me. I want to be as good as you are. I want to deserve to have you love me back. And you need to know that I don't love you because you're easy to love, even though you are, and I don't love you because you were here and convenient, and I don't love you because you're super hot when you're holding a baby, even though, again, you are, and I don't love you because I want Remy back, even though I —oh my god, I miss him. I can't even look at him in case he disappears again. But I love you because you're *you*. And you made me believe in me. And I let you down, and—"

"I forgive you." Three of the most inadequate words I've ever said in my life.

But her face crinkles, half-smile, half-tears, and she whispers, "Really? Because I have this huge romantic gesture planned. With a marching band. And Mardi Gras beads. And fries from Beach Burgers, because I love their burgers, but their fries are really where it's at. And I also trained all the cats to do the wave, because—"

I set Remy's carrier on the ground and close the space between us. "Stop. You're fucking *perfect* just the way you are, whether you're done working on you or not. We're all works in progress. All of us. But you—god, Daisy, you're everything that's right in the world. This heart? That doesn't need improvement."

"This heart missed you." She looks down, pink staining her cheeks.

I tilt her chin up. "I don't need grand gestures, but if they make you happy, I'll sit here with you while you finish planning it all."

Her smile's starting to peek through. "And you weren't supposed to hear me ordering pizza. Why are you here?"

"For you."

"For real for me, or because you think I secretly hid some of Remy's baby stuff in my closet so I could sniff it? Not that I'd...okay. Yes. I kept some of his little onesies. But in my defense, he was going to outgrow them anyway in another few months."

"Daisy."

"Yes?"

"I love you too."

"Still?" She blinks rapidly, and her chin wobbles.

I brush an errant tear from her cheek. "Probably. Do you still have that mechanical unicorn?"

"Yes."

I pretend to wince. "Oh. Then I might have to rethink—"

She shrieks and leaps at me, and I catch her, twirling as she attacks me with kisses to my chin, my jaw, my cheeks, and my nose while she chews me out. "You—awful—terrible—mean—wonderful—amazing—perfect—unpredictable—everything—man."

She's what I've been missing in life.

The *fun*.

But also her pure heart.

I squeeze her back as hard as I can without popping her lungs. She's *so* fucking right in my arms, and I've missed her more than I ever thought I could miss anything in my life. Holding her again is like holding the sun. "I missed you so much," I breathe into her hair.

She laughs, but it's a half-sob. "Telling you to go was the hardest thing I've ever done in my life, but I wanted—I wanted you and Remy to be safe."

"I know, Daisy. I know."

"*Remy!*" she suddenly shrieks.

I set her on the ground, and she dives for the baby carrier. "Oh my god, he tripled in size. He's sucking his thumb. Were his eyes always that shade of brown, or did they get darker? Who dressed him? These little turkey pajamas are adorable."

She has him out of his carrier and pressed to her shoulder, squeezing, her cheek on his hair while he gives me a look that clearly says *now you've done it, and I'm never going to have a moment's peace again.*

I smile at the little guy. He's changing so much every day, getting more and more aware of the world, and I'm only mildly terrified of the mischief I can already see brewing deep inside him.

The next eighteen years are going to be a special, perfect kind of fun.

"Oh my god, he smells so good." She sniffs him, strokes his silky hair, lifts him and holds his gaze while her eyes start to leak again. "Remington Nathaniel Roderick, are you actually here?"

"He's here," I assure her as he squeals and kicks his legs.

"And you're safe?"

"He's safe."

"He can hold his head up."

"Little bit, yeah."

I slip my arms around both of them, and she leans into me, cradling Remy close again. "I need more arms to hold both of you."

"I got you."

"Forever?"

It's a whispered plea that makes my heart both swell and ache. She should know how much she deserves to be loved forever, and I'm going to spend every last minute of my life making sure she knows it. "Forever," I agree huskily.

"I love you so much."

"I love you more."

She laughs, finally, that gloriously happy sound that gives my heart wings, and she lifts her eyes to mine. Sparkling, twinkling blue seas shine at me. "So that's how it's going to be, is it?"

I shrug. "Just want you to know what you're up against here." My own smile is making my cheeks hurt.

This isn't the family I pictured for myself. Or the kind of settling down I thought I'd do.

But Daisy and Remy—and whatever comes next—are everything I ever wanted, and so much more.

She sucks in a sudden breath and straightens. "West—I did something else," she whispers.

I lift a brow and smile, though her own face is

pinching again. "Knowing you, you did several somethings."

"I...found Nina and Baxter."

My lips part.

All the air leaves me.

Is it possible to be so incredibly happy with the woman I have, while still missing a part of my past?

"Actually, Baxter found me," she rushes on. "After all the media coverage—he recognized you—and he—they— they want to know if you're up for flying into South Carolina for coffee sometime."

Fuck.

Just *fuck*.

"They do?" My voice cracks, and I don't care.

This.

Here.

My Daisy.

Our son. By choice.

And the family I thought I lost.

She nods, and her smile goes watery again. "I told them I'd let them know as soon as we could get there. Also, since they're technically underage, I talked to Sierra, and she approved everything. So, maybe tonight?"

"I fucking adore you," I tell her. "Thank you. Just —*thank you*."

"Love is meant to be shared," she says. "And you deserve all of it."

She goes up on tiptoe to claim my lips, and I realize I have one more thing left that I haven't given her yet.

"You remember the night we met?"

"I *love* the night we met."

"I never did finish that striptease for you."

A spark of intrigue lights her blue eyes. "You're right. You didn't."

I nod toward the pool house.

She kisses me again.

And I know we're going to have the wildest, most unexpected, biggest-hearted, *best* next forever in the history of forevers.

EPILOGUE

Daisy

When West asked me where I wanted to get married, I suggested at the bottom of the ball pit.

The crazy man agreed that squeezing all of our friends and family into the balls was a brilliant idea, and I realized I actually had finally fully met my match.

I blinked first, which amused the hell out of him. I didn't know the man could laugh that hard, but he did, and it was so hot that every pair of my panties burned up in the resulting lust fire.

Or so I told him.

Also, I like going commando. And he likes it too. I have this strange suspicion that Remy won't be an only child for long.

I'm daydreaming about our honeymoon as I prop an elbow on the bar at Mordecai's, where our party has taken up almost the entire bistro for Drag Queen Brunch the day after Christmas, waiting for a bartender so I can ask for a special drink just for my surprise groom, when someone bumps into me from behind.

"Oh! So sorry," she says.

I look behind me, about to tell her it's not a problem, when I realize it's the unicorn author.

I know celebrities. And rock stars. And sports stars. And politicians. I can talk to any of them.

But I'm suddenly completely starstruck as I meet her gaze.

"I lost my keys," she says, gesturing to her overflowing purse. "I had to have them to *get* here, but now I can't find them anywhere, and I already lost a set at home once, so I...sorry. You didn't need to know that."

"You do you," I tell her. "Just don't ever stop writing. You're not leaving, are you?"

"No! I left my notebook in my car, and—are you here with the single dad? He should really be on the cover of a book. *So hot.* Good for you!"

"He should," I agree. I reach into my purse and pull out a card. "Drop me a note. We'll see what we can arrange."

She bites her lip, then grins and nods. "Thanks."

Excitement bubbles over in my veins even as I realize West is going to kill me.

And then I'll apologize and do a striptease and seduce him until he can't remember what I did this time, and I'll make sure I'm the first one up with Remy the next morning, and he'll forgive me.

Actually, he'll forgive me even if I don't do all that.

Turns out, he *likes* having fun. It's been missing from his life for too long, with all the military time and being the oldest for so long before that. But the man is lucky enough to be stuck with me forever.

Almost, anyway.

I order him a strawberry daiquiri, tell the bartender to put everyone's drinks on my tab today, and head back to my usual table with my besties.

It's much tighter with Derek, Jude, Beck, and West squeezed in with us, but I like squeezes.

And Remy loves being passed from aunt to uncle and all around.

West's parents, sisters, their families, and even Tyler are here with us this morning, though at the closest tables instead of on top of us. So is my mom. Alessandro and Tiana, naturally. Baxter and Nina, who we call West's *first kids*, and who are both really fucking amazing young adults. And my grandmother, who's decided to retire and take up groveling for a hobby.

It seems she's finally realized that her funeral would look a lot like Julienne's if she didn't start showing her human side.

Plus, I have this suspicion that West might've gone to visit her during those ten years we were apart.

I mean, ten days. But it felt like ten years.

I haven't asked. He hasn't offered. But my grandmother *definitely* has some respect for him that wasn't there before, and he's more tolerant of her when she's annoying than he was before.

"Is this for me to drink, or for me to accidentally spill all over your dress?" he asks me when the bartender arrives with his pink froufrou drink.

"It's just a reminder of how far we've come," I tell him

with a grin. "In case you miss the Strawberry Daiquiri suite too much."

He laughs and kisses me. "Some days, I think I'm crazy for loving you."

"But it's the best kind of crazy."

"You ready for this?"

"Are you kidding? I was *born* ready."

He chuckles again, and I nod to Lady Raquel, who stops in the middle of the dining room and claps her hands. "Excuse me, ladies and gentlemen. We have a special brunchtime entertainment for you today," she announces.

My soon-to-be-sisters-in-law all go wide-eyed and squeal, turning their attention to West and me as we scoot out of the booth. He takes Remy back from Beck, who's just as natural with babies as he is with dogs.

My mom dabs her eyes.

West's mom does too.

Other than the romance novelists and our families, the only other patrons here today are residents of Bluewater, which I'm not sure they all realize, but it's utterly perfect.

"Y'all thought you were coming for brunch, but turns out, you're here to witness a wedding," Lady Raquel continues. "Daisy, girl, bring that handsome man and that baby over here and get up on this table so we can do this right."

I follow directions, stepping onto a chair, and then onto a table, West helping me and hopping up too while my security team gathers around us, just in case. We *are* standing on a table with a baby, after all.

I'll let them get their boxer briefs in a bunch over me standing on a table. But just this once.

Lady Raquel steps up onto a chair—those heels are seriously fabulous, and they put her at eye level with me, anyway—and begins the ceremony to officially make the three of us a real family in front of our friends, family, and favorite romance novelists.

I might tear up a little, but when it's time for the vows, I look up into West's eyes, those magic color-changing eyes that are on the sea green side today, and I don't want to be at a party, or off on my yacht, or in Bora-Bora, or at a club.

I want to be right here. With this amazing man who's helped me find inside of myself so much of the acceptance and belonging I was always looking for with the hundreds of acquaintances I've made over the years.

I still love a good dance party. And I adore people. And I've gone back to Carter International Properties temporarily to make sure all of my former employees will be well taken care of by whoever replaces me.

But I don't need to be popular to know I'm loved. Or that I'm worthy.

And I'm supposed to say my vows to this perfect man, but all I really want to do is kiss him.

And so I do, because what's Lady Raquel going to do?

Refuse to continue the ceremony?

West is smiling as I pull out of the kiss.

"I love you," I tell him.

"Now that's the kind of vow I'm talking about," Lady Raquel says while everyone around us claps and cheers.

We say our *I do*'s, kiss again, and everyone cheers.

Except Remy.

He poops his pants. As babies do.

And Emily isn't cheering, but she's dashing for the bathroom with her hand over her mouth like she's going to puke. Poor thing. Pregnancy isn't agreeing with her all the time yet.

Music pumps through the speakers, and the staff clears away a few tables for a dance floor. The grandmas fight over Remy, and as West pulls me into his arms for our first dance as woman and husband, he also holds up a manila envelope.

I sway my hips into his and we rock to the music. "What's this?"

"Adoption paperwork. To make our little family official. Because you and Remy need each other just as much as I do."

My eyes sting. My throat burns. And I leap onto him, my legs going around his waist while I attack him with kisses.

I might not be the classiest woman in the world.

But I'm loved. So, so loved.

And I'm going to spend the rest of my life giving back every last bit of all the love I have for them.

ARE YOU CAUGHT UP?

Did you miss a Bluewater Billionaires novel?

Emily has a billion-dollar deal that's falling apart and a naked stranger in her bathtub who says he can make all her problems disappear in The Price of Scandal by Lucy Score.

Cameron is reluctantly saddled with an overprotective bodyguard in The Mogul and the Muscle by Claire Kingsley.

Luna loses the public's adoration after a corporate scandal and there's only one man—a big, bearded, dog-rescuing biker—who can help her save it all in Wild Open Hearts by Kathryn Nolan.

The Bluewater Billionaires Series (Complete)
The Price of Scandal by Lucy Score

The Mogul and the Muscle by Claire Kingsley
Wild Open Hearts by Kathryn Nolan
Crazy for Loving You by Pippa Grant

PIPPA GRANT BOOK LIST

The Girl Band Series (Complete)
Mister McHottie

Stud in the Stacks

Rockaway Bride

The Hero and the Hacktivist

The Thrusters Hockey Series
The Pilot and the Puck-Up

Royally Pucked

Beauty and the Beefcake

Charming as Puck

I Pucking Love You

The Bro Code Series
Flirting with the Frenemy

America's Geekheart

Liar, Liar, Hearts on Fire

The Hot Mess and the Heartthrob

Copper Valley Fireballs Series (Complete)
Jock Blocked

Real Fake Love

The Grumpy Player Next Door

Irresistible Trouble

Three BFFs and a Wedding Series (Complete)

The Worst Wedding Date

The Gossip and the Grump

The Bride's Runaway Billionaire

A Thrusters x Fireballs Mash-Up

The Secret Hook-Up

The Tickled Pink Series

The One Who Loves You

Rich In Your Love

Standalones

Until It Was Love

The Last Eligible Billionaire

Not My Kind of Hero

Dirty Talking Rival *(Bro Code Spin-Off)*

A Royally Inconvenient Marriage *(Royally Pucked Spin-Off)*

Exes and Ho Ho Hos

The Happy Cat Series (Complete)

Hosed

Hammered

Hitched

Humbugged

Happily Ever Aftered

The Bluewater Billionaires Series (Complete)

The Price of Scandal by Lucy Score

The Mogul and the Muscle by Claire Kingsley

Wild Open Hearts by Kathryn Nolan

Crazy for Loving You by Pippa Grant

Pippa Grant writing as Jamie Farrell:

The Misfit Brides Series (Complete)

Blissed

Matched

Smittened

Sugared

Married

Spiced

Unhitched

The Officers' Ex-Wives Club Series (Complete)

Her Rebel Heart

Southern Fried Blues

ABOUT THE AUTHOR

Pippa Grant wanted to write books, so she did.

Before she became a *USA Today* and #1 Amazon best-selling romantic comedy author, she was a young military spouse who got into writing as self-therapy. That happened around the time she discovered reading romance novels, and the two eventually merged into a career. Today, she has more than 30 knee-slapping Pippa Grant titles and nine published under the name Jamie Farrell.

When she's not writing romantic comedies, she's fumbling through being a mom, wife, and mountain woman, and sometimes tries to find hobbies. Her crowning achievement? Having impeccable timing for telling stories that will make people snort beverages out of their noses. Consider yourself warned.

Find Pippa at...
www.pippagrant.com
pippa@pippagrant.com

www.ingramcontent.com/pod-product-compliance
Lightning Source LLC
LaVergne TN
LVHW092142130125
801208LV00028B/121

* 9 7 8 1 9 4 0 5 1 7 7 2 8 *